AGE OF STONE

RISE OF MANKIND INCLUDES:

AGE OF STONE

AGE OF BRONZE

AGE OF IRON

AGE OF STEEL

AGE OF FORGED STEEL

AGE OF GLASS

AGE OF EXPANSION

AGE OF CONQUEST

JEZ CAJIAO

AGE OF STONE

—RISE OF MANKIND—

1

AGE OF STONE
Published by AETHON: Vault
In association with Aethon Books

ISBN 978-1-63849-347-1 (hardcover)

First AETHON: Vault Edition: Summer 2026

Printed in the United States of America.
1st Printing.

Aethon Books
www.aethonbooks.com

Vault Storyworks
www.vaultstoryworks.com

Book design and illustration by Adam Cahoon.
Print formatting by Kevin G. Summers, Adam Cahoon, and Rikki Midnight.

AGE OF STONE

IT'S THE END OF THE WORLD (AS WE KNOW IT...)

HIGH MATRIGAN FINNABARR watched the final phase-one satellite float free from the cargo bay of his ship, and he unconsciously released a little warble of regret as its engines flared, shifting its trajectory to match up perfectly with the rest of the net.

He'd been here...in orbit...above this tiny blue, green, and brown ball, which the inhabitants called Earth, for almost two solar cycles now. He'd spent that time seeding the orbit with the satellites required to open the warp, and not a single day had passed when he didn't regret the necessity.

He'd known it was a mistake when he started to watch the denizens, but he'd been bored, despite the significant resources that the clan had expended to fill his ship with every conceivable diversion, and if he was being truly honest, he'd felt curiosity regarding the lives he was about to change.

Most of the council had agreed that his race's primary trait was, in fact, curiosity to such a degree that it should have rendered their species extinct millennia ago, and yet, they had persisted, and had even risen to fill almost the entirety of the council's scientific arm.

A fact which he deeply regretted now, as he observed the small propulsors emitting a burst of gas to shift the device's orientation before the tiny ion drive engaged, pushing it into its new orbit, along with the hundreds of other Distortion Engines needed for this most desperate, and most terrible, of projects.

He'd been so in awe of the science when they'd solved it, he and his brood-pair had laughed and celebrated, dancing the night away when they believed they'd finally discovered the final combination, and leaving the prototype to be rendered overnight. He'd awoken early the next morning, bleary-eyed, his mouth tasting like dried klaar droppings and his horns throbbing in response to the horrified look on his broodmate, Margolan's, face.

He'd awoken early, he told Finnabarr, his words falling over themselves as he tried to explain. He'd gone to check on the prototype, expecting it to still be hours away from completion in the nano-vats, only to find the utter devastation of their lab.

After months of painstaking investigation, it became clear that a tiny Sea-squirrel had swum in through an open purification grate and somehow, against all probability and the manufacturer's persistent denials of responsibility, it had made its way into the lab.

The transformation of that tiny amount of life-energy into mana had been enough, in turn, to level an entire three hundred vani building, *all four floors,* and had instead, created a garden of life-energy-emitting geodes, the likes of which hadn't been found in millennia.

It was enough to create six entire cores, for Frak's sake!

Now here he was, at the end of the line, orbiting in a place where his science and exploration had brought him. Despite all he now desired, each step he'd taken had been full of logic; a small change here, a push there, and now…this… It had taken ten solar cycles, and dozens upon dozens of prisoner sacrifices, but they'd done it…to his eternal shame.

The Intercom chimed, and he snuffled, wiping his crevices. Turning, he slowly walked across to the command chair and sank into it with a groan as he flicked the receiver on, the main screen shifting to reveal his Clan-Leader, Trin'eian.

The enormous Cinthian shifted in the support brace and nodded to Finnabarr in respect, the same sadness he expressed reflected in the colors declared across his crest.

"Finnabarr, Second-Son of my third line, we are here. We know what you do, and that you make this sacrifice for all of our people. As such, the burden is never yours alone. We share in it, and we weep with you." Trin'eian intoned as other screens flickered to life, displaying numerous members of his pod, and lastly, his brood-pair, coming to life on his personal screen. The mana-crystal they shared across space pulsed with their collective love for him as he clutched it tight.

"Thank you, thank…**humph**…thank you all," Finnabarr said quietly, clearing his throat before reaching out and gently caressing the raised nodules of the Primary Distortion Engine controls. He slowly but firmly pressed the keys in turn, slid the dial, and felt the device query his embedded crystal to confirm his identity. Activated, the most valuable cargo that any Cinthian ship had ever carried was released into the ether above the small world below.

Out of the six cores that had been formed by the Sea-squirrel's presence, the resulting information provided them with the information their technology had been lacking. Within a full orbital rotation, they had generated a total of one hundred and sixteen individual Dungeon Cores. As they matured, the Cores were dispatched into orbit, the tiny forms of their fairies each encased in a protective crystal attached to every delivery device. The telemetry that had populated on the fifth screen since loading indicated that the fairies and their bonded Cores were still in perfect hibernation, both halves of the infant Dungeons attached to each other and ready to play their part.

Trin'eian nodded in respect and sympathy as Finnabarr reached for the final control. He touched it gently, feeling it shiver in response, all too aware of the terrible changes its activation would bring. Then, slowly, after looking around the control room and at all his clan, feeling their love and affirmation, he depressed it with a loud 'click'.

The web of satellites responded as one, linking their thrusters and taking aim. A shuddering passed through them as they warped space, linking the small blue and green orb to the subspace rift and allowing the power of Mana to flow through, altering reality.

The world below might never know why they had been chosen for this, a gift, a punishment…a terrible event that would become forever variously known as the Awakening, The Fall or The End. It was even more unlikely that they would ever discover who had bestowed it upon them, but Finnabarr and all his kind would remember them and thank them eternally for their unwitting and unwilling sacrifice.

For the Orakai were coming, and no race, not even one as preternaturally gifted at war as humanity, could hope to survive without the advantages of mana…

Finnabarr turned his ship around, weeping gently as the screens dimmed, his clan signing off to reflect upon the horror of their actions. Behind them, one hundred and sixteen new Dungeon Cores hurtled forward, their ion-pulse engines flaring to guide them to the sites that would provide the most benefit to humanity, giving them at least a faint chance to survive.

As the ship angled away, a barrage of small gravitational effects appeared in orbit as the ship fell into warp, much to NASA's confusion. A small section of an old cold war satellite, desperately in need of decommissioning, bounced off another, heading at an oblique angle to cut across the earth's upper ionosphere.

In and of itself, it was nothing unusual; the trash belt, as it'd come to be known, was full of minor fragments from ships and satellites, but this one, as it spun end over end, cut across the predetermined path of Dungeon Core 112.

A tiny fragment of metal following the main section hit the Core, penetrating deeply enough to cause a small crack in the shield.

As the Core fell, its vessel frantically began to make constant tiny adjustments as it attempted to realign itself. A tiny amount of air escaped from the crack, and slowly, oh so slowly, the Fairy that had been chosen, grown, augmented, and educated to guide the infant Dungeon Core, asphyxiated.

She died in orbit, completely unaware, and the outgassing of the protective atmosphere within the crystal added a slight directional change, shifting a meticulously planned landing off its axis by a single degree.

Empires have fallen from less…

ONE

I LAUGHED, CLAPPING CHRIS on the shoulder, and shook my head at his last comment, amazed the crazy guy could still remember anything of our holiday last month in Greece so clearly. It was almost all a blur for me, only coming back in little bits, like the terror of going through customs and them finding the icing sugar in its little glittery pouch that someone had packed away for a laugh?

That stuck with me. Oh god, that had stuck with me. Three hours of questions in a small cell until they examined it properly, then the subsequent joy of finding that my flight home had, in fact, been delayed because of a safety issue. It had meant that I'd still been able to get aboard, instead of missing the one weekly flight to Newcastle, and as I settled back into the cheap, uncomfortable little seat, seeing the island disappear below me into the distance, I'd felt a relief unlike any I'd ever felt before or since.

Greek Police were NOT to be trifled with.

I smiled, pulling myself away from the memory as I looked at my insane friend, now across the pool table from me. He was still shaking with suppressed laughter as he spoke about one of the guys we'd been drinking with; the way we'd kicked in his door and hit him with the 'Super-Soakers' when he'd had that girl with him, and the look of fury and outrage on his face. Despite being nearly doubled over with amusement at the retelling, the bastard still managed to pot the last red, leave his white in a good position, then toss a wink as he sank the black.

Four games to two, he'd won now, meaning it was my round again, *again*!

"You've been practicing, you filthy bastard…" I grumbled as I picked up our empty glasses and headed off to the bar, weaving my way through the crowds and exchanging a speculative smile with a pretty blonde girl who I'd seen earlier.

She smiled at me, looking me over, when her friend said something to her, grabbing her hand and pulling her away before I could try to introduce myself.

"Ah well, easy come, easy go," I muttered to myself, squeezing past two guys with biceps bigger than my thighs, and who reeked of aftershave. I shook my head subconsciously. The pair of them, I swore, were wearing *fake tan*. Their eyebrows looked like they trimmed each hair one by one, and their clothes clearly must have been meant for someone half their size.

I snorted as the barman, who'd just served them, rolled his eyes at the effort they were putting in. We exchanged a look and that clearly said; *'What are they playing at?'* and nodded in shared agreement.

"What can I get you, mate?" he asked, and I scanned the pump labels quickly.

"Uhhh...two pints of Carling, and a shot of the filthiest rotgut you've got," I said sadly. The barman raised his eyebrow in question, and I shrugged. "It's a forfeit," I explained, jerking my thumb over my shoulder in the direction of the pool table. "I've lost two in a row."

"Ha! Keep doing these, and you'll lose a lot more!" He grinned, pulling a shot glass out from under the counter and pouring a measure of something green into it. He slid it across to me, then went to pull the pints. As the man next to me moved away, taking his drinks from the bar, a familiar mass of long blonde hair took up the space he'd occupied.

"Hi! I'm Kelly." The voice of an angel sounded in my ear, and I turned to find the girl I'd noticed on the way to the bar. This time, she was alone, her friend nowhere in sight, and she was smiling up at me coyly.

"Hi Kelly, I'm Matt," I said, grinning back at her and enjoying her reaction to my accent. She was pretty, beautiful even, but not so much in the style I normally went for. She was well-dressed, her outfit flattering but tasteful, rather than the slutty look I tended to gravitate toward. Her figure was athletic, complimented by long legs, a reasonable chest, and nicely toned arms. I usually went for shorter, very busty girls, but her eyes...

I gazed into them, the brightest blue eyes I'd ever seen, and that smile...

"So, are you going to offer me a drink?" she laughed after a second, and I blinked, realizing I'd just been staring at her and smiling.

"Damn, sorry! You're beautiful." I chuckled in return and shook my head ruefully. "What do you want to drink, then?" I added it to my order, getting a knowing look from the barman when he came back. I swiped my card across the reader, trying not to wince at the expensive cocktails she'd ordered for her and her friend.

Thankfully, it went through, but it would take a chunk out of the limited money I had to see me through to the end of the month. If she was planning on drinking those all night…I looked her over again as we talked, taking the chance to admire the view when she turned to pass the second cocktail to her friend, who magically appeared, took it without a word, then vanished again.

"Wondered where you'd gone…can't trust you foreign types not to bugger off when it comes to paying up…" a voice scoffed at my ear, and I turned, startled out of my ogling. Chris shook his head at me as he slid into the space next to me, pushing me along a bit and accidentally-on-purpose knocking me into Kelly, making her smile up at me as we shuffled along.

I introduced Chris, apologizing for abandoning him, and passed him his pint. I grimaced as he pointedly reminded me of the forfeit, much to his and Kelly's amusement, as I gagged after knocking it back. Her friend, who turned out to be called Michelle, appeared at some point, leaving wherever, or whoever she'd been with up till then, in favor of Chris, the handsome bastard. The night devolved into a blur of bars, ending in a nightclub with Kelly and I in a corner, pressed up against each other, kissing fervently as our hands explored.

We all eventually staggered outside at kicking out time, blinking blearily at the heavy rain as we tried to find somewhere to stand without getting soaked while waiting for the taxi.

"Here's my number. Call me tomorrow, okay? And thanks for the coat…" Kelly whispered breathily into my ear, kissing my cheek and going back to inputting digits into my phone. I took it as she saved it, and hit 'Call.' Her phone lit up, verifying that she had my number in return, and that she'd given me hers correctly.

She smiled at me, and we started kissing again, hands roaming, and I tried to convince her, unsuccessfully, not to go back with Michelle and to instead come to my flat.

In the end, as the taxi honked its horn, she broke away with one last kiss, wrapped my coat around herself, and ran for the car door, her legs gleaming wetly in the rain as she jumped inside and giggled at her friend, who started telling her off.

The door closed, and the taxi pulled away, a spray of cold water shooting up from a puddle to drench my lower legs and shoes. I immediately regretted that I'd given Chris my taxi so that I could spend more time with Kelly.

I stood there, shivering, looking around, but after a handful of seconds, I shrugged and started to walk. My shoes squelched, full of muddy water, as I trudged off.

I waited until I was out of the majority of the rain before pulling up the local taxi app and confirming what I already knew from getting Kelly's taxi sorted for her…there were no more cabs available for at least another hour.

I was only a few miles from the flat, so after popping into an all-night pizza and kebab shop for a tray of French fries and soaking them in vinegar and salt, I set off home.

Forty minutes later, six texts to Kelly, two to Chris, a random argument with another drunk, and a tray of fries that was holding more water in the bottom than it'd originally held food, I staggered up the short series of stone steps to the house, shivering and exhausted.

It had originally been a big old Victorian house, but it'd been converted into three flats, and mine, the top one, was finally within reach as I hunted for my keys…I patted pocket after pocket, before starting to swear loudly.

They were in my damn coat.

I shook my head, banging my forehead slowly off the doorframe of the building as I continued to swear. I was freezing cold, locked out of my flat, my phone battery had died about twenty minutes before, as I'd used the last of it in an attempt to convince Kelly to get a cab to mine, despite knowing damn well there were no cabs to be had.

I'd spent the entire night thinking with the little head, and now the bill had come due.

The bottom flat was owned by a guy named Paul, who worked offshore and wouldn't be home for at least another three days, if I remembered right. A miserable couple lived between us both in the middle flat, and they fucking hated me.

They'd already called the police on me once in the past month after I'd had a party, and twice on Paul downstairs for making 'a disturbance'. The guy had been having sex with his partner; it wasn't his fault that there was an old chimney that ran up one side of the building. It'd been blocked off long ago, but it still carried 'noises' if they were loud enough.

The couple—neither Paul nor I had really bothered to learn their names—had moved in five weeks ago, and were quickly shaping up to be the neighbors from hell.

I stood on the stoop, dripping wet, shivering, and feeling practically sober, as I considered if it was worth waking them up to buzz me through the outer door so I could at least sleep on the mat outside my flat, or if I should just wait.

My options were limited. Chris' place was one of the closest, out of my local friends, and he was about a two hour walk away…plus he'd be passed out drunk by now, much less when I could get there. Alternatively, I knew there was a little old bakery shop about ten minutes' walk in the opposite direction. They'd be opening in about another hour, if I remembered right.

I nodded to myself; the combination of a desperate need to wee, the thought of fresh baked bread, and the vague recollection of one of the guys who worked there having the same model phone as me, decided it. I'd go get some food, charge my phone if I was really lucky, then call Kelly and get my goddamn keys. Hey, maybe I'd even get asked to stay out of pity, I hoped. Looking down at my drenched state, I certainly felt pitiful.

I walked down the steps again and set off up the street, pausing long enough to pull my left shoe off and empty out a very wet stone that had somehow gotten inside. As I wandered up the street, I reflected on how the week before had been clear skies and warm nights.

"Sod's law, I got locked out on a night with a thunderstorm…" I muttered. Hearing noise in the distance, I paused and looked up.

I blinked in confusion, wiped at my eyes, and tried to make sense of what I was seeing. There were…lines in the sky.

Glowing red…yellow…well, fiery, I guessed, judging by the colors…lines that crisscrossed the sky. I turned, tracking one, and realized that they spanned from horizon to horizon, slowly spreading out to link up, making the night bloom into an early dawn. They were faint through the cloud cover, but still bright enough to see and to tell the color, which meant that around the world, they had to be going nuts.

I twisted around, trying to make sense of the lines, and had a sudden fear race through me. I'd done a couple of lines at the end, in the club with Kelly. She'd pulled them out and offered them, laughing when I'd tipped the little container out on her arm and did it there, kissing her afterwards and swearing it was sweeter…

Now I wondered what the hell had been in it. Had she given me some weird shit cut with baking soda or something? Was it melting my brain?

I gaped at the sky, trying to make sense of what I was seeing, as the creak from a window nearby opening pulled my attention. An older man leaned out, staring up at the sky, stunned.

"Hey!" I called, and he jumped, banging his head on the window frame. He began rubbing it and glowered at me. "What's that?" I asked him.

"Think I know, kid?" he growled, pulling his hand back to check, presumably for blood. "I just woke up for a piss and saw it. What do *you* think it is? How long's it been like that?"

"I…I'm on my way to the bakery…" I stammered, shrugging. "It wasn't like that five minutes ago. It was like thunder; then they just started spreading."

"Weird." He shook his head. "It'll be those goddamn contrails from the planes, chemicals! Mark my words, boy, you want to get inside!"

"Locked myself out…" I admitted sourly, gesturing to the house further down the street, and he laughed at me.

"Been there a time or two, kid." he admitted, smiling at last. "Top of the road, go past the baker's and take a left. There's an odds-and-ends corner shop; you know it?" I nodded.

"The guy there opens at seven. He's an ex-locksmith, crotchety old fart, but a friend of mine. Tell him Peter sent you, and as long as you can prove you live there, he'll pop the lock for you. Maybe charge you a couple of quid, but that's it."

"Oh, thank god," I muttered, hope filling me along with relief. "I will, and thank you, mate, you're a lifesaver!" He nodded and waved, muttering about the government and shutting the window with a thump as the old, warped wood resisted.

I drew in a deep breath and made my way up the street, checking my watch as I went. It had been my grandfather's, and I loved it. The smoothly whirring parts indicated five twenty-six in the morning, practically 'O-Dark Thirty' as I'd heard it called in the movies. I grimaced as I wandered up to the corner shop, continuously glancing at the lines in the sky that burned and glimmered. They slowly grew dimmer as I went, until, less than half an hour later, as I waited outside the bakery, they finally dimmed to the point of invisibility.

I was torn. I'd desperately wanted a decent photo of them, but every time I tried to turn my phone on, I got nothing, not even a flicker. I had to admit that I felt relief at them fading away, as well.

I wasn't one of those conspiracy theorists who thought the government was out to get everyone; not because I thought they wouldn't—if they could make a profit for themselves, I was sure they damn well would—but because I viewed the government as completely incompetent.

'Management is nature's way of removing idiots from the workforce.' I'd seen it on a sign once, and damn if it wasn't true. The political 'class' seemed to be comprised of the most incompetent wankers in the world, and it was only that fact that saved us all.

I had no doubt that if they thought they'd be able to get away with it, most governments would have us all branded and collared. It was just far more likely that they were too busy trying to bang their secretaries, get a backhander, or secure their speaking career after their time in office was over, that saved the common man.

I shrugged and leaned back against the wall of the bakery, listening to the sound of people shouting and arguing inside. I distractedly attempted to make out what was being said as I checked my watch again. Three minutes until they opened. I moved across to the bench seats. Soaked, they might be, but so was I, so what did I have to lose?

I sat down, deliberately facing the closed doors and hoping my sad, bedraggled state would earn me some sympathy.

Twenty minutes later, I gave up and got to my feet, walking over to the bakery doors and banging on them, hard.

There was a sudden silence from inside, then a minute later, the sound of bolts being drawn back. The door was pulled open, shuddering as it moved the first few inches.

A small man in a white top and pants and a silly hat, with flour dusted everywhere, glared up at me, before clearly forcing himself to wipe the snarl from his face.

"Sorry, son. Power cut, so we're closed." He shook his head, waving me off. "Might be open later, though; depends on the power."

"Seriously?" I asked him, aghast. "I've been waiting out here for nearly an hour. I'm soaked!" I desperately attempted to play the sympathy card again.

"More fool you, then, son. Should have brought an umbrella." He scowled at my sodden state, totally unimpressed.

"Look, man, I'm locked out and I need somewhere to wait out the storm. I'll be out of your hair in like, half an hour. Just let me stand somewhere warm, and I'll buy anything you want…" I pleaded, hoping he had something warm ready.

"Told you, son, power cut. The ovens are off, the TV's down; hell, even the damn phones don't work." He pinched the bridge of his nose and sighed, before looking me over. "You waiting for Markus?" he asked. I frowned, gesturing in the rough direction of the corner shop, and he nodded.

"Yeah, I was told he can open it," I said, shivering.

"Ah…oh, to hell with it. You can wait in the front of the shop; just try not to make a mess, okay?" He raised an eyebrow at me. I nodded thankfully, and he let me in, saying nothing when I darted for the toilet. When I came out, there was a day-old sandwich in the shop's branded wrapper and a can of soda waiting for me, as well as a towel.

I dried off as best I could, called through my thanks, which was totally ignored, and settled down to wait. The sandwich was awful, egg and cress, possibly my least favorite combination in the entire frigging world, but it went down, partially because I didn't want to be rude, and partially because I was still at least half drunk. The soda mercifully washed the taste away, and I sat watching through the holes in the metal shutters as people began to walk past. I groaned internally at how unlucky I was to need to borrow a phone charger in a blackout. *Not much point there…*I reflected.

A few passersby walked up to the closed doors, cursed, and walked away, while others struggled past in the rain. I watched a bedraggled young woman sloshing along with two kids in tow, and then it struck me: what I hadn't seen yet.

There wasn't a single car moving on the roads. There'd usually be a steady rumble of traffic by now, cars and vans passing through on their way into the city, but today, it was ominously silent. As I glanced along the street, I noticed that no lights were on anywhere, not in the surrounding streets I could see from the shutters, anyway.

Another ten minutes or so passed, with me growing considerably more tired and almost falling asleep on the bench seat, until the short, dark-haired baker came back through and startled me.

"I've just seen Markus ride past, lad; he'll be headed for his shop now," he said, not unkindly, as I straightened and let out a jaw-cracking yawn.

I stiffly stood, thanking him and offering to pay for the food and drink, getting only a shake of his head as he indicated the powerless card reader.

"Don't worry about it. And sorry if I was short with you; not going to be a good day without power here," he apologized.

"No! God, man, you let me in, fed and watered me, and let me use the toilet. I owe you. I'll call down later on today or tomorrow, make it right then," I offered, and he simply shrugged off my insistence.

"Just get yourself home, and get a warm shower, and put yourself to bed. lad. You stink of booze, and you're covered in lipstick. Must have been a good night?"

"Aye, it was…" I said, grinning despite myself, and he laughed, clearly thinking of similar nights in his past as he opened the door and gestured me through. "Go on, then. Bugger off."

I walked out, thanking him again over my shoulder as I heard the door close behind me. Trudging through the puddles, I crossed the street and took the side street off it, walking down to where the corner shop stood. As I approached, I noticed the front door slightly ajar, with an old bike leaning against it.

"Hello?" I called in, peering into the dark recesses of the shop, and heard a grumbling voice call back a few seconds later.

"Be right with you!"

I waited, leaning against the door in a feeble attempt to stay out of the rain, until an older eastern European man eventually appeared, pulling the door further open.

"Sorry, mate…" he said apologetically. "Bloody power cut. All the fridges and freezers have leaked!"

"Ouch!" I winced, remembering how many of the old things the shop had, and imagining the amount of money he was losing as they defrosted. "Anything I can do?" I offered automatically, and he laughed, gesturing at me.

"You kidding? You're soaked through, lad; what happened to you?" He smiled warmly, and I smiled back, shrugging.

"Locked myself out. A guy on my street said to come see you; said his name was Peter?"

"Ah, that miserable fart still alive?" he quipped, shaking his head and smiling. "Name's Markus, by the way."

"Matt," I responded, holding my hand out to shake, and he took it automatically, despite the horror of the last few years' pandemics. The late vaccine program had finally allowed for people to have normal social contact again a few months ago, and practically everywhere you went now, someone wanted to shake hands, hug, or touch you one way or another.

If you were lucky, anyway. Dating in the aftermath was brilliant fun.

"So, what do you need?" he prompted. "And where's 'home'? I can't go far; damn car's not working. You've clearly not got one..."

"I'm at the bottom of Osborne Avenue," I said, shrugging. "Ten minutes' walk, maybe?" I guessed, and he waved dismissively.

"Lot less than that for me on the bike...think you can keep up?" He raised his eyebrows questioningly, and I nodded quickly. He grinned at that and disappeared into the darkness of the shop, reappearing a few minutes later with a small, clearly much –used, laminated sign.

'Popped out, back in ten.'

He pulled a backpack on and gestured me out to the street. I moved back, and he pulled the door closed, locked it with an insanely long key, and grinned as he caught me inspecting it.

"Ain't letting someone break into my place easily, lad. If they can pick that lock, they deserve whatever they can take!" he crowed, climbing nimbly onto the bike and turning it around.

I set off jogging alongside him as he asked me about the street, how long I'd lived there, and about the girl whose lipstick I was apparently covered in.

I told him about Kelly, and about the street, explaining that I'd bought the flat about two years ago, and in seemingly no time, we were there. I showed Markus my driver's license, and he grunted at the address match, pulled out a few thin, randomly bent rods of metal, and had the front door open in under a minute.

He pulled his bike inside and propped it against the entryway wall, and we climbed the two flights of stairs to my flat. Again, he worked his magic with the bent rods, and thirty seconds later, the door popped open, much to my amazement and slight concern.

"There you go, lad," he announced, clapping me on the shoulder and smiling as he stood back up.

"Bloody hell, well done!" I said in shock. "That was amazing! How did you do that?"

"Legacy of a misspent youth, back in the old country." He winked at me, packing his tools back into the old, battered backpack. The bag was yellow with orange trimming and looked like it'd been dragged across the planet, and it clinked as he shifted it about until it was comfortable.

"How much do I owe you?" I asked, pulling my wallet back out.

"Come by the shop, start using it instead of the supermarkets now and then, and we'll call it even," he offered, and I nodded gratefully.

"Definitely!" I promised, and he shot me another good-natured grin before turning and hurrying to the stairs.

"Well, I've got a shop to open and a floor to sort. Get some sleep, lad," he insisted, vanishing down the stairs.

"I will, and thanks, Markus!" I called, probably louder than I should have, considering it wasn't yet eight in the morning, but I was so relieved and tired, I didn't care. I walked inside and kicked my shoes off, heading down the hall to the bathroom. I dropped my waterlogged socks in the sink, emptied my pockets, and pulled off my watch. I set everything on the windowsill of the small bathroom and stripped off, dumping the rest of my clothes into the sink with a wet squelch.

I turned the shower on, thankful for once that it was such an ancient system, it didn't need electricity. I managed to warm myself up before the hot water ran out, dried off, and collapsed into bed.

I was asleep before my head hit the pillow, dreaming of a pretty, sweet, blonde girl.

TWO

IT WAS EARLY afternoon when I woke up, and I groaned at the light shining in through the window, I threw my arm across my eyes a few times, trying to block it out, drifting off, and then waking up again, before I finally gave in and got up. I'd intended to close the blinds and go back to sleep, but the silence made me look outside, and I swore as I realized the power was still off.

I relieved myself, washing my face in cold water, and made a sandwich, attempting to open my fridge for the absolute minimum time possible. Every click and clatter set me wincing as my head pounded from the hangover.

Without any power, I still couldn't charge my phone, but I remembered that Chris had mentioned he was meeting an old friend from Uni this afternoon, and I knew that he kept a battery charge pack for emergencies in his car. He was planning to catch up with them at *'Dirty Molly's,'* so all I had to do was sort out some clean clothes, drive over, and borrow it. Then I could charge the phone, call Kelly, and booyah, dinner, drinks, and (I damn well hoped) some sexy time.

With that in mind, I tidied the flat, chucked some washing in the machine to wait until the power came back on, got rid of the dishes, and even changed the bedsheets. Then I hid all the random shit I'd need to explain, like the inflatable T-Rex outfit.

Occasionally, people would ask me why I had one. In response, I'd get dressed up in it, and they'd laugh their asses off. If they didn't, fuck it; it was their loss. When someone didn't appreciate a giant T-Rex outfit, it was their problem, not mine.

I looked around the flat and nodded to myself in satisfaction. It was passable, nothing too bad on display, just a few stacks of DVDs and my gaming chair. The VR headset I'd spent far too much money on, and the slabs of beers waiting to be drunk would take some explaining, but that was life.

I wrung out the still-soaked clothes from last night, chucked them in the washer with the rest, and checked over the bits I'd had in my pocket. Some coins, my dead phone, and my wallet joined my watch on the bed.

I finished getting dressed and put some aftershave on, checked my reflection to verify that I looked good, just in case she was free then and there, then fished out my spare keys and closed and locked the door. I wandered downstairs, passing the middle flat and sneering slightly at the sound of yet another argument filtering into the hallway.

Once I was outside, it struck me just how damn quiet everything was. Occasional people were wandering around seemingly aimlessly, but most of the area just seemed abandoned.

Weirdly, there were loads of cars in the street. During the day, they were usually all out, even on a weekend…I pressed my key and pulled on the door handle to my car and frowned when I found it still locked. I tried again, not even a beep.

I looked at the key, then the door, then at all the cars around me, and my hungover hindbrain started screaming for my attention that this was very, very bad. I checked the key fob itself, and sure enough, there was a physical key hidden inside. It took a few seconds of pushing and prodding to work it free, but I managed to unlock the car eventually and get inside.

Having seen it done before, I popped the 'Go' button free of the dashboard and found a key slot underneath, inserted the key, turned…and nothing. Not even a cough from the engine turning over. The damn thing was totally dead. I sat there for a fair amount of time as I puzzled through what had happened.

The phones, the cars, household electricity, everything was dead, and that made me think of only one thing: an EMP blast from a nuke. I had a long second of my heart racing before my brain kicked in and took over.

There was no way a nuke would have made those patterns in the sky, and if a nuke had hit us, it was only logical to expect that there'd be more of an effect than just all our electrics dying. Whole streets vanishing into flames and bits of people flying everywhere was probably just Hollywood's version, sure, but still.

"Okay…" I muttered to myself, drumming my fingers on the steering wheel. "Option two: solar flare. They've been reporting shit about those interfering with electrics for years, so maybe that's it?" I contemplated the minimal facts I knew for a long moment before shrugging noncommittally. "Maybe option three should be that the Matrix is broken, then. That's the only thing that makes sense with the sky; maybe it's a grid system that's been upgraded?" I snorted at the ridiculous train of thought and shook my head. "That means someone in the heavenly IT department is panicking right now as their bosses scream at them to fix it before anyone notices…" I shook my head again at the insanity of working in the IT sector, as I had for the last four years, before sighing and pulling my key free.

I was hungover, tired, and the world had gone to shit. It was way above my paygrade to deal with this crap, so I decided to go back inside, sleep the damn hangover off, and see if it was better tomorrow. Tomorrow was Monday, after all, and I'd get ready, walk to work if necessary, and find out what was happening. The company I worked for had government contracts, so they'd be in the loop about fixing shit. Naturally, that also meant that I'd be insanely busy, probably for weeks to come. On the upside, though, overtime was good money.

I got out of the car, locking it and putting the key back together as I strolled up the steps to the house, then wandered up to the flat, closing and locking the door. Absently, I chucked the keys into the bowl I always used for them and looked out of the window in the direction of the city center.

I could see plumes of smoke rising in a few places, and I suddenly got a horrible feeling of impending doom.

"What if the power doesn't come back on?" I whispered to myself, before shaking my head and scoffing at my overactive imagination. It would. Everything would be back to normal in a few weeks. I was big enough, and ugly enough, to manage without my phone, and…

"That's it!" I said suddenly, grinning. "My phone!" It had been dead before the outage, no power at all, so all I had to do was find a way to charge it. If it came on, then I'd know that there hadn't been an EMP, as anything electrical wouldn't work. It wouldn't be able to call anyone else, if their phones had been caught in it, or if the cell towers had been affected, and I was fairly sure I'd heard something about EMPs only affecting things that were in use at the time…but hell with it. At least I had a plan. I'd head to my office; we kept a ton of random gear there, including a generator in the basement, so I'd be able to jury-rig some gear for a few science tests, at least.

Sure, my memories of school physics classes were spotty, mainly revolving around how tight Lyndsey's shirts were and how her boobs were going to escape one day, but that wasn't the point…at least I'd know that electrics worked, and from there, it'd be a short step to starting to fix shit.

If the EMP *had* wiped out all active electronics, the phone would be fine, as it'd been dead at the time. If not, it wasn't an EMP, and that was also fine, because at least I would be one step closer to knowing what it was, and from there, the solution. Pleased with my critical thinking process, I stripped off. I'd been wearing a nice shirt, fresh jeans, and some of my nicer looking shoes, but that was no good for what I needed now. Closing the blinds against the piercing sunlight, I crawled back into bed, groaning happily at the simple comfort of clean sheets and a soft pillow. At least there was one benefit to a power outage on a Sunday. There would be no noise to interrupt my hangover slumber.

Feeling refreshed and much more like myself on Monday morning, I contemplated my wardrobe, keeping in mind that I'd likely be up to my eyeballs in work as soon as I got to the building. My working 'tactical' pants were made of much stronger fabrics than my jeans and had a million pockets. Paired with an Under Armor top, a hooded jacket, and my work boots, I collected my Leatherman and various small toolkits and loaded up the pockets.

Grabbing my shoulder bag from its usual place by the front door, I chucked in a change of clothing, some energy bars, a canteen filled with juice, and my phone, and I left in the standard engineer's complement of random crap I was used to carrying. There was no way of knowing when a first aid kit, dozens of network cables, my network crimping tools, and a plethora of random crap might come in handy.

Every time I picked it up, I'd tell myself that I needed to clear it out, but then, invariably, I'd need some random thing at work within the next day or two, and I always ended up keeping it as it was.

I cinched the straps tight, made sure everything was comfy, and piled some towels under the fridge, as it was already starting to leak. Then I set off, jogging down the stairs and passing the asshole from the middle flat. He watched me go, waiting until I was almost at the front door, then called down, wanting to know if this power cut was my fault.

I stepped back inside and stared up at him.

"What?" I asked, unsure I'd heard him correctly.

"I said, 'is this mess your fault?' The power, everything? You've been messing with shit you shouldn't, haven't you! Don't think we don't know our electricity bill is higher than it should be! We already reported you to the company. We know you've been using ours somehow!"

I gaped at him in disbelief for several seconds, before shaking my head at his stupidity. I had nothing to do with his electricity bill, and no idea why he'd decided the outage had anything to do with me, so I turned around and started back toward the door.

"Hey!" he shouted, starting down the stairs after me. His horrible wife followed him out to shout down at him as he went. "I'm talking to you…!"

"Is it him?!" she screeched, moving out of their doorway and pointing a finger at me. "This is all your fault, you ass! Isn't it?"

"My fault?" I repeated, stunned. "You think the fact the entire area is without power, and the cars and phones are all down, is because of me? What the hell do you think I do for a living?!" I asked.

"Probably a terrorist!" she squealed, pointing at me. "You've all got that filthy foreign skin!" I froze, totally amazed and shocked to my core.

I was six-foot, with dark hair and blue eyes, of mixed American and Mediterranean descent, which resulted in giving me olive-toned skin. Most people were jealous of my tan, since I was slightly darker than the average European in the winter and usually tanned well in the summer, but that was it. I'd never been accused of being a terrorist before, let alone racially profiled by a white woman who looked like she was channeling a popular female pig puppet from one of my childhood shows at the best of times.

"Are you for fucking real?" I snarled, dropping my bag onto the floor and starting back towards them.

"You better not think I'm afraid of you!" the guy said—Gerald, I thought his name was—and he was visibly thinking he'd rather be elsewhere.

"Are you off your fucking rocker?!" I leveled a finger at the fat cow glowering from behind him on the stairs. "Listen, you racist piece of shit, I was born here. My parents moved here from fucking Atlanta, and even if they hadn't, what the hell gives you the right to start that shit? It's people like you that are fucking the world up! We used to be all about helping each other! Hell, I used to be proud to be British; now we're a fucking international laughingstock because fat old fucks like you wanted to relive the glory days *that never happened!*"

I hated politics, but man, I hated racists more than anything else. I had friends of all colors: black, white, Asian, whatever. In the IT field, all anyone cared about was if you could do your job; it didn't matter if you were fucking green, or blue, even. I was an orphan. I'd been the only survivor at the age of fifteen when a hit and run had driven our family car off the motorway into a support for a bridge. I'd spent the last few years of my childhood in and out of foster homes, with only the occasional visit from my asshole cousins and uncle from America, who evidently just wanted a photo opportunity.

The best home I'd ever had since then, one which I'd only left because I was old enough to get my own place, I had still visited regularly for years afterwards, was 'Mama Aurelia's.' A tiny house that always had the heating on full–belt, filled to bursting with an enormous Caribbean woman with a heart the size of the house. Nobody *ever* went hungry in a ten-mile radius of Mama Aurelia; she was a woman out for all she could give, and her funeral six months ago had sent me into a black fit of depression and rage that I was only just starting to get over.

Growing up in and out of houses and foster homes meant I saw the best and the worst of people, and it had fueled my passionate hatred of racism.

My accent hadn't helped, which even I admitted was American, thanks to my parents and the holidays we'd taken to regularly visit the family that had abandoned me after their deaths.

"People like *you*," I spat at the fearfully glowering excuse of a man, "are why racism is going mad. People like *you* are why there's so much shit going on now. And as for you, ya fat cow…" I called up, switching from her pathetic excuse for a husband and pointing up at her. "You can get fucked! You'll want to learn to keep your mouth shut, because there's nobody that's gonna come help you if the shit hits the fan!"

I clamped my mouth shut, forcefully cutting off my tirade, and as I turned away, stalking toward the door and reaching for my bag, I could feel my blood boiling. Man, I wished the last guy hadn't sold the flat to them.

"You better watch yourself!" Gerald threatened, grabbing my arm. I spun, punching him in the gut once. He was maybe forty, flabby *and* skinny in the weird that combination some people managed, with a pot belly and the muscle tone of an over-stretched elastic band. He just folded around my fist, collapsing to the ground and wheezing painfully.

I froze, looking down at him with my fist still clenched in anger, and I started to panic. I hadn't meant to hit him. Hell, I'd been in fights as a kid, who hadn't? And I'd done some sparring in martial arts, but only for a few months here and there. I didn't really get into trouble, so it wasn't a skill I'd ever refined.

I suddenly realized as his wife's squeals and his groaning broke through my fog of contemplation, that I might have made a terrible mistake. Our government contracts, which were a seriously big part of my job, required enhanced criminal checks.

If this asshole pressed charges for me hitting him, I could lose my job! My brain was racing, and I said the only thing I could think of.

"You try anything—touch me again, call the police, anything—and I'll make sure they need a dentist to 'ID' you." I snarled, picking my bag up and walking out of the door.

I hurried down the steps and turned left, jogging down the street, before crossing over the road and taking a right to head for the city, I'd need to pass through it to reach my office, where I'd be able to find any and all gear I needed to power the phone.

As I went, I replayed the scene back in my mind constantly, thinking about the consequences that could come from it, but after half an hour of self-recriminations, I'd come to a decision.

There was nothing wrong with me punching the miserable bastard, and the old argument of 'self-defense,' combined with the fact that it was their word against mine, would probably see me through it with nothing more than a slap on the wrist.

Hell, if the police were actually involved, they'd have to meet the pair and probably give me a round of applause for punching him anyway.

Calmer now, I jogged for a bit, then walked, then jogged, covering the distance quickly, until I started passing more and more people. Couples and families were out for a stroll, kids playing, intermingled with people like me, moving with a purpose. Everywhere I looked, people were on edge. There was that intangible feeling of fear in the air, and the closer I got to the center of the city, the worse it became.

I crossed under the main ring road around the core of the city and soon passed the university campus. The smoke which I'd seen earlier had blackened the walls of one building, with firemen standing around talking to people, and dozens of empty fire extinguishers stacked off to one side.

I hadn't even thought about what would happen with the emergency services out of action until now, and the sudden, horrible thought of the hospitals, the intensive care wards, hell, the delivery suites and all their gear not working came to mind, making me blanch at the thought.

I swallowed hard. I felt an instinctive need to go talk to the firemen, to ask a person in authority what was happening, but as I passed the crowd that surrounded them, I heard enough floating through the concerned voices.

"…as I said, I've no idea why the fire engine won't start, but…" Concerned, I turned away, heading on down the road.

I passed squares and long streets that were normally choked with cars, instead encountering people wandering aimlessly at finding that all of the shops were closed, as they had no power. Even the die-hard shoppers were stuck.

I'd secretly hoped the power might be working over here, and as I passed my favorite burger place, I swallowed the disappointment and went on, my stomach complaining loudly that it just wasn't right to pass by without stopping in.

Another ten minutes, and I was past the city center, heading down another street to the south of the city, when I heard a crash, glass shattering, and a scream for help from around the corner ahead. I started running instinctively, reaching the intersection in time to see a pair of men running off, abandoning a broken window of a nearby shop. The empty jewelry stands on display and the shocked and terrified face of a young sales assistant greeted me as I skidded to a stop.

The thieves were fast, disappearing down a side street in seconds, as the assistant shouted after them in rage.

"Are you okay?" I asked her cautiously, and she turned to glare at me.

"No! No, I'm fucking not!" she half-snapped, half-cried as she came out of her shock.

"Did they hurt you?" I clarified, and she shook her head.

"Then all this can be replaced." I gestured at the window and the stripped display. "You can't be, so don't worry about this sparkly shit."

"You don't understand!" she wailed. "The cameras aren't working, and the owner told me to put the security mesh down! I forgot when I closed up yesterday; that's why I'm here now! She's gonna fire me…" She started to cry.

I patted her arm awkwardly, unsure of what else to do, and gave her a shoulder to cry on, suddenly noticing a few other people walking by and eyeing the windows speculatively.

"Look, let's close the mesh now, okay? I can go looking for the police." I took her by the shoulders and peered into her tear-stricken eyes. She nodded and wiped her face, shuddering as she cried quietly to herself while pulling on the levers. The mesh came down smoothly over the intact window, and I pulled the one down over the broken side.

"Okay," I said, getting her attention. "I'm going to go. I'll head over to the police station, I'll tell them what happened, and give a statement, and send them to you, all right?" She nodded gratefully wiping her eyes.

"Thank you," she said with a little sniffle, and I smiled at her reassuringly.

"It's okay, don't worry about it," I shrugged. It didn't feel like I'd done much, except calm her down.

"I'm Sarah." She stuck her hand out to shake, which still felt a little odd, given the strictly enforced lack of contact during the pandemic, but I returned the gesture.

"I'm Matt," I replied, and she forced a smile.

"Thanks, Matt," she said, and I stepped outside, pulling the mesh down over the door so she could lock it from her side.

"Not a problem, Sarah; nice to meet you." I meant it. It would have been great to meet her, normally; she was pretty and seemed a friendly enough girl. While I liked Kelly, I'd literally met her yesterday, and I'd been drunk. Under typical circumstances, I'd have asked for Sarah's number, but today...wasn't normal. I shook myself from my thoughts and waved to her as I headed off, even more determined to get to work and figure out what the hell was going on.

I crossed two more streets, doubling back on my trajectory at an oblique angle to reach the police main station, and I felt my heart drop as I got closer.

A crowd had amassed outside the station, and two harassed and annoyed police stood in front of the building, dealing with the clamoring people. I joined the group and waited my turn, snarling once at a guy who tried to cut in front of me. Beyond that, I dealt with queue jumpers the British way, which was to say, glaring at them and grumbling under my breath until they realized they'd been spotted and moved back.

The entire time, as I moved forward, I overheard the complaints of the people around me. My first instinct had been to push forward; after all, I had a real crime to report, but I quickly realized, so did they.

Dozens upon dozens of people were reporting the same. From houses to shops, to vans and workshops, looters were going for gold today.

When I finally made it to the front forty minutes later, I gave an explanation to an impatient officer, who wrote it down in a notepad and scrawled his signature on the back of half a raffle ticket.

"Have the owner bring that down to the station tomorrow at some point," he ordered, handing it over, and stapling the other half to the report. "They'll be dealt with then, but unless someone was hurt, we've not got the resources to deal with it today."

"Uh...okay?" I said, astonished. It was a basic premise of modern life; if you were in trouble, you went to the police, and they'd deal with it. To find them this over-run, this stressed, brought the whole thing into focus. "Do you know…" I started, and he sighed, shaking his head in exasperation.

"Look, people!" he called, holding his hands up. "I'll say it *again*, for those who didn't hear last time! We don't know what happened. We're working on it, and when we do know, you'll know. Until then, make your report and move along!" He dropped his hands and gestured to me to move on, turning to the next person in the line.

"No, wait a second…" I started and he glared at me. "I'm a network engineer," I hastily explained. "If you've got any signal from the network, I might be able to help you get the systems back online." He paused briefly before nodding once to me and turning to his partner.

"John, I'll take this guy inside; be right back," he said. His partner looked me over and gave him a single nod in return. "You'd better not be lying, kid," the first policeman said, leading me inside through a magnetic locked door that had released automatically when the power had gone out.

"I'm not; I work with data networks for a living…" I wondered if the datacenters were intact, or if they'd been wiped. Most people had no idea, but the data they accessed was all stored in 'datacenters,' hubs for all the high-tech storage devices that were replicated all over the world. The buildings themselves were generally well-secured, but the more important and therefore more secure centers weren't on any maps. Those were usually housed on sites that were guarded by armed security, even here in the UK, where guns were rarer than in America. The sites were often heavily shielded and had backup generators, as well, so for the first time since entering the queue, I started to think things might be fixable.

"Hmmm, well, we've already got some techs in here…" he said, opening a side door and leading me down to a basement level. I grumbled a bit under my breath as we descended into the bowels of the old building. I privately reflected that it was just like typical bureaucracy to always put the IT guys out of the way in the shitty sections of the building, not realizing until something went wrong just how much they needed us.

We finally entered a room that was full of cables, computer parts, and swearing, and I grinned reflexively. I was home.

"Hey guys, got some IT geek here, says he can help?" the copper called, and I glared at him.

"I *said* I was a network engineer, and that I *might* be able to help if you had a signal," I clarified. A head popped up from the other side of a desk, jam-jar glasses inflating his eyes to owlish proportions.

"Tell me you're a sys-admin?" the figure asked, and I smiled reflexively.

"Network, mainly..." I replied. "Mostly layer one, but I can do two to four."

"That's great, I'm all about the layer seven," he countered in geek-speak, and the copper who'd brought me down shrugged and walked off, leaving me with the guy.

The next hour passed in a blur as I was introduced around. Martin and Danny were the two engineers' names, and I was quickly brought up to speed on the things they'd already tried. We pulled fresh kit out of sealed boxes and connected it all up; the generator in the basement was getting worked on by a different team, and we tested all the gear as best we could until it was all ready. I was sitting on a table munching on a packet of crisps when Martin came looking for me.

"Sorry, man," he said, holding up a powerbank. "I could have sworn I'd charged it as well, but I must have forgotten..." He looked worried. I shrugged and swallowed my mouthful, getting off the desk and checking the device over.

"It's all right; I'll just wire one up from the battery packs I've got in the office, once we've tested this..." I said, both of us ignoring the possibility that it *had* been charged and was now dead for a different reason.

"Well, they think they're ready to start the generator now!" he said. A few minutes later, a clicking sounded from a few rooms over, followed by a lot of swearing.

We prodded the power button on the gear we'd put in place, and then tried the light switches, before looking at each other in mutual annoyance.

Martin left the room to see what was happening with the generator, while Danny and I argued over possible reasons it might not be working. He'd settled on the Matrix idea as the most likely, while I was convinced of a serious fuckup in the area, possibly some lab testing something they shouldn't have and buggering up the electrics...although I couldn't explain how.

We debated over candlelight and tossed increasingly stupid ideas back and forth until Martin returned, sitting on a desk nearby and removing the enormous jam-jar glasses to polish them.

"Right," he started. "The generator works, sort of. At least, as near as anyone can tell."

"But there's no power..." Danny said, and Martin held up his hand to stop him.

"I know, that's what I'm telling you. The *generator* works. It's old school, a diesel genny, but the *electricity* doesn't, and I can't explain why. It just...doesn't work." He rubbed the bridge of his nose. "I think we need someone who's really into this kind of crap, because we're way past my level of understanding for it. As far as I know, it *should* be working; there's just no logical reason why it wouldn't." I sat back, thinking over the possibilities, and spoke up after a few seconds.

"What about the University?" I asked. "There's got to be someone there who knows about it; physics lecturers, or chemistry, or whatever..."

"Chief already sent a couple of the senior team to the Uni, and some to the council buildings. Guess we just wait around now, see what we can come up with..."

So that's what we did. We sat around, talking shit and trying to figure things out, until we ran out of candles, and we were all forced upstairs by necessity.

We huddled together out in a quiet area, talking about possible ideas, until Martin and Danny were pulled away to an emergency meeting, which I was clearly not invited to attend. I took my leave, accepted their thanks for my help, and set off to my office once again.

It took another two hours to reach it, crossing over the Tyne River and down through meandering streets. Occasional shouting and more and more broken windows were interspersed by grim-faced individuals who sat outside their shops and homes, some with cricket bats, others with metal posts or other improvised weapons on clear display. I sighed each time I passed one of them.

The sight of the fall of civilization so quickly was hard to watch, and even more so when I passed down into a normally grim estate on the outside of the industrial estate which housed my office. After a few minutes of walking, I became aware of people walking down the adjoining streets in the same direction as me. They were clearly watching me, and they weren't the kind of people I wanted to be followed by.

I glanced behind me, counting four lads following there as well. Two of them carried baseball bats, and one had a damn replica Japanese sword, of all things. In broad daylight. The last one had a knife that looked like Rambo would be missing it, and I swallowed hard, hoping it was a coincidence.

I took the next intersection quickly, noting the two lads to my right in the adjoining street were there again, staring at me, and were moving at the same speed as I was, a brisk walk.

I kept my gaze focused ahead, knowing this wasn't likely to end well.

The estate I was in was rough; abandoned cars were burnt out at the end in the parking lot of a supermarket that had closed down years ago, and the woods nearby were badly overgrown. The fence that had collapsed on one side of the lot allowed easy access to the back of a church and the graveyard attached to it. The industrial estate where I worked was on the far side, but as I hurried along the street, I started to panic.

The four of them were still behind me, two to the right that I'd seen. There was nowhere to go to my left, due to being the backs of houses, with a barbed wire roll across the top of the walls. That meant the only way to go was forward. The houses would end in a few more meters, and I'd have to decide.

Either I bluffed it through and hoped I was wrong about what was coming, and maybe they would all meet up and bugger off, or I'd get some abuse but be let go. Or, more likely I suspected, I was going to get mugged.

If the second option was the one they were going for, they'd want me as far from people as possible, so they'd wait likely until I was in the graveyard or the first few units of the industrial estate, as they were all abandoned, due to having been robbed so many times. That, or they'd follow me to work and try and rob the place as well.

The building I worked in was still about a mile away, on the far side of the estate, located next to the banks and shops that made it look all 'up and coming'. I desperately hoped that some of the team would be in today, already working on a solution, because if these thugs followed me all the way there and it was locked up tight, I knew that this was going to end badly.

I tightened my backpack, cinching the straps and taking a few deep breaths as I approached the end of the road, and I groaned internally as I observed three shadows peeking out from the end of the street, where someone was clearly hiding. The footsteps behind me were getting closer, faster.

"Oi, you! Stop, we just want a word…" a voice from behind called out, and my nerve broke.

I set off like the cry was a starter's gun. Despite the bag on my back, despite all the gear I now passionately wished I'd left behind, and despite the fact that I was wearing steel toe-capped boots and had the end of a hangover to contend with, I ran like I hadn't run in years.

My feet powered me forward across the broken glass, fag ends, and random shit that covered the estate end, racing past weeds that had cracked the pavement decades ago. I sprinted past the three that stepped out, a hand grabbing at my sleeve and nearly sending me flying before I broke free and ran even faster, if more unsteadily.

Whoops and hollers rose behind me, and the sound of feet bursting into pursuit arose. Shouts to others were answered from somewhere up ahead, and I felt my heart drop, while the rate of beats was simultaneously going through the roof.

I careened across the dilapidated, abandoned parking lot, jumped the small twofoot high retaining wall, and barreled into the cover of the trees. The asphalt of the carpark crumbled to hardpacked dirt. Thorn bushes, backed by green trees, surrounded me. As I raced down the path, a single lad up ahead stepped out of a concealing bush with a wicked grin on his face as he hefted a baseball bat with barbed wire wrapped around it.

"Stop right there," he growled threateningly, and I swallowed hard, my steps faltering slightly.

"Fuck it," I whimpered to myself, doubling down instead and sprinting right at him. I saw the surprise on his face before he stepped back into a batter's stance and drew the bat back. I jinked left, then right, the narrow path effectively constraining my options until I was nearly within reach of him, then turned fully left, hurtling into the trees and graveyard proper.

I felt it then. I had thought I might have managed to dodge the thug's reach, but I'd been wrong. Something hit my right arm between my shoulder and elbow, and the glancing blow was enough to break the bone, I knew immediately by the hot, numb feeling, the taste of panic rising in my throat as the barbed wire tore deep into the muscle.

I screamed, grabbing at the bat with my left hand and running on, but by then, I'd lost my momentum and my balance. I tripped over a root, went flying, and rolled, coming up in time to see a gleefully grinning, shaven-headed thug closing the distance, his right foot drawn back, and his Doc Martin boot flying toward my face.

It hit me high on the right side of my cheekbone, slamming my head into the ground. I tried to grab at something, anything, to defend myself. My desperate fingers grabbed my Leatherman from my right thigh pocket with my left hand, or tried to, until a boot slammed down, and I twisted to the side, opening my mouth to shout for help.

Before I could manage a peep, 'The Boot' made a return appearance, slamming into my face a second time. I went flying, my nose breaking, blood spraying, and I went down again, this time to stay, curling into as much of a ball as I could. The group appeared all around me as the world spun, and I was suddenly surrounded by a maelstrom of boots flying, bats swinging, laughter and cat calls rising. I grunted and cried out in pain and panic, unable to protect myself with my mangled limbs before a cricket bat swung at my head turned out the lights.

THREE

IT WAS DARK when I regained consciousness. Hours had passed, and I was in serious pain. I was freezing cold and my right arm was totally numb, or so it seemed, until I managed to move it slightly, whimpering with the pain.

I hurt everywhere. Breathing was terrible. I could feel bits of my chest moving in ways it never had before. My right arm was useless, my left was a mess, and I couldn't move my two bottom fingers on that hand. I lifted it up and could faintly make it out in the darkness, but I could only see out of my left eye, and I realized matted, dried blood was caked all over my face as I touched it.

A great big cut ran across my scalp, going from below my right eye back into my hairline until it nearly reached the top of my head. Touching it made me want to vomit. It didn't help that I could feel…stuff…in it, and my eye was swollen shut.

The laceration was filled with dirt and leaves. When something crawled across my questing finger, I cried out, jerking my hand away, and I whimpered again as the fast movement made broken bones shift. For what felt like hours, I just lay there, tears streaming down my face, pain wracking me, as I tried to make sense of what had happened. I ran my tongue over my teeth and felt where one was missing, and several more were jagged and cracked, sobbing as I imagined what I must look like.

It was just a day. A single day, and the world seemed to have gone mad. Only yesterday, I'd met an amazing girl, drank and danced, partied and loved my life. I was earning good money, owned my own flat, had lots of holidays and sex…. and today, I was lying somewhere in the darkness, bleeding, probably scarred for life, and that was only if I survived.

The way I felt, the tight pains in my body, the broken ribs, and how hard it was to breathe? It was making me really scared that the 'for life' part might not be that long, after all. I twisted to my right, moaning as I screwed my one working eye shut in pain. When I could breathe again, I turned further, scanning the area and trying to figure out where I was.

I'd clearly been dragged somewhere, and judging from the angle of the nearby ground, I'd been rolled down a hill out of sight. I knew that the graveyard bordered onto some of the greenbelt land...land that had been put aside and restricted from development years ago, to ensure that cities and towns still had green places around them. I figured I'd been dumped somewhere in there, but I had no idea where. There was no noise from nearby roads, and no light from streetlights. I tried to get up, only to find my left knee was...a mess. It must have been hit with something, because it was swollen to nearly twice its normal size, the tough fabric of my work pants stretching tight around the swelling.

I checked my pocket instinctively. My phone was gone, even though it was dead, as were my wallet, my keys, and...my watch. I checked my right wrist frantically, even though I knew it as soon as I touched it that it wasn't there.

It was a valuable one, a real antique left to me by my grandfather, and it was all I had left of him. I didn't have pictures, or anything else beyond the memory of a man with kind eyes and a wonderful laugh, slicked-back hair, a love of 'Black Bullet' sweets, and that watch. He'd given it to me just before he'd died of cancer, only a few months before I'd lost my parents in the crash, and for the first time in this terrible night, I felt something beyond fear and pain.

I felt a naked, bloody fury. I'd get out of here. I'd find my way back if I had to crawl across broken glass to do it. I'd find the thieving little shits who'd done this, and I'd kill them all, I silently vowed.

As if in answer, something seemed to tug at me, and I turned my head, staring out into the darkness. I felt something...pulling me in, and in the absence of any better ideas, I half-dragged myself across to the trunk of a small tree. I grabbed onto the lowest branch, just within reach, and pulled while forcing my right leg down.

The end result was that I managed to get upright, but just barely, and I was in horrific pain as soon as I tried to walk. I scoured the area with my single eye until I spotted the strap of my bag poking out of a nearby bush.

I hobbled over to it, nearly sobbing with relief when I sank to the ground and tipped it over. Loose cables fell out; the medical kit, tools, and smaller, older Leatherman I had been desperately hoping to find were all gone, as were all the good quality, still-wrapped cables, leaving only the shitty oldest ones that I hadn't gotten around to throwing out.

Even the bag was ruined, torn and covered by my own blood, so I left it, trying to contaminate the crime scene as little as possible. I took half of the longest cables and dragged myself over to a fallen tree branch. Laying it against my leg as a splint, I laid a second on the other side of it and proceeded to tie it in place as best I could, finishing off with my belt tight around my thigh to keep the whole thing from shifting too much.

All in all, it was a terrible attempt at survival craftsmanship, but it did what it needed to, strengthening my leg enough that I probably wouldn't pass out the first time I leaned my weight on that leg too heavily. A single gleam to the left of the bag got my attention, and I almost wept as I picked up my housekeys. The car key was gone, but the rest had been dumped, probably because they didn't been too stupid to check my driver's license to see where I lived.

With grim determination, I set off, slowly, staggering from tree to tree and falling as much as walking.

Three hours later, I was still stumbling along, heedless of the tears that ran down my cheeks, the rasping breaths, and the fact that I was moving slower and slower, leaving a trail of cooling blood behind, when I crested a rise…and found it.

A crater lay in the middle of the small valley below. It wasn't big, maybe a dozen feet across, with something glimmering weakly at the bottom. I immediately fixated on the strange object like a dog after a rabbit. I managed a half dozen more steps before my lack of attention nearly killed me, when my left leg got caught on a stone. I twisted, and the pain screamed through me. I turned back instinctively, overcompensated, and lost my balance, then fell, rolling over and over, sliding until I hit a bramble bush. The prickly branches tore a dozen new cuts in every exposed area of skin and pulled at the fabric of my tattered, bloody clothing.

I sprawled on the ground, panting weakly as the world spun, and once again, I felt the pull that had drawn me all the way here. My resolve was stronger now, steady and insistent, and I growled, my last reserves of strength powering me upright with a hiss through gritted teeth.

I twisted and tore myself free of the grasping shrubs, turning in the direction I could feel calling to me, and I staggered on, desperation, fury, and insanity warring with exhaustion and blood loss.

Ten more minutes passed, and with the world spinning and my breath ragged, with my body shaking from cold, despite the warmth of the summer night, I finally pushed through the last of the bushes and trees and reached it.

It rested on its side in the small impact crater, a stream which cut through the valley pooling around one end of it. I stared, frozen in utter shock. It was a missile, or something like it, my brain insisted.

The sides were burned and scoured; symbols that had once identified it were mauled and illegible, the sections of torn metal all that remained to indicate that something, presumably guidance fins, had once been.

My brain was fogged to all hell, and I stumbled around the edge, my mind latching onto bits and pieces, such as the power loss and this missile, and trying to make sense of everything. I knew, just *knew*, that if I was whole, I'd be able to put all the pieces together, or at least more than I could at the moment.

I followed the pull to the far side, splashing through the shallow stream and up the other bank, to get a closer look at…

Something that wasn't right. Even in my current state, my brain told me that this was wrong as I stared at the cracked crystalline mesh lining the inside of the metallic frame. It looked as though a crazy crystal spider had webbed a weirdly glowing cylinder into place inside the missile, and the luminous container had come loose when it'd crashed, dangling from the top and swaying gently in the nighttime breeze.

I reached out and tried to grab the cylinder, feeling a shock roar up my arm as soon as my bloody palm touched it. The world vanished again as I was blown from my feet by the concussion.

I was unconscious for a long time—how long, I didn't know—but this time, when I opened my eyes, I saw the characteristic red-gold light of a sunset overhead through the trees. I heard the warbling of birds as they settled down, and the buzz of insects in the foliage. I twisted my head suddenly, following a bat that blurred past in hot pursuit of a moth, and I grunted as pain flared through my skull. It had been night when I'd woken up before; surely I hadn't been out here, alone, for another full day?

I froze at the thought, then turned my head, trying to see what was blinking orange off to my right. There was nothing there, but as I stared harder, I realized I'd just been mistaken. It was further to my right than I'd guessed, right at the very edge of my vision…

I tried again, and again, twisting further each time, until I abruptly realized what I was doing. I'd turned around almost entirely, and I was looking out of both eyes!

I was still in pain, sure, considerable pain; enough that I'd be at a doctor's, given the chance, but before I'd passed out, I was in need of an accident and emergency team. Now I was just…aching and sore.

I lifted my right arm, wincing at the pain, but I could move all of my fingers. I mirrored the same movements with my left, and though the broken fingers throbbed, they had healed to the point that I felt like I'd had a good week's worth of healing already, making me worry about how long I'd been lying down here.

I reached up and gingerly felt the cuts on my face and right upper arm. They were scabbed over, but they felt as though they'd healed for a week or so as well. *I'm hungry, seriously hungry, but not a-week-unconscious-in-the-forest hungry, surely?* I wondered, then I forced myself to my feet and staggered across to the stream. Lying down, I dipped my hands into the water, then lifted them to slurp the clear liquid noisily from my cupped palms.

I repeated the process a few times before getting back up and looking around, and finally properly inspecting the missile that rested across the clearing. I'd been trying to ignore it for some reason, no idea why, just the human mind playing its tricks, and filtering out other details when I'd really, really needed a drink.

I slowly circled the metal object, my mind noting in passing that it was weird that I didn't need to relieve myself, and that thankfully I hadn't shit myself or anything when I was unconscious. The missile, or craft, or whatever, was maybe six meters long, badly damaged, and hollow, with a weird pattern dried on the inside of the thing. A single crystal cylinder laid on the ground underneath it, maybe twenty inches long and six wide. I reached out hesitantly, tapping it with a finger, then retreating, before tentatively picking it up. My mind vaguely registered that this small cylinder had been part of a larger one before, one I'd not been able to take my eyes off of. This section…it filled me with a sense of sadness, and mild regret, for some reason. I turned it over in my hands, frowning as I stared at it, trying to make out what was inside.

I shook it a little, and something clattered around inside. Washing it carefully in the stream, I made sure to keep the cracked section away from the water, just in case it was valuable.

When I thought it looked cleaner, I straightened up, hissing in discomfort. Using the hem of my shirt, I wiped the surface again, leaning close and staring into it before dropping it with a yelp.

I backed away quickly, scanning the area and then warily eyeing the container and the tiny, desiccated body inside. It took a few minutes before I worked up the courage to pick it up and peer inside again.

This time, I stared at it in wonder. The creature was tiny, maybe six inches tall and maybe one wide. The remains of wings jutted from its back, with the majority of the pinions and one arm lying broken in the bottom of the cylinder…presumably from my thoughtless shaking.

I swallowed hard, then glanced around again. Seeing nothing else in the area, I also found no sign of the larger, ominously shining crystal that I'd touched before. I searched the area quickly, pausing to examine my wounds as best I could. Ultimately, I decided that discretion was the better part of valor, and that I'd bring the authorities here later, let them see what the thing was, and maybe get a nice finder's fee out of it.

I didn't trust that it wouldn't disappear once they got ahold of it, as I now fervently believed it was an alien craft of some kind, but I'd also seen enough 'Alien Invasion' movies to know that the dude who tried to hide the whole thing usually ended up dead, and I wasn't looking to be a redshirt.

I turned back in the direction I thought the city should be and started walking, carrying the cylinder carefully. After a few minutes, I slowed to a stop, frowning. I couldn't see any landmarks, I was surrounded by trees, and the sun was vanishing somewhere in the distance past the trees. I had no idea where I was, but I also *knew* that I was six-point-four miles from my home, and that the nearest road was in *that* direction.

I paused for a dozen long heartbeats, trying to make sense of how I knew these things, until the sudden bite of a fly on my neck startled me from my daze, and I decided to test it out by doing what I could. I set off walking again. I ached, I was sore, and I felt seriously ravenous, but I moved steadily, knowing that I could be home in a few hours, and hoping that something had been figured out with the power by now.

As I made my way slowly up and down banks and across a field, passing from the shadows of the trees out into the evening light, I paused, turning my gaze to the sight of Newcastle in the distance. I was maybe a mile to the south of the estate where I'd been attacked, and as I continued to look, I thought I could just about figure out where the crash had been.

I carefully mapped it out in my brain, then blinked in surprise as it shifted. The mental image I'd made of the area rapidly altered itself to razor sharp clarity, and the crash site suddenly became marked with a single pulsing dot. That triggered another of the orange-amber pulses in the corner of my vision, and I unconsciously muttered aloud as I tried to turn my head.

"What the hell is that?" I said, freezing in shock as my vision shifted without my conscious control.

The world seemed to blur out of focus as a series of small boxes popped up in my vision. Staring at them for a moment, I blinked and jumped as they vanished, presumably in response to my desire to be rid of them. To my surprise, they reappeared when I mentally focused and 'pulled' them 'up' again.

I focused in on the first one, which grew slightly and centered itself, overlapping the others.

Dungeon Core assimilation is at 12%

Full assimilation cannot be completed until ambient mana in the surrounding area reaches a high enough level.

Do you wish to view Host capabilities?

Yes/No

I read it through three times before it made any sort of sense. I had no idea what a 'Dungeon Core' was, but I knew what mana was; it was a common resource in all of my RPG games. At a thought, another pop-up shifted forward into view.

Ambient Mana is at 6%...

Estimated time to complete permeation is 387 local days.

Communication array is unavailable at this time. Fall back on secondary role: Construct Dungeon and begin local area cleanse.

Recommended difficulty level for local inhabitants: 4.

"What the hell is this?" I asked aloud, but there was no response. After a few seconds, I pulled up the first prompt again and mentally selected 'Yes,' getting a new screen.

Name: Unnamed	
Modifiers: ***Broken!*** *16 bones are currently healing. This modifier restricts the speed of the Host by 25%.* ***Drained!*** *Rapid healing has drained the Host of reserves, leaving it mentally and physically impaired. -3 to control.*	
Species: Human	Bonus: None
Level: 0	Progress to next level: 0/10
Assimilation: 12%	Dungeon Level: 0
Control: 3	Dungeon Capacity: 0
Host Powers: 0	Dungeon Spells: 0

Stat	Current points	Description	Effect	Progress to next level
Agility	6	Governs dodge and movement.		0/100
Charisma	8	Governs likely success to charm seduce or threaten		0/100
Constitution	7	Governs Health and Health Regeneration	HP: 7x10	0/100
Dexterity	11	Governs ability with weapons and crafting	+2% Increased chance of improved result	0/100
Endurance	7	Governs Stamina and Stamina Regeneration	Stamina: 7x10	0/100
Intelligence	7	Governs base manapool, standard intellectual capacity, plus Control when combined with Wisdom and divided by 2	Mana: 7x10=70 Control: 7+5/2 = 6	0/100
Luck	6	Governs overall chance of bonuses and critical hits	Average chance of bonus - 40%	0/100
Perception	8	Governs ranged damage and chance to spot hidden items/traps	Average chance to notice important details - 20%	0/100

Strength	6	Governs damage with melee weapons and carrying capacity		0/100
Wisdom	5	Governs mana regeneration and Control, when combined with Intelligence and divided by 2	50 mana regenerated per hour Control: 7+5/2 = 6	0/100

I perused it thoroughly, asking myself the first question that popped into my head, aloud.

"Well, what the hell is the average?" I'd always had a sneaking fear that I was below average, secretly worrying about it most of my life. It had driven me to excel at school, and thankfully, in the bedroom, but no matter what was said, there was always that little niggling fear…

Human: Homo Sapiens
Classification: Common, Local Species Variant, Humanoid
Average Speed: 45KM/H
Average Height: 1.65m
Humanity on this world has evolved to a basic state of consciousness. The current variant is held back by incomplete genetic sequences and variances that are sub-optimal.
Current averages are as follows, and are calculated across the species:

Statistic Identifier	Level
Agility	6
Charisma	6
Constitution	5
Dexterity	5
Endurance	7
Intelligence	5
Luck	6
Perception	5
Strength	5
Wisdom	5

"Oh. Okay, so I'm fucking awesome then…" I started to say, before another prompt popped up.

Current Host age, gender, and genetic variant comparison:

Statistic Identifier	Average	Host
Agility	8	6
Charisma	9	8
Constitution	11	7
Dexterity	10	11
Endurance	9	7
Intelligence	10	9
Luck	7	6
Perception	10	8
Strength	9	6
Wisdom	6	5

"Wait, what?!" I muttered, poring over the table. "So across the species, I'm looking good, but in comparison to other men my age, around my height, and with similar genetics, I'm…below average?! Motherfucker! I knew it!" I spat, shaking my head. The world immediately spun like crazy, and I staggered, the prompts vanishing as I desperately tried to focus.

As soon as I got control again, I stood still, my breath coming in ragged gasps as I tried to make sense of the world around me. Somehow, I was seeing prompts, specifically descriptions of the world and my place in it. I was curious whether I could summon up descriptions of the details of the prompts, so…

Assimilation: 12%

Dungeon Core Assimilation is currently at 12%. Increase this to augment the power of the Dungeon and to grow your Dungeon Host abilities.

Warning!

Dungeon Host is a physical, mortal being. This is a sub-optimal security solution. Recommend relocation of core to physical structure designed to ensure longevity of Dungeon.

Dungeon Level: 0

This references the current level of your Dungeon, the floors it can presently create and control, and the current condition of its Core. Once the Core is fully activated and is installed in an appropriate location, the Dungeon Core will reach level one and begin to earn mana and experience towards its first Core Evolution.

Dungeon Capacity: 0

This references the current number of creatures which the Core or Host can summon to defend the core, explore the surrounding area, or populate the Dungeon. This number is calculated by multiplying the Dungeon's level by the Host's Intelligence and Wisdom scores combined.

Dungeon Spells: 0

This references the specialized Dungeon Spells that a Dungeon Core can access, which will increase with each rank. Spell development will be based on the Dungeon Core's actions, surroundings, and Host.

Host Powers: 0

Assimilating a Dungeon Core into a mortal Host will grant the Host powers. These will begin to manifest at an Assimilation level of 25%. Current Host likelihood of termination increases by 2% per point increase of Assimilation from 0.

Control: 3

This references the current Host's level of physical and mental control. In order to fully activate and bond with the Dungeon Core, this must reach a minimum of 10. *(Current negative modifiers of -3 exist due to injuries and rapid healing debuffs.)*

I read over the details slowly, a veritable dump of information hitting me all at once, and I started to piece things together, albeit slowly.

"So..." I muttered aloud. "The Core of a Dungeon was in that ship, and somehow, it's now in me? It's got a two percent chance to kill me with each level of Assimilation it reaches, and it's currently at twelve percent, so twenty-four...wait a fucking minute! This thing had a one in four chance of killing me already, and it's only going to increase?!" I growled, anger flooding my mind, along with fear.

Do you wish to eject the Dungeon Core at this time?

You will have 108 seconds to place the Core and activate it before it will become unstable and detonate.

Warning!

Host's current Control level is too low to be able to bond with this Dungeon Core. The ejected Dungeon Core will identify Host as hostile, provided the Dungeon Core does not detonate immediately upon ejection.

Yes/No

Estimated area consumed by Dungeon Core Detonation: 1.672sq miles.

"Well, that's just fucking peachy." I groaned, selecting 'No' and leaning back, suddenly aware that at some point, I'd sat down. The pain was shifting from the level it'd been at when I first awoke, to, well...moderate aches and discomfort. The intensity felt more like a toothache in my bones, paired with weariness, rather than the horrific levels I'd felt not long before.

"So, I can't 'eject' the core yet, as it'd kill me and anyone nearby, and I can't keep it in me as some kind of battery, since it'll kill me that way too. How long until the Assimilation level is too high?" I asked aloud, smiling slightly when a pop-up shifted to answer me. It seemed that the Core couldn't talk to me directly; it didn't seem sentient, but it was responding like a computer. If I asked the right questions, it would respond with the data.

Current Level of Core Assimilation: 12%

Estimated time for increase of Assimilation level is 0.5% per hour in current low Mana Density. Move to an area of higher Mana Density to decrease this time.

"Or I could fucking not, and maybe live a bit longer..." I muttered, dismissing the prompt.

I could see that I was near the estate that I'd been attacked in, and I didn't particularly feel like getting my ass kicked again. Instead, I decided to head to the left, carefully skirting the estate and heading home as quickly as possible.

From where I stood, I could see the side of my office building in the distance. There weren't any lights on, and the shutters were down, so I didn't think heading there would help at all.

Adding to that my disheveled state; I was covered in dried blood, mud, and probably stank to high heaven. The best I could expect, if I did bump into someone normal, was having the police or an ambulance sent after me.

If they could contact them, I reflected grimly.

I set off, slowly moving through the woods and then emerging out onto the paths that ran along the southwest boundary of the estate. Cars and vans cluttered the roadside, abandoned haphazardly. Their doors swung in the breeze; peeled paint, rusted exteriors, and charred remains of upholstery indicated that they'd been torched some time ago, then left to deteriorate, as not even the police wanted to spend time in this area.

I'd never realized it was so bad. I'd known it was a bit shitty, and there was a high crime rate around here, but I'd walked through it twice, both times with friends and in broad daylight, when help wasn't far away with a simple call to the police.

Now, I realized just how rough the area was, and I wished fervently for my own damn car. I walked, staggering occasionally, for another twenty minutes, before a strange pulse of warning seemed to pass through me. As I turned, I caught the flash of a head as it disappeared below the top edge of a wall in the distance, and my heart dropped again.

Feigning nonchalance, I flexed my knee, grateful to find that it was significantly better than it had been, but knowing it was still nowhere near good enough for a run. Unfortunately, I was painfully aware that I didn't have much of a choice.

I picked up the pace, deciding the best chance I had was to get to a better area fast, and hope for a wandering police presence or a good Samaritan, rather than continuing along the outside, now that I'd been spotted.

I shuffled along as fast as I could, leaning heavily on the nearest wall as I went. As I began cutting across a road and heading up the middle of the street, the feeling of warning grew increasingly stronger as I went.

Nervously, I ducked down an alleyway, planning on running to the end as best I could and then erupting out onto the ring road that separated the estate from a much nicer one, when I came to a sudden halt. I found myself face to face with one of the thugs who had beaten me earlier.

He was alone, the cricket bat he'd used on my face nowhere in evidence as he almost walked into me, coming the other way. His eyes opened wide as he recognized me, and he dropped the sandwich he'd been eating, reaching into his right tracksuit pocket quickly and pulling out a Leatherman in an old, battered case.

I recognized my stolen tool and heard an almost animalistic growl fill the air. I was shocked on one level to realize it had come from me, but I knew as he grabbed the sheath and tried to free the blade, that I didn't have time to try and talk my way out of this, nor did I want to.

I grabbed his right wrist with my left, balled my right fist up the best I could, and punched him in the face. It was a terrible punch. He barely rocked back, and the only reason he didn't beat me senseless was that he was still fixated on getting the blade free.

Taking advantage of his persistent attempts to free the tool, I punched him again, and again. Grabbing at his ear, I pulled, twisting it, and brought my knee up to hit him in the stomach, while releasing him with my left hand as he dropped the Leatherman and tried to defend himself. He doubled over in shock, so I jumped on him.

We collapsed to the floor and rolled, punches flying wildly, both shouting and kicking. When he grabbed my right shoulder, I saw my chance, and I bit down on his wrist with my broken teeth, clenching my jaw as hard as I could.

He cried out, and we rolled again. My fist caught him under his jaw, and his head rocked back as I tasted blood in my mouth from his ruptured skin. He screamed, tearing his wrist from my bite. Blood spurted from the vein, and I kicked out, tripping him as he tried to get away. He fell, and as if in slow motion, his body landed on the road, but his head hit the curb with a loud crack, like a branch being broken.

He slumped, his body unresponsive as he glared up at me from suddenly terror-filled eyes, managing to croak out a single word.

"Help..."

It infuriated me as much as it terrified me, that he dared to ask my help. Shouts arose in the distance, coming closer. I reached out and grabbed my Leatherman, pocketing it and searching him quickly. I didn't care about anything else but the watch, but it wasn't there. I sobbed in my panic, scrambling to my feet and starting to run, ignoring the flashing notification warning at the edge of my vision.

I ran, and I ran. I stumbled, I fell over, and I ran again.

I passed people who pointed at me in shock, and others who called out, asking if I was all right, if I needed help.

It was all the same to me, houses and estates passing in a blur, until at last, practically gibbering in fear, panic, and shock, I clattered my way into the lobby of my house. I crawled up the stairs, my frenzied dash having robbed me of almost every ounce of energy and sanity I had left.

I passed the middle flat on my way up the stairs and I heard the door open, saw the hate-filled eyes of 'Miss Piggy,' then the shock and the horror as she registered my battered state, followed by her slamming her door in my face, and the clanging of bolts being driven home.

I dragged myself up the last dozen steps, managed to open my door, and fell inside. I barely managed to kick the door closed behind me before I passed out on the floor.

FOUR

THE SHADOWY OUTLINES of my furniture greeted my bleary eyes when I finally woke up, and for a while I just laid there, face pressed to the wooden floor of my flat, staring into the semi-darkness. I could barely make out the shape of the doorway from my prone position, with the lounge on my right, and I guessed the faint light filtering in from the windows must be starlight, but I didn't have the energy to care.

I remained motionless until the insistent call of my aching bladder grew too strong and I dragged myself upright, surprised by the lack of pain, and went to relieve myself. I flushed afterwards and paused, wondering if I'd just used up a serious amount of water I was going to need later. There was no getting it back, however, so I shrugged, walking sullenly out of the bathroom and stepping over the sticky, congealed mess my unconscious body had left behind on the floor.

I'd felt it when I had gotten up, but I couldn't face trying to clean it up at the moment. I went down the hall, moving in the opposite direction from the lounge into the bedroom, the stars shining through the window providing just enough light to see by.

At first, I just stood there. My mind kept starting down the route of, 'I need to do…' and I'd stop it. I knew I was dying. I'd taken a hell of a beating, and then *something,* a…Core…had ended up inside of me. The thought was all it took, and a notification popped up in my vision.

Current Level of Core Assimilation: 17.5%
Estimated time for increase of Assimilation level is 0.5% per hour in current low Mana Density. Move to an area of higher Mana Density to decrease this time.

Great; so the area that I was standing in was no worse than the forest. That was good, right? It was going to take me a few more hours to die…maybe. I didn't want to think, I didn't want to do anything, but my stomach rumbled insistently, and my throat was parched. I figured, what the hell. Might as well eat a little, make the last few hours slightly less unpleasant.

I scanned the room and slowly made my way to the shelf where I knew I'd left the little chef's blowtorch I'd bought for a laugh. It was hidden behind a candle, one that had been intended to make the room a little more romantic with an ex, fat lot of good that had done.

The sight of the candle always sparked that memory of her text. I'd lit it, knowing she was on her way over, when I got a text saying there was something waiting outside for me.

I'd gone down to it, excitedly opening the door, and boom: a small cardboard box. I'd looked around, confused, thinking she was hiding somewhere. Finally, I'd picked it up and looked inside, only to find my stuff. Everything I'd left at hers or lent her. Joy.

I'd gone, in one day, from being happily in a relationship, to nothing, nada, dumped. She'd blocked my number and ignored me when I tried to talk to her in person. I'd complained about it to a friend in the pub, grumbled, and went on with life, confused.

Then a few weeks later, I'd bumped into an old friend and his fiancée. He'd just returned from a six-month deployment, and practically the entire time he'd been away, fighting for us all, I'd been happily screwing his girl. And I'd had no idea.

It had broken me for months. I'd done the usual: drinking, gym, sleeping around, but I'd been distant with everyone, mates and dates, as I felt I didn't know who I could trust. I'd finally started to feel like my old self again, and boom! The world went to shit right after I met a cute girl.

Typical.

I shrugged and deliberately banished the memory, flicking the starter and pulling the trigger on the blowtorch…a click, and nothing else. I frowned, verifying that the gas registered as full, and I could hear and smell it coming out, but no spark…

I checked the batteries and found they were dead, totally dead. I fished out another after rooting around in a nearby 'junk' drawer and unpackaged it, slotting it inside, and…dead.

I glared at the battery in my hand and tried the remaining couple in the packet with equal success. Cursing under my breath, I hunted out a packet of matches in the drawer instead and sparked one to life, using it to light the candle.

The room was instantly so much more comfortable, it was unreal. I put the candle back on its shelf and looked in the mirror, catching sight of my battered state and froze.

The last few hours crashed back down on me as my eyes traveled over my reflection, taking in the bloody, dried mud, general dirt, and ruined clothes. I also saw various scabs covering wounds, but there were surprisingly few of them. I swallowed hard and moved closer to the mirror, opening my mouth to find clean, white, regular teeth.

I stared in shock, remembering the jagged remains of my teeth cutting my tongue at several points…or was I going mad? I hurriedly checked my right upper arm; the cloth that covered the limb was shredded, as the baseball bat had been wrapped with barbed wire, but the skin…

It was almost healed, white and red scars livid against my tanned skin. Beyond that…the bone ached, but that was all. It felt as if I'd overdone it at the gym, not broken it?

Maybe it hadn't been broken? I wondered. *Maybe I'm going mad? A psychotic break, or whatever they call it?* I tried to make sense of it all, but I just couldn't. Nothing seemed right, but when I lifted a hand to scratch at the day or more's growth of beard on my chin, I paused.

My hands, forearm, hell, my clothes; I was covered in blood. My gaze shot back to the mirror, taking in the blood on my face, around my mouth and across my cheek. I remembered biting down on that guy's wrist, and the blood spurting out. I'd gotten it in my mouth!

He'd…oh god…

"I killed him…" I whispered, feeling my stomach roil. I barely managed to make it to the bathroom, leaning over the toilet and bringing up a thin, acidic liquid that burned as it left my stomach.

I hunched over the receptacle, alternatively sobbing, swearing that it wasn't my fault, and retching, until I finally collapsed onto the floor and passed out again.

When I awoke once again, daylight streamed in through the windows, and I laid on the cool tile, staring blankly up at the ceiling.

Current Level of Core Assimilation: 22%

Estimated time for increase of Assimilation level is 0.5% per hour in current low Mana Density. Move to an area of higher Mana Density to decrease this time.

I stared at the prompt sightlessly before I finally sat up. My mind felt clearer than it had since this had all started, even though my stomach thought my throat had been cut, and I was more desperate for a drink than I could ever remember being in my life.

"Okay..." I whispered hoarsely. "We're at a forty-four percent chance of death now, and my control is..." I briefly thought about it and *knew* it was at six. "Okay, so I either die, and damn soon, I'm guessing, considering in six hours I'll reach a point of 'fifty-fifty' death with the Assimilation. Not where I want to be. Or I find a safe place to eject this thing, away from people, and hope that's safer than Assimilating it."

I sat up, grimaced at the state of my hands and shook my head. Stripping off quickly, I dumped everything into the sink with my wad of filthy, wet clothes from yesterday. It was overflowing now, but that was the least of my concerns.

I turned the shower on and grinned when it worked. It was cold—my god, it was cold—but I forced myself to stay put and scrub myself clean, making sure I got every inch before I allowed myself to escape.

I shivered, my towel doing little to replace the heat I'd lost to the icy deluge, and checked myself over in the mirror. My wounds were all scars now, including the extensive one that ran from under my right eye up to disappear into my hairline. It actually made me look dangerous as fuck, and I grinned a little at that, until yesterday's encounter came back and forced me to acknowledge that I was dangerous in appearance only. I drew in a deep breath and glared into the mirror, critically eyeing the toned body I'd worked hard for.

There was no good reason that I was a victim. I was jumped by a gang of thugs who were all armed. I wasn't weak. I wasn't a failure. I wasn't a coward. I said it over and over again in my mind, until I felt like I almost believed it, and then I finally allowed myself to leave the bathroom. I padded into the kitchen, pulling a warm soda from the fridge and chucking the soaked towel from the floor in front of it into the sink.

I practically downed the lukewarm beverage in one gulp, then cracked another one and pulled out the protein bars I'd stockpiled for the gym, munching my way through three of them before I could stop myself. I took two more and a protein shake into the lounge, which adjoined the kitchen due to the open layout, and sank into a chair, uncaring that I was naked, or that with the floor to ceiling windows to my left, I might be scaring the neighbors with my ass.

"Time to man up," I muttered aloud, and I concentrated, bringing up the notifications which I could feel waiting for my attention, the steadily blinking orange light in the corner of my vision making sure I couldn't forget about them.

Congratulations!
You have defeated an opponent classed as 'Local Thug'

Thug level: 0
Your level: 0
XP awarded: 25

Congratulations!
You have gained one level in Unarmed Combat!
You receive 2% increase in your chance to inflict critical damage.
Increase your skill to augment your ability further.
You have reached Level One!
You have five Stat points to invest.
XP required to reach next level: 85/100

"Okay, now what do the stats do, and how do I allocate them?" I muttered, pausing in my attempts to read all of the notifications. I concentrated and brought up the stats screen again, taking the time to read through the details with a mind that wasn't in shock. While Strength and Endurance were standard, as were most of the others, there were a few that seemed more interesting.

"'Intelligence: Governs base manapool. Standard intellectual capacity plus Control, when combined with Wisdom and divided by two. Each individual level provides ten points to the pool, while every ten points raises the multiplier by ten…' Okay, so if I have seven in it, I've got seventy; but if I have eleven, I've got two hundred and twenty, as it goes from seven times ten to eleven times twenty. Weird, but okay," I absentmindedly mumbled the calculations to myself, fully absorbed in the intricacies of the stats.

"'Wisdom: Governs mana regeneration and Control, when combined with Intelligence and divided by two. Each individual point invested will increase your ability to absorb ambient mana by ten points per hour.'" I stared up at the ceiling, deep in thought, and decided that while putting all five points of my 'stat increase' into, say, Wisdom would bring it up to ten; ten-add-seven was seventeen, divided by two was eight and a half, which was too low to eject the Core safely.

"Do I have to kill someone to get XP?" I asked aloud, and the first prompt flashed up again. I read it carefully and realized that it said 'defeat'. "So as long as I kick their ass, I'll be okay?" I asked aloud, but I got no answer. "Okay, I got twenty-five points for kicking his ass, and I need eighty-five for the next 'level', as it looks like to go from level zero to level one takes ten points maybe? So, if I was to go back and kick the ass of four more of those assholes, I'd get another level?"

Progress to next level: 15/100

"Okay…" I said, dismissing it with a thought. I was trying not to think about what that actually meant for me, and how shit my chances were of success…but these assholes had literally beaten me half to death, then dragged me out into the forest and left me to die. They'd stolen my grandfather's watch, my gear, and who knew how many others they'd attack if I left them to it.

"Well, I've got two advantages, I guess…" I admitted, staring out of the window as I thought. "They don't know I'm coming, and they don't have levels…do they?"

Current Mana Density in surrounding area is at 4%. Mortal Mana interaction systems are estimated to activate at 10%, depending on individual and capacity.

"Okay, not really sure what all that means, but that's fine," I grumbled, bringing up the stat screen again. "So I need to increase my control to get this thing out of me and not have it detonate or view me as suddenly hostile, which means I need to increase my combined Intelligence and Wisdom score to twenty overall. I'm at twelve, so I'll put three points into Intelligence, and the last two…well, I need to be able to fight, so I guess, Strength?" Suddenly I remembered the pop-up on 'averages' and I compared that to my scores. The one area I really stood out in, with my genetics and everything being taken into account, was Dexterity, which apparently covered weapons and crafting. I guessed it the reason I usually won at computer games, and why I was so good at manual skills like typing fast. I decided to trust the 'system' and dropped the two points into Dexterity instead.

Confirm Point allocation:
Yes/No

I focused on 'Yes,' and my brain almost exploded. It felt like someone had flicked a switch and plugged in a few extra Gig of RAM; everything seemed suddenly easier to understand, and I sat there stunned for quite a while. When I finally pulled myself out of my self-induced brain fog, I nodded, grim-faced as I reflected on what I had to do. I had both a limited time until I died, and a limited time during which, for whatever reason, I was the only one who was leveling, at least as far as I knew.

Once those thugs realized how things had changed, and how they could improve themselves, it'd be open season on anyone they met, so I had to act fast. I strode through to my bedroom, only pausing briefly to consider the bloody mess on the floor by the door and the crystal that held the small creature. At some point, I'd let go of the construct when I'd been unconscious, but I was glad I'd kept it, rather than losing it or leaving it behind. I ignored the blood, placing the corpsicle on the table in my room.

I sorted through my dresser, thankful that I had multiple pairs of strong work pants. I paired them up with a training top that would keep me cool, then dug through my closet until I found an old shoulder bag. Moving quickly, I filled it with some bandages, some protein bars and another canteen of water, as well as some more clothes.

Once I was satisfied that I'd packed most of the useful supplies I had on hand, I grabbed my running shoes and my black leather gloves. I'd wait to put them on until I needed them, but I didn't want to leave any evidence behind. I also chucked some bleach wipes into the bag, figuring I could use them as well.

With that, and not a single weapon to my name, I headed down the stairs. I paused at the middle flat at the sense of being watched through the door, and I walked across to the small peephole, slowly and deliberately extending my middle finger and glaring through it.

We all have fallings out with people, I reflected, *but seeing your neighbor practically bleeding out on the carpet and slamming the door in their face? Asshole move…*

Snorting dismissively, I set off again, jogging down to the entryway, then paused and grinned to myself as a memory hit. Instead of going out the front, I detoured to the back garden, walked up to the shiny, brand new shed, pulled out my Leatherman and used it to strip the lock off the door. The doors swung open smoothly to reveal a showroom-condition Boardman road bike.

It had belonged to Gerald, or whatever the fuckhead's name was. Now it was mine, and I didn't feel even slightly ashamed about it. I wheeled it out, faced up at the windows, and was unsurprised to find them both staring at me. They ducked out of sight, like the cowards they were.

"Thanks for my new bike, Fucktard!" I called up, then calmly unbolted the back gate and mounted it, heading up the street.

It took me only a few minutes to reach Markus's shop, and I growled angrily as I saw the damage to the front door where someone had clearly tried to kick it in at some point. I gritted my teeth and pushed on it gently. It opened, and a voice called out from the candlelit gloom within.

"Sorry, but I'm closed!" Markus's voice yesterday, or the day before, I couldn't be sure now, had been friendly, happy-go-lucky and eager to help. Now it was low, almost a warning growl.

"Markus?" I called, and a second later, he materialized out of the darkness, a cricket bat in his hand.

"Boy?" he said, frowning at me. "Let me look at you, son…" He stepped forward, and I turned my head obligingly when I realized he was inspecting my scar. "Damn, boy, what the hell happened to your face?! Matt, isn't it?" he asked, and I nodded.

"Yeah, it's me. I got mugged, then healed insanely fast. No idea why," I lied.

"Huh, tell me about it. My old bones usually keep me awake at night, damn arthritis, but now? I could do squats all day. You all right? What happened?" he repeated, concern tinging his voice.

"Like I said, I got mugged; bunch of little shits. I was walking to work, trying to figure out how to help things out, then boom. A load of them with bats jumped me."

"Hmmm. I hope you kicked their asses?" Markus pressed, glowering at me. "Some little shits thought they could help themselves to what they wanted here, too. Made them aware of the 'realities of life…' if you know what I mean." He grinned darkly, punctuating the implication with a single slow wink.

"Glad to hear it, and unfortunately, no. I caught one of them later, but there were too many, so I ran. I'm going to go see if I can find a few more now, quietly…" I explained, giving him a wink in return.

"Well, you go teach them a lesson, boy. You got something you can use?" he asked, and I shook my head. "That why you came here?" I paused awkwardly.

"Not really…you were good to me, so I wanted to check that you were okay, that's all. If you've got a spare bat, though, I'd not say no…"

"This one's got sentimental attachments…came with me to this country, but I've got something that might suit you. Come in and lock the door." He turned and shuffled off into the gloom. I followed him inside, dragging my bike in and locking the door, before following.

I wandered through the shelves and into the narrow backroom, finding a dual staircase, with one side leading up and the other down. Markus was heading down, his bobbing candlelight all that illuminated the darkness, so I followed, feeling my way carefully down the steps.

"You'll have questions about what I show you, lad, no doubt about that, so I'll just lay it out nice and straightforward. You ever hear of HEMA?" he asked, and I shook my head.

"Uh…no, not really?" I said after a second, once I realized he couldn't see me.

"Well, HEMA stands for 'Historic European Martial Arts.' It was all the rage where I grew up in Germany. I expected it to be the same here when I arrived, but I was disappointed. Tried to start a club up a few times, but I never drummed up enough interest, so I gave up in the end," he explained, leading the way to a large box in the corner of the room. It came up to my shoulders, about a meter wide and deep, and when he slid the lid back, I whistled reflexively.

"Them's German Longswords, lad, Federschwert. Now don't get excited, they're all training weapons, blunt…and I'm not giving you a steel one. They're worth hundreds of pounds each. I will give you one of these, though…" He pulled a black blade out and passed it to me.

I hefted it, judging by the feel that it was coated with rubber, or plastic, or some such material. I couldn't decide which, but the weapon itself felt real; the weight was good, but it'd never hold up against…

"I know what you're thinking, boy, but believe me, that's all you need and more. It's got a steel core inside; that's the weight you feel. You'd need to put a lot more strength into it than I think you've got to break that…Company who made them went out of business when someone died after being hit with one the wrong way; modern ones are a lot softer."

"Okay…" I said cautiously, looking it over and then glancing back at the gear in the box.

"I'll give you a pair of gloves and a shoulder scabbard for it, if you want. It's too long to wear on your hip, but be warned! It's a bitch to draw in a fight. Best way is to pull it off and chuck the scabbard aside. You ever used one?" he asked, and I shook my head sheepishly, eliciting a sigh from him.

"Fine, come on. We'll go in the backyard." He picked up another training blade and passed me a pair of gloves and a scabbard. I followed respectfully as he wove his way out of the basement filled with old stock, up the rickety stairs that creaked with every step, and a minute or two later, we emerged in the small concrete yard at the back of the building.

"Right, then; first and foremost, feet!" he barked, and I looked down, puzzled. "Standing like that is no use. Watch!" he commanded and shoved me roughly. I staggered back and nearly fell over, having not expected the blow.

"Hey!" I complained.

"Bah, you see what was wrong there?" he asked, and I snorted.

"Yeah, you pushed me…"

"Smart arse," he muttered, shaking his head. "No, your stance was shit. Look, stand with one foot pointed towards me, the other back behind you, shoulder width apart, angled at forty-five degrees outwards, like this…" He proceeded to shift me around, indicating minor adjustments with taps to my limbs. "That's it; now, front leg bent at the knee. Aim for the knee to be directly over the heel, back leg extended slightly, heel lifted, and balance on the ball of your foot…" I did as he asked, and then he tried shoving me again. I didn't move, not even a hair, and when I tilted him to the side slightly, he was the one who went staggering.

"Good!" he said, grinning. "Now reverse it. You right-handed?" I nodded, and he gestured to my left foot. "Then you want the left advanced to start; best way for you. Now, step forward and swap over, so you're in the same stance, but right foot forward, left back." I followed his instructions, swapping back and forth a dozen times until he was satisfied, then he started pushing and shoving me as I switched.

It took a while, an hour or more perhaps, but I enjoyed it, and clearly so did he, as he kept adjusting my positioning until he felt I could drop into 'stance' without thought.

"Good lad. I want you to practice that, and I mean a lot. Do it for an hour a day, nothing but foot work, and you'll be amazed at how quick you learn. Now, I've shown you the basic stances, but you need to be able to move around. Quickly now, as I know you've got somewhere you want to be; you move like this…"

He showed me to lunge and retreat, to circle around in triangular patterns, and finally to cover short distances fast with bursts of speed. After another hour had passed, we were both knackered, although he definitely looked the worse between the two of us. He was easily in his fifties, if not older, judging from the comments he'd made as we'd sparred. I had to admit I really liked the old sod.

"Right, last point. Although it's the most important to you now, or so you think, believe me, practice the feet and the rest will be fine! Grab your sword, hold it like this…" He gripped his sword with his right hand at the top of the hilt, left hand loosely grasping the pommel, a good four or five inches below the right on the long hilt.

"People think you need a death grip. Rubbish!" He scoffed, shaking his head. "Think of it like you're holding your lady's hand. Good grip, but don't crush her. Left hand is like holding your wee kiddie's hand: loose, you're using it to direct your swing, but be ready to tighten if you need to!"

I did as he directed, learning the paces of a drill. The sword started point down, resting against the ground, then was pulled back, pommel resting against my right hip, sword point angled upwards at forty-five degrees towards the enemy. Then the blade was raised overhead, the point angled down, then switched to being held directly upwards as though a line ran from my chin to the top of my head at ninety degrees, with the sword extending the line.

From there, he showed me a series of cuts, swinging down from the right to draw an imaginary line across from his left shoulder to right hip, stepping forward as I delivered the attack, then switching my lead foot to bring the sword back up to reverse that move, before flipping over as I switched feet to slash from my opponent's left hip to right shoulder, flip and reverse.

We repeated the strokes for ten minutes before he nodded in satisfaction, then swung his sword at me without warning.

I dropped into defense and slashed back at him, mirroring his action. Our blades clashed briefly as he continued the pattern, each swing more graceful and fluid than I could manage by far, but in fighting back, I realized those four simple cuts were suddenly also four simple blocks, each one an easy counterattack that I was amazed at.

"Well, lad, you're far from good, but you learn fast, and you should have a better chance now…still, do me a favor and let me know you're okay later, all right?" he asked kindly, and I smiled as I clapped him on the shoulder.

"I will, Markus, and thank you. It'll make a hell of a difference," I replied, and he smiled sadly.

"Honestly, lad, it will, IF you remember to do it, in the heat of combat. Many a good fighter has forgotten everything, and that's in tournaments… judging by that look in your eye, what you're going to do is a damn sight more dangerous. I don't want details, just in case, but come back safe, and if you ever want to train, I'm here…"

"I'll be back," I said in my best Austrian-American accent, winking at him, before swallowing hard. The time I'd spent here, while making a hell of a difference to my chances, I was sure, had also increased my Assimilation level by another point and a half, and as I watched, it inched up, becoming two points.

Current Level of Core Assimilation: 24%

Estimated time for increase of Assimilation level is 0.5% per hour in current low Mana Density. Move to an area of higher Mana Density to decrease this time.

"I'm sorry, Markus, I have to go…" I dismissed the prompt, grimacing when I saw the look of confusion on his face. "Look, all I can say is that if you start to see, I don't know, a flickering light at the edge of your vision, or something like that, just concentrate on it, okay? Read what you see, think on it, and I'll be back to talk to you about it soon."

"A light…son, are you having…visions…?" he asked, suddenly a lot less sanguine about arming me and training me.

"Hah, trust me, I'm not mad…although mad people never think they are, do they? Either way, I have to go, before those scumbags find someone else…" I shot him a reassuring smile, turning and heading for the shop.

I was nearly at the door when he called out again, and I turned to catch the can he threw at me. I grinned, appreciating the size of the Redbull, and I thanked him as I slid my head through the strap for the scabbard. Once I'd settled it comfortably onto my back, I pulled the gloves on, surprised by how flexible they were despite their bulk, and tucked the can into my small bag that hung off my opposite shoulder.

"Good luck, son," Markus said to me, patting me on the shoulder as I mounted my bike. "Stay safe, beat those assholes, and help people where you can; that's all I ask."

"I will, my friend," I promised, shaking his hand. I raced down the street, calling back to him as I went. "Now get inside and stay safe, you old sod!"

FIVE

I PRACTICALLY FLEW DOWN the street, taking the corners faster than I'd gone on a bike in years. I couldn't help marveling at the difference between a road bike, one that probably cost thousands, and a cheap steel frame mountain bike, which was all I'd ever been able to afford as a kid.

With the cars being out of action, I used the roads, weaving smoothly around the occasional car that must have died when the event happened, and dodging pedestrians.

There were a lot less of them than there had been the first time I'd traveled this way, and those that were braving the streets glared and looked at me suspiciously.

Everyone hurried about, bags on their shoulders, and many had clubs on clear display. One man pointed a damn shotgun at me, but thankfully, he just grumbled and lowered it when he saw I had no interest in him or the shopping trolley piled high with tinned food that the child with him was pushing.

What had taken three or four hours to walk, not counting my stops the first day, only took me about half an hour on the bike, and as I came close to the estate, I felt a combination of nerves, fierce determination, and a desire to be anywhere else but here.

I skidded around a building and flew down the street that led to the estate. Three lads lounged in various positions on the low wall on the corner, watching everyone passing wide of them.

As soon as they saw me, they were whistling back into the street, out of sight, and I swallowed hard, knowing it was on.

I headed straight towards the street, swinging wide of their position. I was about to turn in, when two more thugs, both on bikes themselves, burst from a side street to intercept me. I changed direction, swerving and dipping between their outstretched hands, heading downhill, as though trying to get away.

They both pedaled after me, grinning, and their friend hollered and screamed at them to get me. Arguments broke out among the runners over who was getting my bike, and I grinned ferally as I skidded around another corner, making sure the cyclists saw my trajectory.

We cut down two more streets, and I managed my speed carefully, making sure they weren't far enough back that they'd just give up, but also drawing them far enough ahead of their friends that I felt I stood a decent chance of winning the fight before they could get to me. I took another corner fast, shooting around it and fighting to stay upright.

As soon as I was out of sight, I didn't let off the brakes. Instead of running, I jumped off, dumping my bike against the wall. Knowing I had mere seconds to prepare, I shrugged out of my scabbard, drawing the sword and tossing it aside as Markus had taught me.

I dropped into stance, moving up to the edge of the street, and drew the longsword back. As I gripped it tightly with both hands, Markus's voice echoed in my ears, and I shifted my grip. The top hand, my right…was for punching forward, he'd said, while the bottom hand was to pull, guiding the sword and directing it. It seemed weird, especially after years of watching Hollywood do things totally differently, but the way Markus had moved, it was like a dance, one with deadly consequences for everyone else.

I heard their panting shouts to each other as they closed in. The leader was saying something about my bike being his, and the second was complaining that 'the boss' wouldn't like it…

I drew back further, forcing myself to breathe slowly and calmly, judging the distance by the sound of their cries, and then I forced myself into action.

I deliberately—for the first time outside of school, which didn't really count, or the Bigg Market, when being blind drunk— acted to hurt someone, and badly at that. The changes they'd forced on me with the beating…no, the attempted murder…had changed me.

I was terrified. I knew I was broken inside. I'd partially come to terms with that on the ride over, because this wasn't normal. It wasn't something a 'good man' did.

But punishing people like this, stopping them, was something a man had to do, or at least it was something I knew *I* had to do, especially if I ever wanted to be able to look in the mirror and not hate myself.

It helped that I was also pretty convinced that my only chance at survival was to fight them. As I was fighting the growing certainty that I could die at any point as the Assimilation level increased, at least I didn't have to worry about a jail sentence.

I swung…and I swung *hard.*

It was more or less on target, which was as much luck as intent. The 'more or less' was because I'd been aiming to hit him in the chest. He'd been standing up on the pedals when I'd last peeked back at him, but as he took the corner, he'd sat down, so the sword hit him two thirds of the way down the blade, nearly wrenching itself free of my grip as it hit him in the throat, catapulting him backwards into a flip and onto the street.

He landed with an audible crunch and flopped bonelessly to a halt, as I gaped open-mouthed at what I'd done, before the second one shouted something, not far behind. New instincts powered by fear and fury kicked in.

I'd automatically returned the sword to the 'guard' position Markus had taught me, and I swung again, too soon, and he swerved, but the shock of a sword appearing out of nowhere caused him to lose control and crash, rolling and shouting as he bounced across the asphalt.

I moved as quickly as I could. This one, I'd recognized from before. He'd laughed as he stomped on my fingers, breaking them. I growled in anger as he looked up, stunned. My first blow took him across his upraised right arm, and I felt the jarring reverberation along my sword as I broke the bone.

The second strike was flipped over and in reverse, as I'd been taught, but instead of going from right hip to left shoulder, if he'd been standing, it ended with his jaw, spinning him sideways, unconscious, with a spray of blood and teeth.

I stood over him, panting as he laid still, blood pooling around his mouth. Confident that he'd been incapacitated, I turned to the other one, noting that his head was lolling at an unnatural angle. He was dead, judging from the glass-eyed stare, and the second one…I moved back to him, feeling for a pulse, but it was weak, since he was bleeding heavily. His jaw was fractured, and it looked like he'd be on soup for the rest of his life…however long he had left.

I couldn't help it. I vomited everywhere.

I knew I needed to do this; that they deserved it. Hell, I'd never thought that anyone besides a kiddie-fiddler could deserve this level of violence until now, not this viscerally. Intellectually, it was one thing to say, 'they deserve to be killed for doing that,' but to do it myself? To set out, lure them into a trap, and actually do it?

Totally different.

I was shaking, still fixated on the pair, when I heard a shout in the distance, and the world came crashing back to me. I hunted around frantically, nobody in sight, but when I ran to the corner of the road, I caught sight of three more coming down the hill. They were panting heavily, but they all had bats and clubs, and they were maybe thirty meters away, searching for indicators of which way to go. I'd poked my head out too far, I realized, when one of them pointed at me and shouted a question. I ducked back, ignoring his words, and thought quickly, I could either run, or check them over and then fight the next three, but I couldn't do both.

It came down to maybe finding Grandad's watch, or definitely not, and losing the element of surprise and the chance to try again. I knew, despite the flash of notifications, I wouldn't have enough XP for the level I needed; not yet.

I had to go on.

I moved back from the corner, slipping into a recessed doorway, and waited. My breath came far too loud to my ears as I tried to hide. I closed my eyes, listening as hard as I could and repeating the mantra from a favorite book over and over.

"I must not fear. Fear is the mind-killer…" I muttered aloud, quickly moving through the mantra, memories of watching the original movie years ago coming to mind and calming me.

I froze at the sound of a gasp, accompanied by slapping footfalls, and my eyes flared open. I acted before I thought, moving out into the street as the first of them scrambled to a halt nearby, staring in shock at his friends.

I sprinted straight at him, and he twisted around, startled to find me closing the distance. He turned to face me, legs planted side by side, and swung his bat like he was trying to send me to Mars.

I stepped aside, falling into stance as the bat whistled past, jerking him off balance, and we both watched it in shock: him, terrified that he'd missed, and me, amazed at how accurate Markus's words had been. He'd commented that the sword, huge as a German longsword was, was also a finesse weapon. If you used excessive force, it was impossible to recover before you were dead.

It was better to hit and need to hit again, or to slice the opponent as you drew back, rather than attempt to cleave them in half, as most likely, if you did manage a hit like those in the movies, you'd end up with a sword that was wedged inside a corpse, and then you were fucked if anyone else had an issue with what you'd just done.

We blinked at each other, and he tried to yank the bat back, but his shitty footwork meant he was off balance, and he started to fall. I flashed my sword forward, connecting the pommel with the back of his head as he fell. The blow accelerated his dive, allowing me to draw back and kick him in the gut, hard. I turned back to the street as the second, and a heartbeat later, the third thug arrived.

The two newcomers gaped at the bodies, the pooling blood, and me, but I was in full swing now, raging as I'd recognized another of them, one who'd kicked me in the face with his shiny, shiny fucking shoes.

He'd laughed as I'd cried out, but he sure as shit didn't when I swung for his throat. He dove aside, hitting the ground and rolling as I recovered and swung again. The reverse attack served nicely for his friend, with a little correction.

As my sword swung up, his scream rose in pitch as his balls cushioned the blow to his pelvis, and I stepped forward, my left hand releasing the pommel of my sword to grab his shirt collar. He dropped his bat, and I drove the pommel into his mouth harshly, yanking him forward at the same time, before pulling back and smashing the cross guard into his temple.

He fell to the ground, groaning as I released him, and I turned around, jumping backwards and stumbling over the moaning man as the second swung for me with his cricket bat. I backed up again, falling into stance out of habit. As he swung, I countered, his overhand meeting my own, and as I grunted and shoved, I threw him off balance. The footwork that Markus had drilled into me saved me, and I followed him, reversing the swing and striking upwards, catching his attempt to bring the bat around and smashing it from his hands.

I swung my blade up, flipped sides and brought it whipping around to smash it into his neck with a scream of effort. Time seemed to drop into slow motion as the blunt blade brutalized his neck, the flesh bending to one side, while his head and body seemed to fold around the blade. I felt the neck snap, and I pulled back, twisting at the hip and kicking him in the chest, 'Sparta' style.

The corpse collapsed as I turned to face the remaining two. The second was still kneeling on the ground, clutching his privates in his own personal world of pain, while the first had forced himself up, his bat in hand. He was clearly still dazed, but his stupor warred with the principles of my entire life, being taught that violence like this was wrong, and feeling sickened by the lives I'd already taken.

I forced the thoughts down and slashed out at him. He jumped back, causing me to panic as he regained his footing and advanced, too fast for me to dodge. He brought his bat up over his head, about to smack it down onto me. I couldn't bring the blade around fast enough, and he was inside its length anyway, so I lunged for him instead, dropping the sword and grappling with him. We both fell to the street, rolling, punching, and shouting in an animalistic brawl. The world reduced to a confused blur as we both reacted instinctively, lashing out ineffectually, before we rolled again, and he came out on top.

He wrapped both hands around my throat and squeezed as hard as he could, pushing down and crushing my windpipe more and more by the second. I panicked, flailing at him, and tried to pry his hands away frantically. Seconds passed like hours, until I finally remembered a scene from a movie. Desperate for air, I reacted as the world began to grow dim around the edges.

I let go of his hands, the shallow furrows I'd torn with my nails ineffective, and instead grabbed his head by the temples, driving both thumbs into his eyes They felt like over-set jelly, a slick coating on the outside. Just as I was beginning to black out, my thumbs popped into the sockets, squashing the malleable orbs to the sides. He released me with an awful scream, and I shoved him back, twisting aside and grabbing at my throat as I hoarsely wheezed in a breath of sweet, sweet air. I panted and coughed, crying as I got enough air to restart my brain, and I glanced over at the man I'd just blinded.

It was telling that here, even in broad daylight, nobody was in sight. Here in England, 'Estates' meant something very different to what they did in America I'd learned, there they'd be known as 'slum ghettos' and worse...and clearly in this estate, cries for help were ignored as signs of weakness, even before the world had gone to shit. I rolled over and forced myself to my feet, wiping eye-gunk from my thumbs as I picked up the nearest weapon: a cricket bat. I turned back to face the man who was screaming and pawing at his face, drew back as I sank into my stance, and swung for the fences.

The crack was loud enough that I was never sure afterwards, even as I replayed it in my mind, if it was the bat breaking, his skull shattering, or both. Either way, he collapsed soundlessly to the earth, blood pooling around his head.

I felt ice cold, empty inside, as I scanned the street. They were all dead or unconscious, save one; the man who'd never have kids.

Not that any of them ever would now, if they hadn't already.

I discarded the useless remnants of the bat, snapped in half as it was. The top only hung on by a splinter. Picking my way around the spreading pools of blood, I bent to collect my sword, sweeping it up and glaring down at the lone survivor as he tried to drag himself away. Clearly, I'd done more damage than I'd thought, as his left leg evidently wasn't working. He didn't make it far.

"Why?!?" he cried, rolling back, and looking up at me as I loomed over him. "Why are you doing this?! Please…no…" he blubbered. I felt my lip curling back in disgust. This little fucker was a murderer, or at least an attempted murderer, and he and his friends had chased me down, intending at minimum to mug me. They'd already tried to murder me once, even if he didn't recognize me today. Now, because he'd lost, he wanted mercy? Because he was on the receiving end, he thought all should be forgiven? I growled as I reached down, grabbing him by the throat.

"Tell me where it is…" I said in a low, hoarse voice.

"Wh…what?" he stuttered fearfully.

"WHERE IS IT!" I screamed at him, shaking him back and forth like a rat caught by a terrier. "WHERE'S MY WATCH!" I demanded furiously, but he just gaped at me in confusion. Then I saw it. The light dawned, and he stared at my right cheek, following the thin scar that ran up and disappeared into my hairline.

"No, you…you're dead…" he whispered. I smacked him back, slamming his skull off the asphalt and making him cry out.

"LAST CHANCE!" I raged, straightening up and stepping over him. I lashed my sword down, as hard as I could, smashing him in the left clavicle, the snapping sound forcing his scream.

With his left arm entirely useless and his right reaching to cradle the fresh injury, I braced my foot onto his throat and pressed down just enough to cut off the air.

"Where's my fucking watch…" I whispered icily, watching his eyes bulge. He tried to grab my foot, but he had no leverage where he was, and he knew it.

I pressed down harder, and he tried to talk, the smell and spreading darkness across the front of his jeans revealing that he'd lost control of the remains of his cock. I let up slightly and he wheezed in a breath, gasping out a single word.

"…boss…"

"Where?" I growled, and he answered, tears drawing tracks in the dirt on his cheeks as he whimpered out all I needed to know.

I glowered down at him, and I knew I'd done more to him than hurt him. I'd broken him, inside. He was no threat now, and with a little push, he never would be again.

"Listen to me…" I said quietly. "I'm going to kill him, and everyone else in your shitty little gang. You're going to live, but only for now, because if I ever hear about this shit happening here again, I'll come for you. I don't care if it's got nothing to do with you; it's still you I'll come for, you and everyone you love, so remember that. Next time you see some little shit acting up, you'd better stop it before I have to, or you'll be the first one I come for…"

With that, I removed my foot, turning away from him in disgust. Something inside me had changed further. What had begun with the attack, the fight, and then the sight of 'Miss Piggy' and her husband closing the door in my face, had been finished here.

'Matt the Nice Guy' had died somewhere along the line. This new world didn't have room for a nice guy; not anymore. It might in the future, but right now? It needed something else…something *more*.

I didn't know what it was yet, but I knew I was going to find out.

SIX

I QUICKLY SEARCHED THE others, finding nothing of value besides a nice diving knife strapped to one guy's ankle. I took it, attaching it around my own leg and rolling my pants back down to conceal it.

Sighing, I picked up my sword and examined it sadly. The blade had a kink in it, and the hilt was loose. The pommel tightened up when I twisted it, but shaking the weapon caused it to slowly loosen again. Despite that, it was the weapon I was going to use to clean the estate up. I took a minute to use the bleach wipes on everything I thought I'd touched, not that I thought I needed to now, but it was better to be safe than sorry.

I found the scabbard, sheathed the battered blade, and shrugged it onto my back again, then got onto my bike. Without a backward glance, I pedaled back up the hill. It was slow going, especially as I was aching in various places. Aside from all the fighting, I hadn't cycled in years, and my throat was throbbing painfully, but I fought to ignore the pain and glared ahead as I went. I turned back onto the adjoining street, pedaled up to the top of the road, and then out onto the main road again, finding it strange to realize how silent it was.

There was nobody but an old man in sight in the distance, and there'd been a lot more people walking around when I'd come in the opposite direction....

"The screams..." I shook my head in disgusted understanding. "They all ran away, rather than trying to help," I muttered to myself. The old man was panting, yet still steadily making his way in my direction. I looked at the box he was carrying, noticing the bandages and medical supplies that filled it, and I frowned, pedaling up the hill to greet him.

"Are...you okay...?" he asked me, trying to catch his breath. The man was genuinely concerned, I realized, as I came to halt.

"I am. Are you?" I asked.

"I...I heard...screams...shouts for help..." he said, pointing over his shoulder to the houses further up the street on the far side. Some of the structures were okay, neatly maintained, rather than the majority nearer the estate, many of which had steel shutters covering broken windows. "I had to go…to get my box…" He was shaking, and I felt terrible for him, both for the world we were suddenly thrust into, and the state he was in. He must have been in his late eighties, at least, and yet here he was, trying to help.

"It's okay," I reassured him, but he shook his head anxiously.

"No! No, it isn't! You don't understand…those boys, they *do* things… terrible things! They've got someone…they must be hurting them…I heard the screams…I tried to call the police, but there's no power. The phone…it won't work…" he insisted, clearly panicking.

"No, look…what's your name?" I reached out and placed my hand on his shoulder, my heart clenching at the fear and desperation on his face.

"I'm…I'm Wilfred…Wilfred Owens…"

"Mr. Owens, you're not wrong about what they do. Those 'boys' are like rabid animals. In this world, when the police don't come when you need them, there's only one way to deal with a rabid animal. Do you understand? What do you do with a rabid animal?"

"You…put them down…I had a dog once, as a boy…" He began shaking, gaping up at me with horror.

"Yes, you put them down. I'm sorry, Mr. Owens, but they tried to kill me, and I did what I had to do. It was their screams that you heard. They won't attack anyone else. Not ever again," I said firmly.

He stared at me in silence. Slowly at first, then with increasing speed and surety, he shook his head, glaring up at me as he took a step back, followed by another.

"No, son. No, you didn't." He glared up at me. "No matter the stuff those boys been doin', they're just kids. They need to go to prison, or in the Army; that'd sort them out…You don't put a man down, not like a dog…" He started to back up slowly, eyeing me like I might attack him at any second, suddenly noting the blood spatters that covered my clothing.

"Well, we'll have to agree to disagree, Mr. Owens, considering they tried to kill me yesterday…" I said, pointing to my face. He peered at the healed injury myopically, then shook his head.

"Son, that scar's a month old if it's a day, so don't try that shit with me. Those boys weren't anywhere near so bad, till that Damon got back outta prison, and he's only been back a week!"

"Damon?" I asked, leaning forward. "The one they call 'the boss'?"

"Huh. Doesn't surprise me; that boy's always been trouble…but you listen here…those boys ain't all bad. Yeah, maybe some should be…put to sleep…but we don't do that, not here. That's something for the police to take care of, not the likes of you and me."

"And if I ride on? And Damon sees you with something he wants? Sees someone you love, alone?" I asked, and he paused, standing there for a moment. His eyes clearing, he looked back to me and cocked his head to one side.

"You thinking of going looking for him? Boy, you don't stand a chance. He's bigger than you in every way, and he's not just bad. That kid's *evil.* Bad in the bone. Last time I heard he lost a fight, he was twelve. Got caught hurtin' a puppy, and the guy who loved that dog kicked his ass. A week later, that guy was in intensive care. Burglars, the police said. Never caught them, but we all knew. Kid was taken away for a while, then he was back, then off to prison, and now he's back again. Every time he comes back, he's worse…but…"

"Then it's time he didn't come back, isn't it?" I insisted. He hesitated, considering me, the knowledge of the threat the kid posed, warring with years of closely held beliefs and a fear of being involved. He opened his mouth a time or two, but he ended up shutting it each time without saying anything. I nodded to him slowly.

"That's what I thought, too," I said quietly. "One of those 'boys' you tried to warn me about is probably still alive back there, but he won't be feeling good, I promise you. If you want to help him, he's in that direction, bottom of that street," I pointed down the hill behind me. "You'll probably be able to see him from there. The rest of his group… well, they're not going to be a problem anymore. Good luck, Mr. Owens. I hope you get through this, either way." I nodded respectfully in farewell, turning and glancing along the road. I drew in a deep breath as I thought about what I was about to do, and the decisions I'd made to get to here, and I decided it was time to check the notifications before I did anything else.

Current Level of Core Assimilation: 25%

Estimated time for increase of Assimilation level is 1% per hour in current low Mana Density. Move to an area of higher Mana Density to decrease this time.

*

Congratulations!

You have defeated five opponents classed as 'Local Thug'

Thug level: 0
Your level: 1
XP awarded: 125*

Congratulations!
You have gained a level in Ambush!
You receive 5% increase to damage dealt while evading detection. Because you have gained this level in a sub-skill of 'Stealth,' you have also received the requisite levels in 'Stealth', granting a 3% reduction in chances of being spotted. Increase your skill to further improve your damage bonuses.
*

Congratulations!
You have gained a level in Dodge!
You receive 1% increase to chances to evade damage. Increase your skill to augment your ability further.
*

Congratulations!
You have gained three levels in Longsword!
Because you have gained this level in a sub-skill of 'Blades,' you have also received the requisite three levels in 'Blades'. Increase your skill to improve your abilities with this weapon.
*

You have generated a Quest!
Quest!
Clean up the Estate.
You have learned of a small gang intent on building their own fiefdom in a nearby estate. Remove the gang by any means necessary, and you will receive the following bonuses:
+1 to top three Attributes
+1 Skill point to allocate
+1 Class Perk
250 XP
Note: *Rewards have been increased on this quest due to level of difficulty.*
*

You have reached Level Two!
You receive five Stat points to invest in your attributes, plus one Skill point.
*

You have five Stat points to invest.
XP required to reach next level: 160/200

I read through the notifications hurriedly, noting that the rewards were no different for killing or sparing an opponent. As long as they were considered defeated, that was good enough to gain the XP. The next level required two hundred total XP to reach it, and I currently had forty points 'in the tank,' as it were. Adding to that, I guessed that I got a skill point every other level; maybe more, maybe less, but I had one now. I considered putting it into Blades, but as I'd leveled it three times in a single fight, I decided there wasn't an immediate need. I'd save it.

I also gathered that if I took care of the gang, I'd at least reach another level as well. I could then use those points to boost my Wisdom, and as such, my Control, up to a level that would enable me to eject the Core and install it somewhere safe.

That meant I had to decide. Did I put these five points into definitely getting the attributes up in an attempt to deal with the Core now, or did I risk it all, dumping them into something that would help me in the fight, and go clean up the neighborhood…I considered for several seconds, seconds that turned into minutes, but when I looked over my shoulder, I saw the disappearing back of old Mr. Owens as he vanished down the indicated street, hurrying off to help the kid I'd just fucked up.

That made my decision for me. He, and others like him could hate me all they wanted for what I did, as long as they were alive to do it. If I left him, left the gang alone for now, by tomorrow, they might have killed him or someone else already.

I pulled up my stats and skimmed them quickly. So far, I was above average in both Intelligence and Dexterity, but I was going to face a gang, and one that loved dealing out punishment. I had three logical places where I could commit the points, which I believed would make an immediate difference: Strength, Endurance, or Agility.

Strength would give my attacks more damage. Endurance would allow me to fight for longer, which was appealing, as I'd definitely been lagging by the end of the fight there, and my breathing had come hard and fast. Agility would hopefully boost my ability to dodge attacks.

I considered them for a minute, before deciding if I was going all out and risking it all, then I might as well risk it all properly.

I slammed all five points into Strength and confirmed it, grunting in shock as my body felt like it was being torn apart. I hunched over the handlebars, clenching the grips in pain and trying not to scream as I felt my muscles writhing around. It took less than a minute, but when I could breathe again, I flexed my arms and stared in amazement. My top had been reasonably tight-fitting before; not insane, but fairly tight. Now, I was moderately concerned that if I sneezed, I'd shred it. I reached out and felt my biceps, my forearms, my traps and thighs…I was a beast!

Seriously, my muscles were hard, healthy, and I felt a subtle ache like I'd just finished a damn good workout. My first thought was that I needed a mirror, and the second that I was seriously pissed about all the hours I'd wasted in the gym over the years, when all I had to do was kick some assholes to shit.

My next thought was that if the gang 'boss,' Damon, had found out how to level, I might be fucked. I swallowed hard and looked around counting the streets that led off the main road where I stood, thinking about what the kid I'd questioned had said.

The third street leading off on the left-hand side, I decided. That was probably the one he had meant. I stood up on the pedal, and pushed down, skidding slightly as I took off like a rocket! I had pushed off hard, sure, but I was headed slightly uphill. Instead of starting off a bit quicker, I must have nearly doubled my speed, and as I pumped harder, I was amazed at the result.

The change to my Strength hadn't been a minor one, and it was affecting *everything*. I mean, that upgrade must have piled the muscle on everywhere. I felt...stiffer...and not in a fun way. I mainly noticed it across my shoulders and hips, and as I cycled forward, I could feel slight restrictions in the way I moved that I'd never noticed before, not to mention how uncomfortable my clothes felt.

The thing was, though, my legs were so much stronger, it was insane. I could feel the changes, and when I considered how I'd normally work at the gym, I thought I knew why. There, I'd concentrated on my arms, my shoulders, and my stomach, as that was what society said a man should do. I knew that I should do my legs as well, and I did, a bit, but that wasn't so much what women seemed interested in, so I'd neglected it in comparison.

The stat boost had fixed that by essentially almost doubling the muscle mass and efficiency across my entire body, and I guessed that I would look insane now when I was naked. The thought of my ex seeing me like this, considering the guy she'd left me for, made me grin for a second, until I realized in my daydreaming, I'd passed the street I wanted and was heading off on a tangent.

I turned down the next one instead, figuring I'd take it and take a left at the bottom, which would ultimately take me to the same place, but as I turned down the street, I suddenly found myself weaving in and out of parked cars. This street actually still had people living in it, or so it seemed. Windows were shuttered, but I caught glimpses of fearful faces peering out, and I growled to myself as I tore down the bank, headed to the bottom of the street.

The decline was steep, and by the time I'd passed the dozen or so houses sheltering people, I found the estate falling deeper into disrepair again. Blazing down the last stretch, I shot out onto the street at the bottom, taking a left, and again, I found myself surrounded by boarded-up houses. There was silence down this way, and the stink of smoke hung in the air. I followed the directions I'd been given, taking another cross-street to the right and heading down to the old railway tracks and the abandoned munitions plant.

I slid to a stop in the middle of the street, looking around. I was standing where he'd told me to go, I was sure of it, but the house he'd said to look out for, a big one with a blue door, wasn't there.

I searched the surrounding buildings, trying to work it out, when a burgeoning sense of danger rose in my mind. I frowned, looking around in an attempt to figure out where it was coming from. That hesitation nearly cost me my life.

I stretched while I scanned the area, trying to loosen up the muscles in my back and neck without thinking about it. Luckily, it was that change in posture that caused the arrow to hit me in the thick muscle of my shoulder, rather than sinking into the back of my head and killing me outright.

I cried out in pain, staggering to the side, then saw a man rise up from the flat roof of a nearby house and draw his arrow back, his bow bending as he took aim.

I froze, then took off, tripping and staggering as I jumped off the bike and ran for the nearest cover, a recessed doorway that was boarded up. Two more arrows hit the ground near me as I ran, and shouts and laughter rose around me from the houses I'd ignored.

I grunted in pain, reaching over my shoulder and grabbing at the arrow that was already stuck in me, fighting down panic as I realized I couldn't get it. My 'brilliant' idea of boosting my muscles like an Olympic athlete had left me unable to bend in certain ways, and the god-damn arrow was literally just out of reach!

To add insult to injury, I couldn't get back out of sight in the doorway without driving the arrow in deeper! I slapped at my shoulders, then twisted back as another arrow clattered off the brickwork near my head, and I growled in anger. I didn't have time to fuck about with this! I grabbed my scabbard and gave it an experimental tug, feeling it catch on the arrow, and nodding to myself in grim determination.

Then, before I could think better of it, I yanked the scabbard forward and off my shoulder. The strap, which had been on the far side of the arrow, hit the shaft and half tore it out, before something gave way in my back and the arrow bent. It was hanging from my torn skin, and I was trying not to bite my own tongue off as I slapped my hand back, finally catching the trailing fletching's of the arrow and pulling it completely free.

"Hey, asshole!" a voice jeered, and I thoughtlessly leaned out, before jumping back to flatten myself against the door again as two more arrows ricocheted off the stone near me. "Pass my arrows back, will ya?" the voice continued, to the rising laughter of others.

"You want the arrow?" I called out, looking around desperately. I grinned to myself as I realized the wood at the top of the door was hanging slightly loose.

"Throw them out nice and slow!" the man replied. Ignoring him, I turned, grabbing onto the boards and heaving with my new strength. They resisted for a second, but a loud crack resulted in half of the covering coming away in my hand. I spun, bracing it out into the street, and an arrow slammed into it a second later.

"Well, come and get them!" I shouted, turning back and punching the old door as hard as I could in the middle of the center panel. It cracked easily, and I yanked my fist back, punching again and splitting it wider. Reveling in my new strength, I continued wrestling a section free, pulling some of the surrounding material with it, and exposing the dark interior. I drove myself inside, struggling through the jagged opening, but managing to pull myself through. In the chaos, I took an arrow in my calf, while others slammed into the ground and doorframe around me.

I fell to the floor, my sword still in the scabbard, and grunted with the impact. Fighting through the pain, I dragged myself to my feet and hobbled out of the hallway. I hurriedly took the second door, finding myself in a small, bare room. The windows had been boarded over, and a stinking puddle of standing water and mold festered in one corner, rising damp and spores spreading across the inside of the walls.

I grimaced as shouts filtered from outside, and hid behind the door as best I could, again cursing my new size, as it felt harder than it should have been.

Voices raised in question, then anger, followed someone shouting orders. A few minutes later, as I worked the arrow out of my leg, clattering and crashes grew louder as the front door was forced in fully.

"Come out, come out, wherever you are…" someone called in a sing-song voice, and I gritted my teeth, waiting for them to advance down the hallway.

"Look!" another voice said, clearly calling back to someone else. "Blood! I told you I got 'im!"

"Bollocks! That's probably from my shot!" the singer retorted, and I peered down at the arrow clutched tightly in my right fist. The ceilings were too low in here, and the hall was too narrow to use the sword, so it looked like I would be defending myself with an arrow, and…I reached down, gently bracing my sword against the wall, and drew the diving knife, swapping the arrow to my left hand and gripping it halfway along the shaft, tip upright.

The sound of footsteps drew closer, accompanied by doors being opened, before they paused right outside of the room…

"There! More blood; he's in here!"

I closed my eyes for a second in self-recrimination. over my stupidity, then stepped out to stand in front of the doorway. Steeling my nerves, I drew a deep breath and crouched, as though getting ready to run a hundred-meter sprint. As soon as the door opened, I was off, clearing the tiny distance as the man on the other side came into sight, his hand leaving the door handle and going back to his bow.

I covered the space between us in a heartbeat, slamming into him and stabbing the knife into his gut, then the arrow. Roaring, I spun my suddenly screaming, shocked, and surprisingly light meat-shield to the right, using him to intercept the arrow his friend fired off, and lifted him using the convenient handles I'd just driven into him.

He screamed again, dropping the bow to grab at the knife and arrow, as I rushed forwards, slamming him into his friend. The pair went down, and I swept up the second guy's bow, grabbed an arrow and fired it out of the door, getting a scream as someone didn't dodge fast enough.

I lashed out, kicking and stamping the two on the floor, concentrating mainly on the man under my shield, as he still had a chance at survival, while the dark, fast flowing puddle of blood on the floor said the first didn't.

Dropping to a crouch, I pulled up a handful of the first man's arrows from his hip, then stabbed them all down at once into the second's throat as he managed to shove his friend off him. His eyes went wide as his fingers came up, and I plucked one arrow back out, ignoring the spray of blood that was released.

Once I nocked the arrow correctly, I drew back on the bow and waited. I'd never used one of them before, but the flashing orange light gave me a hint, and I concentrated while aiming.

Do you wish to assign your unused Skill Point to Archery?
Yes/No

I frantically spammed 'Yes,' and the opaque screen vanished just as a head popped up in the doorway. I fired, missing, unfortunately, but the Skill Point had delivered a rush of vague knowledge, and when I yanked free the second arrow, I held both it and the bow slightly differently.

I drew back smoothly and when the head popped up again, the man stepping into view with his bow drawn back, my arrow flew first, and it flew true. The bolt slammed home into his chest, just below the sternum, sending him crashing to the floor with a scream as his arrow arced out of sight. I draw a third arrow from my impromptu quiver, which had just stopped twitching and spurting, and I fired it at my opponent as well, grimly satisfied as it sank deep into his chest on the left side. I knew it would have struck a lung, and that should put him out of the action.

I grabbed more arrows, sheathing my knife, and slowly backed up, ready to fire. I kept my eyes trained on the end of the hallway, ignoring the weak burbles and wheezes from my first meat-shield, and the much louder cries for help from the man I'd just riddled with arrows.

Backing into the room where I'd taken brief refuge, I grabbed my sword and hurried upstairs, the narrow, steep path nearly making me fall as my leg screamed at me. Somehow, I made it, ducking out of sight to the left as more shouts came from outside.

I moved through the rooms, searching quickly until I found what I needed: an old, boarded-over balcony door, one which led out onto a small area that overlooked the side garden to the right and the street to the left. I peered out between the slats of wood, counting four of the thugs there, with three more hurrying across nearby roofs to join in.

From this angle, I could see the plank walkways that had been cobbled together to let the gang run from house to house, all but invisible from the outer streets. I also spotted a house further in, a street or so away. The windows revealed people moving around inside and occasionally looking out, clearly trying to see what was going on.

A small balcony on one of the upper floors supported a huge man. A young, dark-haired, topless girl stood next to him, holding onto his waist as he drew on a cigar and watched his men.

The 'boss,' as I guessed only the boss would be that unconcerned at watching his people die, was easily six and a half foot. His build was heavily muscled, despite his size, as so many that tall were typically weedy. He had poorly drawn tattoos sprawled across his chest, a close-shaven scalp, and a goatee. Ratty blue jeans, gold 'bling' on his wrists and around his neck, judging from the shine in the sunlight, and silver aviator glasses further enhanced his thug demeanor.

I glared at him, even knowing he couldn't see me, then turned my attention back to the men gathering below me. Studying the windows, I realized the boards were on the other side, so it'd be obvious when I forced my way out. When I tried the nearest window, it didn't budge. Inspecting the frame closely, it was clear that it'd been nailed shut at some point in the past, and someone had painted over the nails, so that wasn't going to open anytime soon.

I decided I needed a two-stage approach to the next fight. First, the simple bit: kill as many of those fuckers as I could. Second, I needed something to open the window with, and there were at least seven more mobile battering rams below, so that was useful.

I didn't really know where the change I'd experienced was going to take me, the loss of fear, to some degree, and the determination to take this gang down, but I was starting to see what the marines meant when they said that thing about enemies to the left, to the right, behind them, and in front…that meant they're exactly where you want them.

I couldn't remember exactly what it was they said, but it was something like that, and I was really starting to feel it. Each opponent was walking XP, as far as I was concerned.

I peeked back through the boards at the house at the end. The man I assumed was Damon picked up a shotgun and pointed it into the air, some of his men cheering as he did, and I did a double-take as the girl walked back out into view.

"What the hell?" I muttered, unsure if I should be appreciating the view, or feeling scared. She still had her impressive tits on display, but for some reason, she had donned shoulder pads and was settling spiked headgear into place over her dark, curly hair, one that looked like it'd started life as an American football helmet. Her jeans appeared to have armor stitched onto them, and a baseball bat reflected the sun disturbingly as she lifted it into the air with a bloodthirsty scream. "Are those fucking razorblades?" My jaw dropped in horrified disbelief.

I'd been thinking I might need to rescue her, and that she might even be grateful when I did, but judging by that display, hell, no. She was clearly there by choice. She and Damon vanished inside, and I swallowed hard, rethinking my plan. Armor would stop the arrows, and I only had five more. I had a knife, which was good, but no armor, and my sword was too big to be used indoors.

I shook my head in frustration as I considered the numbers arrayed against me. I just needed to defeat them, not necessarily kill them all. Ultimately, I needed to destroy the gang, effectively breaking them up. That'd be enough to finish the quest, I somehow knew.

Damon and his girl emerged from the house at the front of a group of five, maybe six people. I'd taken five down earlier today, one yesterday, and killed two downstairs, leaving a third that was dying right now. That made a total of nine. Seven milled outside the front of my building now, and seven or eight more were incoming from various directions. My best chance was to break them up, 'defeat them in detail,' I thought it was called.

I took a deep, determined breath, then eased my way to the top of the stairs, leaving my sword by the window in the front room I'd just left. I stabbed the arrows into the rotten wood of the floorboards at the top of the stairs to keep them close at hand, embedding the knife into the plasterboard of the wall nearby, where I could grab it easily.

I took a single arrow, fitted it to the bow, and kept the point trained on the floor below. My eyes followed the shadows moving as the gang made their way inside, blocking the limited light. I took care to keep out of sight as much as I could, as one of them started peering around the corner of the stairs. I'd ducked back just in time, it seemed, as I heard him whispering to his friend before he started climbing up the steep stairs. I took a couple of deep breaths. When he was nearly at the top, I spun, leaning out.

I'd had my foot drawn back, ready as I twisted around, and I drove it forward with as much force as I could muster. The steepness of the stairs and the way he was leaning forward combined to bring his head close to the perfect height.

My foot slammed into the bottom of his chin, driving his head back with such terrific force that he was literally lifted his from his feet, the blow cutting off his surprised cry of warning…with the end of his tongue.

He was apparently one of those people who habitually gripped his tongue with his teeth when he was nervous or excited, and that ended badly for him as he cartwheeled backwards, blood spurting from between clenched teeth and the remnants of his tongue.

I swore in sudden pain, staggering as I tried to put my foot down, and I felt the result of my kick. I'd forgotten that I'd changed into my trainers, and the difference between using steel toe-capped boots and trainers to land a powerful kick on bone was immense.

Hissing, I pulled back and straightened up, drawing back on the bow and aiming as they fell down the stairs. The first man was squealing like a stuck pig and thrashing around, while the second tried to catch himself and figure out what was going on.

The pair of them fell backwards, clattering and screaming, and I fired, missing completely. I swore viciously and grabbed a second arrow, drawing back and aiming, waiting until they came to a bone-crunching stop against the radiator at the bottom of the stairs before firing again.

I ignored the first man, who had gone still after slamming into the radiator; dead or unconscious, I didn't really care. This time, the arrow sunk deep, slamming into the second man in the groin and making him scream, over and over, as he clutched at himself. I stepped back into hiding and waited, listening to the shouted questions and the injured screaming for help.

It took a handful of seconds before someone darted in, grabbing the guy with the pierced pecker, and dragged him out of sight. I waited, watching and wincing as I thought about the pain that guy must be in. I'd had the option to go for the chest, but I'd recognized him at the last second as one of those who'd attacked me. He'd been the one with the barbed wire around his bat who'd cut off my escape and broken my arm, and I'd changed my aim deliberately. I didn't regret shooting him like that; I just hoped it never happened to me.

There were a few moments of relative silence, broken by screams and moans and a bubbling cry, as the man with the severed tongue woke up and started to crawl away, before a voice called up to me from below, out of sight.

"So, who sent you?" someone shouted, and I stayed out of sight and remained silent. "Come on, don't be shy! Was it Micky? Timo? One of the Manchester lot wanting their money? Come on. Either you tell me, and we can sort this out, maybe even give you a job, considering all you've done here, or I set fire to the house, see how long you last?" The last bit carried a tone of hunger, and I guessed that was what he was planning on doing either way.

"Last time offered, but hell, maybe I'll send up some more people to play first. See what you have to say for yourself after that," he offered, waiting for a beat before moving back and saying something I couldn't make out. Then someone stepped around the corner, and I felt my butthole twitch. It was a bull of a man, one I'd not seen before, and he was holding the section of the door covering that I'd ripped free earlier. The bugger wasn't that tall, but fuck, he filled the stairwell, he was that broad.

"Well, fuck," I muttered under my breath, stepping out as the huge man lumbered up the stairs, hauling back on the bow, and then freezing in shock as the man stopped partway up, grinning up at me malevolently. He ducked back down, and a shotgun appeared over his shoulder, pointed right at me. I tried to move, but I was too slow. Raucous laughter burst up from below.

It fired, dozens of pellets piercing my skin as I frantically dove aside.

I cried out in pain as I felt literal hot lead poking holes into my skin, burying themselves deep in my muscles. I slammed into the floor, gasping in shock as the world briefly flared into white-hot agony.

My adrenaline took over quickly, dulling the pain, and I grunted as I rolled to the side, reaching out with my left hand and grabbing the knife where a stray pellet had knocked it free of the wall. I tried to move my right arm, but it was a sea of pain and blood, and I gave up after a single attempt. Instead, I stabbed out with the knife, digging it into the rotting floorboards and hauling on it, dragging myself forward. My right leg, arm, and chest had taken the majority of the pellets, and I grunted in pain as I kicked out with my left leg, pushing myself forward, desperately trying to escape.

I'd maybe covered three feet, if that, before something slammed down hard onto the small of my back, and I screamed in pain, my left leg collapsing. I tried to move, finding that nothing below the impact point was responding and I almost gibbered with fear. Someone stepped past me and stomped down on my left wrist. I wrenched my gaze up, finding a maniacal grin and a fantastic set of tits that would have normally commanded my full attention.

Today, though, I fixated more on the bat that was being waved in front of my face. Razor blades had been embedded in it in all directions, and they were dripping blood.

My blood…I knew with chilling certainty.

I winced at the crazed look in her eyes as she started to whisper to me.

"You came for us, but you don't know…no, you don't know the truth…the truth of the new world! You think it's still the old one, but it's not. This is our world, where the strong get to do what they want! Your false lord is dead! Priest tried to tell us, tried to say it was wrong…guess what we did to him?" she asked, waving the bat in front of my eyes again. "Hmmm, you gonna guess? I SAID, GUESS!" she screamed, louder than I could believe from such a slender frame. "Guess! GUESS, guess! She started chanting, capering around like a chimp on acid, before halting suddenly, and dropping to the floor to lie next to me and whisper in my ear.

"You don't want to play?" she pouted in a sad little girl voice, before smiling suddenly. "That's okay!" She kissed me quickly on the cheek, bouncing back upright to announce to someone out of sight. "He doesn't want to play!" she called happily, skipping back to kick me in the face hard, sending me spiraling down into darkness.

Again.

SEVEN

I HAD NO IDEA how much longer it was before I woke again, only that I'd not expected to, and that multiple notifications were flashing for my attention.

I was tied to a chair, upright, and in a hell of a lot of pain. I tried to lift my head and got a surprise when I felt something in my mouth. Pushing at the obstruction with my tongue, I tried to shift it, realizing it was a ball gag. I had a horrible thought about who might have used it before me. Then my hind brain shouted up to my full brain that it was far more important to wonder how the fuck I was going to get out of here, rather than whose kinky sex shit this was.

Luckily, it had only been wedged in my mouth and not braced, so I managed to spit it out after a few seconds, and then spent a few seconds more of spitting in an attempt to get the taste out of my mouth.

I shifted my head, looking around the room blearily as I worked my aching jaw I was tied up in a small, dark room; what looked like bedsheets were stapled to the windows, and bare floorboards had been covered in a collection of mattresses, used needles, and empty cans.

Two figures lay slumped in the darkness. One was staring unseeing at me in some drug-induced catatonia, while the other snored his head off in the corner.

I shifted, biting down hard on the inside of my lip at the pain, but after a few seconds, it died away, and I tried moving again. My hands and ankles were tied to the chair, an old office piece with the castors ripped off the bottom.

The arms of the chair rattled as I shifted, and I visually followed the cable ties that dug into my skin. They'd been attached under the arms of the chair, so I couldn't simply pull them off, a small analytical part of my mind noted.

I started shifting slowly, testing my body and my restraints. After a few minutes, I slumped back, breathing hoarsely in pain. I looked around the room again, but nothing had changed. Druggie one was still staring, but could have actually overdosed, and I wouldn't be able to tell, thanks to the horrific smell and lack of movement. Druggie two was still snoring.

I took a deep breath and brought up my notifications, scared of what I was going to see. Whatever changes touching the Core had wrought on me with my sudden hyper-speed healing ability was great, as I now had the use of my body again; it was just painful. But the Assimilation…

Current Level of Core Assimilation: 29%
Estimated time for increase of Assimilation level is 1% per hour in current low Mana Density. Move to an area of higher Mana Density to decrease this time.

"Fuck." That was a fifty-eight percent chance of dying now. Not good at all. I guessed that meant I'd been out around four hours, and judging from the faint hints of daylight around the bedsheet curtains, that'd make sense. Shouting and cat calls sounded in the distance, and somewhere closer, overhead, I could hear rhythmic grunting and moaning. Clearly, 'Batshit Betty' was having fun.

I tried to get my hands free again as I brought up the next prompt.

Congratulations!
You have defeated five opponents classed as 'Local Thug'
Thug level: 0
Your level: 2
XP awarded: 125
*

Congratulations!
You have gained two levels in Ambush!
You receive a further 10% increase to damage dealt while evading detection. Because you have gained this level in a sub-skill of 'Stealth,' you have also received the requisite levels in 'Stealth', granting a further 3% reduction per level in chances of being spotted. Increase your skill to further improve your damage bonuses.
*

Your progress to Level Three is at 165/200.

"Well, that's just fucking peachy," I muttered, shaking my head, as a long-drawn-out scream of pleasure rang out above. "Glad someone's having a good day, though…" I shuddered, forcing my thoughts back to my current predicament.

I reached down under the arms of the chair and started feeling around. After a few seconds of blind groping, my fingers found something: a wingnut. The metal screw was holding the arm in place, and I grinned with relief as I started to slowly twist it. It took longer than I expected, mainly because, while my left was okay, my right arm was still considerably weaker, and the more I moved, the more little rivulets of blood escaped from my wounds.

A handful of desperate minutes passed with me slowly turning the nuts as best I could, feeling the arms growing looser and looser, until I heard footsteps approaching outside the room. I quickly lowered my head and pretended to be asleep, unconscious, or dead…whatever.

"Hi! Whatcha doin'?" a voice called from the doorway as my head hung down. By sheer force of will, I kept my eyes closed, ignoring the crazy lady. The soft sound of bare feet padded across the floor, then a hot breathy whisper brushed my ear. "You awake? Want to play? I can play niiiiice…" she promised huskily, and I felt a hand slowly run up my left leg before settling on my crotch.

I kept as still as possible, doing everything I could not to respond, not to flinch, or…well…stiffen. I managed it at first, but after several panicked heartbeats, her voice changed, no longer speaking to me. Now she sounded like she was talking to herself. "What's in here, then? D won't mind if I just take a little look…" The hand undid the zipper of my jeans, pulling it down and reaching inside. I felt her take ahold of me, freeing me from my pants, before the hot breath I'd felt on my cheek was suddenly playing elsewhere, lower…

"I wonder what you taste like…hmmm? Maybe just a little lick. What Damon doesn't know won't hurt him…or me…or maybe it would. Maybe he'll hurt me gooooood…" She mumbled and moaned, and I flinched as I felt her shift her grip, forcing me to respond, despite my fervent wishes.

She looked up, shocked, as I moved, and I reacted instinctively, stiffening but staying as still as possible, given that she was holding onto me far too tightly for me to do anything else…I just sat there, staring furiously into her eyes at a range of an inch.

"What the ever-living fuck are you doing?" I whispered to her in shock and disgust, remembering at the last second that when I had been tied up, I probably looked like I was dying. Bang; there went the element of surprise…

"You're awake…" she purred with a feral grin. Checking to verify that my hands were still tied, she shifted her grip, wrapping her fist around me comfortably, then slapped her other hand down hard on a very sensitive part of my anatomy like she was determined to get the last bit of ketchup out of the bottle.

"Aaaaah!" I cried out, and she jumped back, laughing, then turned around and shouted upstairs.

"D! He's awake! Can I play with him?!" There was a brief pause, then a deep voice called back down tiredly.

"Have fun, babe…just make sure he's ready to talk when I come down…" She turned around slowly and fixed me with a mad smile, then brushed her hair back from her face, sauntering in. I'd been deliberately not looking before, but now I couldn't help but notice her shirt, unbuttoned down the front, black lacy panties and stockings. She grinned at me as I looked and ached.

"You like? Maybe if I'm nice to you, you'll tell me what I want to hear?" she asked in her best sex kitten voice, and I grimaced.

"Lady, you're all kinds of fucked up..." I muttered, not sure where I'd heard the line before, but determined it'd never been more suited to someone.

"Oh, I am..." she whispered in delighted agreement. Dancing across to the guy that was staring fixedly, she reached down and prodded him, then poked him in the eye. He didn't respond at all, and I mentally moved him from the 'drugged up' box into the 'dead from drugs' box. She leaned down, sniffed him, then licked his cheek. She maintained eye contact with me as she giggled and sauntered across to the snoring man, then danced back a step or two, wound up, and kicked him as hard as she could.

He awoke, crying out in pain, wheezing and clutching at himself as she giggled again. He instinctively rolled toward her, growling, then saw who it was and backed up.

"Oh, come on! Nobody wants to play with me! You know?" she pouted, turning back to me and dancing across the room, before spinning around and darting back out of the door. I started yanking at the restraints again, feeling them give more and more, but it wasn't enough to free me before she returned.

She dragged a chair in with her, excitedly yanking it along, before plopping down into it across from me. Two other gang members walked in after her and settled down on the mattresses to watch, but she seemed oblivious to them, even though one started flicking his lighter so it sparked to life, then blowing it out and doing it again, over and over.

"Soooo, D wants you to talk..." she whispered, biting her thumb nail and staring at me coquettishly. "Wanna make a deal?" She leaned forward, smiling sexily, before leaning back and putting a foot on either of my shoulders, then nodding downwards.

I stared fixedly at her, not giving her the satisfaction, and she huffed out a breath, sitting back upright and staring into my eyes so closely, our noses were touching.

"Look, I need you to tell me what you know, so here's the deal...okay? You tell me everything, and I'll give you a niiiice long, slow blow, right? Orrrr..." she whispered, leaning back to pull something out from behind her back. Holding the object up between us, she shook it so that I couldn't help but recognize it.

It was a fucking cheese grater.

"...or I play with this, hmmm?" She pouted, lifting her hands and pretending to cry anime-style.

"Or, we go for option three…" I whispered to her, shifting as best I could in preparation.

"Okay…what's that?" she whispered excitedly, leaning in to put her nose against mine again, a huge, insane smile stretching her cheeks.

"I break outta here, fuck you up, kill all your friends, and walk out the front door, after setting fire to the house and pissing on your boy 'D's' corpse." I forced a smile in return.

"Oh, I like that! How? How are you gonna do it?" she breathed excitedly, and I flicked my eyes to her breast pocket. She looked down and then back up, understanding what I'd seen when she leaned forward: a small flick knife.

"My knife?" she asked curiously in her little girl voice. "But even if I let you have it, you're all tied up…"

"Yeah…except for one point…" I whispered to her, jerking my head back and to the right. She grinned at me and leaned in again. "I've…broken…the… chair…" I slowly whispered into her ear.

She looked back at me, then down, then back up, as though not understanding. Taking advantage of her momentary confusion, I jerked my hands up with all my now-considerable strength.

The arms on the chair, loose as they were, barely slowed me as they broke free of the rusted chair. I grabbed her by the throat with my left, tore the knife free with my right, then pulled her close before throwing her back from her chair into the guy closest to her, who was struggling to his feet.

She tumbled into him with a squawk of protest, and the effort sent me over backwards. I flicked the blade free and yanked at the restraints on my ankles, digging the blade in and cutting them away, nicking myself shallowly on both legs in the process.

Rolling aside, I jumped up and drew the knife back, flinging it at the man on the far side who was also climbing to his feet, slowed by shock and drawing his own knife. My appropriated blade smacked into his head high on the right side, drawing a scream from him as it cut him deeply before glancing off. The other two were still shoving at each other, trying to get up, as I stepped over to them and loomed over the girl. I picked her up by the shirt collar and one thigh, dragged her backwards, and spun her around like I was trying out for the shot-put before slamming her into the guard, hard.

They went down with a sound like coconuts hitting at the fair, and I jumped on the guy who'd been kicked by her, punching him hard and knocking him out easily enough. With everyone in the room taken down, I strode to the door, cautiously stepping to the side of it and sweeping up the knife dropped by the guy with the head wound. He looked up at me from between hands that were covered in blood, shouting out in alarm.

"He…he's free!" he screamed, and I glared at him, swallowing hard before stabbing down, taking him in the throat as he gurgled in horror.

I kicked him back and waited, the sound of running feet and voices rising in question. I waited until they got closer…then stepped out, punching forward with the knife to take a guy with a mohawk in the stomach. I quickly tore it back out, grabbing ahold of his shoulder, and pumped it back into him again and again, before yanking it sideways and shoving him back as his guts fell out.

Two more thugs were barreling down the hall. Running feet echoing from elsewhere in the building told me they were all coming for me. I realized suddenly that I wasn't afraid, not even slightly. I'd gone right out the far side of fear and into full-on beast mode, with a side of disgust. These people were scum, not even human to me now, and they needed to be removed from society.

I lunged at the next guy who was sprinting at me, shabbily dressed in jeans and a 'Death-Metal' t-shirt, a pathetic attempt at a beard that was just painful to see, no chin, and a long, greasy ponytail made me grin, knowing I was actively doing him a favor by killing him.

He raised his club behind his back and screamed at me, swinging it high overhead, obviously planning on smashing it down onto my skull. Unfortunately, he'd forgotten two important details. First, I wasn't going to stay still long enough for him to hit me. Secondly, and arguably most importantly… he was indoors, in an old house with low ceilings.

His club hit the roof, bouncing backwards and hitting the guy who was running behind him. The grease-ball turned to see what had happened, then clearly remembered where and what he was doing and spun back around, just in time to take the punch I'd wound up for him.

He fell like he'd been hit by a thunderbolt, and with my strength being at Olympic levels now, it probably felt like one as well. He collided with the man behind him, who was already clutching his face and slowing from his friend's blow. I stood over them both, stabbing down with the knife, once, twice, three times, pulling the blade back as blood sprayed up. I lifted my gore-spattered face, glaring at a guy who skidded into the hall, bounced off the wall, and then turned and tried to reverse course.

He tripped over his panicked feet and slid across the floor, kicking and slapping at the ground as he tried to stop. I reached down to my right, swapping the knife to my left hand and swept up a club, heading after the guy as he scrambled to his feet and sprinted for the stairs leading up.

"Yooo-hooo, 'D'!" I called up. "I'm coming for you…"

My shout was cut off by the boom of a shotgun, and the guy who was sprinting upstairs fell back down, half his head blown away. Swearing filtered down from upstairs as 'D' shouted to someone else.

"He's half dead! You saw him when we tied him to the chair. Get down there and finish the fucker off!"

"*You* finish him off! All I've got is a knife!" someone else called out, and I grinned, turning and heading back to the other end of the hall. Two doors led off the hall on my right, one on the left. As I'd come from the first one on the right, I checked the left, finding a small room full of boxes, TV's, computers, coffee machines; all sorts of appliances and electronics were stored there, boxed up and abandoned. Clearly, they'd looted some major store or something. I looked in on the room I'd come from as I passed it. The girl was stirring, but the guy I'd slammed her into wasn't. I clenched my fist and moved on, unsure how I was going to resolve that.

I'd been raised to believe that no man should ever hit a woman. Using her as a club had kinda swerved that issue, but I knew it wasn't going to go away.

I pushed open the next door and glanced inside before pulling back as an arrow slammed into the doorframe right next to me.

"He's here!" A panicked, high pitched voice shrieked from inside, and a second arrow slammed into the far wall. I debated what to do, before grinning as I remembered something I'd seen one of the guys in the first room playing with, and I ducked back to collect it, ignoring the moaning and dazed crazy girl on the floor.

It took a second or two, but I soon found the lighter. Stepping to the storeroom, I found a rolled-up pile of bedding that stank to high heaven. I bit back a gag as I wrapped it around a club that was on the floor next to one of the corpses, then lit it, waited until it was burning merrily, and returned to the room with the archer hiding inside.

I waved the torch in the doorway, and a second later, an arrow glanced off it. I risked a glance inside, briefly glimpsing the man hiding at the far end behind a pile of crates and boxes. I located a good target and twisted, lunging across to the far side of the doorway as he frantically drew back and fired another arrow, which bounced off a wall inside.

I stepped back out into view and threw the burning mess off to the right, where it smashed into a cupboard, wiping out several of the half-empty bottles placed on top of it. They fell, as if in slow motion, and we both stared at them as they tumbled over and over. The crash and tinkle of breaking glass as the bottles hit the floor was eclipsed by the 'wumph' as the alcohol hit the flames, then spread across the narrow walkway between the boxes.

I glanced up, catching the look of horror on the skinny guy's face as flames licked up across the space between us. I nodded to him once, stepping back out into the hallway and closing the door. He started to scream as I turned around and made my way back to the room I'd first woken up in. I moved quickly to the girl, who was just starting to sit up, rubbing her head. She glared up at me through a mess of blood, her nose having clearly been broken when she impacted the other man, and her eyes blazed at me, as though I'd been the unreasonable one.

My cock was still throbbing, and not in a good way, as I came to a halt over her, hauling her upright and spinning her around. I twisted one arm up behind her back and put the knife to her throat as I forced her out of the door and towards the stairs.

"So…wanna have some fun later?" she asked me, trying to reach up and lick my cheek.

"Shut the fuck up, you crazy bitch!" I muttered in her ear, shifting her so her face was further away from me. She moved up the stairs happily as I directed her, before stopping halfway and pressing her ass back against me and giving a little wiggle.

"I can be good…" she whispered, licking her lip clear of blood, and I pressed the knife harder against her throat.

"You'll be fucking dead if you don't do as I say!" I growled at her.

"Mmmm, tell me what to do, then…" she whispered playfully, and I glared at her, unsure how to handle her. I was certain of two things; no matter what I said, she was going to have an answer for it, and she was clearly all kinds of crazy that I really didn't want anything to do with, despite how pretty she was. Topping it all off was the sure and certain knowledge that sex with her would be an experience. One I'd probably not survive.

I shoved her up the stairs and called up ahead of us.

"Put the gun down, Damon! I've got your girl…"

"Keep her!" a voice called back down, and I growled to myself as I forced her up onto the next floor. We emerged into a hallway that led both to the right and left, with two doors on the far side, one behind me at the other end.

"Where are you…?" I muttered aloud, unthinkingly.

"He'll be in our room, at the end…" she whispered to me, winking. "Or maybe I'm lying…?"

"Die!" Someone screamed from my left, and my head whipped around as the thick-bodied bull of a man sprinted out of the door behind me at the end of the corridor, even as I heard the boom of the shotgun again from the opposite end.

I grunted, feeling a few stinging cuts as pellets tore across my flesh. The girl, however, screamed in pain, sagging in my grasp.

I dropped her in shock, looking up in time to see Damon pumping the spent shell out of the shotgun before lifting it again, aiming for me. I pushed off as fast as I could, colliding with the big man and twisting my body around. The second shot went off, taking a nearby section of the wall out, while a few more pellets buried themselves into my skin.

The big man also grunted in pain as his larger bulk took a few projectiles, but it didn't stop him from grappling me to the ground, his left hand grabbing my right wrist and slamming it down hard as I tried to stab him.

I brought my knees up between us, pushing him back and punching out with my left fist as he focused on slamming my right hand down repeatedly until I lost my grip on the knife. He went for it, while another man approached with a meat cleaver. 'D' hovered somewhere behind him, swearing venomously as he tried to get his shotgun reloaded.

"I'll kill you!" the big man swore down at me, his breath foul, as I punched him, my left fist glancing off his cheekbone. He lunged again as I tried to shove the dropped knife further away, and I felt his weight shift across my legs. Man, the fucker was heavy, but we were also at the top of the stairs, and he'd given up all stability in his desperation to reach the knife.

I grabbed onto his top and pushed up with all the strength I had, shoving him aside into the bannister. The rotting railing lasted less than a second before it snapped, an entire section of the wooden spindles fracturing as he fell through them with a cry and disappeared down the stairs.

I rolled to my side, twisting as the meat cleaver slammed down inches from my head. Instinctively, I grabbed the knifeman's arm with my left hand and started punching him desperately with my right while whipping my right knee into his face.

He fell to the side, I instantly rolled onto him, ripping the meat cleaver out of the wooden floor and slamming it down with a strength driven by desperation. He tried to block with his forearm and screamed as the blade sank through flesh to smack into the bone.

I yanked the blade back as his blood spurted out, spraying across me, and I grabbed his arm with my left hand, pulling it aside as I struck again. This time, the hit was good, sinking into his skull with a crunch. I tried to lever it out but couldn't, just as 'D's' grunt indicated that he'd finally managed to get the shells into the shotgun and close it back up.

I got to my feet, seeing only one way to go, and sprinted at him as he levelled the shotgun. I dove to the right, making it most of the way into the nearest room before he managed to pull the trigger.

I screamed as my left hip took most of the blast, knocking me off course and sending me to the floor with blood running from my side. Before I could think of what to do, 'D' was standing over me, panting in rage, fear, and adrenaline.

"You're a dead man!" he screamed at me. "Who sent you? WHO?!?" His eyes bulged with fury as the shotgun's barrel wove back and forth over my face at point blank range.

"Your…*Cough*…mum," I said, grinning up at him as I laid back, relaxing despite the pain. I couldn't see any way out of this, and I could hear the crackling of the flames downstairs as the building was consumed. I might be dead, but at least I would have managed the task I'd set myself, and the surrounding area would be safe from this gang. "She said…she wished she swallowed you…" I muttered, then lifted my right hand and gave him the finger.

"You're a fucking dead man," he whispered, moving the barrel to aim directly at my forehead.

"Yeah, well, it's been…tried before…" I said, shrugging, pretending not to care, and refusing to be afraid. I closed my eyes as I coughed again, swallowing hard and preparing myself, fully expecting to die.

A scream rang out, followed by the shotgun blast close enough to my head that I felt my eardrum on that side burst, but the buckshot slammed harmlessly into the floor at my side as my eyes flew open. I looked over to see 'D' falling backwards, blood spurting from the back of his legs as his girl grinned at us both.

She lay where she'd dragged herself, her left arm, most of her chest, and lower body a complete mess of shredded flesh. Blood visibly pumped out of her countless wounds. With her right arm extended, the knife she'd used to hamstring her former partner and killer clattered to the floor as 'D' landed, clutching at his leg.

I rolled over, the world seeming to spin and pulse as my head pounded in time to the blood that dripped from my ear. I glanced back at the girl, who was grinning at me with bloodstained teeth, before 'D' heaved himself sideways and bashed the shotgun butt into her face.

Her head slammed back into the floor with a crunch, and he screamed something incoherent at her, hitting her again, and then pulling back to repeat the blow a third time.

I lunged for him, grabbing his uninjured leg and hauling myself up his body as he spun the shotgun around and planted it against my cheek.

We froze, looking into each other's eyes, and stayed like that for a countless series of heartbeats.

"Back away..." he growled after a handful of seconds spent in joint paralysis, and I frowned. Why hadn't he pulled the trigger? He...the last few seconds came back to me, and I counted. One blast in the hallway, and one in here, into the floor...

"You're out of rounds..." I whispered, the fear in his eyes confirming the truth as he tried to deny it. I grinned, and he pulled the trigger defiantly. We both froze again, but only for a second as the click of an empty chamber echoed around the room. I drove the shotgun aside and hauled myself further up his body, ignoring his attempts to hit me with the stock, and punched him in the face.

He let go of the shotgun and grabbed my left hip, where his second to last shot had caught me, and I screamed in pain, using the agony to drive my next punch. I felt his left cheekbone and nose break as my punch landed, the back of his head smacking into the floor and rebounding. He tried to grab onto me, his fingers wriggling to get inside my skin, and I roared. His eyes widened in shock at my unhindered attack, stunned as my fist landed again. I drew back and shifted my weight in order to use both arms and started punching. After a dozen blows, he wasn't moving any more, and the mass I was punching had become far more shapeless. Huffing from the exertion and adrenaline, I scanned the room to check for any further threats, when my questing gaze fell on the girl's face. Grateful that her eyes had already glazed in death, I interlocked my fingers, lifting them overhead and slamming them down in a hammerfist that smashed the front of 'D's' skull in.

I collapsed to my right, panting and coughing as the smoke rose, and I reached out to her, gently closing her eyes. She was batshit crazy, but her help was the only reason I'd survived. She must have known she was dying, and had instead decided to get revenge on her boyfriend for abandoning her as expendable.

The room was starting to fill with smoke, and I laid back down, in too much pain to care that it'd all be over soon. I swatted out at a blinking light that was annoying me, until I realized what it was.

I coughed again and pulled up my notifications for what I thought would be the last time, my mind idly reflecting on how weird my life had become.

Quest Complete!

Clean up the Estate

You have defeated the gang! Their headquarters is in ruins, and less that 10% of the gang still live. Those who do live have sworn in the darkness of their souls to do better, lest they attract your ire again.

+1 to Agility, Constitution, and Dexterity
+1 Skill Point to allocate
+1 Class Perk
250 XP

*

Congratulations!
You have defeated ten opponents classed as 'Local Thug'
Thug level: 0
Your level: 2
XP awarded: 250

*

Congratulations!
You have defeated one opponent classed as 'Gang Lord'
Gang Lord level: 0
Your level: 2
XP awarded: 50

*

You have reached Level Three!
You receive five Stat points to invest in your attributes.

*

You have reached Level Four!
You receive five Stat points to invest in your attributes and gain one Skill Point to allocate.

*

Your progress to Level five is at 115/500.

*

You have ten Stat points, two Skill Points, and one Class Perk to allocate. Please allocate these within the next 24 hours, or they will be assigned randomly for you.

*

Congratulations!
You have gained two levels in Dodge!
You receive 2% increase to chances to evade damage.
Increase your skill to augment your ability further.

*

Congratulations!
You have gained four levels in Unarmed Combat!
You receive 8% increase in your chance to inflict critical damage.
Increase your skill to augment your ability further.

*

Congratulations!
You have gained three levels in Small Blades!
You receive 6% increase in your chance to inflict critical damage.
Increase your skill to augment your ability further.

I remained on the floor, my head spinning as I tried to make sense of the welter of notifications flooding my vision. I read through them as quickly as I could, coughing more and more as the room began to fill with smoke, before I grinned to myself. I still had a chance!

I pulled up my character sheet, quickly slamming the points home in a frenzied attempt to save myself. Five points into Wisdom to bring my Control to ten. Two points into Constitution, bringing that one to ten as well and triggering the increase in the value of the health it generated from ten to twenty. I held off on assigning the remaining three points, just in case, and confirmed my choice, before screaming until I broke off into a coughing fit.

I writhed around, coughing until I retched and threw up a thin bile across the floor, but as I blinked my eyes open, I found that I could see and focus much more clearly.

I slowly pushed myself upright, grimacing as I felt the pain of my injuries rippling through me. Thankfully, it was manageable now, and I could feel the pellets being slowly pushed out of my body as I healed. I peered around the room, then growled aloud as I spotted the watch on 'D's' wrist. It was my Granddad's watch, and I moved quickly, stripping it from his cooling corpse. The timepiece was covered in blood, both from him and me, but I felt immeasurably better to have it back.

I coughed again, turning and considering the flickering flames that were climbing the stairs. Feeling the wash of heat that rolled through the room, I was dismayed to realize that there was only one window, and it was small, barricaded with a crossbar that had been nailed across it. I shook my head; I wasn't getting out that way.

I slowly pushed myself upright, continuing to cough, and made my way to the doorway, wincing as the heat intensified. I backed up, covering my mouth, and then ran out into the hall, turning right and heading to the furthest end of the hallway, away from the stairs and the corpses.

I staggered into the room at the end, finding that it was indeed, as I'd hoped, 'D's' room. The entire space had been stuffed full of loot, piled around a massive bed and a sex swing rocking gently in the breeze from a harness chained into the ceiling.

Shaking my head in wonder at the pair of them, I moved on quickly, stumbling to the double doors that led out onto a balcony. I threw them open, peering along the side of the building. Flames rose from the windows and open door below me, the concrete yard appearing to be the only place I could safely get to.

I swore, looked back inside, and grimaced. There was a way to make my landing softer, but it'd no doubt be less pleasant than landing on the concrete would have been. Despite my rapid healing abilities, I knew it was better not to push my body any harder today wherever possible, so I hobbled back in and grabbed the mattress, dragged it to the balcony, and threw it over, trying to touch the thing as little as possible.

I took one last look around. Seeing my sword propped against one wall, I grabbed it and left behind the rest of the crap that they'd filled the room with. I clambered over the balcony railing, hissing with pain as I threw myself over.

I plummeted to the mattress, bouncing and tumbling off it, feeling defiled for touching the damn thing after having heard the pair of them going 'at it' when I'd first reawakened.

I lurched painfully through the old wooden gate and managed to make it a dozen or so steps down the street before I fell. Once I'd caught my breath, hissing with the pain, I forced myself back upright and made it another twenty yards, only to slump down against the wall, watching the flames rise as I collapsed fully, groaning softly.

EIGHT

I LAID MOTIONLESS FOR another twenty minutes or so, watching the house burn down, and noting the total lack of anyone coming to help or to investigate.

Sighing, I concentrated hard, and a screen popped up for me.

Do you wish to eject the Dungeon Core at this time?
You will have 108 seconds to place the Core and activate it before it will become unstable and detonate.

Host has a sufficiently high enough level of Control to be able to assume full command privileges over this Dungeon. Do you wish to assume control?
Yes/No
Estimated area consumed by Dungeon Core detonation: 1.672sq miles.

"What happens if I take control?" I wondered aloud, only for a second screen to pop up.

If the Dungeon Host ejects the Core and assumes full control over the nascent Dungeon, Host will be able to design, assign, and alter the Dungeon priorities, including but not limited to:
-Growth
-Loot
-Dungeon Creatures
-Research and Development
-Mana Purification Control

If this is the Host's intention, it is highly recommended that the Dungeon Core is relocated to a high mana density area before placement.

"Okay, define the priorities, please?" I asked the air nervously, well aware that the longer I kept this damn thing inside me, the better the chances that I'd die, and I was already bleeding heavily.

Growth

Dungeons require Mana to grow and to maintain essential functions. There are three accepted methods for the dungeon to access said mana:

Ambient Mana Collection*:* Mana is drawn in from the local area, purified, and released back into the ether. Unpurified mana greatly increases the chances of monsters spawning in the surrounding area, while purified mana has been linked to increases in the health, wellbeing, and intelligence of creatures in the surrounding area.

Direct Assimilation: Mana is drawn from a direct source of mana, such as a nearby sub-space rift. This is by far the most effective method to grow a Dungeon, but also the most expensive and difficult to arrange.

Mana drawn from lifeforms: This, combined with the Ambient Mana Collection, is the standard method of growing a Dungeon. When Adventurers or living creatures enter the Dungeon's area of influence, it begins to draw the corrupted mana found within their forms into itself. Mana released by lifeforms at the point of death is absorbed at a higher rate.

Loot

Dungeon fairies traditionally assign a portion of the collected mana to generate random loot in order to entice Adventurers into the Dungeon depths, as opposed to those who simply gather at the Dungeon entrance to cultivate mana, enjoying the increased purification that the Dungeon provides.

Dungeon Creatures

Each Dungeon generates creatures to roam its depths, stirring up the mana that accumulates and gradually increasing the mana of one strand or another. Depending on the overall aim of the Dungeon fairy, certain creatures may be prioritized over others.

Example: Goblinoid races generate Earth mana consistently, while Nature mana may be drawn from Woodland Beasts, such as bears, panthers, and horned rabbits.

Research and Development

All Dungeons that are designated to grow more efficiently must eventually unlock research and development options, enabling directed growth.

Example*:* A Dungeon specializing in metal production may choose to develop base Golems that are armed with drilling tools, to replace the standard first level 'Rockworm' design of gatherer.

Mana Purification Control

Specialized mana purification Dungeons have been set up on several Cinthian worlds to cleanse, purify, and regulate ambient mana. This has the environmental effect of systematically raising the local lifeforms from their low-level existence to a tier two, three, or even four civilization. A Dungeon set up for exclusive mana purification will draw in the local mana and purify it at a much greater rate than a standard dungeon. As such, standard dungeons on these worlds are deployed on a 1:6 ratio.

"What the fuck…?" I muttered, reading over the details and shaking my head as I made the connections. "Is this a 'Cinthian World'?" I asked, but there was no response. "Hey! I asked you a question!" I shouted, then groaned as pain shot through me at the movement.

There was an abundance of silence, and I slumped back, listening to the crackle of the flames and hearing the occasional crash as glass shattered from the heat. Luckily, the house was a freestanding one, so I hoped it wouldn't set fire to anything else, but still.

"Okay…" I continued under my breath. "I guess the creature in that crystal was the 'Dungeon Fairy' that had been assigned to the Dungeon Core. Well, it's toast, and I'm now the host…I could eject it, but it'd still kill me if I didn't claim it. Simplest solution is I claim it, then, so I can set its priorities. I can make it purify the area, fair enough; that'd probably be a good thing, but there's no way to tell for sure, really. The way those prompts were laid out suggests that this is now classed as a Cinthian world, and that they've seeded these fucking dungeons around." I shifted, gritting my teeth as I forced myself to my feet and started to walk along the wall slowly, heading back toward the house I'd been captured in.

"That means they've got plans for us, possibly to 'raise our tier,' whatever the fuck that is. Either way, though, I'm betting this means the power isn't coming back on, and that the whole world's gone to shit." I scrubbed my face with my gory hand. "And I've clearly gone mad, talking to myself. Meh. Only way I'm going to get a good conversation, I guess…So, world's gone to shit, and I'm in control of a Dungeon, one I need to eject fast, before it kills me. Where the hell am I going to find a 'high mana area,' though…?"

A map popped up in my vision, the local area overlaid in blues, greens, yellows, oranges, and reds. I searched for my current location, discovering that it was classed as a yellow zone, and where I lived was orange.

"Okay, so if here is green, at one point an hour, and home is orange at half a point, I guess the reds are, what…no mana? Logically then, the blues are the place to be…" I muttered, absentmindedly rubbing my chin and missing the flakes of dried blood that fell off.

I studied the map closely, figuring out locations and trying to guess where I could set up that nobody would notice, as the last thing I wanted was for people to actually stumble into the Dungeon. Maybe one day, yeah, fine, but for now, I needed to figure this shit out, and once the government got wind of it, they'd no doubt nick it, if it had half the potential I was starting to suspect it had.

I traced out streets and locations, grinning to myself as I fixated on a bar I'd spent many a happy night in. It was on Collingwood Street, a great little bar and nightclub called 'House of Smith,' and it'd closed down a week ago for renovations. Given the way the world was going, it'd probably never reopen, and it was slap-bang in the middle of the deepest blue area I could see.

Feeling unexpectedly pleased, I selected that as my intended location, and grinned as a softly glowing star appeared on the map before I banished it with a thought. Now that I was able to see properly again, I looked around, trying to figure out which house I'd been driven into earlier. I found it after a minute and staggered over to it, but when I reached the doorway, I started to curse.

I hadn't held onto much hope as I'd walked, but seeing that my new bike was missing, I shook my head dejectedly. That had been my best chance to get to Perdu without dying, and it was gone. One of the little turds I'd been fighting had probably nicked it, parking it up somewhere stupid. Knowing my luck, it was charring nicely in the damn house behind me.

I sat down, grumbling to myself, and tried to come up with another plan. I was still bleeding, and once again, I'd lost my damn bag. Unless…

I headed deeper into the house, searching quickly and stepping over the bodies that were beginning to reek of death. It took a few minutes, and a lot of cursing, but eventually, I found my bag. They'd clearly missed it in the corner of the room, behind the door, as its contents were undisturbed. I sighed gratefully as I dumped out bandages, protein bars, and drinks.

Quickly stripping off down to my boxers, I used a wadded-up bit of bandage soaked in antiseptic to clean my wounds, then set to putting bandages over them. After ten minutes, I eventually gave in and changed the bandages to just cover the biggest wounds, as there were far too many to bind them all individually, and if I managed it, I'd end up looking like a mummy anyway. I dressed in the spare clothes I'd brought, and feeling at least a bit better, I headed back downstairs, dismissing the prompt about leveling up my first aid skill.

I stepped out into the setting sun and checked my surroundings. The house was still blazing merrily, but still, there was nobody about. Considering the way that kids would travel miles to see a fire, yet there were none in sight? The entire area must have learned not to come this way.

I set off walking, cutting down alleys and up streets, passing old, red-bricked houses from the forties and white stucco coated houses from the seventies, wandering through overgrown gardens and past yards abandoned by all but the weeds, and wondered what the hell had happened to the estates over here. I'd known they were rough, but damn…behind the main streets, it appeared as though people had just slunk away to live anywhere else.

I eventually made my way back to the main road, and started to encounter occasional people again. They were few and far between, but every so often, I'd hear the sound of kids playing behind a wall or shouting at each other, quickly shushed by an adult.

By the time I got out of the area and had crossed into Gateshead properly, the sun had fully set, and night was falling quickly. Occasional candles lit up windows here and there, while the majority stood dark. People had already learned not to draw the attention of outsiders. I assumed they opted to stay in rooms that weren't as visible from the road.

By that point, I was feeling much stronger and healthier, thankfully. Whatever change the Core had wrought, with regard to my healing, was lovingly accepted. I checked my hip during one of my breaks, finding that the bandages were actually holding half a dozen pellets that my healing body had evicted. I checked over my body and found a few more in other bandages, as well as a load of sore spots, with fully healed-over skin where the wounds were shallowest.

I was still walking carefully, thanks to my bruised tail, primarily due to Batshit Betty's attempt to 'get out the ketchup'. I'd checked it when I got changed and found that it was black with bruises, making the second time that had happened in my life, and for a far less fun reason than the first. I dismissed the idle thoughts and moved on, hoping it'd heal soon.

As a new notification bloomed for me, I sped up, motivated by the warning that I really didn't have long left…

Current Level of Core Assimilation: 31%

Estimated time for increase of Assimilation level is 1% per hour in current low Mana Density. Move to an area of higher Mana Density to decrease this time.

Knowing that I was now facing a sixty-two percent chance of dying with every single percentage point increase made my heart race, and I swallowed hard, shaking myself and starting to jog, despite the pain it caused me.

I passed along Durham road, coming up to pass the Saltwell Park turnoff, when it hit me like a bolt from the blue. A circus had been set up on the fields there. I'd heard about it; it was supposed to be there for two weeks. If memory served, I'd actually been told about it by Kelly. She said she lived over here somewhere…I knew I'd never be able to find her house. Hell, all I knew was that she could see the park from her bedroom window, but what she'd said came back to me suddenly.

"…these beautiful, big horses; they're running all over the field with the gypsies watching over them…"

I couldn't remember much more, but it didn't matter. That was what I needed! A damn horse! I changed direction, jogging down the side street past the care homes and the new estates built after the college was torn down. Once

I turned right I could see the park, despite approaching it in utter darkness. The clouds that scudded low overhead were thick and black, the promise of rain clear enough in the air that I knew I needed to move quickly if I didn't want to be soaked. Right now, however, that was the least of my problems.

I could make out the boundaries of the park by the mass of black shadowy trees, but little else was visible in the gloom, and I stumbled on, keeping my right hand on the railing as I jogged along, hunting for the gates into the park. The area here was so dark, I had to resort to feeling the bars as I walked.

It took a while. I was gloomily convinced that I'd probably started about a foot from one of the entrances, judging by how long it was taking to find a way in, but eventually, I felt it. The tall, spike-topped fence gave way to an arched opening…one that was in turn filled with a ramshackle wooden barrier.

I halted, running my hands over the rough boards and squinting, trying to see, as I felt the first few light raindrops landing. I started to swear.

Someone had made a barrier across the entrance, a big one, which ran at least as high as I could reach and filled the entire space. I searched the opening back and forth, before growling to myself and setting off jogging again. I couldn't help wincing at each foot fall as my remaining wounds were jostled. I ran off and on for nearly ten minutes before I found the next entrance. I cursed softly at finding it similarly blocked off, but this time, at least I could see better, the trees being further back and not casting as deep a shadow.

I searched about, finally finding a handhold I knew I'd be able to use, and started to climb, disappearing upwards into the darkness. It took far longer than I'd expected, having to feel each time for a handhold as the heavens opened above me. A long, low rumble of thunder filled the night as I finally felt the top of the arch and clambered over it.

I dangled over the other side, still unable to see anything, before closing my eyes, dropping into the darkness, and landing hard. I fell to the side, hitting a square-shaped brace that my hands determined to be a park bench support.

I pulled myself up onto the bench and sat there, listening and hoping that nobody would come, while simultaneously hoping that someone would, and that they'd help me. Finally realizing that I would likely die of exposure if I stayed where I was, I clambered back to my feet and set off. Whoever had closed the park entrances had clearly wanted to keep everyone out, so I had to guess they'd have a way to make sure nobody did what I had just done…I walked on, arms outstretched and ears listening, my eyes little use to me under the trees.

I tripped over what seemed like everything in the park, only my memories keeping me even headed in the right direction for the field. Eventually, my ears perked up at the sound of laughter up ahead. I slowed, listening hard, before moving closer. I'd been hoping to do a deal with the gypsies for a horse, but now, I was starting to worry. The time I'd spent lumbering around in the trees could have gotten me at least a mile down the road, probably closer to two or three, and I had to bet the gypsies weren't going to want to part with a horse for anything I could afford.

I cautiously came out of the trees near the boating lake. The sound of heavy rain drumming on the water to my left encouraged me to turn to the right, squinting hard and stumbling along, trying to make sure I didn't fall in the lake. Despite the downpour I was trapped in, that was all I needed. I knew if the gypsies were here, they'd have to be close by, as the other fields were smaller and separated off by things like tennis courts and play areas. The main field would be the best one for their tents and caravans, and I thought that should be located to my right. I wandered forward blindly for a dozen or more steps, before feeling the edge of the lake suddenly come up and jumping back, only to knock over a stacked pile of beer bottles with a tinkling crash of glass breaking.

The cacophony of startled dogs frantically barking rose somewhere ahead, and I almost wept with relief, even as shouting rose to join the barking.

"Who's there!"

"What's that?"

"Shu'rrup, ye damn dogs!"

That last shout was followed by a yelp, and the barking from several dogs broke off, while one sounded like it'd been kicked. I growled to myself, my hopeful outlook on this little adventure suddenly dropping into my boots. I hated people who were cruel to animals. I couldn't care less about people, generally, although beating kids was a big no-no, but hurting your own damn dog?

"Speak up! Who's there!" a new voice called out, female and full of authority, and several lanterns were lit off to my right. The flare of a match moved from one to another, carefully shielded against the rain. Suddenly, more appeared, until at least a dozen were lit, and people started to move outward. *Looking for me,* I realized.

"Shit…" I muttered, shaking my head at my stupidity and sending droplets flying. "I'm here!" I called out, watching the majority of the lanterns snap around to my direction and start heading towards me, with a squelch of muddy, water-logged ground. The other lanterns seemed to be searching around, just in case. "Look, I'm alone…I just need some help?" I called out, and a handful of seconds later, a trio of lanterns were in close enough proximity to me that I had to lift my hand against the glare.

They'd put mirrors in the back of the small square boxes, with a handle affixed on the top. The result was a reasonably powerful, easily directed light. A collection of different-colored candles puddled in the middle of each box, giving the air a slightly odd mixture of scents.

"Who be you, laddie and why do you be here?" a man's gruff voice demanded. I rubbed water back from my face, looking in the direction of the voice.

"I'm Matt, I'm lost, it's pitch fucking black, and I really need some help. I'm trying to reach the gypsy camp…" I called out, before getting cut off by the same voice replying in a growl.

"Ye've found the camp o' the Traveling People. What de yer want with us?"

"Fuck," I murmured, realizing that I'd pissed them off already, yet having no idea why. "Look, I need to buy a horse. That's all!" I called back to the owner of the voice, only to be met with laughter…laughter that rose all around me as shuttered lanterns were opened to shine on me.

"Horses be worth more than sports cars these days, bonny lad. Ye carryin' a gold bar in that bag?" a female voice asked from my left, the rolling burr of Ireland clear in her voice.

"I wish," I said, shaking my head and looking in the direction of the lady's voice. "Look, seriously, I don't need it for long. I just have to get to the center of town, tonight, and then you can have the horse back…"

"Ye think ye be the first t' plan on helpin' yersel' to a horse of ours, laddie?" the female voice called out, and I spoke up quickly.

"I don't expect it for free. I can pay, or at least I can give a cheque? Hell, I don't even want to keep the horse, I just have to get to town tonight!" I said desperately.

"How'd he get in?" someone else called. "If there's a breach in the fence, we need to fix it immediately!"

"Shut it, Dara," the male voice near me snarled, stepping up close to me. "Well, laddie? Where'd yer get in?" he demanded.

"Ah, Christ, look at 'im!" the female voice interrupted again, stepping forward into the light of the lanterns and pointing hers at my face, then moving the light over my body. As much as I'd managed to heal since the fight, I was still clearly injured, and the torn mess of my clothes, mixed with the blood-soaked bandages, showed clearly that I was hardly a threat to a big group. "Ma! We've got a wounded one here…" A handful of seconds hung in the air before another female voice rang out in response.

"Bring 'im in, Hannah…and someone get the King," the voice replied, scratchy and filled with irritation.

I was grabbed by the scruff of the neck by one of the men, who tried to drag me forward. Finding me heavier than he expected, he grunted and tugged again as I slapped his hand away, glaring at him.

Two more grabbed onto me, and the barrel of a handgun was suddenly pressed to the underside of my chin, making me freeze in place.

"Ah'll tell ye now, laddie, dinna mistake the lady's kindness fer weakness, all right? You'll no be the first ah've killed..."

"And neither will you," I snapped back at him before I could think better of it.

"That so, is it?" he asked softly, moving in close and staring searchingly into my eyes. "Aye, maybe it be true, at that..." he muttered eventually, then turned his head to call out into the darkness. "Brian, Hannah, keep yer guns on 'im. Got the look of a tiger, and he's killed before, he says...Ah believe 'im."

Behind the lights, the clicks of safeties being taken off was the only response, and I grimaced, thinking about how it was really time I learned to keep my fucking mouth shut.

"Come on, then, let's go see the King." The man nodded to the side, his gun trained on me, and I felt a sudden lightness on my hip. I reached down, finding the knife I'd had folded up and sticking out of my right pocket was gone, and I swore again, splashing through the puddles after the girl who was leading the way.

"We take 'im to Ma. She'll have t' King woken and brought t' her. This one won't last long if he does no get some help," the female voice—Hannah, I guessed—said decisively, prompting a growl from the first man.

A dozen steps more, and I was ducking under a dark canopy, then being led through a maze of interlocking cloth barriers, until I emerged into the middle of a clearing, one that was suddenly well lit by a campfire. I turned around in confusion, not understanding how they'd hidden this.

"Oilskin cloths on the outside," one of the men said, grinning when he saw the confusion on my face. "Reflects the light and heat back inwards; makes the camp warmer, and keeps prying eyes out."

"More overhead, and you'd be surprised by how much cloth it takes to make a big top tent," the girl said, stepping in close and examining me, before nodding and leading me off to one side. "We put up the Big Top, pushed the vans around it, and covered them in oilcloths. Ain't nobody findin' the People when we dinna want te be found."

"It's impressive..." I admitted, following her to a section of the big tent which appeared to be an aid station. As I looked around curiously, I observed that the interior had been portioned off into smaller private areas, with a communal area for food prep, storage, even what looked to be a section for the animals off to one side.

I couldn't help but smile at the dignified nonchalance of a large black cat that strolled through the middle of the tent, rubbing up against legs and being cursed as he tripped people who weren't expecting him.

"Over here, bonnie lad," the girl said, and I hurried to catch up, then slowing as a tall, raw-boned woman stepped out of a section that had been out of sight and gestured to me to follow her. We moved into a cordoned-off space, and I found her sitting down on the far side of a small brazier, staring at me.

"Let's be seeing to the wounds first, laddie," she said, and I shrugged.

"I'll be all right, don't worry, It's a horse…" I started to say, only to feel the cold press of the handgun at the back of my head again. "…or I could shut up and let you have a look?" I amended quickly. She smiled coldly at me, shaking her head once in annoyance.

I quickly stripped off my soaked top; then, at a nod from her, I sighed and removed my trousers as well, with the younger woman undoing my bandages. I reached for them once and got the handgun jammed into my ear in warning.

"Listen, I've had a really bad couple of days…" I growled at the guy behind me with the gun. "So how about you quit that shit right now?"

"Or ah could just shoot yer now, make sure yer not a threat, aye?" he sneered. The tall woman snorted at him.

"Or yer could all stop yer shit. Keith, drop the attitude, and you…" she said her eyes pinning me to the spot. "Quit rubbin' him the wrong way…"

"I'm sure as shit not rubbing him the *right* way…" I muttered, catching a snort from behind me as the gun was taken away.

"Right, then. I'm Queen Esme. I do all the doctorin' for the People. Who be you, and why are ye so covered in wounds?"

"I'm Matt…" I said after a pause, in which I considered lying, and figured I didn't need to; I just wouldn't tell the whole truth. "I got jumped by a gang of thugs along the road to the industrial estate in the valley. They tried to kill me. It ended badly for them," I said simply.

"An' nearly for you too, laddie," Esme countered, slowly circling me as she inspected my injuries. "I'm seein' the wounds, and the healin'…so how about you cut the crap, and we make a deal? One time offer only?"

"Go on?" I said, watching her warily as she circled me. Keith and the girl who I assumed was Hannah leaned against posts on either side of me, watching the exchange.

"Yer seen anythin'…unusual…of late?" she asked slowly, watching my eyes as she came to a stop. I flinched, and she nodded. "That. That's what I thought, laddie. Tell me what yer saw, tell me what yer know, an' why, an' maybe the People can make a deal with ya."

"I…" I stopped. I couldn't tell them about the Dungeon Core. First, I'd sound mad. Second, if they did believe me, it wasn't something I could prove without ejecting it. That could destroy the area unless, I planted it, and this place was shit for it. If they did believe me, I didn't see a way out without a fight for control of the Dungeon either. I sure as hell wasn't going to tell them about the ship…but maybe…"Look, I don't know what's going on, but I'll do a deal. One of you lend me a horse, or even just ride along with me on the back; drop me off in the city, and fast, and you take the horse back. Do that, and I'll tell you what I suspect, and what I've seen…Deal?"

"Depends on the tale, laddie…" Esme said, sitting back down on an old rocking chair and watching me. "Hannah, go hurry up yer Da. Somethin' tells me he'll want to hear this, an' only the King can make a deal this strange…"

"But Ma…" the girl, Hannah, started to complain.

"But nothin', lassie! Get yer Da. Mr. Muscles will still be here fer yer to leer over when yer get back, iffin' yer be quick." She waved Hannah away, never taking her eyes off me.

"Fine!" She snorted, turning and heading off. Our little section of the tent was silent for a long moment before I finally asked the question.

"So, are you going to help me with my wounds, then?" I said, looking at Esme.

"Do we need to?" she asked, and I froze, getting a cackle from her as she scored another point. "Yer need to learn to lie a bit better, laddie. That 'rabbit in the headlights' look is gonna get yer killed…"

"Well, shit." I glanced around the room. Another chair sat off to my left and I made my way over to it, ignoring Keith as he reached for his gun again. Whatever these people had going on, I was becoming more and more certain they weren't going to kill me yet, not unless I made them do it. And yet, something felt very…wrong here. I dragged the chair back to where I'd been standing and put it down.

"How about some dry clothes and a hot drink?" I asked, getting a snort from Esme.

"How about the truth first, an' then we'll see? I ain't wastin' gear on someone we're gonna be buryin'."

"Well, I…" I started to say, trying to figure out what I could, and what I *should*, say. Something felt really off, and not least the fact that they had guns, let alone in open sight. Guns were common when I'd visited family in America, but here in the UK? It was only a few years ago that the Armed Police stopped getting huge complaints when they were seen out and about with weapons. The fact that they had them here, and…

"Who's this, then?" a voice interrupted from behind and I spun around to see a new man enter the room. He was short, middle aged, and had a wide, friendly smile on his lips, clapping Keith on the shoulder as he passed him, before sitting down next to 'Queen' Esme and folding his hands over his belly. "Seems you've got a tale to tell me, my lad. Better be a good one, or I'll not be pleased at bein' roused outta bed…" I noted the way he squinted at me, then glanced at Esme before forcing another smile.

"Little early for bed, isn't it?" I asked carefully, and he glared at me. "Uh, okay, moving on…I got jumped in the estate next to Team Valley…and…"

"Let's start at the beginning, laddie," Esme said flatly. "I'll be bettin' you've no always healed this fast?" I glanced down at the exposed wounds, and one picked that exact time to slowly push out a shotgun pellet. It fell to the floor, and Hannah swooped in, picking it up and examining it.

"Shotgun…looks like birdshot, Ma." She tossed the shard underhand to Esme. The tall woman examined it and passed it to the King, who glared sourly at not receiving it first.

"Look, it's not like I know a lot, okay? I was on my way home a few nights back, drunk outta my skull and soaked to the bone when the sky went mad; lines and fire, all over it. The clouds were heavy, it was pissing down, but I could make the lines out even through them, so fuck knows what it looked like elsewhere…." A short, middle aged man strolled in, looked me over, and went to stand next to Esme, his hand resting on her shoulder as I talked, with Hannah following him and stopping on the opposite side of Esme to listen. "I'd lost my keys, so I ended up wandering around a bit out in the night, waited the rain out near a baker's shop. Once the fire in the sky died down, I got someone that was opening up his shop to get me back inside my house. I crashed out for a bit, came to, and there was no power. Assumed it was a power cut, but clearly, it's still going. I tried to go to work; I work in the 'Valley'…and I got attacked on the way, mugged. Long story short, now I'm here, heading back to the city. Weird thing is, I'm healing fast…like insanely fast," I finished.

"I bet yer could tell the history o' the earth in less time than it takes to boil an egg, laddie," Esme muttered, shaking her head. "What yer said might even be truth, as near as ah can tell, but there's a lot yer not sayin'."

"What about you?" I asked shortly. "I don't know any of you; you expect me to tell you my life story?"

"I offered a deal, laddie, an' you've no broken it…yet. But I've no heard anythin' that makes me want to help yer neither."

"Well, you've told me fuck-all yourselves!" I growled, drawing a laugh from the seated man.

"True. Matt, is it?" he asked, and I nodded, still bristling. "Well, Matt, you see, we've been attacked three times, and that's just today, by people tryin' to steal our horses or our gear. We've had lit torches thrown at us, and turned away beggars by the dozen. Almost a hundred new families have joined us, claimin' some old Traveler blood, so it's a time of change, all right. Now you've come here, demandin' a horse, one of the most valuable things we own, and you're tellin' us nothing. A few details isn't that much to ask, now is it?" He smiled genially and spread his hands wide. His voice was smooth, relaxed, and his accent gentle, the Irish burr almost hidden, but his eyes…I instinctively didn't trust this man in the slightest. His smile never reached those predatory orbs.

"Look, I don't know what happened. Do you think I'd be here if I did? I'd have fucking armed guards and be working for the government…" he snorted at my proclamation and shook his head.

"Nobody that knows anything would be working for the government, Matt. Those that know what they're doing make the government work for them…"

"Yeah, well, I don't know about that," I muttered. "I just need to get back to the city."

"Tonight?" he asked, grinning deeper at my affirming nod. "Why not stay a while? We've got food, and I know that's in short supply these days; only goin' to get worse…and you're injured…"

"No." I said shortly. "I have to get to the city, now, tonight!"

"And why is that, hmmm?" The predatory gleam in his eye sharpened.

"I…I just do…" I started to say, and he cut me off.

"I don't think so, Matt. There be somethin' you're no saying. Clearly, you've lost a lot of blood, but you heal fast, faster that any I've seen, and you know somethin', somethin' your eyes say is important…"

"Fine. If you're not willing to help me, I'll just get dressed and go…"

"I think not," he said coldly. "You've as good as admitted you know somethin', and what kind of a host would I be if I let a guest go out in the middle of the night? No, you'll stay with us tonight, an' we'll talk in the mornin'. Maybe then we'll send you on your way with a little help… maybe not. And just to make sure you tell us the truth, you'll be stayin' the night with a few other 'guests'."

I looked to the others in the room, reading disappointment from most, and maybe disgust on Hannah's and Esme's faces, but Keith just grinned at me, stroking the butt of his gun.

"You can get dressed now, boy. You'll be staying in the special quarters at the back," the King said, walking out of the small, enclosed area. For the first time, I noticed the man who left with him. He was short, blond, and rough-looking, but it was the gear he wore that got my attention. It a was filthy but clearly new set of police-issue body armor, spotted with dark patches, which I guessed with a sinking heart were blood, and he was carrying a semi-automatic rifle. As soon as he stepped out of sight, another man stepped in, a club in his hand, and he glared at me, softly patting the end into his other hand.

"So that's it? I come to the Traveling People asking for help, and I'm a prisoner?" I spat at Esme, and she shrugged, looking slightly ashamed but firmly following the 'King's' orders.

"A prisoner? No; a wee 'honored guest,' that be all. An' yer about to meet the animals! Time was, people paid a lot o' money t' meet them as close as you'll be…Besides…times be hard, laddie. Maybe this'll help ye to remember that nowt be free. You think on tellin' us what ye know, and a word to the wise, lyin' be a big mistake…"

"Now, Ma, he just be tired, stressed, an' hungry. Maybe we could help him a little? Give him a drink and some food?" Hannah asked, glaring when Keith blinked at her in shock, then shook his head.

"It's a new day, Hannah; don't you be forgettin' it," Keith said, his lip curling in a sneer as he faced her. She scoffed, storming off in disgust. Esme glared warningly at him, sitting down heavily and staring off after her daughter, clearly thinking. Keith drew his gun again and told me to get dressed. I pulled my sopping wet clothes back on, shivering at the frigid touch, before being led by the other man from the little private area.

They guided me, none too gently, to the back of the area, past a dozen or more families, and then out into the night. Once we stepped out into the rain, I froze for a second, hoping that they weren't just going to shoot me. Grunting their annoyance, they shoved me forward, then turned and walked along the outer edge, ducking back inside another, smaller tented area.

This one was totally different. Where the main tent had been warm, full of light and laughter, even a little low music from a few people in the center, this tent was lit only by a single lantern, and had been filled with large cages set around the perimeter. The first one held a bear, the second and third contained a lion and pair of Hyenas, respectively, all of which were fast asleep. The others, I didn't get the chance to focus on before Keith shoved me again.

I loved animals normally, and I'd usually have been over the moon to see them up close, despite the cages, but it was the other occupants of the cages that made me swallow hard. A divide had been placed within each cage, a loose one that would be easily withdrawn, I guessed…and in the other half of each cage was a collection of men. Three in with the hyenas, two each in with the lion and the bear, and as I was roughly shoved to the back, I saw what I'd missed when I entered. The fourth cage, one without a barrier, was getting one slotted into place, and the occupant of it, a large white Tiger, didn't seem happy about it.

"Guess who?" Keith called out to the big cat, ignoring the other two men who were guiding the divider between the bars. As soon as it saw Keith, the Tiger's ears flattened and it hissed at him in fury. He spat at the tiger, gesturing to the small space in the cage that had been cordoned off. "There's your bed for the night, 'Matt'. Bet you can't wait."

"In there?" I squeaked in a seriously unmanly way. I swallowed and tried again. "Okay, you've had your fucking joke. Now seriously, I'm leaving..." I started to say, when the lights went out as Keith slammed his gun into my temple, sending me to the floor.

NINE

I WOKE SLOWLY, ANOTHER flashing notification pulsing away in the corner of my vision, making me shake my head as a migraine banged away in rhythm with it. I shook my head again, stopping when the pain made me want to throw up, and I shifted, trying to get more comfortable, only to hear a screech of claws against metal that made my eyes fly open in shock.

I had been laid against the bars of a cage. The floor was wood, the bars metal, and they extended up and over to interlock, curving down to attach to the wagon bed on the far side. The room outside was dark and silent, but the cage itself was partitioned off by a plate of metal, with something on the other side that was growling in fury.

The events of the night came rushing back, and I swallowed hard, pushing myself back as far from the divider as possible. The flimsy metal trembled as something slammed against it. I kept telling myself it wasn't really the tiger; people didn't do this kind of shit, not really…but peering around in the gloom confirmed that others had been placed in other cages. I heard their soft sobs, saw the defeated, panicked looks on their faces, and I felt an urgent need to use the toilet rising, my cold confidence in the fight against the gang nowhere in sight.

I moved as quietly as I could up against the door of the cage, reaching out and trying to feel for the latch. It didn't take long to find, but neither did the huge steel padlock that kept it closed unfortunately. Dejected, I sagged down before trying to open it anyway. A small, desperate part of my mind told me that maybe it wasn't locked, not really. People didn't do this; it was just a cruel joke…

I tugged on the lock frantically, making it clang and clang as the bolt shifted in its housing. The tiger behind me growled and snarled, banging on the divider. I looked back, shaking in terror, and realized the divider was bending in the middle as the tiger desperately tried to reach me. The ends of the crude metal partition were slowly pulling closer to slipping inside the cage. When that happened, I knew instinctively that it was all over.

"Stop, you idiot!" someone hissed from one of the other cages, but I was past reason, shoving desperately against the lock, and I started to shout, rousing the other animals to roar and scream as well.

"Help! Someone help!" I screamed, shaking the bars. After a few minutes, Keith strolled in with the 'King' at his side. They stood there, watching me and smiling as I panicked. "Fucking hell, man, come on! I'll tell you everything!" I called to them, desperation filling me. I'd won the fights against those scumbag thugs because they were thugs, but this was a fucking tiger, a creature that evolved to kill, and I was in a tiny, enclosed space with it, unarmed and terrified.

"And just what do you think I need to hear?" the King asked calmly as he lit the end of a cigar, puffing it to life.

"There's a Dungeon! I've got the Core!" I shouted, and he tilted his head to one side in question.

"A what?" he said slowly.

"A Dungeon! Look, I don't know why. It was in a ship, a fucking spaceship…" I shouted, seeing them exchange a long look. "It's controlled by the Core, but I need to get it to the city so it can feed off the mana. If I don't, it'll explode!"

"Sounds like somethin' I'd be interested in seein'…" The King shrugged. "Thing is, though, we've already gone through the bag you have. Ain't nothin' interestin' in there…"

"It's in me!" I interrupted, my words falling over themselves in my desperation to get them out. "I've got the core in me!"

"Really…what, stuck up your arse?" Keith asked, snorting in laughter.

"No, you fucking idiot!" I snarled at him. "It's inside of me! I can't eject it without a place to put it, or it'll fucking explode!" I pressed myself against the bars as hard as I could, desperately trying to get through them as I fixed the King with one eye. "If I eject it, it'll explode, but the longer it's in me, the better chance it'll explode anyway! I need to get downtown to get it out safely!"

"Really…well, maybe tomorrow, we can talk about it, when you've calmed down." The King eyed me dismissively, starting to turn away.

"I won't be here tomorrow, you fucking asshole!" I screamed. "And neither will you!"

Current Level of Core Assimilation: 34%

Estimated time for increase of Assimilation level is 1% per hour in current low Mana Density. Move to an area of higher Mana Density to decrease this time.

Estimated area consumed by Dungeon Core Detonation: 1.672sq miles.

"Sixty-eight percent!" I shouted as he looked back at me. "I've got a sixty-eight percent chance of dying in the next hour, and the fucking detonation will cover...one point six-seven-two square miles!"

"That's very specific." He scowled suspiciously, moving in closer to me. He reached up and tapped the bars of the cage, eliciting a snarl from the tiger, who clearly hated him. "Listen, Matt, I don't care what kind of shitty issues you've got goin' on in that tiny brain, but yer goin' to tell me what I need to know, because yer not comin' out of there until you do!"

With a cruel smile, he took a deep drag on his cigar, blew it out into the tiger's face, and walked away. I yanked on the bars and shouted for him to let me out, and that I needed help. The tiger next to me went crazy, spitting, hissing, and smashing into the barrier between us, and the world broke down into an insane mess of howling, growls, and screams.

It felt like forever, the time passing in a cacophony of noise and fear, but eventually, I felt hands wrapping around my own where they clutched onto the bars frantically. I looked up slowly, my eyes taking a long while to focus, until I saw her face. It seemed like hours before I remembered who she was. Hannah.

In all that had happened so far, I hadn't paid attention to her looks before now. She was short, red haired, and round faced, with enough curves that she'd get a second look in almost any company, and those deep green eyes were full of smiles. I gazed desperately into them, and she kept talking softly to me, making me realize she'd been speaking for a while.

"...it's all right. Shhhh, just calm down, bonnie laddie..." she whispered, and I nodded, stifling my panicked cries. "...That's it, just breathe with me, slow. In and out; come on, let's get that heart rate doon..." I swallowed, my throat feeling like it was full of razorblades, and coughed, an involuntary sob escaping me as I tried to understand what had happened. I glanced fearfully to the side, my panic spiking at the sight of the bent metal divide and the bloody furrows carved into the floor where it had twisted, rising up far enough that the tiger's claws could get underneath by a few inches.

I gaped back at her, my eyes going wider, and she shook her head.

"It's all right, Matt, do no worry. Simo is calm, me Ma made him a wee snack. He's eatin' it now, with a few extra 'herbs' on it, so he's not gonna give a shit about anythin', so long as you do no rile 'im up, okay?" She rubbed my hands soothingly. I nodded slowly, not trusting my voice, and tried to shift my hands, wincing as pain lanced through them. I'd been holding the bars so tightly and for so long, my fingers had cramped, and then I'd kept at it. Now they were like claws as I pulled them free.

Hannah reached in through the bars, and I flinched back. She backed up, nodding in understanding, and spread her hands wide to show me she wasn't going to try anything as she continued speaking in a low, calm voice.

"Me Ma talked the King into lettin' me calm yer down, as people were startin' to get scared." She shook her head. "People still be gettin' used to the ways o' the People, and they do no need to hear ye screamin' fer help. He's told them all yer a dangerous criminal; said yer attacked a wee lassie an' tried to rape her, so most o' them don't mind yer being kept in a cage, even if they dinna know you're sharin' it…" She explained, shrugging. "Thing is, Matt, in a camp o' the Traveling Folk, there be an unofficial leader, the one everyone listens to, but he's got little more power than that. Then there be the King. The King o' the Roma be our true King, an' we all swear t' obey 'im. He makes the laws, and his people enforce 'em, but with the world all gone to shit, me Da decided we needed a new King, especially as so many want te join us now. So…he and me Ma are the new King and Queen o' the Roma, fer us at least. That means he needs t' be seen as a father figure, nice and kindly, while his men, like Keith, they do the enforcin'. Ye understand? He's got a lot o' stress, and he's just tryin' te find his way. Now, I was outside the tent, so I heard what yer said to me Da, but I need to hear it true for meself. What's going on? What's this about a ship? An' a Dungeon? Come on, lad; tell me an' let me help ye."

"It's a Dungeon." I whispered, sagging against the bars, too wiped out to try to hide anything anymore. "I found a ship crashed in the forest, some kind of alien thing, I guess; found the Dungeon Core, and it went…. into…me somehow. Now I'm its Host. It said it needs a mana-rich area, or it'll fail or die or whatever, and if I 'eject' the Core, I have to plant it, or it'll explode. Until it gets planted, though, it's still collecting mana, and every time it ticks up a point closer to being full, there's a significantly higher chance that it'll explode inside me."

"What's the chance now?" she asked casually, and I looked up at her sharply, catching a sudden caring smile. I shrugged, even as a warning feeling pulsed through me, making me pay more attention.

Current Level of Core Assimilation: 35%
Estimated time for increase of Assimilation level is 1% per hour in current low Mana Density. Move to an area of higher Mana Density to decrease this time.
Estimated area consumed by Dungeon Core Detonation: 1.672sq miles.

"Seventy percent," I said, and she nodded slowly, clearly unsure if she should believe me or not.

"So, if it's real, this Dungeon thing, what could it do?" She leaned in, gripping my hands tighter. I paused, wondering at the new look in her eyes.

She'd gone from friendly, concerned, and caring to…hungry? I coughed, rubbing my head as I tried to think, and her demeanor shifted, smiling again and rubbing my hands with her thumbs as I tried to decide if I'd seen what I thought I had.

"I don't know. It makes things, I guess, loot and monsters, buildings…I don't know." I said eventually, exhaustion filling me. "I literally just know that it's dangerous if I don't get it out and set it up, and that it's valuable, but beyond that…" I slumped, my knowledge and my energy spent. She nodded slowly, releasing my hands as she looked off into the distance.

"A Dungeon, ye say, one tha' might be able to make things. Could it make food? Medicine?" she prodded, and I shrugged.

"I guess so. If it's anything like I'm imagining, it could make anything. It's already helped me to heal…Look, Hannah, I just don't know, okay? Can you get me out now, please? I told you everything…" I whispered, swallowing hard.

"Soon…do no worry, Matt. This will be all over soon." She promised softly, and this time, I saw a clear look of greed flash across her face for a second before she smoothed it away again. I paused in thought, then spoke up quickly.

"Oh…it's classified me as the 'Host' so I'll have control over it. I think it dies if I do, even once it's deployed," I added quickly, just in case, drawing a smile from her.

"Oh, don't worry! I'll make sure you're okay," she reassured me, smiling as she moved in close again. When she reached out and offered her hands, I took them, hesitating and wondering if what I'd seen was all in my head. "I'm goin' to go talk to me Ma now, see if I can get her to help me, and we'll see what we can do. You just stay here, calm an' quiet-like, okay?" I clutched desperately at her hands before she pulled them away. "It's all right. Do no rile Simo up, and yer will be fine, okay?" She flashed a smile, then rushed away.

I looked back at the metal barrier, my scalp prickling at the way it'd bent and the marks carved in it, and tried not to give in to the panic I felt building. I sat as far from the bent divide, and by extension, the tiger, as I could manage, huddled up to the bars as I tried to get my brain working again.

Hours seemingly passed, but I couldn't say how many, or even if it truly was hours, rather than minutes…but Hannah was finally back, slipping into the room and hurrying across to me. Crouching, she pulled keys out from her pocket, pressing a finger to my lips as I started to speak.

"Listen, I got a friend to help. He's keepin' watch out the front, so let's go. I've got a horse out the back. I'll take yer back to the town, and yer can show me this Dungeon, right?" she said, smiling at me. "Maybe I can stay wit' yer for a bit, make sure yer okay? Just tell me where the Dungeon is, just in case we get separated…" She kept her voice low and her eyes friendly, though that hungry edge was starting to return to both.

"It's part of me, so it isn't set up yet…" I muttered, then reading the darkening look in her eyes, I went on hurriedly. "I'll let you know where to go as I know; it'll tell me." She glared at me for a second, before smoothing her face back to her usual friendliness.

"Okay, you direct, an' I'll get us there. But yer got to be quiet, right?" she said, and I nodded my agreement as she unlocked the small door and helped me to crawl out of it. I almost fell to the floor as she let me out, backing away warily as she closed the cage quietly, locking it up and ignoring the other whispered pleas for help. I suddenly noticed that the door in the tiger's cage was far too small to be for the tiger, and I frowned, trying to figure out why it'd have a small hatch as well as an entrance, but I gave up, feeling too tired, stressed, and ragged to care, even as I tried to ignore the others the way she did.

"Here…" she murmured, passing me a handful of things; my wallet and keys, I realized, pocketing them. "I couldn't get the rest, but I figured you'd at least need these? Come on, this way…" She grabbed my hand and led me to the back of the tent, lifting a flap slightly to uncover a peg that had been tugged free of the ground. We crawled out, and I caught the disgusted look she gave me as I passed her, my pants displaying clear evidence that I no longer needed to use the toilet. I almost said something, something pointed about being locked in a fucking cage with a goddamn tiger that was trying to kill me, but in the end, I bit my tongue. I needed her help, and I saw the way she tried to hide her revulsion behind a kind smile.

She guided me through the darkness, running across the field to a line of horses that were tied up nearby. Gesturing silently, she took me to a single horse on the end of the row. The animal had its bridle on, with a blanket draped across its back, presumably because a saddle for two wasn't invented, or comfortable, or whatever. Either way, she mounted the horse and swore at me when I suggested taking a second horse for myself.

"No!" she snapped. "There's no time. They'll find yer gone soon! Yer don't want to go back inside, do ye? In the cage with the tiger?" she hissed threateningly, glaring at me in the darkness.

"Okay, no, I'm sorry…" I said quickly, fear making my voice crack. Taking her offered hand, I almost managed to accidentally pull her off the horse as I clambered up. It was uncomfortable; my only experience of horse riding had been limited to a holiday with an ex, which had left me crippled for days. I held tight onto Hannah as she slowly directed the horse across the field in the darkness toward a hanging lantern. Two men were stationed by a gate that was open, and she kicked the horse hard, sending us through the gap before they could do more than shout half-heartedly after us. I looked back as we galloped into the night to see them simply watching us, and my bad feeling grew worse.

"Where we headed?" she asked me again, and I brought up my map in my vision, telling her to take a right at the end of the path we were on. The loud clatter of hooves and her seeming unconcern, made me more and more sure of what was happening.

I directed her as we went, clattering along the dark streets and across the highways. It didn't escape my attention that she shut down any conversations that didn't revolve around the Dungeon as 'too risky to talk right now.' When we finally made it across the High Level Bridge into Newcastle itself, my anxiety started to spike further.

The occasional thugs and idiots that were drawn out into the night by the sound of the horse's hooves always fell away behind us as Hannah dug her heels in. I hung on for dear life, the intensifying mana concentration making me feel sicker by the minute.

We passed the old castle, and I had a momentary thought about using that instead of 'House of Smith', fantasizing about having a castle, until I saw the flickering candles glowing through a curtain high up. Someone had already moved in, it seemed, so I shrugged and checked the latest flickering notification.

Current Level of Core Assimilation: 41%

Estimated time for increase of Assimilation level is 5% per hour in current higher Mana Density. Move to an area of higher Mana Density to decrease this time.

Estimated area consumed by Dungeon Core Detonation: 4.324sq miles.

"Oh, shit!" I gasped, and Hannah froze against me.

"What?!" she asked sharply, pulling the reins and bringing the horse's canter down to a slow walk. I started to speak, then picked up the sound of dozens of horses behind us somewhere and stared at her wordlessly. She forced a look of shock, then spoke up. "Oh no! They must have followed us!"

I recognized the look in her eyes, the contempt she was badly hiding behind the mask of beauty, and I forced myself to stay calm, acting like I believed her, while I wondered how stupid I had been to fall for her false kindness for even a second.

"Yeah, we need to split up," I said abruptly.

"What? No!" she snapped. "I mean…you'd get lost without me…" She grabbed onto my hand as I started to take it from her waist.

"No, you don't understand! I just got a warning…I'm not going to last!" I cried, tearing my hand free and tumbling off the back of the horse, somehow barely managing to keep from slamming into the pavement. "The Dungeon is the Castle, you see? Up there?" I asked, pointing upward at the light that flickered gently. She glanced up, then back to me. "That's my partner. Look, draw them away, then circle around. If there's no explosion, then come back, meet me there, and I'll show you the Dungeon, okay? You trust me after all, don't you?" I snarled, at her, my anger at being conned leaching through into my voice at the end.

I darted forward and slapped the horse on the arse as I'd seen on TV, startling it and making it bolt while I turned and ran for the castle. She struggled to get control of the horse again. Once she'd calmed it, wrenching its head around hard enough that I thought she was trying to break its neck, she raced back to where she'd last seen me, swearing sulfurously.

I'd darted across the street when she'd been preoccupied with the panicking horse, ducking down the alley between two bars and trying to ignore the things I might be stepping in as I tried to get out of sight. The thunder of dozens of horses drew close as Hannah shouted out into the night. She'd evidently raced across to the castle and noticed what I'd seen earlier in passing: the gates were closed and locked solidly.

"I know you're here, Matt!" she called, all trace of false friendship suddenly gone as the other horses drew in around her. "We'll find you, and whatever you're hidin'!" The voice of the King rang out, calling instructions to the other riders.

"Find him, find out what he's hidin', and do it quick!" he snarled. Panting heavily, I frantically raced along the alleyway. By the sounds of their hooves, the horses were starting to spread out and lanterns were being opened to lend higher visibility to their hunt.

I ran, the alleyway unfortunately leading me away from my intended destination, but as I took a right, sprinting and grunting in pain and fear, across the road I wanted to be on, I caught glimpses of the lanterns swinging from riders' hands as they started to search the streets.

"Move out, get a perimeter, then close in toward the center. Don't let him outrun ye!" I heard Hannah shout, and I cursed myself for thinking she was pretty.

My heart hammering, I sprinted up to the next street, taking another right into an alleyway and crashing into the tightly locked gates with a groan. I'd forgotten about the fucking gates!

I looked up, squinting into the gloom. I was sure that someone would have heard that noise, and nearly gasped with relief when I spotted a section where a bit of the ornamental scrollwork had come away. It was narrow, and jagged, but it was my only way into the back alley, and I took it, clambering up desperately.

Hoofbeats clattered along the streets, moving closer, and I pressed myself into the brick façade tightly, barely fitting behind the outcropping as a light shone down in my direction, freezing me against the wall. I waited breathlessly, listening to the horse snort as the rider did something, but then, blessedly, they moved on, and I grabbed the loose section. Flaking rust came away under my grip as I pulled as hard as I could. The sharp, degraded rusty metal edges cut into my skin, but I barely felt the pain in comparison to the wave of relief when it moved. First one, then another rivet popped free, before it began to peel back easier. I stopped, leaving a space that was tight—damn, it was tight—but I needed to be able to close it after me. I pulled myself up, shoving and wriggling my body into the gap and through, leaving skin and blood behind, but the hardest part, once my upper chest was through, was having to yank my body after it, clinging to the bars and knowing what was coming.

As I dragged my legs through, with nothing to hold onto above that section of gate, I fell headfirst onto the cobbled street.

I grunted, slamming into the stones and rolling as best I could. I winced at feeling the fresh injuries, my nose breaking again, another tooth possibly… no, definitely being lost. A noise from the street sent me frantically crawling to the side of the bins I could smell in the darkness. I dragged myself into the piled up, reeking bags, and curled up as best I could, thankful that the bins were overflowing, while also being disgusted by the squish and stench.

I laid there, shivering in the weird warmth of rotting garbage, choosing to be thankful that it hadn't been the glass bins, when a light shone down into the alley. I stayed as still as possible, while the beam angled around, before letting out a little sigh as it finally moved on. The sound of hooves traveling down the street in the opposite direction made me sag in relief.

I stayed put for a slow count of thirty, just in case they were fucking with me. Confident that no sound or light had returned, I crawled out and headed deeper down the alley. One hand on the wall guided me along, my fingers feeling in the pitch darkness for the familiar outline of a carving on the wall.

I almost missed it, but years of sitting next to it made me almost laugh out loud with relief as I felt it. I traced it to be sure, suddenly more grateful than ever that I'd frequented the multiple bars that opened out into the shared alley so often. I moved the three feet along the wall until I found the edge of Florita's emergency exit. I carefully felt around the top of the doorframe, knowing what I was looking for after a friend who worked there had taught me about it. My fingers rummaged around the outwards projected lip of the door…There! A little bolt that was stuck upwards!

"Thank you, cheap-ass bar managers!" I muttered gratefully, pressing down on the bolt. It resisted for a second before clunking down and releasing the latch. I had no idea why it worked, and I didn't care either. It had something to do with the remote locks, Ben had said. I didn't give a shit. I just slipped inside the bar, closing the door softly behind me, and breathed a sigh of relief.

I moved across to the bar top, knowing even in the pitch black that it would be to my right. My hands found the long dust sheets that hung down to protect the stock. I moved around the edge of the bar, slipping behind it. My hands reached cautiously along the counter as I stared blindly, searching under the bar for the manager's stash.

It took a full minute, and I was starting to worry that they'd removed it while the refurb was taking place, but eventually, I found it: a little lacquered box at the back behind a pile of paperwork. Pulling it out, I popped the lid, feeling the familiar cigars and…an old Zippo lighter.

The damn thing was older than I was, probably by a factor of three, but it worked when I sparked it to life carefully. I knew the front of the building was well secured against thieves, so I wasn't too concerned about anyone busting in by surprise, and I set off through the adjoining room, making my way into Madame Koo's.

It had been bought out a few months back and annexed to be part of the new 'House of Smith,' as three bars rolled into one: Madame Koo, Florita's, and the original House of Smith. After talking to Ben, I'd learned the new design had a lot of additional space in the basement, space that would be fantastic for my specific needs.

I hurried downstairs, almost falling in my rush, and opened the heavy double doors into the stripped-out nightclub.

I lifted the Zippo overhead, ignoring how hot it was getting, and grinned. It was perfect! The mirrored wall reflected enough light that I knew where I was, even as I headed across in the floor to the manager's office at the back. I felt a twinge of disappointment at finding the room had been stripped of everything, bar an old, well-worn chair, a bottle of whisky, and some paperwork on a desk, with a half empty steel wastepaper bin. I lit the paper in the bin, closed the lighter, and dragged the blazing bin and the chair out into the center of the room. Finally safe for a moment, with a source of light, I sat down with a groan.

Sighing, I pulled up the prompt and took a last look at it.

Current Level of Core Assimilation: 43%

Estimated time for increase of Assimilation level is 6% per hour in current Mana Density. Move to an area of higher Mana Density to decrease this time.

Estimated area consumed by Dungeon Core Detonation: 5.189sq miles.

Do you wish to Eject the Dungeon Core?

Yes/No

"Yes," I said simply, and the world dissolved before me.

TEN

I BLINKED, NO LONGER in darkness as the world transformed. Wireframe drawings of this building, and those that surrounded me, flared to life. Red outlines of people and horses were frozen in the act of exploring the street above me, and smaller shapes glowed below and around the room I was hovering in.

I could see sewers, pipes; hell, I even saw the tip of a large cave system deep, deep underground beneath my location, a hundred meters or more down. I saw everything, the entire building and all of those in the local area, and I zoomed through them mentally as a single glowing star of Energy pulsed and flickered before me.

I darted back to where my body remained physically, to find a green figure collapsed in the chair, arms thrown back as though in pain.

"Well, fuck, this doesn't look good," I commented to myself. A flicker caught my attention, and I turned my vision sideways without moving. I couldn't describe it better than that, even to myself. I just seemed to slide the world along, while my sight remained in exactly the same place. Suddenly, a new screen waited for me, one that was steadily counting down. As it fell, a figure alongside it grew less and less defined.

That figure was me, I realized, and I froze, then frantically inspected the screen. It was the same map I'd seen before, just localized in the room I was in, and I suddenly understood. Whatever I'd done in ejecting the core, the process had slowed time locally somehow, but that action was using a tremendous amount of mana to maintain it.

It was ticking down, increasing the chance of a failure and a detonation, as well as my own personal death, for every second I wasted.

I frowned, trying to figure out what it wanted. A second later, it became clear as I unconsciously shifted the glowing star, and the room altered with it. I needed to pick a position for the Core, and I needed to finalize the design for the room before it would…do whatever it was going to do. Be born, I guessed.

I concentrated and shifted the Core back to the most solid wall and imagined it being secured there, safely fixed away from the plumbing, just in case.

The room blurred as time resumed, and I collapsed to the side, the chair tipping over and sending me crashing to the floor. I laid on the floor for a while, groaning, as I pulled up the notifications.

Current Level of Core Assimilation: 0%

Dungeon Core has been placed and is absorbing mana. Full control privileges will be released at 100% charge. It is recommended the Core is not disturbed until primary activation has occurred at 10%.

Current Charge: 7%

Estimated time to full charge: 15 hours local time

Basic functions will be made available to Dungeon Master in 1 hour 6 minutes.

I collapsed back with a sigh of relief, dismissing the prompt and slowly climbing to my feet. Once I'd set my chair back upright, I turned to face the glowing Dungeon Core.

It hovered in the air between two spikes of a silvery metal that protruded from the floor and ceiling. The shining surfaces sharpened to a keen point around an inch from either end of the Core, which spun gently in the air between them. The Core itself was the size of my thumbnail, and it glowed with a gentle radiance. I slowly approached it, staring at the actual core and wondering what the hell it actually was to be able to float like that. It was clearly crystal, and probably naturally grown, judging by the rough, unpolished edges.

I reached out to touch it, then thought better of it and moved back, sitting in the chair and sighing with relief. For the first time since I'd left Markus's shop, I felt safe.

More or less.

I'd been stabbed, shot, clubbed, and beaten, thrown into a cage with a tiger, and subjected to a horse ride that had mainly been intended to injure my balls, judging from the way Hannah had ridden, but at least I'd made it here alive.

Hannah…now there was a debt I'd have to settle at some stage. Hannah, the King, Keith, all of them. I wondered just what was going on there, and how many of the people they were sheltering actually knew what they were up to.

Well, for the first time since waking up in that forest, I wasn't close to death, or even dying at all, as far as I knew, so I did what any man would do in those circumstances. I took a damn big swig of the whisky I'd found and settled back in the chair, going to sleep.

It was a good few hours later when I opened my eyes again, awoken this time by a tingle of warning and a sense of desire, a hunger. I sat upright, looking around blearily, but I found nothing. The wastepaper bin had long since gone out, and the steady glow of the Core filled the room.

I frowned, staring closely at it, and I concentrated on the feelings coming from it. An image appeared before me, showing the area again. More people were moving around, including some at the front of the building I was in. I almost panicked, thinking they were the gypsies, until I realized they were wandering up and down the street outside.

There weren't many of them, and they seemed to be walking with purpose, but…I almost slapped myself as I realized what they were. They were people, just walking wherever they wanted in the city!

They weren't out to get me, they were just…out.

I watched them for a few minutes, sorting through the feelings. After a few moments of investigating, I was able to identify the warning as coming from the Core because people were so close to it, and the hunger, because it wanted… to eat them? No, that was inaccurate, I knew immediately. It wasn't interested in them, per se; it specifically wanted the corrupted mana that they'd absorbed.

I suddenly knew that life attracted mana, and that unless a person cultivated it, purified it, and worked with it, improving their body, the build-up would not only eventually kill them, it could transform them, converting a normal lifeform into a mana-twisted version of itself.

A sudden thought of mana twisting people, and turning them into savage, feral nightmares, came to me, a warning of sorts. I also knew, although how, I couldn't say, that if the feral monsters grew powerful enough, they'd come for the Core.

One of the Core's defenses, when paired with a Dungeon Fairy, was to build multiple floors. Each one would be filled with traps, and the Core would circulate the corrupted mana into designated areas, where it would build up naturally.

The Core would concentrate on gathering and purifying the corrupted mana, and it would use that mana to create 'Dungeon Monsters'. These were creatures that it either researched, found, or designed to perform functions of the Dungeon, including drawing in Adventurers, clearing the local area, exploring, or even performing specific tasks for the Dungeon, such as crafting or research.

I sat there, working through the processes in my mind.

There were multiple types of focus for the Dungeons, but the main reason they existed, at least as far as I understood, wasn't to kill people, despite what I'd learned from the games I'd played. They were purposefully seeded to cleanse the mana in an area, to stop the corrupted mana from becoming too strong and warping people and animals into Ferals, who'd seemingly kill anything. The Dungeons' primary purpose was to clear the surrounding area of harmful shit, and within that designation, they were compelled to construct items and grow.

I had sudden visions of shining cities that flew through space, havens of safety and tranquility where nobody wanted for anything. Items ranging from glowing swords and armor to small spacecraft were grown and given to the residents as they went out to save others.

That was a genuine possibility, I suddenly knew. As my Dungeon was now, those benefits were at the far end of the spectrum , but it was doable, and what did I have, but time?

I concentrated, and a screen popped up, indicating that the Dungeon was at forty-two percent charge, and full functionality would be granted at one hundred percent.

The ten percent minimum had been surpassed, though, which gave me access to the screens I needed. I started to flick through them, reading and learning what the hell was going on. I quickly realized there were five established pages. The first, and clearly considered to be the most important, was Manaflow and Core Status; the second was Dungeon Design; then Monsters; then Loot; and finally, Research and Development.

Manaflow and Core Status was simple enough. It showed the current state of the Core, which was charging and at forty-three percent. The percentage ticked up visibly while I watched it, but was currently classed as a 'Stone Core' and as I focused on that label, a new detail popped up.

<u>Stone Core:</u>
'Stone' is the assigned designation for the primary Dungeon Core and represents the first of many of the accepted 'Ages' of most starfaring civilizations. Increasing the quality of the Dungeon Core through direct upgrades, mana infusion, and redesign will result in higher grade mana absorption rates, as well as increases in the size, quality, and capabilities of the Dungeon. For further details, please see the assigned Dungeon Companion.

"Well, that's just fucking peachy," I grumbled aloud, grimacing as I considered that the 'assigned Dungeon Companion' was dried to a husk and sitting on my bedside table at home at the moment.

I shook my head and moved on, noting the representation of the Core resembled a pebble. Finding nothing of further immediate value, I dismissed it and went to the next page, figuring I'd get more details once it reached one hundred percent.

Page two was 'Dungeon Design' and indicated a grand total of about a foot and a half in radius around the softly glowing Core. There was, of course, bugger-all I could do there, so I moved on. Monsters and Loot were both much the same; each was greyed out as currently unavailable, but it looked like anything that I created as a Dungeon Monster would need a portion of the Dungeon's mana to keep it going. Loot was assigned from any blueprints the Dungeon had access to, and would drop upon the death of a creature, or when a receptacle, like a chest, was generated. Current loot blueprints…none.

I snarled with frustration, flipping irritably to the final page, 'Research and Development,' letting out a relieved sigh when I saw that there were finally options.

I could assign a portion of the absorbed mana to a Research Node, and it would slowly chug along until it unlocked a blueprint. I guessed that they were all locked away inside the core, somehow, but I wasn't sure. Maybe the magic friggin' pixies delivered them when I was sleeping and nicked any teeth that were going spare on the way out. I shrugged, dismissing the method as unimportant, while bringing up the options.

<u>The following Research is available:</u>
Core Upgrades*:* Research into Core improvements will unlock the path to higher tiers, increased mana absorption rates, and increases in the size, quality, and capabilities of the Core.
Dungeon Upgrades: Research into Dungeon upgrades will provide blueprints for specialist structures, facilities, traps, and special magics.
Monsters: Research into Monsters can provide upgrades to existing Dungeon creations, provide insight into hunting and eliminating mana-warped threats, and further options, depending on the specializations chosen.
Loot: All loot must originate from somewhere. Loot research reveals methods to upgrade the standard basic designs, provide magic options, stat boosts, and higher-tier drops.
Research Nodes: Investing in research can provide a Dungeon with additional research nodes. Please note: the maximum research points assigned will always affect the outcome and quality of completed research.

I sat there for a while processing all the options, trying to get them settled in my mind. As near as I could figure, I had a few priorities.

First and foremost, I had to defend myself. There was no point in doing anything else if I was dead. I had to get the Dungeon to take control of the entire building, and then I could reinforce it, or whatever. Second, I needed food. God, I needed real food! I didn't know what the chances of a steak dinner were, but I'd take anything over the goddamn protein bars. Adding to that, the entire world had relied on transport facilities that were now toast. Ideally, I needed to set something up that would enable me to provide food for others. At minimum, I wanted to be able to bring a few friends inside, to keep them safe, so that must fall under the Dungeon facilities, I guessed.

An odd thought ran through my brain, that if I could find that Kelly, having her here would go a long way toward making my life better. Hell, any kind of company would be good; just someone to watch my back! I needed Monsters to protect the Dungeon, yeah, but for now, I needed to hide. No need to draw attention when I couldn't defend myself yet.

Third, I needed to start generating loot. If I could just drop the loot into a chest or something, there was nothing stopping me from picking it back out! That could solve my food problem, and give me some clothes as well, which was something I desperately needed.

Research felt like a tricky decision. I'd always loved games like Civ, and the Infrastructure versus Production versus Research decisions were traditionally something I loved to balance. Now, I was pissed that it even existed, with how limited my resources were, but I decided I'd figure it out, somehow.

For now, I needed to wait, letting the Core charge up fully. Once it was full, I could get started on the next phase. Maybe tomorrow, I'd head out and try to find some food and a change of clothes. For now, I needed to stay hidden, and that meant scouring the building like a starving rat, praying there was food to be found somewhere....

I got up and took my new best friend, the lighter, to start searching around. The downstairs bar area, where I'd placed the Core, had nothing. Neither did the surrounding rooms, which were set up to lead off the main dance floor. Luckily, on the upper floor, I found and kicked in a locked door to a storeroom that held all the stock that they'd decided to keep safe from the renovation. There wasn't much in the way of food, since most of it was alcohol, but three boxes of crisps, what the Americans called chips, had been stacked in one corner, and at the very back, furthest from the door and buried beneath a crate of vodka, was a crate of mixers, so at least I wouldn't be down to drinking booze constantly. I made a few trips to bring most of the fruit juices and the crisps down, then I spent over an hour cursing and losing my temper as I wrestled the biggest, comfiest couch that I could find down to my new Core room.

It was a pain in the ass, but eventually, I maneuvered it inside the space and collapsed onto it. I drank some fruit juice, made a trip to the mercifully still plumbed in and working toilet, and spent the next few hours walking back and forth around the room, most often with the map up, so I could be sure nobody was trying to get inside.

It was early evening, by my watch, when the Core finally reached full charge, and I sagged into the couch in relief, bringing up the Dungeon Core management screen.

Dungeon Core:
Classification: Stone
Charge: 100%
Ambient Mana Absorption: 6 Points per hour (pph)

I studied the self-explanatory details, few as they were, and I nodded in comprehension. There really wasn't much I could do with it yet, beyond checking to verify that it was okay, I guessed. I moved to the next section, glad to see that Dungeon Design was unlocked, and that there were options available to me.

Current Dungeon Area: 16m2
Options available:
- Alteration/Expansion

Once again, the interface seemed clearly simple and designed for fast access. I looked around the room, suddenly aware that the area where I stood looked slightly different to the rest of the room. My immediate surroundings, presumably inside the Dungeon's area, were slightly sharper in texture; at least, that was the best way I could explain it. Colors were brighter, and it was as though I was watching the room in HD, as opposed to SD, on a movie. I walked over to the edge of the Dungeon's influence, and stared. After a few seconds, I found the boundary on a wooden plank on the floor. A line of slowly-growing detail inched along the floor, almost unnoticeable, but when I made a mark with a fingernail and watched intently, the detail gradually absorbed it.

I straightened up, nodding to myself in satisfaction. Clearly, the dungeon took time to claim the area, and the options I'd been given were limited to concentrating on growing that claim or working on it as it was. I sat down on my couch again and selected 'Expansion.'

Instantly, I felt my point of view change, and I shook myself, landing back in my body a millisecond later. I tried again, and once again, I shifted, seemingly fading out of my body and into the Core. I looked around the room and found my usual battered meatsuit slumped on the couch. With a little effort I mentally zoomed over to it, its form highlighted in my ethereal vision.

Human Host
Class: Unassigned
Level: 4
HP: 200
MP: 200
STM: 70

Permeate?
Yes/No

I hastily selected 'No' and moved back. In a fit of curiosity, I reached out to the office chair I'd been using before I had liberated the couch.

Simple Office Chair
Class: Furniture, Non-magical, Non-enhanced.
Level: N/A

Permeate?
Yes/No

I selected 'Yes' and felt a dip in the mana stored in the Core. I watched curiously as the chair was slowly saturated with mana, and a second prompt appeared.

Design accepted.

That was it, nothing else. I waited, but when nothing happened, I focused in on the chair again, this time getting a new series of options.

Repair/Absorb

I selected 'Repair,' and the chair seemed to melt partially, the cracked and battered leather flowing, then reforming, the metal frame tightening. The chipped paint seemed to become liquid for a second, then flowed back to 'normal', and I grunted in surprise.

The damn chair looked amazing, like it'd just been bought! I shook myself out of the Core and stood up, moving over to examine the chair and running my hands over it. It was a seriously huge improvement, and I grinned, thinking about what I could do with my clothes.

I flew back into the Core again, examining my tattered, filthy clothes. Elated, I was about to start repairing them, and by extension, cleaning them, when I noticed the Core. It was down to seventy percent.

"Shit, really?" I groaned, realizing that it'd take at least the rest of the energy in the Core to make my clothes fresh again. I concentrated on the chair again, bringing up the same options, but this time, 'Repair' was greyed out, leaving only 'Absorb'.

I shrugged and selected that the solitary option, watching closely as the chair seemed to dissolve into a rush of matter that streamed into the Core...

Core Charge level: 100%
Excess Matter has been lost.

"Seriously?!" I cried out, back in my body as I gestured angrily at the Core. "You couldn't have warned me of that before? Like a 'Hey, by the way, there's more here than I need to recharge, are you sure' or something? Motherfucker!" I growled in annoyance as I stomped around the room. I tried not to think about the fact that I could at least be wearing some clean clothes at the moment, but it was hard.

I forced myself to sit down, still muttering, and I pushed myself into the Core again, looking out at the world. I reselected 'Expansion' and felt something... different, but in what way, I couldn't say. I moved out from the Core to inspect the area where the Dungeon influence and the real world seemed to meet.

I could feel a change, a resistance, along the edge, and I reached out, feeling resistance, like a rubber membrane stretched between me and the world. I pushed out, and the Dungeon area slowly flowed forward, the mana from the Core sinking into everything around me. It was weird, as I could feel the mana permeating the air with little resistance, but as I pushed over to a series of recessed booths in the wall, places where I'd sat and shot the shit with friends dozens of times over the years, the mana seemed to slow, taking longer to sink into the wood and leather.

I moved slowly, steadily pushing out around the room and 'claiming' it all. By the time I'd reached the far side of the dance floor, near the restrooms, I was exhausted and happily fled back to my body.

Core Charge Level: 16%

I flopped back on the couch, breathing heavily, and took the time to rest. I was finding the expansion process a weird experience, as my physical body felt totally fine, but my mind was wrung out. I felt as if I'd just finished a nightmare exam or something.

I checked the Core and found that, with the increased area covered by the Dungeon, I had more options to absorb stuff. I pulled one of the booths apart, refilling the 'tank' to nearly fifty percent. Satisfied for the moment, I moved to the Research screens, selecting 'Core,' and read through the options spread out before me.

'Core' was at the top, with three lines leading out from it, heading downwards. Going from left to right, I saw 'Tier One: Bronze', 'Mana Absorption', and 'Upgrades' as options. Selecting each gave me a brief impression of the details.

'Tier One: Bronze' was an overall Upgrade to the next Tier, as 'Stone' was apparently Tier Zero. Upgrading to the next level would be a serious upgrade, something I mentally compared to going from a tiny Fiat car to a small one. It was still a little car, with limited luxuries and capabilities, but it was an upgrade to everything.

'Mana Absorption' was a specific upgrade to, surprise, surprise, the rate that I could draw in Mana. I compared this to upgrading the engine of the car; it wasn't going to suddenly be able to do two hundred miles an hour, but it'd be faster than it was, and it would go up the hills better. It was always going to be a limited upgrade, as it was constrained by the size of the car, and the design, but it was better than the bog-standard version they sold it with.

Lastly, I looked at the 'Upgrades' tab, finding that it gave the sense of minor changes, like replacing the stereo or changing to leather seats. Minor details, but significantly cheaper to do than a full turnkey upgrade. Unfortunately, it required prior research to populate the options, or required that it be done 'manually' somehow.

I sat and thought for a while, staring away into the distance, not really seeing anything. I knew I needed to improve the Core, otherwise it would take forever to get anywhere with it. Ideally, I needed to push the Dungeon area out to the street and all the way to the top of the building, claim all of it, and then reinforce it. To reach that boundary as things were now, the job would probably take close to two weeks, judging from the time that last expansion had taken, and while I could absorb things, using them to recharge the Core, I needed to save some for emergencies, and some for, well…life.

I settled on 'Mana Absorption' as a compromise. I needed to pick up the speed, and while I wanted to jump all the way to the highest Tier of Core right away, thank you very much, I knew it wasn't going to happen like that. As soon as I selected the research, I got a slider, asking how much mana I wanted to invest into RP, or Research Points. They worked on a one-to-one ratio, it seemed, so I put three out of the six coming in into it, sighing as it flashed in acceptance and vanished.

Looking back around the room, there was nothing else I could do but wait, so I had a few packets of crisps. Cheese and onion, thankfully, was an option. I also took the time to have the Dungeon absorb all twelve bags of tomato sauce flavor with a shudder of disgust. I got three points of mana for the lot and viewed it as a good trade.

I settled back to drink some lukewarm orange juice, then relaxed, waiting for something to happen. I wondered how my friends were doing, worrying about what could be happening to them while I idly chilled in my Dungeon basement. I wanted to go to them, to get out and help, but I knew I couldn't. I needed to get the base ready first. Then, and only then, I could get out there and bring people back. I couldn't afford to let someone else steal it from me.

With that pleasant thought, I shifted around, trying to get comfortable, until I finally fell asleep.

ELEVEN

I WOKE UP HOURS later, bleary-eyed, as a terrible sense of foreboding filled me. I sat bolt upright, searching the room. Seeing nothing out of the ordinary, I then reached out to the Core, and my heart started to race.

I could see the outlines of figures moving around upstairs in Florita's. While I could sense their location, I wasn't able to determine who they were or why they were there, and I frantically dived into the Dungeon design section, fleeing from my body back into the Core.

I was at sixty-eight percent mana, and the space controlled by the Dungeon had grown, seemingly infinitesimally, past what I last remembered it being. I ignored the rest of the room, though, and floated straight to the stairs leading up to the next floor. I pushed and prodded, moving the bubble of control steadily through the door and to the bottom stair, then slowly edged upwards. Each step took more energy than the one before it, and I saw my charge dropping quickly. I reached ten percent mana with six steps to go, and suddenly felt a change, as the Dungeon refused to push any further. I started to panic at the sounds of people moving through the building, clearly searching.

I dove back downstairs and grabbed at the remaining two booths in the room, absorbing them both and receiving sixteen and twenty-two percent, respectively, due to their size. It took over a minute to convert each, and when I flew back to the stairs, now at forty-eight again, I could not only hear people clearly talking, but I could see the flickers of light as they searched through the bar.

Almost gibbering with the fear of being discovered, I claimed all the way up to the doors, deciding to include them too. I wracked my brain frantically for a way to protect them, then dipped into the 'Alteration' option, highlighting the doors thinking I needed to change them.

Limited options flooded my mind. They were simple—god, they were depressingly simple—but they were all I had. I could cover them to look like a plain brick wall, like the ones downstairs, remove the doors altogether, or fill the space with wooden planks. I could also transform them into solid stone, but

I didn't have enough mana. It also seemed that I couldn't make anything that wasn't creatable by a similar level of technology to the Stone Core's tech level. There had been other options to replace the doors with other types of doors I'd examined downstairs, but they'd been marked as too advanced for the Core and remained greyed out.

I decided on the brick wall; the bar had put them up over all the standard grey concrete walls, and there were more upstairs, so hopefully it'd blend in. Failing that, I didn't know what I'd do.

I selected the wall, and the view changed to allow me to place it, lining it up and smoothing the edges as best I could into the existing, unclaimed brickwork. It would take a few minutes, and the façade would never stand up to real scrutiny, but it was all I could do with the time I had left.

As soon as I confirmed my choice, the mana flooded out, sinking into the doors and blurring them. The wood ran like honey, slow and thick, seeping out and shifting in size and color. I sensed one of the figures on the other side move into the room I was working on, and I prayed fervently that he wouldn't spot the wall that was growing across the doors.

"What the hell?" I heard a rough voice call out, and I froze, opting to frantically force more mana into the process a second later when the voice went on. "Look at this!" he hollered deeper into the building to someone else. "Jackpot!"

A second, then a third figure joined the first, striding straight past the wall that was forming in the darkness as they headed into the open storeroom I'd raided earlier.

"Looks like someone found it already, but there's still loads of booze!" a sharp voice said excitedly. "Get out there and get the cart; we'll get it loaded up and clear out as much as we can. Jonny, you're staying here. Make sure nobody comes back for this shit. It's ours!"

I heard laughter and agreement, and I sighed as the wall finished forming, thankful for the combination of darkness and poor light from the torches, paired with greedy idiots, to let me hide the stairs.

I fled back to my body and watched them on the map for a while. Their red figures moved backwards and forwards to the alley outside, clearly robbing the bar blind. I felt my anger growing as I watched them. I knew it was ridiculous—after all, I was literally stealing the building—but they were robbing my favorite bar.

I growled softly as I watched them, wishing there was something I could do about it, before I felt my eyes drawn to the 'Monsters and Loot' tab. I smiled evilly. As I pulled it up, I saw that I had three options for monsters at the moment. They were all greyed out, but that was fine, I was down to twelve percent charge, after all.

Monsters

Common Grade:

Vermin: Rats are a common pest that are ubiquitous across the universe. Vermin of this type vary in size and limb count, but often conform to similar local design.

Cost: Vermin spawn in packs of three for 5 mana each. Maintenance is 1 mana point per day, per individual.

Mammal: Goblins as a species have multiple variations, ranging from the lowest caste, who are barely sentient, to the High Grenai, a race that suffers little interaction with 'lesser' species, due to the enormous gulf of grace and beauty between those races and their own. The most basic can be spawned as Dungeon Monsters. Utilizing their species' polymorphic tendencies results in greater enhancements than are commonly available.

Cost: Goblins spawn individually for 5 mana each. Maintenance is 2 mana points per day, per individual.

Reptilian: Kobolds are a common, highly structured, caste-driven species. Semi-sentient Kobolds are a standard sight in Dungeons, due to their advanced trap-making skills and low cost.

Cost: Kobolds spawn in packs of three for 10 mana each. Maintenance is 1 mana point per day, per individual.

I read through the details quickly, nodding in consideration as I calculated the initial and ongoing costs. I was glad I had some basic options, but also not too pleased about the amount of mana they would require to maintain. I moved on to the loot section and discovered I had to research any weapons above a crude stick. The weapon subcategory was split up into three sections: Offense, Defense, and Miscellaneous.

Offence had literally a stick in it. A wooden stick. That was it. Defense had a set of fabric clothes that not only looked terrible, but I was ninety-nine percent sure would feel like sandpaper as well. At least Miscellaneous held a bit more, including a design blueprint section that had the chair I'd scanned, along with everything else I'd examined in it. I shook my head at the blueprints section, not seeing any possible use for it, and went back to the main Miscellaneous section. It had been populated with a list of small items like nails and the lock from the door I'd examined, planks of wood etc, and there, amongst all the rest of the random details, were the goddamn tomato sauce crisps.

"I don't care what else goes wrong in the world; that's a line I won't cross," I vowed to myself, staring in disgust at that affront to the gods. I found a load of random things, but nothing that was useful, until I came to the bottom of the list. I froze in shock.

Spellbooks, Skillbooks, and Magical Items:
Spellbooks Skillbooks, and Magical Items are limited by the Dungeon level, available technologies in the local area, and materials, but there is a chance that these items will drop randomly each time a creature is killed in the Dungeon.
Current chance of drop: 0.01%
Do you wish to adjust the chance of this drop?
Yes/No

"Hell yes, I do!" I muttered, grabbing it and sliding it along to the maximum. Unfortunately, it really didn't change much; even if I invested ten points of mana an hour, the maximum for the Stone Core and more than I even passively earned at present, I would manage to raise it to only a one percent chance. "Dammit!" I groused, slumping back on the couch, before sitting back up as I realized something.

I'd been planning on summoning creatures as a last resort, something to defend my Dungeon against the assholes out there, but now…now I wondered if there was a better way to use it. I could summon the weakest creatures available and kill them myself. Yeah, it would cost me in terms of mana expenditure, that was a given, but if I did it say, once a day, to use it as a training method, I could get myself up to the point where I could defend myself properly, and I could collect all the loot. Even better, I could use only what I wanted and absorb the rest back into the Dungeon!

I could research weapons that I wanted to use, armor…hell, I could find a goddamn gun, and then just shoot the fuckers!

I started to get excited, before remembering the issues I'd had creating the wall across the entrance to the stairs, and I dove back into the screens, reading and examining the details. After another hour, I felt I had a better grasp on things, and I dismissed them while I considered what I'd discovered.

The tech I could replicate was dependent on the Core and its capabilities, which meant I was stuck with extremely low-level tech for now. That explained why the weapons were limited to a stick, rather than starting with a sword or anything more useful. They'd be available only when I lifted the Core to a level of 'Bronze' or 'Iron'. It seemed that I could absorb anything, and certain items were omitted from those rules, such as food. I could make the crisps, after all, so it was a relief to know that 'food' was apparently not going to be limited to grains and shit. A brief note had indicated something along the lines of 'sustenance differing to such extreme variables among worlds that it was exempted from the Core level requirements.' All I needed to do was absorb examples of different foods, and I could have the Core produce them for me. I nearly wept with joy.

I also learned that I could repair more complex things, like the chair, but I couldn't actually make them from scratch yet. That meant, in my mind at least, that it was a setting in the Core, a program that said 'If 'X,' then 'Y'. It was also waaaaay beyond my ability to change it, though, considering the fact that the Core could somehow alter matter at a fundamental level.

I resolved not to touch it…at least not for a long time.

Realizing that I had been reading for a while, I checked the Research tab, pleased to find that the Mana Absorption was ticking away nicely and had a countdown timer of ten hours to go. I got up and started wandering around the room, bored to all hell, when I froze in sudden fear, looking up at the ceiling as a horrible thought occurred to me, before letting out a relieved sigh a second later.

I'd blocked off the upper stairs with a fake brick wall, but there were open airducts still in place, so even though there wasn't power, there was at least a way for the air to get in. I'd had a sudden terrible fear that I was going to have to knock that wall down or suffocate. I was about to laugh at my baseless panic, when I grunted in shock, as I realized what else I'd forgotten about in a place like this…namely, that it had to have an emergency exit!

I pulled up the Dungeon screen and found the doors a few seconds later. They were on the far side of a side room I'd not permeated yet, which was why I'd missed them. I'd seen them earlier, when I was exploring a bit with my Zippo torch, but they hadn't registered, as fire doors tended not to, when you didn't need them.

I made a mental note to change them to a door only I could open as soon as possible. The charge level was too low to be able to do anything at present, and there was literally bugger-all I could do with everything else until that improved. With nothing else left to investigate, I settled down to watch the people moving around on the map and trying to sleep as much as I could.

It was boring, seriously boring, but I just couldn't risk more, not yet. I was terrified of losing the Dungeon Core to someone else who found their way in, or being captured by the gypsies or another gang again.

I laid there in the semi-darkness, the only light in the room being the glow of the Core, and I tried not to imagine the shit I could be doing right then. I thought about the foods I needed to collect samples of, for the Dungeon to absorb and learn. I started a mental list of all the amazing stuff I could get from the nearby supermarkets, and…

I sat upright suddenly, realizing what I'd been ignoring. The rooms around me were full of cleaning products, stock for the club, chairs, building gear, all of it, and I'd been thinking like I was under siege, planning on holding onto it all for an emergency! There were even two more booths in the back of the room, and all I had to do was reach them! I bounded to my feet and rushed to the nearest storeroom, grabbing a case of vodka and dumping it on the dance floor inside of the Dungeon influence area, then went back for more.

I spent an hour stripping the room out, piling everything up, before I pulled the screen up and began to absorb it. There was a certain amount of wastage—I guessed that was the nature of things—but a handful of minutes later, I'd refilled the charge, and I was off again, pushing the boundary out. I moved in and out of the various rooms, stopping long enough to absorb random stuff, but leaving a single room that was full of random shit as my emergency stockpile.

The rest of the stuff I came across fueled my expansion, and in three hours, I'd reached the emergency fire escape. I absorbed enough that the charge was back to a hundred percent, and then started to permeate the big steel and composite doors. Once I'd fully acquired them, I kept pushing out into the hallway beyond, slowly moving up the stairs.

I spread my influence evenly as I went, taking in the walls and floor, the metal stairs, and absorbing any electrical bits as I went. Those were pointless at this stage, after all, so they served to fuel my expansion.

By the time I reached the doors into the alleyway, I was exhausted again, and I had to stop and rest for a few hours before I could permeate them. I couldn't stop grinning to myself when I'd finally managed it, because it didn't just mean I had closed off unauthorized access to the Dungeon now; it also meant I had a secured way in and out!

I found that I could control the doors mentally. They unlocked and locked again at my unspoken command effortlessly, and that meant I could leave! I could go into the city for supplies or weapons and get back in!

I fled back to my body on the couch, opening my eyes and staring at the Dungeon Core as I thought about the possibilities. I knew the safe option was to stay inside, to stay hidden, doing nothing that could bring attention to me. However, I was bored out of my tiny mind, not to mention wearing filthy clothes, starving for real food, and well, I needed a few creature comforts.

I didn't really see any point to staying in my flat anymore, not when I had an actual home that I could endlessly modify, especially one that would be safe and could generate everything I needed. All I wanted was the gear I had in my flat, my personal effects, mementoes of my family, photos, my bed, and god, my books! I'd spent a fortune over the years on my book collection. It was mainly Sci-Fi and Fantasy, but there were all sorts of adventures in there, and they'd help me while away the hours, weeks, and possibly years it'd take me to get this place set up properly.

I especially needed to get that goddamn fairy corpse, as it might be possible to learn more about what was happening by having the Dungeon scan the thing.

I resolved that I would go home today, get a suitcase of gear, clothes, a few bits and pieces, and some creature comforts. Then I could have the Dungeon scan them and remake them, if anything happened to the originals.

Pleased with my flawless plan, I used the Dungeon interface for two things. First, I made myself a stick. It was a crappy weapon, but it was still a weapon, and then I checked on the Research, finding that it was possible to queue the research up. I chose the stick from the menu and selected 'Upgrade'. The bar appeared to show how long it would take, but without a mana allocation, it was empty. I shrugged and moved on, taking the time to stretch, use the toilet, and drink some warm fruit juice.

Then, when I couldn't justify putting my departure off any longer, I went up to the door with equal measures of trepidation and excitement. I checked the surrounding area, found there was nobody in the alley or in sight, then I cautiously ordered the doors to open and stepped out into the warm morning.

I looked around, slightly paranoid that people would be about anyway, but when there wasn't a single soul in sight, I nodded to myself in satisfaction and mentally closed the doors.

I took a single step away from my sanctuary, then spun around and made the doors open again, then close, then reopen, just to be sure I could, before nodding again and heading to the edge of the alley, gripping my stick tightly in a white-knuckled fist.

I peered both ways, made sure there wasn't anyone in sight, then set off, heading north towards my home. I soon saw my first people, and I noticed the way they froze, glaring at me, before changing direction and scurrying away as quickly as they could.

That was the new way of the world, I found, after an hour, by which time I had made it across the city center and was moving quickly up the main road towards my old flat. Each encounter with people resulted in silent stares, followed by watching me as I passed. The people further back in the city, closest to the high mana concentration areas, were the worst, either standing their ground and glaring or running like frightened rabbits, but everywhere I went, people were hesitant and distrustful.

I diverted to head past Markus's shop, figuring I could check on him and let him know I was okay, maybe drop a few hints and make sure he was ready to join me when my Dungeon was up and running. He was someone I would want to help, and he'd seemed like a good guy, not to mention he'd probably be damn useful.

When I got to his shop, though, the doors hung wide open, and goods had been strewn everywhere. No food, just packaging, and when I went inside, it had obviously been ransacked. I headed in deeper, finding nobody home, and when I went downstairs, thankful for my little lighter, I found that even his training sanctuary had been looted. The good steel swords, the gloves, all of it was gone, leaving only a handful of the practice swords in a box at the back.

I felt better having another practice sword, gladly dumping the stick, but I still left the building in a much worse mood than when I'd entered it. I also noted the looks I got from residents peeping from their windows; the hatred, disgust, and fear was clear on their faces. When I called out to ask what had happened and if Markus was all right, though, I got no answer. People hid, rather than replying.

I'd taken a small carrier bag of things I knew would come in useful from Markus's shop; flour, powdered eggs, no milk or butter, of course, but jerky and a handful of tins. The little sewing kit I'd spotted on the counter in particular seemed like it might be useful, but the various home staples, like painkillers, candles, matches, and so on, stuff that would be really useful, all had been taken long since.

I continued down the street quickly, hurrying back to my place with as much speed as I could manage without running. As I marched up to the house, I furtively glanced around . A burgeoning sense of danger grew in my mind again, and I hurried inside, eager to avoid another confrontation.

I tried the bottom flat, hoping Paul would be back, but there was no answer, so I started up to the next floor, passing the assholes' flat. I was unsurprised when the letterbox opened and a voice called out to me.

"Where's my bike, you thief!" I turned and glared at the malicious gaze of Gerald, squatting down to reply.

"I gave it to a whore for a blowjob; why?" I said, blurting the first thing that came to mind that I figured would annoy him the most.

"WHAT?! That bike was worth thousands! You fucking idiot! I already told the police! They said they'd be coming for you; you see if they don't!" I grinned at him and flipped him the finger before starting to straighten up. I paused, then sighed, and squatted back down to look at him as he screamed to his wife about what I'd done.

"Look, I'm sorry. I didn't, really. I just wanted to piss you off, okay?" I said, and he spun around, glaring at me. "The world's gone to shit out there. I got attacked and they took the bike. I took it because I was angry at the way you both turned away from me when I was hurt and needed help. I...."

"You admit it! You admit you stole my bike!" He snapped, and I snorted.

"Yeah, I admit it, okay? Look, neither of us likes the other, and that's fine, but seriously, it's getting really bad out there, people are...they're like animals, so just...be careful if you go out, okay?" I said, swallowing my dislike of the pair of them. Just because they were assholes, didn't mean I was, and the least I could do was warn them.

"You don't need to tell me that. The world's full of it! This is all your fault. If your kind just went home, and left the civilized people to it, we'd be all right..." Miss Piggy started up, and I snarled, straightening up and marching on upstairs towards my room. The door opened a crack, and I saw her face filling it as she screamed up at me.

"And you can tell your friends to keep the noise down! We'll be reporting you to the landlord's association for this when it's all over! See if we don't!" I froze, frowning at her in confusion. She nodded at me in satisfaction, thinking she'd scored a point, and went on. "That's right! They'll make you move out, and we'll get some good, respectable white people in here instead, not like you and that filthy Scot downstairs!"

I glanced at the ceiling, wondering who she meant, and hoping against hope that Chris had come around, that he'd stayed, waiting for me for some reason, or hell, maybe it was Kelly. I'd left my keys in the coat I'd lent her, after all...

"You just see what the landlord's association has to say about this, you..."

"Shut the fuck up!" I snapped at her, shaking my head. "We own our flats, you stupid bitch. Even if there *was* still a landlords association, they'd have nothing to do with us. Now fuck off!"

I stormed away from her, hurrying up the stairs and wondering who was waiting for me. Running through the short list of possibilities, I reached the door and pulled my keys out, and...looked at them...

These weren't right.

My keys had been replaced. There were a half dozen on the ring, but they were all wrong. All that was right was the keyring itself, with the picture of the dog I'd had when growing up on it. I stared at the unfamiliar bits of metal, confused, until the door handle shifted and opened from the inside, revealing a swarthy, grinning face I recognized, and a handgun barrel that was pointed at my face.

"Fuck…Keith…" I muttered in shock, and Keith the gypsy backed up slightly, gesturing to me to come inside with his gun.

"Aye, yer wee snot, now get yer arse in here, or I'll fuckin' shoot yer right there!"

I swallowed hard and stepped inside, my heart in my boots and my butthole puckering like it was trying to decide if it was tighter than a duck's arse or bracing itself for a weinering by an elephant.

TWELVE

I MOVED THROUGH THE door, closing it behind me at Keith's gesture, and glared at him.

"How did you get here?" I demanded, and he snorted scornfully, tossing his head.

"It wasna hard. We got the address from yer wallet, swapped yer keys out before Hannah gave 'em back to ye. Now, me an' Barr have been bored shitless waitin' fer yer to show up. We almost gave up, then I look out the window and there ye are, strollin' along, happy as can be." He grinned cruelly at me, and I glanced toward the other end of the hall as a second man stepped out, a cosh held loosely in his hands as he smiled.

My balls shriveled up at the sight of the weapon. I'd seen one years before, used on a roof tile by a mate who wanted to show it off, since they were illegal pretty much everywhere. It was basically a short handle with a thick spring on the top, tightly wound, and a solid lead tip. When they hit anything, the force was magnified by the coiled spring, and they shattered bones like glass. I remembered the tile smashing, then the cosh bending backwards on the rebound after it'd hit the pavement below. The spring had struck his little brother's hand, who'd been reaching over, too eager for his turn to wait. The howl as the bones shattered in his hand had been terrible.

I knew upon seeing that, and considering who had been waiting for me, that this wasn't a fight I was going to walk away from with just a few bruises. They were going to cripple me at the least, and most likely kill me.

"So, put that thing down, and the bag…now. Then you can tell us all about where you've been," Keith growled, and I slowly swung the sword around, off my back, thankful I'd found another scabbard.

"This?" I asked, dropping the bag of things from the shop and lifting the sword out sideways, so the tip was about a foot from Keith's stomach.

"Aye; we know it's rubber, so don't try anythin' 'smart,'" the other guy—Barr, I assumed—said.

"Oh, okay then," I said innocently, wrapping my left hand around the pommel and shifting my right up to grip the top half of the hilt properly, the way Markus had shown me.

"I said…" Keith started to repeat, and I lunged, yanking back towards myself, hard, with my left hand, while I drove the sword into his stomach with my right.

It had the effect of moving the sword point faster than Keith could see, and it knocked the barrel of his gun aside as he fired. The bullet flew down the hall and lodged in the doorframe next to Barr's head, forcing him to duck aside with a curse as I stepped in closer to Keith.

I shoved the gun aside, letting go of my sword with the left hand, and slammed the hilt of the sword into his face with my right, knocking him back. Before he could regain his balance, I dropped it and grabbed his t-shirt collar, yanking him into a headbutt.

The gun went off again as he tried to shove me away with his left arm, his right pulling the gun back as I grabbed at it, and I hissed, feeling the bullet score across my ribs before heading down the hall again, and making Barr shout.

I shoved Keith back into the wall, finally managing to get ahold of the wrist of his gun arm and cracking it against the wall next to his head. I leaned in, twisting around and shoving my back against his chest. He grabbed at my face with his left hand, but I shook it off, yanking his arm harder than he thought I'd be able to, and I pointed the gun at his friend, who was running down the hall, now only a few feet away.

The gun went off with a boom, the third shot flashing out and slamming into the charging man. The impact hurled him from his feet in a welter of blood and bone fragments, sending him crashing to the floor with a pained squeal.

"Barr!" Keith bellowed, finally grabbing a handful of my shirt with his left hand. I'd frozen, having never shot someone before, and before I could reorient, Keith shoved hard into me, twisting and slamming me headfirst into the wall opposite. The gun was torn loose from both of us, clattering away into the bloody debris on the floor near Barr, who was thrashing and clutching at his chest.

Keith started punching, slamming fist after fist into me, howling like an enraged bear as I tried to defend myself. I twisted and kicked out, managing a glancing blow on his hip that forced him back a step, and I lunged back at him. Ducking down and wrapping my arms around his waist, I lifted him and rushed through the open doorway into my bedroom.

He was raining blows down on me, kicking where he could, as I half carried, half threw him, slamming him into the dresser. His bulk made the whole thing collapse, as cheap as it was.

The clothes, panels and various crap that had accumulated over the years on top of the dresser fell onto him, burying him as he struggled back upright. Unfortunately for him, his face got to meet my fist coming the other way as he swiped a shirt off his head.

This punch was much better aimed, and I followed through better than I had the last few I'd thrown. My anger at this scumbag breaking into my home to clearly murder me helped to power it, and it connected full force with his nose and upper jaw.

His head slammed back, smacking off the wooden remains of the dresser as blood sprayed from his flattened nose, and I stepped in closer, slamming my left in hard, then my right again, as he attempted to defend himself. He was clearly more skilled than I was, but thanks to my Stat increases, I had the musculature of an Olympian, and while my Dexterity had been constrained by the increased muscle mass, it was still well past the average, at least for now. I slammed fist after fist into his face, before grabbing him by the throat and yanking him upright, staring into his one remaining good eye. The other had begun swelling shut already, and had clearly filled with blood.

"Where are they?" I asked him, my voice a low growl. "Where are the rest of your friends?"

He started to speak, coughed, then spat a tooth out, and managed to glare at me.

"Go fuck yerself," he managed to rasp out, and I sneered at him, slamming him back into the wall with my left hand.

"Wrong answer," I snapped, punching him in the gut, then I shifted, hammering first the bottom left, then the bottom right, short ribs. I could feel them snap under my blows and making him gasp in pain. "See, this is how it's gonna work..." I whispered, glaring at him. "Every time you give me a wrong answer, I snap some ribs; then it'll be fingers, then arms. I'm leaving here, right after we talk, and I'm gonna leave you to bleed out on the floor. If you're good, maybe you'll still be alive when Hannah and the others come looking...maybe I'll even give you a message to pass on. Or maybe you'll be dead, just like your mate."

He glared at me, blood dripping from his chin and started to speak, then lashed out, punching me in the face with his right hand as he grabbed at my wrist with his left, trying to break my grip.

I shook my head, shaking the blow off, and glared at him. The taste of blood filled my mouth from what felt like a busted lip, and I slammed him back again, letting go of his throat and grabbing his right arm instead, twisting it and slamming my fist into the wrist, feeling the delicate bones as they fractured.

He screamed, and I grabbed him by the hair, lifting his head and punching him in the face again.

"Maybe I don't need you alive to pass a message on, eh? Maybe I should just fucking kill you and write it down?!" I snarled to him. He spat out a gobbet of blood, coughing and snarling a response.

"I…said go…fuck yerself…" he managed to get out, and I snorted, shaking my head.

"Typical Gypsy," I growled at him. "Never give up, eh…Fine." I drew my fist back and punched him as hard as I could, letting go with my left as it landed, and he slammed back into the wall, slumping to the floor.

I wanted to kill him; fuck, I really did, but I didn't need to kill him. I could just leave him, and what happened, happened.

I checked on the other one, verifying that he was dead already. Blood spread out from the hole through his chest. I picked the gun up, shoving it into my jeans waistband after putting the safety on, determined not to blow my own dick off.

I grabbed the cosh as well. A thick leather loop on the base could be closed over the top of the spring, compressing it and making it more or less 'safe'. With all the weapons in my possession, I checked Keith over, finding he was unconscious, and pulled a handful of bullets for the gun from his pocket and a big bunch of keys. The thick roll of cash he had in his pocket might not have much value anymore, but I snagged it too, leaving the pouch of drugs behind… then I took them on a whim. I didn't trust what he might have, for all I knew it was a trap, but I might be able to use it in the Dungeon.

I knew the gunshots would attract attention, as would the blood that I had no doubt was seeping through the floor of my hallway now, so I moved quickly, searching the bedroom. I pulled out my old suitcase, a big one on wheels, thankfully, and flipped it open, chucking a few pairs of boxers, some socks, and a half dozen tops in, making sure I had some thick, some thin, some sports clothes, and some winter ones, as well as a pair of good boots, and stripped off, quickly.

I knew I didn't have time for a shower, so instead I got changed and made do with that, dumped the little first aid box I had, mainly bandages and bits and bobs like aspirin, into the bottom of the case as well. I glanced around quickly, grabbing photos and a few keepsakes, then frowned and started looking harder.

After a frenzied search, I stood in the middle of the floor, swearing like a pirate. It was gone; the Fairy corpse in its crystal container. Some fuckhead had taken it! I knew who it'd be, as well, and I spat on the floor. I slapped Keith a bit and poured a can of beer over his face. I refused to waste water, and it was only Fosters, anyway, but it was no good. He was out for the count.

I stood thinking furiously for a few more seconds, then started moving again, grabbing shower gel, aftershave, and the various other products I used regularly, shaving gear and a toilet roll…By this point, my suitcase was getting full, so I shoved half a dozen of my favorite books in, before filling up every last available space with individual foods from the kitchen, including a very soft bar of butter, which I put in a bag, along with a handful of condiments.

I felt a bit daft, considering I had two people bleeding out in my flat, one dead, and one clearly not far from it, but that was the way the world was going, and I'd given up on most of normal life already.

I checked around for the last time, hoping against hope that there was nothing I was missing, then grabbed the rolled up sleeping bag from under my bed and my pillow, having made my mind up that some things weren't luxuries, and I didn't care what I looked like.

I left the flat, knowing it was almost certainly for the last time, leaving a note for any friends who came looking in the middle of the bed. I knew it was a risk, but I felt it was worth it.

Guys,
Remember me at the end of the night.
- M

I figured it might read more like a goodbye to anyone who wasn't part of our group, but it was a phrase we used regularly, meaning that if we'd passed out drunk, or off our heads on the drink, then we'd need to be taken home. As we almost always ended the night in Koo's, it would be enough for the lads to understand, but almost impossible for anyone else, especially without access to our social media.

I carried the case out of the door, stepping over the corpse, and snagged a long coat on the way out, along with the sword in its scabbard, before setting off down the stairs. I paused, looking at the door of the middle flat as I passed, then called out, knowing they were listening.

"They weren't friends of mine. They were there to rob me. They're dead now, and I'm going to Scotland to stay with my family. Good luck." Then I turned and clunked down the stairs, wondering if they'd stay there, or run away. Either way, at least if someone asked them where I was, it might leave a false trail. The lads knew I had no family, so they'd know it was bullshit; the Gypsies wouldn't.

I got outside and started off down the street, deliberately heading as though I was going to leave the area, until I was out of sight of the flat, then changing direction down a side street, and heading back towards the center.

I saw a handful of people as I trundled along the streets, my case rattling as it bounced over the uneven paving stones, and I nodded to the few people that didn't seem hostile. Even so, the vast majority either ignored me or actively avoided me.

The only person who spoke to me or made any kind of an effort to be nice was an old priest, when I passed him sitting on a park bench halfway to town.

He was old, like in his eighties or nineties, and not healthy, like some older people are at that age. His skin was like paper, his hair transparent, and his eyes rheumy and barely able to see me a few feet away.

"Hello?" he called out in quavering voice, and I slowed, looking first at him, then glancing around to make sure it wasn't a trap.

"Hello, Father," I said quietly. "Are you okay? Do you need help?"

"A…a little news would be good; nobody seems to speak anymore…" he said, forcing a smile.

"Of course…" I said, straightening and putting my case on all four wheels, dipping a hand into the carrier bag I'd brought with me. "Do you need a drink, Father?" He smiled genuinely.

"Ah, no; thank you, my son. I gave it up long ago…"

"A soft drink, then?" I offered, holding out a bottle of still juice. He took it with thanks and opened it, taking a long drink.

"Thank you," he said afterwards, moving to pass it back.

"You keep it. Do you need anything else? A little food?" I asked, and he opened his mouth, then seemed to think better of it.

"No, my son, I think you should keep the food. I don't seem to need it as much now…" he whispered and I smiled at him, uncomfortable, but not wanting to just ignore him. "Do you have news, then?" he prompted, and I blinked, remembering that had been his first question.

"Not so much. As near as I can tell, there's no real news about the world. The power is off, probably gone forever, and people are…changing. They're attacking each other, killing and taking. It's not good, Father," I said sadly.

"I know," he whispered, wiping at tears that appeared suddenly. "The apostate has come, the darkness has risen, and the end of days is upon us. The living envy the dead, and beasts are desecrating the graveyards…we have been abandoned!" His hands clutched at each other, and he twisted them, as though trying to wring the fingers from their sockets.

"Oh…sorry." I said, wincing, knowing it was a terrible thing to say, but having no clue what I could say to make it all right. It wasn't as though me saying 'oh, it's okay, it's not your faith, it's a bunch of aliens, I think…' was going to make him feel any better. Still, I had to try.

"Uh, look, there's a lot of evidence so far that it's aliens, not Judgment Day, okay?" I said, my explanation sounding weak as hell even to my own ears.

"It's the end of days," he repeated, slowly shaking his head. "It may not be the way we envisaged it, but we were warned that the dead would rise, the good to the resurrection of life, and the evil to judgment…I've seen them, I've seen the evil, crawling across the graveyard, feeding…".

"Wait, what?" I asked, looking at him in shock. "You've seen the dead rising?" He nodded slowly, still wiping tears from his cheeks. "Fuck's sake, Father, look at me! You've seen the dead rising?" I snapped at him, and he fixed me with a look that told me to watch myself, or he'd scrub my mouth out with soap.

"Some have already dragged themselves from their earthly graves…they've started to gather. They feed on the weak that try to pass through. I…I have to try to exorcise them, I have to try to save them, but I cannot…I'm weak, my faith is weak…" he mumbled, going back to wringing his hands and softly weeping.

I tried to talk to him more, asking him questions, but he started to rock slowly, singing to himself, and I couldn't get through to him again. I set the bag down, pulling a few chocolate bars, another drink and two cans of food out, setting them next to him before awkwardly making the sign of the cross over him and moving on. I wasn't a believer, and I didn't know if I'd done something appropriate, but I knew it had felt like the right thing to do.

I considered trying to get him to come with me, but I knew in my heart that I wouldn't be able to, and that he'd never understand.

I wished him good luck and set off again, trudging on as the early afternoon sunlight changed, the clouds rolling in. I picked up the pace as the wind changed, a chill, blustery squall evident in the distance. I began to grow nervous that I wouldn't make it in time as I started down Northumberland street, eying the clouds over Gateshead that were growing darker. The few people that were still about moved quicker, as well.

I took the side streets, passing as quickly as I was able, up and down, crossing the city in as direct a path as I could manage, glad when I reached the edge of the high mana zone fairly quickly. This time, in an attempt to avoid notice from anyone else in the area, I'd taken a different path.

As I passed the old cathedral, I heard sounds from inside, rising through the broken ground floor windows on one side, and I noticed the burgeoning feeling of danger again. I paused, thinking at first it might be the priest I'd seen before, as I heard what sounded like someone crying. I moved closer until I heard giggling, which froze me in place, before a sharp snap of something and growling rose from inside.

"No! Mine!" I heard a high pitched, croaky voice say, followed by the thump of something hitting flesh, hard. There was a whine, followed by the sounds of someone eating, crunching and gnawing on something, and I shook my head, deciding I wanted nothing to do with whatever was inside.

I started moving away quickly, but as my case dropped down from the curb, I hit a glass bottle, sending it clattering away. I glared down the street at the bottle as it rolled away, then looked back on a whim.

I froze in truth. Staring back at me from the window was a face.

It looked like a little girl, her brown hair still plaited and partially covered by a dirty off-white headdress of some kind, the veil twisted and hanging half off. But her face…She stared at me, open hunger in her eyes. Her skin was grey, and her mouth ragged. Blood coated her tiny lips and dripped from her chin, falling out of sight. Her eyes were bright blue, but in a way that I instinctively knew was all kinds of wrong. They seemed to glow, and as I watched, she shifted, moving to another broken window, one that was closer to me. She vanished from sight, then reappeared at the other, in less time than it would take me to travel the distance. Fair enough; sometimes kids are surprisingly fast, I knew, but as she smiled at me and tilted her head, the movements were sharp, like a bird's, and the second 'wrong' thing became clear…

The section of window she was looking at me from was at least ten foot off the ground, and she'd run to it like she was on level ground. I'd been in that cathedral before. An ex had taken me in once to look around, and I *knew* that there was nothing on the far side that she could have walked across.

I heard snuffling coming from inside again, then growling, and when I looked back at the girl, she grabbed some of the glass and tore it free to get a better look at me, ripping the material as though it was paper, not stained glass reinforced with lead.

She reached a hand out, as though expecting me to come and take it, and I backed away fast, making her hiss in displeasure. Her flesh was grey and filthy, smeared liberally with blood. The nails were sharp, more like talons, and the skin looked to be…scaled…

I started backing away faster and faster, and she started to keen at me, clearly angry, and the sound cut through me, making me feel cold and alone. I swallowed hard, feeling numb and afraid.

There was no point, a little voice said inside me, *no point in going on, not if I was going to be alone. Instead, I could go inside the cathedral. I could be with the girl...and the others...I'd never be alone again! No more fear, no more pain...*

My foot caught on the curb behind me, tripping me and sending me falling. My case and bag clattering to the ground with me, while the sword hilt banged me in the side of the head...and I suddenly felt like someone had poured a bucket of cold water over me. I blinked, and shook myself, hearing another hiss, one of fury this time. Wasting no time, I grabbed my gear, darting to my feet and fleeing from the creature.

My stumbling feet still going on autopilot had been all that saved me back there, I knew, and I was determined to get as far away as possible, as the keening lifted into the air again behind me.

I ran, my arms full of my possessions, and my heart thudded in time with my feet. I took the far corner as quick as I could, slipping on the cobbles, and had to jump aside as I nearly ran over a short, fat man coming the other way.

"Look out!" he snapped at me, jumping back as I dodged to the side.

"The...cathedral!" I said to him, trying to catch my breath. "There's something in there! Don't go near it!"

"Idiot!" the man snapped, shaking his head as I tried to rearrange things in my arms. "You're another fool that's running away because of a power cut! Well, go on, get out! The city and the rest of us will be better off without your sort!"

I looked at him, my fear clear on my face, and he paused, considering me. I thought maybe, just maybe, he'd listen...then my hand caught a packet in the bag, accidentally tipping it onto the floor along with a tube of toothpaste and some toilet roll.

We both ignored the common, sundry items, but the little wrap of white paper unfurled, gleaming white powder as innocent-looking as snow blowing from it, and the atmosphere changed again. The man sneered at me in disgust, spitting at me and stalking off, heading toward the cathedral.

"Goddamn druggies!" he snarled. I shook my head, calling out and trying to explain, but he ignored me, marching on.

I watched him go before gathering everything up and moving again, heading up to the alley. The gates were still open, presumably from whoever had robbed the bar last night. I moved to my doors, and they opened for me at a mental push. I ducked inside, dragging the suitcase, feeling relief filling me as

I did so, until an agonized scream echoed up in the distance, and I knew it came from the man, having strayed too close to that creature.

I panicked, dragging my gear inside and ordering the doors to close before hurrying down the stairs in the dark and rushing out into the Core room. I threw myself into the couch and pulled up the map, making sure there wasn't anything in the building or anywhere nearby.

I scoured the image for a long time, making sure the area was clear before finally relaxing. The adrenaline crash made me shake like a shitting dog.

I pushed out with the Dungeon senses into the room instead, going through the bag first, scanning and making sure it could reproduce the patterns for the food and various items I had brought back. Then I rolled the sleeping bag out and curled up in it, eating some chocolate and trying to calm myself, before I finally fell asleep.

THIRTEEN

IT WAS HOURS later when I woke up. I knew because I was desperate for the toilet, and when I checked, I couldn't see anything happening on the streets outside. My watch had stopped; the wind-up mechanism needed to be rewound, but I had no clue what time it was now, so I shrugged and accepted that it probably didn't matter anymore.

I used the toilet and checked the research screens, seeing that the 'Mana Absorption' research had finished, and the stick was nearly two thirds of its way to an upgrade as well. I pulled up the completed one, seeing that it was now a blueprint, and it had been automatically added to the list I had access to.

Mana Absorption Upgrade 1

Improved conduits have been uncovered, allowing an increase of 0.75 Mana per collector, per hour. Complete further research to improve this rate of absorption.

When I looked over the blueprints, I couldn't make sense of them, but when I opened the design screen, I discovered that the conduit that reached out from the Core into the air, apparently just large enough that I could actually see it with the naked eye, could now be improved. I zoomed in, using the Dungeon senses, and examined it. A dozen small filaments reached out from tiny holes in the Core and stretched into the air. I selected them, finding that each could access a small amount of the ambient mana and was collecting it, drawing it inside.

"How much mana is in the air?" I asked the room in general, but I got no answer. I watched the process for a while, noting the way the thin strands moved, as though blowing in a non-existent wind. "Can we extend these?" I muttered, reaching out with my mind and 'pulling' on them, excited to feel them slowly lengthening. I tried harder and then stopped dead, as one of them came away in my mental grasp, and the mana absorption rate, which had been slowly climbing as I drew the strands out, dropped again, this time to five point six, despite the improved collectors' research.

I swallowed hard and started again, mentally prodding at the now-empty hole where the mana collection strand had been. After a few attempts, I got a single strand to emerge again. It was a fraction of a hair in thickness, but as I concentrated on it, I sensed different metals and possibly organics inside of it. I stared at it fixedly, feeding mana into it and carefully re-growing it.

It was slow, painstaking work, but after an hour, the Core was back up to six points, and two hours after that, I had refined the process down enough that I was up to eight points per hour now. I sagged back, my mental goal reached, and I fed the additional two points per hour into research, joining the previous three.

The stick upgrade was complete, having finished at some point while I was working, and I pulled it up, groaning as I looked at it.

Crude Stick > Rough Stick
Your starter design 'Crude Stick' has been successfully upgraded to 'Rough Stick,' improving both durability and damage. Increase this design further to unlock additional capabilities.
Damage 2 > 3
Durability 4 > 6

"What a waste of time!" I muttered, shaking my head. It'd finished, finally, but man, that 'upgrade' was shit. I pulled up the 'defense' section, dejected to find a collection of 'rough spun' clothing, consisting of pants, soft shoes, and a smock. I just shook my head. Wasn't happening. Nothing in the miscellaneous section was useful either, but bringing up the 'Dungeon' section, I saw there were a few new options available. They were split into Facilities, Blueprints, Traps and Magics.

I looked over each one quickly, pleased to find that the Facilities tab offered living quarters as one of the first upgrades, amongst dozens of others. They were classed as 'Crude' living quarters, and I doubted they'd have a more luxurious bed than the one I already had in my sofa, but the thought of running water really made me consider it. I had no idea if that would be part of the design, and betted that it would be a tap if it did, not a power-shower, but still…

Blueprints were random, it seemed; I might get a really useful blueprint, or I might not, but a 'feeling' told me that blueprints were much easier and faster to upgrade than solid items, so that was a definite option as well.

Traps, I dismissed out of hand. I needed them, but if I ever got the kobolds as creatures in the dungeon, they'd make the traps anyway.

The magic, though? That, I was interested in! There was one spell available currently: Fear.

Dungeon Spells

Fear:

Fear is a standard general purpose spell, used primarily to drive away low level adventurers or monsters while the Dungeon is being remodeled.

Cost*:* 100 mana to cast, with a further 10 mana per minute active.

AOE*:* 5 meters, but can be increased for a further 10 mana per meter, per minute active.

The upgrade path was slightly different, in that it went from level one to five, reducing noticeably in cost and increasing in effect, and there was a new spell to research. The next spell available was 'Burning Hands.' I considered it, I really did, as that could be awesome; not so much Fear, although that could be useful, but Burning Hands sounded both awesome, and like it'd help me make short work of the creature in the Cathedral.

Lastly, I pulled up the Nodes options, and my jaw dropped at finding they were essentially magical item generators! They were split into three sections: Research, Environment and Mana. Apparently, I could use Research to create a secondary spin-off section that the Core would then physically have to build, but once it was done, it would act as a secondary generator of research, which would be great, if I had the mana to run it.

I looked through the Environment version, and found it would either generate a secondary 'bubble' that would slowly grow out, attaching a secondary location to the Dungeon, or create a specialist environment in that area. I could see that being useful, depending on how efficient it was, but there was little specific detail on either option. Once again, I needed the mana before I could claim a second area, and unless I could recreate the beach in Crete, with the hot sun, sand, and sea, *plus the booze, food, and women*, I wasn't sure about it yet.

Lastly, though, Mana raised some interesting possibilities, as it was a specialized node that would suck in the ambient mana and convert it to a specific form; the notes used 'nature' as an example, being a mixture of 'Air, Earth, and Water Mana' that would increase growth of crops in a set area. Or Dryads, apparently…

Again, interesting, but not really useful at this early stage.

I sat thinking, trying to figure out the best way of doing this. I knew that I really needed everything, but in the end, I decided that what I needed to concentrate on was me. The Dungeon was seriously important to my survival, I got that; but for now, at least, it wasn't going to bring in a great deal of anything until it managed to upgrade. I could run it like a game, focusing on building up the infrastructure, or doing research, so that I was ahead of other 'players,' if there were others out there, but this wasn't a game.

It was my life.

I needed to do whatever gave me the best chance of survival, and falling into the trap of treating this situation like a game could kill me. Especially with that creature out there.

I needed to be as strong as possible, and I needed to get that goddamn fairy corpse back. I especially needed to be ready if that creature came sniffing around, or if the thieves from upstairs managed to get inside.

For now, that meant a slight restructuring of the Dungeon and my own priorities.

I had eight points per hour coming in right now, so I could recharge the Core to full every twelve and a half hours, if I put them all into it. For now, I directed six points into charging, and two for research, and I determined that I needed to increase the Dungeon above ground, claiming the next floor and all of those that came thereafter. For my security and the safety of the Core, I needed to secure the facility, and with that in mind, I pulled up the Core Research tree and assigned both points to the improved Mana Absorption option, knowing it'd take a while to get there.

Then I emptied out the bags I'd brought and pulled up the Dungeon Design tab, using the facility to scan everything I'd brought. It took literal hours, examining them one by one, and several times, I accidentally did the same one more than once, when my mind wandered through boredom.

Some items, I could assign as loot straight away with no problems, such as food, which was a vast relief. Bandages were available as well, as was the sewing kit, but only a lower-leveled version. The kit contained rough thread and had stone needles, for example. I'd found that items such as my sword would be reproduced as a wooden club; it just made a bigger one than the standard version.

In the end, though, I was ready for the final phase of my master plan.

I got up, cleared everything away, and took a few deep breaths, acknowledging my notifications and swiping them aside.

Congratulations!

You have gained one level in Firearms!

At level One, you gain an increased chance to hit your target by 1%. This stacks with the class of firearms, such as a 5% chance to hit with energy weapons becoming a combined 6%. 1% chance of familiarity with unknown firearms, also gained. Increased familiarity with said Firearm will increase this chance.

I grunted, dismissing it and moving on.

Congratulations!
You have defeated two opponents classed as 'Gypsy Thug'
Thug level: 0
Your level: 4
XP awarded: 50

I was at one hundred and sixty-five out of five hundred XP to reach level five, and I took the time to drop the three points I'd kept in reserve into Luck, figuring I was going to need it.

Then I concentrated and summoned my first goblin, after tying a packet of cheese and onion crisps to it as a loot drop, along with the thing I really wanted…a Skillbook, Spellbook, or magical item. I had literally a one-in-ten-thousand chance of it dropping, but that was why I'd increased my Luck.

The creature began to take shape before me, tiny infinitesimal motes of light streaming out from the Core and flooding the area. I watched in fascination as it built up slowly in a manner that seemed weirdly like a 3D printer, layer upon layer, until it slowed, and then stopped altogether, the final motes settling onto a rough, green skin and sinking in.

The creature blinked at me uncertainly, then looked around, as if unsure of what was going on. It was short, maybe two feet tall, bipedal, with long, sharp-looking claws at the tips of its three-toed feet and hands.

The hands were webbed at the base, with three long fingers and a stubby thumb, and its head was massive for its tiny body, with huge ears that trailed behind it as it turned its head. The mouth was downturned, like a fish, with only a few large, pointed teeth in it. Black eyes with red pupils inspected the walls, and a little tuft of hair lifted from the top of its head, wafting aimlessly.

It was built more like a toddler than a small man, with the large bulbous belly that protruded out far enough that it looked like it might overbalance. Thankfully, it wore a tiny loincloth.

It looked up at me, chuffing out a sound, but when I didn't respond, it started scratching itself and dropped to all fours, sniffing around the room and wandering here and there.

Clearly a creature summoned by myself didn't view me as a threat, I guessed, and I faced the first major hurdle of my plan.

Could I murder a creature I'd just created?

I watched it for a minute, until it caught a scent and raced across to my piled supplies. It dove in, and a few seconds later, it reappeared, dragging the mixed box of crisps I'd not opened yet. It shredded the cardboard with its nails and plunged its nose inside, sniffing loudly.

"Hey!" I called, annoyed. "Get off that!" I started forward, and it lifted its head, an unsealed bag of tomato crisps clutched in its teeth. It backed up, tugging at the bag and growling, until the crisps fell free and it started munching on them.

"You sick little bastard…" I muttered, shaking my head as I saw its choice.

The head came up again, and it growled at me, looking from me to the box of crisps and back, before flexing its claws in clear threat.

I quickly revised the opinion I'd held about them not attacking me, I guessed that I was actually viewed as a neutral entity until I did something it considered hostile. Getting between the goblin and food made me a threat, and that made me feel so much better.

"Oh, thank god," I muttered, drawing my sword back and dropping into 'guard stance,' feet shoulder width apart and right foot trailing, sword held upright, but the point angled at my target at a forty-five degree angle.

It growled at me again, then sprang forward, snarling, and swiped at me. I stepped back, then again, getting an idea of its speed and range of movement and attacking as it made its third leap.

I stepped forward, swinging across my body from right to left, fast, and then stepping back after I'd hit it. It went flying with a crunch of breaking bones, hitting the floor and sliding a good foot before it came to a halt. My sword had impacted just to the left side of its neck as it jumped, snapping the clavicle and several ribs and smashing the small form to the floor, where it coughed out blood and twitched.

I stepped in and brought the sword down on its head, killing the goblin quickly.

As soon as the creature was dead, I got a notification, and I pulled it up eagerly as the corpse slowly dissolved, leaving behind a single packet of cheese and onion crisps. I nodded to myself in satisfaction and looked at the log.

Congratulations!

You have defeated a Dungeon Opponent classed as 'Pathetic Goblin'

Goblin level: 1

Your level: 4

XP awarded: 10

(Note: XP is halved, due to creature being a summoned monster.)

That penalty was something I could live with. I got eight points an hour in mana charge for the dungeon, and the goblin took five per summoning, so I couldn't just pound them out, but as a proof of concept, it worked.

I checked the sword, making sure it was okay, then put the crisps aside, planning on trying them later. I checked the area to verify that nobody was up above, and nodded to myself. It was time to get some shit done.

I had thirty percent charge at the minute, so I needed to bring some stuff to the dungeon to be destroyed. As there was nobody in the alley or the surrounding street right now, that seemed like the perfect time to do it. There wasn't even a figure upstairs in Florita's anymore, but there was also a lot less in the way of stock, from what I could see on the wireframe map.

I decided I'd get as much junk down as I could, then push the Dungeon control out to the gates to the alley and seal them. Once I had control over those, I could start on the surrounding buildings in peace, stripping them to the ground and sealing the whole place up.

I quickly headed upstairs, double checking that the map was clear before moving outside, and then looking around, just to make sure, as soon as the doors opened.

I darted out, picking up the boxes and general debris in the alley, dragging all of it inside the doorway and returning for more, getting everything small that wasn't nailed down, including the bags of rubbish, and piling them inside the entrance, before slipping back inside and closing the doors.

It took less than a minute to select each item and absorb it, and I grinned as the Dungeon jumped up to forty-nine percent by the time I reopened the doors, dragging the big wheeled bins over to the door in turn.

I quickly closed the doors again, and separated myself into the floating, formless control state of the Dungeon. My incorporeal mind passed back through the sealed doors, pleased to see that almost a foot of extra space had been claimed by the Dungeon into the alley than there had been when I originally took the doors. I nodded in satisfaction that it was still increasing its aura or mass or whatever and started to manually push it out again.

The feeling of a soap bubble slowly expanding was there again, and I pressed it gently but firmly outwards, quickly encompassing the entire bottle bin and sinking inside to select all the bottles, absorbing them as quickly as I could.

That gave me another ten points of mana, and I used it quickly, pushing out further and further. I was finding that the cost of manual expansion was roughly equivalent to each small step I took in my mental form taking a single point of mana. I worked that out as roughly a foot per point, and saw that the alleyway, which was blocked by gates that had been forced open on each end, was around a hundred meters in length, and maybe five wide.

That gave me, with a bit of mental math, around fifteen hundred feet to go, if I claimed it all, or, around three hundred, if I went in a straight line, then claimed just the gates, leaving the rest to slowly expand out naturally.

I checked after claiming the space I needed to drain the bin, and found I had fifty-five points left; if I took off the minimum ten that the dungeon needed to keep operating, I could do forty five feet…ish.

Nowhere near enough to claim the section in a day, unless I found a better source of mana.

I slowly pushed along the wall toward the gates to my left anyway, figuring that it was better to be busy, when I sensed something.

It was small, very small, and close by, and it was full of mana…due to its size, it wasn't a huge amount, but still, it was far, far more than the rubbish had given me, and I looked around in confusion, seeing nothing there with my eyes. I concentrated on the Dungeon senses instead, and what I found shocked me.

I'd been subconsciously using the visual equivalent of the sense automatically, as that was what I was used to, but as I concentrated on the mana in the alley, not the ambient stuff that was flowing through the atmosphere, but the actual concentrations, I was shocked to realize that it was everywhere! There were piles of it, huddled in the corners of the alley, hiding in the gutters, just out of sight, in the…in the drains…I 'looked' up and saw more, fluttering from roof to roof, and I realized what the bright spots were.

They were the vermin that the city was full to the brim with; the rats, mice, and pigeons, all the things that, as a city dweller, you just ignored, and that hid from you instinctively. It was all there, and they were full of mana!

I quickly summoned a goblin into the middle of the alley, the swirl of light and energy making things shy away again, but as soon as it appeared, it dropped to the floor, snuffling.

I could sense things from it, when I was in the Dungeon system as I was now, that I'd missed when facing it directly, and I grinned as I found that I could influence it. It wasn't a command system like I was used to, at least, not like a game where I could point and click and give a command. Instead, this was more like suggesting things.

I drew its attention to an accumulation of creatures hiding in a hole in a wall near a drainpipe, and I felt the goblin's focus sharpen as soon as it sniffed them. It scrabbled forward, sniffing, then diving at the hole and ramming its claws in. It scrabbled roughly at the crumbling bricks, until there was a squeak, and a single, small, furry mouse was yanked out of its hole and shoved into the goblin's maw.

It crunched down, chewing noisily and swallowing, before diving back into the hole, widening it and hunting for more, and I mentally nodded in satisfaction at the single point of mana that it gained me. It wasn't much, but the goblin only cost me two points a day to maintain, and it'd only been a damn mouse.

I quickly summoned a second goblin, impressed on them both the need to not leave the alley, and not to be seen by any humans, and set them both at it, the need to 'feed' driving them.

In the next ten minutes, they'd killed eleven mice each for one point at a time, a single rat, which seemed huge to me, and had gained me three points, and a single terminally stupid pigeon, which gained me two points.

I couldn't reproduce any of the creatures, and I assumed that was because the goblins ate them, rather than the dungeon absorbing them, but that was fine, I decided. The cost of the Goblins was ten points, plus two each for the next day's maintenance, and they'd earned me sixteen points so far, but when I reached the closest sewer grate, I decided it was time for them to really earn their keep.

I assumed control over the grate fully, then sank down into it, sensing the multitude of life scurrying around below, including a few creatures that felt…wrong.

I decided to play it safe and summoned two more goblins, bunched all five around the edge of the grate, and then opened it.

Instantly, the scurrying mass of rats and insects scattered from the light, and I directed the goblins inside before closing the grate behind them, just in case. I couldn't see what was going on, now the grate was closed, but the goblins fed back to me a sense of their condition, and I waited.

At first, there was a sense of confusion, then hunger, as they all rocketed off into the darkness, and I hoped they could actually see down there with their weird eyes. The next few minutes were filled with a heady rush of mana and a sense of pain and fear. In the time it took me to shove the bubble out a few feet, the mana stores were almost filled, and I started pushing frantically, forcing the Dungeon's area of influence to grow, trying to make the most of it before the mana reached full and started to be wasted.

When I'd only managed a dozen feet, the charge reached a hundred and I stopped, quickly summoning another five goblins and sending them down into the sewers as well. I grinned to myself, thinking that I'd found a cheat, when a goblin suddenly vanished from the dungeon sense, followed by another, and then two more.

I felt the mana being ripped from them as something else fed on them, and I froze, staring back down the alley to the open grate. I summoned two more goblins, then a trio of rats, and sent them in to reinforce the group, before backing away, and flying back into the Dungeon, closing the doors all but a fraction, that allowed me to look out, wondering what the hell was out there.

The remaining goblins were killed quickly, as were the rats, and I sensed the other vermin in the sewers fleeing quickly as something approached. I shook myself, realizing I was being an idiot, and closed and locked the doors into the Dungeon, before floating through them and starting to push down into the sewer, remembering that I was incorporeal.

I slowly sank down into the sewer; the absence of light meant instead that I saw the mana that was leaked and absorbed by the creatures around me, and I quickly found the corpses of the goblins, the trail of cheese and onion crisps an easy way to identify them. I looked around slowly, seeing nothing else. The goblins had dissolved, fair enough. The outline of the crisp packets glowed with tiny motes of mana, and the various sludge, bits of creatures, and the boundaries of the walls around me made it easy enough to see the outline of my surroundings, but I couldn't see anything else, nothing that could have killed the goblins, certainly…

I reached out, slowly pushing the 'bubble' deeper into the sewer, spreading my influence, when a sudden sense of warning filled me. I knew it was from the Dungeon itself, and I turned full circle, staring about, trying to make sense of the feeling, but I could see nothing.

I could feel the warning growing, though, so I turned and flitted back to the ladder up to the alley above, stopping when I reached it and turning again, thinking to look about, when I saw something move, out of the corner of my eye.

I twisted around, catching a blur of movement as something whipped out of sight, back into the darkness, and I swallowed hard. I'd not seen much, just a flicker of something as it was drawn out of sight, but it'd looked like a tail, a white- grey color with bone ridges and a flexible stinger, and it wasn't near any of the goblin corpses…it was much, much closer to me.

I backed right up to the ladders, then shot up as quickly as I could into the open air, heading straight for the door into the Dungeon, when it struck. I felt pain as something passed through my 'leg', if a mental construct could be said to have one. At any rate, I felt a tug, which vanished as whatever it was retracted, passing through my form, but a second later, I felt something else grab at me, and I sank into the door, passing through and stopping on the far side, fear filling me.

Whatever that creature was, it could hurt me even in this form. I didn't want to go back out, so I brought up the wireframe map of the area, zooming in on the alleyway, and got another shock.

It was empty.

FOURTEEN

WHATEVER WAS OUT there wasn't registering on the Dungeon senses, and it somehow hid its mana signature. The things I'd sensed down in the sewers that were 'wrong' were the size of rats, and this fucker was clearly bigger!

I 'heard' it snuffling on the other side of the barrier between us, then prying at the doors. I fled to my body and slowly backed away, bracing myself against the far wall before slipping into the Dungeon sense again and forcing myself to think about what I was going to do.

I needed to kill the fucker, whatever it was, as it was clearly a threat to me and to the Dungeon, but I couldn't even see the damn thing, so I needed to come up with a plan. First and foremost, I needed to distract the fucker, though.

I quickly summoned two goblins and three rats outside, the first goblin being shredded apart before it was completed, but the second lasted long enough to scream in fear and then pain as something tore into it. The three rats, I drove past the killing area and down into the sewers. The first was killed before it reached them, the second just inside, and the third as it started to flee down one side of the stinking tunnel, but that was all right, because as soon as I felt the second one die, I'd ordered the grate closed.

It closed easily enough, and the death of the third one made me confident that I'd drawn whatever it was back inside, when something hit the grate. Something hard.

It started to take damage, and I instinctively knew it was losing its durability. The ten points I somehow knew the grate had dropped to eight, then seven, then five, then four, and finally stopped at three, as I summoned another three rats at the bottom of the ladder, sending them squeaking into the darkness and drawing the creature away.

As soon as it was gone, I pulled the grate up in my Dungeon sense, staying inside, just in case, and selected 'repair,' or at least I tried to. It was greyed out.

I could open or close it, but nothing else, and I swore, hoping the creature wouldn't come back. I waited a handful of minutes, and was about to give up, when I heard a scream from the alley outside, somewhere down by the end of the street.

I swore viciously, and slowly pushed myself through the door, seeing nothing in the alley. I looked all around, finding thin claw marks in the door I was sheltering behind, and more in the walls nearby. I started to follow them, the sense of danger slowly sinking away, until a second, louder scream came from the distance, and a howl of pain. I heard people shouting, and then more screams, and I looked back at the grate, frantically selecting it. It allowed me to repair it this time, and I ordered that done, as well as the door, which had fallen from thirty points to twenty-six, as I tried to convince myself that whatever was happening wasn't my fault.

A pained scream rose in the distance, echoing off the buildings around me, and I failed utterly. My avatar fled back inside as I wrestled with myself, finally swearing and slamming the doors open, running outside in my own body with my sword in hand. I looked from side to side, then up, making sure there wasn't anything lurking in the alley, then ordered the doors to close as I set off running in the direction the scream had come from.

"This is such a bad idea..." I mumbled to myself as I ran, squeezing out through the wedged bins at the opposite end of the alley to the one I normally left by. The back of the job center sat across the street from me, the cathedral down the road to my right, which I stared at a second, making sure there was nothing in sight, and then I looked up to the left, where all of the bars and clubs up that way were shuttered.

I paused, trying to decide which way to go, then thought 'fuck it' and ran to the right, coming around the corner of the job center and facing the cathedral across the road. At first, I didn't see anything, but then something skittered across the inside of the stained glass in the tower...something that looked far too long and thin.

I swallowed hard and forced myself to look away, down to the left, toward the apartments further down the road. I ran that way, searching as I went, desperately hoping I'd see whatever it was before it saw me.

I both won and lost that hope when I turned the next corner, coming upon two bodies on the ground. One had been torn half apart, a horrifying mess from the waist up; the other...the other was suspended in the air, getting shaken from side to side, as something fed upon it.

As blood sprayed from the bites, the creature would become visible, then the blood would run down, or be shook off, and it would fade from sight again.

Whatever it was, it was tall, standing on two legs that bent back at the knee, like a goat. The tail that flicked and swished in the air was thin, with bumps that made me think of a spine, and finished at the tip with a bulbous stinger, like that of a scorpion.

The upper half of the body was stained by more blood than the lower, and I could see the arms that awkwardly held the corpse aloft. They were rail thin, but filled with a wiry strength, changing below the elbow from wiry muscle into long, solid spurs of bone, one jammed deeply into the corpse it fed on.

The head was the worst, eyeless, with small holes for ears. The humanoid skull was covered with flesh that was apparently smoothed over the eye sockets, no nose, just slits, and a long jaw that was filled with razor sharp teeth. The tip of a long, thick tongue flashed out and wiped across its face, spreading the blood about before whipping back inside as the head came down, biting deep.

It chewed and slobbered noisily, the reek of the sewers clearly rising from it, yet it stood there, unconcerned, in the middle of the street as it feasted. I paused, knowing that there was nothing I could do for the victims, and I wondered if I could get away before it saw me, until a small dog approached from further up the street.

It was a cross breed, my mind, randomly throwing up details, informed me. I stared, hoping against hope it'd choose discretion over valor and flee. Probably a rottweiler and Pitbull cross, judging from the size of it, it was young, still a puppy, but the leash that flapped as it ran forward told me that it'd lost its owner.

Somewhere behind it, I heard a child cry out, calling for the dog, and I had to bite down to stop myself from swearing aloud.

The creature lifted its head, hissing at the dog, which slid to a halt and started barking at it incessantly. The creature dropped the woman's remains and turned, presenting its back to me. It hunched forward, landing on the bone spurs of its lower arms as its tail whipped up overhead, swaying as it aimed for the dog.

Even now, I considered running, or at least slinking away, as I looked at the creature. I was damn sure it was beyond me, until a young girl ran into view at the top of the road, shouting for the dog to 'come here'. At the child's appearance, the creature shifted, focusing in on her, and the tail went still, the barking dog forgotten.

I didn't know why it wasn't interested in me at the minute, or if I'd just been overlooked in the search for more interesting prey, but I was damn thankful. Even then, I considered running, even with the child and a puppy in danger, but when it took its first slow step toward them, I moved as well, forcing myself to act, despite the cowardice that filled my heart.

I ran at it from behind, the noise of my trainers on the cobbles masked by the barking of the dog and the sudden scream of the child as she saw everything: the creature, the bodies, the blood…

The camouflage the creature used was good; disturbingly good. It was fading from view even as I rushed it, but the blood that stained it kept it at least partially visible, and that was enough.

The creature clearly sensed something as I closed the last few feet, as it started to turn, but by then, I'd already swung, doing exactly what Markus had told me not to do. I swung for the fences, a move that, if you missed, left you totally open to a counterattack, as it took you totally off balance.

But I didn't miss.

I slammed the blunt length of steel and rubber into the base of its tail where it joined the spine, and I felt the impact through my hands as it hit. I jumped back as the thing howled and whipped around, the tail sagging and falling to the ground, useless and broken. It screeched at me, fury, hatred, and pain in full force, and I roared back, my fear gone, now that it was too late to run.

I stepped back again and again, shifting my feet as quickly as I could, while I swung the sword from side to side, keeping it back. It glowered at me, its jaw hanging low as it hissed, and the long, prehensile tongue flickered back and forth. It tried to move to my left, and it staggered, its balance off as it tripped on its own flaccid tail. It glared down, wondering what had tripped it.

I saw my chance and stepped forward, punching forward with my right fist and pulling down with my left, my two-handed grip on the sword's hilt enough to whip it around with blurring speed. It connected with the creature's left shoulder and I heard a snap of bones…before the counterattack of the thing's right arm landed, sending me flying.

My leg hit a bollard as I flew back, sending me arse over tit, and I slammed into the ground, face first, grunting in pain and shock. I shook myself, looking up, and shoving myself to the right as the creature landed right where I'd been. I rolled again as it lunged for me, and then rolled back, kicking out at its wounded arm.

It screamed, buckling and falling on top of me. I had a split second in which I heard my own voice saying calmly in my ear: *'Well, that didn't work out quite as we'd hoped, now did it…'*

Then it slammed into me, the next several seconds passed in a blur as we thrashed around. It kept trying to bite me, or to get enough leverage to lift itself up, and I was frantically fighting to not get my face bitten off. I braced my left hand against its skull, shoving it back as it attempted to sink its teeth into me, then punched it as hard as I could, feeling amazement as it drew back. I'd struck bones when I'd punched it, and I was sure I'd felt them give, possibly break...

In that instant, the fight changed, as I went back on the offensive. The horrific creature suddenly shifted from a possibly unbeatable monster...to one of flesh and blood. I changed my motivation from trying to buy the girl and her dog enough time to flee, into a determination to kill this fucker before it got anyone else.

I twisted, grabbing at its throat and punching it again and again. It whipped me from side to side, breaking my grip and throwing me into the air before backing up, hissing at me in fury.

I rolled back to my feet, gritting my teeth and ignoring the pain of being repeatedly slammed into the cobbles as I faced the creature, the dog still barking.

"Get out of here!" I roared to my right, not taking my eyes off the creature. "Get out of here, and take the dog with you!" The creature lunged for me, its jaws snapping shut a few inches from my face, and I punched it, then backed up, glancing around for my sword. I'd lost it at some point; I thought it had been when it'd hit me into the air, but where...

I looked to the right, then the left, searching, and before I could straighten up, the thing was on me, the bone spur of the remaining good arm slamming into me and punching through my upper right shoulder, just to the left of the joint. I screamed, my right arm twisting spasmodically, then hanging loose.

I dangled from the impalement, then I was slammed down into the floor on my back, my head smacking off the paving slabs of the path. Despite the pain, I sneered up at the creature as it hunched over me.

As I'd been slammed down, I'd felt something bounce against my chest, and I reached into my hoodie's front pocket in a stupor, desperate for anything I could use as a weapon. I curled my fingers around the grip and pulled it free, pointing up and grinning at the creature as I flicked the safety off. I mentally kicked myself, suddenly knowing that this whole fight could have ended much quicker, if only I'd taken the time to think, rather than reacting.

It hissed at me, opening its jaws wider, and was about to bite, when I pulled the trigger, once, twice...a third time.

The holes the small handgun blew in the creature were bigger than seemed right to me, but I wasn't going to complain as the bullets slammed home. The first took it in the lower chest, lifting it into the air, the second caused a blossom of blood to unfurl at the base of its neck, as the top of its spine was pulverized and blown into the air out of the back, but the third was the charm. The other two would have killed it, I realized later, but the third impacted just a few inches above the upper lip and took the entire top of its skull off in a welter of blood and brain.

It fell backwards, the force of the bullets hurling it from me as I laid on the ground, staring up at the sky and wondering what the hell was happening to me, that these injuries were my new normal.

I coughed and reached up towards my shoulder, before remembering what was in my hand and putting it back in my hoodie. I reached up again with my left hand, gingerly touching my shoulder, then my head, as I tried to sit up. The world spun from the blow to the head.

I shuffled backward, resting my back against the nearest bollard, and looked around the street. The girl had finally got the leash on the dog and was staring at me, and at the creature. She was young, probably ten or so, but I wasn't really good with guessing kid's ages, and I was a mess right then, anyway.

I coughed and spat some blood on the floor, groaning as I levered myself to my feet. I looked down at the thing, then pulled the gun out and struggled to slip the three loose bullets I'd taken from Keith's corpse into the clip. I didn't know too much about guns, not beyond what I'd seen on TV, and that was the first time I'd fired one outside of the ranges in America, so I resolved to look it over when I got back, to make sure I hadn't damaged it or anything…

"Hey Mister…you okay?" came a shy voice, and I turned around. The girl had moved a bit closer and was staring at me, in between looking wide-eyed at the corpses and telling her dog to be quiet.

"Yeah…" I muttered, then coughed and spat more blood on the cobbles.

"It's rude to spit!" she scolded me, and I grinned at her.

"Make sure you remember that when you're older; it'll make you popular…" I said without thinking, then coughed again.

"What?" she asked, confused, and I shook my head, regretting the throwaway comment.

"Nothing, sorry…just a bit confused." I sighed. "Look, what are you doing here?" I fixed her with a glare. "It's not safe, not around here."

"I…Spot ran away…I had to catch him…" she said in a small voice.

"Seriously, kid, next time, let the dog go," I advised, feeling horrible for saying it, but thinking it was the best way to keep her safe. "Oh…and why 'Spot'? He's not got a single spot on him?" I glanced at the dog.

"That's why!" she said, smiling brightly, and I shrugged, in no state to debate children's logic.

"Where do you live?" I asked and she pointed back over her shoulder in the direction of Gateshead. "Well, that's a bugger. How far?" I asked her, and she sniffled.

"By the park..."

"Saltwell Park?" I clarified, and she nodded sadly.

"Oh, fuck that," I said, shaking my head. "Look, kid, it's..."

"Amy," she interrupted.

"...what?" I looked down at her, confused.

"I'm not 'kid'; my name's Amy," she repeated stubbornly.

"Okay, sorry, Amy, but it's getting dark, and Saltwell Park is a long way from here. Plus, the bastard gypsies are there..." I growled.

"That's not a nice thing to say!" she scolded me, and I raised one eyebrow at her.

"Really, kid?" I asked and she glared even fiercer. "Okay...sorry. Amy. But seriously, that's a hell of a long way to go in the dark...how long were you chasing the damn dog?"

"All day! He got out yesterday. My momma went to the park to ask for help. When she didn't come back and the bad men told me to go away, I went looking for Spot on my own."

"The 'bad men'?" I asked her, then nodded in understanding. "The guys around the outside of Saltwell Park? The gypsies?" She nodded, sniffling and rubbing her nose, and I swore under my breath, having a fairly good idea what had happened to her mom after my own run-in with the gypsies.

"Uh, is she pretty; your momma, I mean?" I asked her, and she smiled through her tears, nodding quickly.

"Momma is the most beautiful woman in the whole wide world!"

"Yeah, I thought she might be..." I muttered. "Look, kid, you got somewhere to stay?" I asked and she looked over her shoulder towards Gateshead hesitantly. "Fuck," I muttered eloquently. "Okay, kid, you can stay with me for the night. I've got enough food, and then tomorrow...well, we'll figure tomorrow out tomorrow..."

"Momma told me not to go with strange men..." she said dubiously, and I looked down, seeing the state of my clothes, torn, bloody, and recalling that I'd literally just put a gun out of sight.

"Yeah, that's good advice, ki...Amy. Thing is, though, I literally just fought some kinda demon thing to stop it from hunting and eating people, so while I'm not gonna force you to go anywhere, I'd ask that if you're not coming, you start running. This area is dangerous, and the further away you are, the safer you'll be."

I pulled the fabric back from my shoulder, inspecting the wound and swearing under my breath, then looked at the corpse of the creature, and at my sword. I needed my sword, but I couldn't help wondering about the creature…I had a Dungeon that could replicate things I brought in, and they left me in control of the creatures I made, more or less. Could I make one of these? Seemed like it'd be a far better hunter than the damn goblins were.

I glanced back at the kid, catching her looking around and clutching the dog's lead tight, as though unsure of what to do.

"Amy…" I said, and I waited for her to look at me before I went on. "I'm sorry about your mum. I don't know what happened to her, but hopefully she's back home now, waiting for you. Thing is, it's honestly dangerous to try to make your way there now. If you wait until morning, I'll take you home myself, okay? I could do with a little help here, and you'll be safe, I promise."

"Promise?" she asked, and I heard the desperation in her voice as she spoke.

"I promise. Anything that tries to hurt you will have to go through me first," I said firmly. She nodded and wiped her cheeks, smearing dirt and tears across her face.

"Okay…but you'll take me to my momma tomorrow, right?" she pleaded, and I paused, thinking how easy it would be to just lie…

"No, Amy…" I said after a few seconds. "I hope your momma is at home waiting for you, but I don't know it for sure. I'll take you back to your home, though, and I'll try to help you. That's the best I can promise."

"Okay…" she said quietly, and I could tell she was on the brink of tears again.

"Right, then, Amy, I need you to keep a tight hold on…Spot…and go pick my sword up. You see it over there?" I asked, pointing to the sword. She nodded, and I moved to the creature's corpse as she grabbed my sword.

"What are you doing?" she asked, horrified and backing up as I grabbed onto one of the arms, hauling it more or less into a fireman's carry over my left shoulder with a pained groan.

"I need it," I grunted out, shifting it until it was as comfortable as I could get it. It wasn't particularly heavy, just awkward;, the damn thing was too long in the arm and leg, and as I started stumbling up the street, making sure to head away from the cathedral, I kept almost tripping on its feet, which dangled in front of my own.

We walked up the street to the middle of the Bigg Market, before turning left, and left again, going back down the street that led parallel, finally ducking into the alley at the back of my building. All the while, I was peppered with incessant questions by Amy, until we got halfway along the alley and a particularly loud 'But why' from her provoked a response from the sewer grate.

It shook, and the screech of bone spurs against metal reverberated through the alleyway, making us both freeze in place. I swallowed, glaring at her, as I'd been telling her to be quiet seemingly every other word since we set off, and she nodded finally, wide-eyed.

I flexed a mental muscle, and the doors popped open to the dungeon. Amy gasped, backing up.

"No!" I hissed to her, "it's okay, that's where I live…" I nodded to the doors, then staggered inside, trying to ignore the screech and battering at the grate. I moved around it quickly and threw the corpse down onto the floor inside the door, kicking it off to one side as she ran in after me, dragging Spot, who had started barking furiously at the grate.

"For the love of god, shut him up!" I snapped at her as I closed the doors and sent my mind into the Dungeon senses. I reached out and checked the grate, chagrined to find that it only had two points of durability left, and that as long as the creature was interacting with it, I couldn't affect it, not even to do repairs.

I swore and shook my head, turning to the little girl and the dog. Suddenly I became aware that it was pitch black inside, and while I was used to it, they weren't.

"Okay, stay still and stay quiet. I'm moving over to you, and I'll carry the dog. You just concentrate on walking down the stairs, all right? There's light at the bottom," I reassured her, moving carefully over to where they had been standing when the closure of the doors had cut the light off entirely.

I'd considered using the lighter, but I figured holding a dog that didn't know me and a flame in the other hand wouldn't end well. I reached out blindly, and after a few seconds, I found the leash. Following it down, I picked the dog up, muttering soothingly to it, even as I felt Amy grab onto my other arm. I fought to stifle a groan as the wound shifted.

We headed downstairs slowly, moving into the Core room after only a minute, where I put the dog down and gave Amy the 'grand tour'. It consisted of; 'leave *that* alone…toilets are over there, there's a couch to rest on, and a sleeping bag, food is over there, and there's my stash of pop and juice, help yourself…'

"Is this really where you live?" she asked me after a few minutes, her eyes being continually drawn back to the rotating, glowing core.

"It is," I said simply. "I used to have a flat, but the gypsies attacked me there, trying to rob me, and now I live here. I know it's a bit weird, but it has its benefits."

"Like what?" she asked, and I opened my mouth before closing it with a click. I'd been about to tell her about the Core, mainly because it was so cool, and I'd not had anyone to really talk to since the end of the world, not normally. I remembered just in time that she was a kid, and she'd tell everyone she met about it if I did.

In the end, I shrugged and finished lamely that it 'just did'. Luckily, a screech from outside interrupted our conversation.

"Quick, hide in the sleeping bag!" I told her, and she obeyed, while I sat down on the couch and dove into the dungeon senses, flying up to examine the alleyway. As soon as I reached the doors, I could sense the snuffling of the creature on the far side. I froze, remembering the way that they'd managed to hurt me, even in this form. Instead, I turned my focus to the corpse on the floor, glad that this form of 'vision' didn't seem to need light.

I pushed the mana into the corpse slowly, permeating it entirely, and grinned to myself when I was given the option to absorb it into the dungeon. I checked the levels, relieved that I was back up to almost a hundred points, so I spent fifty points on goblins, summoning ten of them in the alley. Three were dead before they were fully formed, their coalescing forms torn apart viciously, but the remaining seven appeared intact, and I ordered them to kill whatever was attacking them.

They turned as one, creating a whirlwind of bloody destruction by attacking an invisible mass, their tiny forms jumping onto the creature and mobbing it, claws and teeth sinking in and tearing strips of the creature free.

Unsurprisingly, they didn't last long, even as a group, but they managed to claw and bite the creature enough that, as I sensed the last goblin torn from its leg, the second creature collapsed from blood loss, a lucky bite having severed an artery.

"Okay, so they're crap individually, but as a mob, they're actually useful..." I commented to myself, pleasantly surprised at the discovery. Reaching out and absorbing the first creature, I found the influx of mana I gained to be entirely different.

New Mana Form Encountered!

Your Dungeon has encountered a tier-three form of Mana: Shadow.

Shadow Mana is a mixture of three forms of tier-two mana; Storm, Clay, and Nature. The combination of Mana has resulted in an aberration known as a Lesser Ghast.

Your Dungeon has absorbed the new Mana form, gaining +25 to storage capabilities, +1 additional Research Path, +1 to Agility for all Dungeon creatures.

Find and Absorb additional forms of Mana to increase Dungeon Bonuses!

I could almost taste the difference in the mana I absorbed from the thing, which, according to the Dungeon, was a Lesser Ghast; it was dark, cold, and…hungry. I got an impression of the Ghast as being a creature that wasn't necessarily 'evil,' as it didn't take pleasure in what it did, but it was driven to kill, and to eat, voraciously. It felt as though it would never be satisfied, because it couldn't fill some void inside itself, a yawning gulf of hunger for…something…

I shook myself, and the feeling vanished. The fifty points I got from the creature were enough to bring me up to ninety-seven, out of a new maximum of one hundred and twenty-five. I quickly reached out my senses and found the sewer grate outside, smashed and worthless. I couldn't repair it, as it was at zero durability, and I wasn't advanced enough to recreate it, so instead I filled the passage with stone. I should have considered doing it before, I realized, building blocks like bricks over and over again, filling in the unavoidable gaps with rubbish and anything else I could stuff in there.

Soon, it was filled, and I copied a section of the alley, cobbles and all, over the top to conceal it. Then, with only thirteen points of mana left, I absorbed the second corpse and searched the alleyway for loot. Seven packets of crisps dropped by the goblins. Joy.

I shrugged and retreated to my body, which was being shaken by Amy, who was talking frantically at me.

"…wrong?" she said in a panicked voice, and I blinked, turning to look at her.

"What?" I asked.

"What's wrong!" she said again, louder. "I asked you before, and you just ignored me!" Her bottom lip quivered, tears clear in her eyes.

"Crap," I muttered, shaking my head. "Sorry, Amy. I was concentrating on something, that's all," I said, forcing a smile. "Look, why don't you go get some food, okay? Anything you want!" I told her, nodding at the piled-up food. She looked at me askance and her eyes slowly widened.

"Anyyyyything?" she asked carefully.

"Anything that I have," I said warily. "Seriously, I know there's no healthy food there, but still, just grab what you want. I won't tell anyone if you don't." I smiled, lifting a finger warningly. "Just don't make yourself sick by eating too much, okay?"

"Okay…" She said, clambering out of the sleeping bag and going over to pick through the boxes, asking me in a sad voice if there were any tomato sauce flavor crisps left.

The sick little sod.

It was a good while later when I finally managed to get her to sleep. I'd let her help me bandage up my shoulder, played some guessing games, and played with the dog for a while. As soon as I was sure she was out, I pulled up the details for the Monsters.

I was excited that the Ghast had joined the other creatures, but it was greyed out for now, as it required specialist mana forms to create it. Looking into the details, I soon found that any creatures could be formed from the 'Pure' mana which the Dungeon generated by sucking in the various corrupted forms around us and purifying it, but that it took a tremendous amount of that mana to create creatures beyond the 'basic' ones. As an example, the Lesser Ghast would take either forty Shadow Mana to make, or two hundred Pure mana. I delved further into the information on mana itself, and after some digging around, learned that the various types of mana could be created by combining the purified four elements of mana: Earth, Air, Fire and Water. I tried to modify the pure mana but received a prompt telling me that I needed to create a set of 'Accumulation Crystals' to access that skill.

Looking over the facilities, I resigned myself to having to do a deep dive through them sooner rather than later, but for now, I contented myself with just checking over the most basic facilities I could construct.

The available options were Living Quarters, which I clearly now needed, Halls, a Monster Den, a Kitchen, an Underground Farm, and the ability to build 'freely,' which was basically the smartest way to do it, as near as I could tell. The set designs were hugely mana intensive, while it seemed that I could create the same things for roughly two-thirds to half the mana by figuring it out myself.

I spent a few hours playing with the facilities options before queuing up the research to work on the goblins next. I figured, if I needed to, I could upgrade them to mob the Ghasts, if more turned up.

FIFTEEN

I WOKE THE NEXT morning to Amy whispering loudly to the dog that she'd take him out for a wee and creeping off towards the stairs. Thankfully, I knew that nobody else could open the doors, but still, I got up and yawned hugely, having left her asleep on the sofa while I'd stretched out uncomfortably on the floor overnight.

"Wait a minute..." I called to her, stretching and yawning again, still amazed at my sudden healing ability. Where last night, the deep wound in my shoulder had sent stabbing pain through me, today, there was freshly healed skin, red and sore, but solid. I grinned at the feeling under my questing fingers before getting up and searching around for my sword. I'd used the Dungeon abilities last night to replicate the training weapon in wood, then repaired the steel and rubber one. The scabbard, I'd made out of leather, which I was fairly sure was actually goblin hide, but since the Dungeon had made it, I wasn't going to complain.

I told her again to wait and pulled both swords on across opposite shoulders. The setup was a pain in the ass, as it was literally impossible to draw a sword that was three feet long out of a sheath on your back gracefully without having arms at least two feet longer than the standard, as near as I could tell, regardless of the things Hollywood showed.

Adding to that, a longsword that was three foot, or just over, as mine were, tended to drag along the floor when you walked if you didn't hold the hilt and angle the tip back. After much low swearing and experimentation in another room, I'd come to the conclusion that a back sheath was great for carrying said sword, but when you wanted to use it, you needed to take it off and throw the scabbard aside.

It was massively inconvenient, but trying to draw it from my shoulder meant I got the last few inches stuck in the sheath, and I looked like an absolute tit, staggering about, until I used both hands and shifted my grip to halfway down the blade before pulling again.

It was something that annoyed me to no end.

I'd considered trying to shorten the swords, but I suspected that would just cause more issues, so in the end, I'd just accepted that my scabbards would be spending a lot of time on the floor, and planned to use the wooden sword until it broke, then use the other.

I drew the wooden sword and took Amy and Spot upstairs, carefully examining the alley with my senses, then summoning a trio of rats outside first. I let them sniff and run about for a few minutes, and when they weren't attacked, I sent them to the far ends of the alley. Once I knew they were out of sight, we opened the doors to let Spot do his business.

He, of course, smelled the rats and immediately tried to run after them.

I managed to grab his lead as he shot free of Amy and yanked back, hard, making him fall over as I snapped at him to stop, Amy shouting the same. We managed to get him under control and doing his business after a few minutes, but I'd had to shout at him far louder than I'd wanted to. As soon as he was done, I hustled them back inside, casting worried glances toward the end of the alley.

"What's down there?" Amy asked, and I paused before telling her the truth, figuring it was the best way.

"I don't know, but it's dangerous, and evil, I think," I shrugged uncomfortably. "Something is living in the old Cathedral, and whatever it is, it scared the shit out of me when I saw it. It looked like a little girl, but it wasn't."

"A girl?" She asked, perking up.

"No." I said flatly, crouching down so I was level with her now that we were back in the Core room. "It's definitely not a little girl, whatever it is. It killed a man the other day, so don't think about going to look, okay?" I saw the frightened look on her face and I quickly changed the subject. "Besides, we're going to have some food, and then I'm going to take you back home, right? See if we can find your momma?"

"Really? Thank you!!" She said, a sudden smile splitting her face from ear to ear, and I nodded quickly.

"Yup. Just as soon as you eat some food, have a drink, and use the toilet, okay?" She nodded and rushed off, grabbing a handful of chocolate bars and a bottle of pop, before heading to the ladies' toilets. I shrugged and let her go, sitting down and stroking the dog.

He'd woken up a few times during the night, and each time, he'd woken me, sniffing around, so I'd ended up stroking him and settling him down, in fear of Amy panicking when she woke and found he was missing.

I checked the research, disappointed that it wasn't even halfway to level two of the Mana Absorption yet, so I shrugged and went back to stroking the dog, giving him some crisps and various bits of food, as well as a drink.

By the time Amy came back, both Spot and I were ready, and I decided not to ask what had taken so long, instead making sure the gun was secure, and that she had a couple of chocolate bars in her pockets.

We opened the doors cautiously, my Rats outside once again letting me know it was safe, and stepped out into the alley.

"Where's the monster!" she suddenly gasped, pointing at the clean area inside the doors. "It's gone!" Then she spun around, looking for the sewer grate, and being unable to find it, she started to panic.

"Shit." I growled. "No! It's okay, I got rid of it last night, that's all!" I grabbed her shoulders and made her look me in the eyes. "It's okay, Amy. Don't panic; it's safe, but you need to be quiet!"

"But…" she whined.

"No!" I snapped. "Seriously, Amy, it's gone, but there are other things around here, and we don't need to draw attention!" She bit back tears at the tone of my voice, and I felt bad for snapping at her, but I preferred that she listen and stay alive, than making noise and drawing something down on us. I forced her to look at me and I tried to smile. "Look, I'm sorry, but you have to be quiet. If you don't, we won't get you home. You want to see your momma, right?" I asked, and she nodded tearfully. "Good, so you keep ahold of Spot and stay damn close to me. Don't say anything unless you have to, right?" I asked her, and she nodded again.

We glanced around cautiously, and I started us off towards the other end of the alley, leading us away from the Cathedral. It was a longer route, but I felt it was probably safer. She stuck by me, and Spot did what dogs do, which was stop every few feet to sniff something, and bark whenever he saw something interesting.

Thankfully, the rat I'd sent to this end of the alley was well hidden, and though he smelled it, he was pulled away easily enough.

We took a right up the connecting street, then out into the top end of the Bigg Market, running as fast as we could, all together, until we ducked down into the next street, crossed the next one, and pressed on again, before taking a right, and heading down toward the bridge out of Newcastle. We moved as quickly as we could, but the feel of danger was everywhere.

Several times, I had to draw Amy's attention to things in other directions as we passed bloodstains and broken windows. As we crossed over the underpass,

I looked up at the apartments on our left, observing closed curtains…and a few windows that were covered in gore.

Growling from Spot drew my attention away, and I turned to him quickly. The dog was fixated on the underpass, and I was getting a strong feeling of warning from the Dungeon as something down there moved in the darkness.

"Come on!" I snapped to them, tugging on Spot's lead and setting off running again, forcing them to keep up. A few minutes later, we were on the bridge, and I felt relief as the surrounding buildings fell away, mixed with fear that we were so exposed. As we crossed it, moving out from the cover we'd been using thus far, we saw more of the City and surrounding area, and Amy started to cry.

Huge sections of the city had clearly been on fire recently. Apartment blocks still smoldered, and here and there, the distance was punctuated by shouts and the occasional gunshot or scream of pain.

I grabbed her hand again and hurried her along. After a few more blocks, I found that the improvements I'd made to my body were significant enough that, when she started to flag, it was actually less effort to lift her in a 'princess carry' and run with her like that, than it was to encourage her along and pull Spot away from interesting scents. Thankfully, Spot trotted along obediently, focused on running at pace above all else.

The next hour of the journey was uneventful, besides the occasional movements of people looking out of windows, or a few shouted questions, which I ignored. In passing the few small supermarkets that didn't have huge shutters on them, I saw a fight break out between three men near one of them, and we ducked down into hiding.

One was begging, saying he needed something for his wife, but the other two were threatening him, warning him off. He took a step too close, and one produced a gun, firing at the man three times. The first two shots missed, the third slamming home into the man's shoulder and sending him spinning to the floor with a scream of pain.

"Dammit," I swore, peering over at them. The man who'd pulled the trigger seemed unsure what to do, but his companion simply laughed and told him to 'finish the rat off'…

"Stay here. If I die, run. Go home, okay?" I snapped to Amy, and she looked at me wide-eyed. I'd set her down next to me where we huddled on the far side of a car out of sight, and I'd grabbed Spot's muzzle, keeping him quiet, despite the little dog's attempts to get free. "Okay?" I pressed again, and she nodded to me, fear clear in her eyes. I wanted to go on, to leave these men to whatever, and get the girl home safe. That was the task I'd given myself, but I couldn't just walk on by.

The man on the ground was frantically trying to get away. He rolled onto his side and staggered to his feet, starting to run, when the gunman raised his weapon, taking aim at the back of his head.

"Oi, fuckface!" I shouted, running forward from behind the car, dragging my sword off my shoulder and sliding it free of the leather as I went. He changed his aim, his eyes widening as he saw me. His friend said something I couldn't hear, and the gunman's gaze went cold, the gun bucking in his hands as a bullet flew past me to my right. I ducked back down, sliding behind a second parked car, and I heard the smash of glass as another bullet hit the car near where I hunched. "Why, oh why, did you have to say that, Matt? Couldn't just shout 'hello,' could you? Oh no, you have to be a dick..." I muttered to myself, flinching down again as a third bullet slammed into the car closer to me, my eyes flaring wide as I heard the tell-tale splashes of fuel from a ruptured tank.

I surged to my feet, rushing around the far side of the corner. The injured man dove behind a car on the far side of the street, even as I sprinted forwards, desperate to close the distance between the shooter and myself. He fired one more bullet, this one tearing a furrow in my left bicep, before the hammer came down on an empty chamber and he froze, gaping at the gun in shock.

I closed the last few feet, my sword held overhead in what Markus had called an 'Oberhau,' and I slammed it down hard, desperate to take the first man out. He stepped back at just the right time, and my blade missed him entirely, slamming hard into the pavement before rebounding. A loud crack came from the wood as I grimaced, my palms flaring in pain, and the second man slammed into me from inside the store, taking me from my feet and driving me into the side of a parked car.

I grunted in pain as the glass shattered. Letting go of the sword with my left hand, I slammed my elbow into his nose and sent him reeling back before swinging hard into the side of his head with the sword. Pressed against the car as I'd been, I couldn't get a proper swing going, but it was clearly still painful, as he staggered back with a cry after it cracked into his cheek.

I shoved myself free of the car, shoulder-charging the man to the ground, then swinging the sword round again, this time with more control and finesse. My left hand grabbed onto the pommel and directed the maneuver as the blade tip whistled around to slam into the gun that was being leveled at me again. The fresh clip slid into the butt at almost the same instant the blade hit the barrel, and the simultaneous click of the clip locking into place melded with the snapping sound of the gunman's finger as the gun was sent flying.

I swung the sword around, mirroring the first blow in reverse, which had swept downwards from right to left, by swinging up from left to right. The move took the gunman in the chin with enough force to lift him from his feet, teeth crunching and his jaw fracturing with a pained squeal as he collapsed backward to land on the sidewalk.

"Motherfucker!" I snarled, following and kicking him hard in the face, once, twice, and then a third time, before leaning on my sword and glaring down at the pair of them. I picked the gun up, checked it, and ejected the clip after looking it over for a few seconds. It was a simple enough; a small switch on the left side of the grip I was pleased to find that it was similar to the gun I already had. I put the safety on, slid it into my pants, and swung my sword down across the upraised arm of the man who'd been directing the gunman.

His wrist snapped, and he screamed, then choked as I pressed the rounded tip of the sword hard against his windpipe.

"If I ever see you again, I'll kill you." I warned him. "Blink if you understand…good boy. Now, pick your friend up and get moving. You've got till the count of three before I shoot you." He glared at me but did as he was told, and once I was satisfied they were on their way, I moved over to check on the man they'd shot.

He was crouched behind a car, tears covering his cheeks as he clutched at his arm. I nodded to him reassuringly as I walked around him, squatting down carefully a few feet out of reach. Amy scampered over with Spot a few seconds later.

"Are you okay?" I asked him, and he gaped at me.

"Of course I'm not fucking okay!" he snapped, still clutching his arm. "They *shot* me!"

"Yeah, I saw," I said nodding towards his arm. "Want me to take a look?" I offered, secretly hoping he'd refuse.

"Well…are you a doctor?" he asked, and I shook my head. "A nurse?" he tried again, hopefully.

"Nope. Fuck-all medical training whatsoever," I said bluntly. "Learned the basics watching TV. Blood should stay inside of you; I got that much, and yours isn't." My eyes flickered to the trickle dripping from his fingers.

"What do I do?" he whimpered, and I smiled at him.

"We go inside there, find a medical kit, and patch you up as best we can." I shrugged. "They've got a pharmacy in there, right?" I asked, noticing the sign on one wall, and he nodded anxiously.

"Yeah, it's new; it's why I was there…" He trailed off, wiping his eyes. "My wife…She needs antibiotics…" He took a deep breath and forced himself to his feet, glaring at the men who were watching us and moving away, slowly. "What's wrong with you?!" he shouted at them. "All I wanted was some drugs for my wife!"

"They're ours!" The one I'd just spoken to snarled, halting his backwards walk and glaring at us. "You better watch yourself, you bastard…I'll find you…" He started pointing at me, and I straightened, swapping my sword to my left hand. I pulled the gun from the waistband of my pants, flicked the safety off, and pointed it at them.

"Three," I said, not bothering to count. I'd warned them and given them a chance; this was the choice they'd made. The recoil from the shot was stronger than I'd expected, throwing my aim off slightly as I brought the gun back up for a second shot.

I'd aimed for the center of mass, fully expecting to miss, and I had…I'd hit the second man in the chest, rather than the one I was aiming for, them being side by side.

He fell backwards, blood spraying and a look of shock on his face, as I swallowed and pointed the gun at the first man, firing again.

This time, I missed entirely as he dove behind a car, shouting his friend's name, then scurried out of sight, screaming that I'd regret that.

I already did. Each life I took was both weighing on me, yet strangely, not enough. The 'points' I was getting for basically defending myself and taking out the scum of the planet were helpful and making me want more, which sickened me to my stomach.

I gestured to Amy to come to me, and she dragged Spot over, staring at me wide-eyed and afraid. I led the way into the store, stepping through the broken floor-to-ceiling windows, passing collapsed shelving and piles of damaged boxes as I led them all the way to the back of the room. The faint sunlight filtering in through the grates over the windows was just enough to let me find what I needed.

The Pharmacy at the back was still well-stocked, the secure door hanging broken on its hinges and rocking back and forth slowly in a faint breeze. I stepped inside, searching quickly, gun in my left hand, sword in my right, as I checked to make sure it was safe.

No one else was hiding inside, and I grabbed a first aid kit off the wall and carried it to the man standing anxiously by the counter.

"Right, let me see it," I ordered brusquely, gesturing at his arm.

"I thought you said you didn't know what you were doing?" he whined, and I fixed him with a glare.

"Look, I have somewhere to be. You want to do this yourself? Fine by me; we can fuck off and leave you to it…"

"No!" he gasped, shaking his head quickly. "Please, I'm just…"

"Just an asshole. Yeah, it's all right; I know." I said, quirking a smile. "Come on…let's see it…" He peeled his jacket back and I looked the wound over, glad to see that it looked to have passed cleanly through the upper meat of the shoulder. I poked and prodded at it, making sure no bullet fragments had been left, and ignored his pained winces.

"Okay, first off, you're lucky…I think. It looks like the bullet went straight through. Lots of blood and pain, I bet, but nothing inside. Bandage it up, and hopefully it'll sort itself out, until you can find a medical textbook or a doctor, anyway," I said, pouring out some antiseptic onto a bandage and roughly cleaning the wound, then wrapping it in a fresh bandage and binding it as best I could.

Congratulations!

You have gained one level in First Aid!

You receive 2% increase in your chance to downgrade your targets' damage tiers. Increase your skill to augment your ability further.

Tier	Chance to Downgrade
Minor	0%
Average	20%
Serious	10%
Major	5%
Critical	1%
Deadly	1%

I spent a brief moment looking over the prompt before dismissing it this time, remembering the last few times it'd shown up, and realizing that I'd reached level five in it already. The 'chance to downgrade' was a bit unclear, but as I concentrated on the phrase, I felt a wash of information flood me. Blinking, I knew suddenly that it indicated the chances that if I worked on a wound, I could make it less life threatening, basically. While I couldn't make a minor wound vanish magically, I had a twenty percent chance of taking an 'average' wound and making it a lot less serious.

I nodded to myself in satisfaction and considered the guy before me, who'd been watching me zone out and seemingly 'read' something in the air.

"So, has anything weird happened to you since, you know, the world ended?" I asked him cautiously.

"Besides being shot by those idiots?" he asked, disbelieving, and I nodded. "No, we've been waiting for the police or the army or whatever to sort things out…what do you mean the 'end of the world'?" He looked at me fearfully.

"Never mind," I said shaking my head. "Look, we've got to get on, so take whatever you need, and take plenty of it. You can't come back here now, with that asshole out there."

"I'm not a thief!" He retorted hotly, and I snorted, shaking my head at him.

"Then when the world comes back together, you can come see whoever owns the shop and make things right. Until then? It's your choice of starving if you don't, but either way, not my problem." I turned to Amy. "Amy, I need you to fill a bag with anything you think you'll need for home, okay? Sensible food, please, not just chocolate and shit." With that, I turned away from them both and dove back into the pharmacy section, searching quickly. I grabbed a single packet of everything I could, from condoms to Aspirin, dumping them all in a shoulder bag I took off the wall, along with basics like bandages and antiseptic. I figured if I could get the dungeon to clone all this stuff, then I'd be set; eventually, at least.

I moved out to the front and grabbed a pair of giant cans of Redbull, storing one and popping the top off the other, sighing after a long swig.

"Damn, I needed that," I muttered to myself, then called over to Amy. "Okay, Amy, it's time; we have to move." She just nodded to me, grabbing the last few things she'd wanted and dumping them into a matching shoulder bag.

"Good luck, man," I called over my shoulder, and the two of us moved out to the door, checked around to make sure it was clear, then jogged out and down the street, Spot running alongside us happily.

I let Amy lead the way, down streets that ran parallel to those I'd have taken, but it was her home, so I followed along. After another hour or so, we apparently reached her estate, and slowed, tired. We'd been alternating jogging and briskly walking for most of it. I'd hidden my guns again, but the sword was on open display in my hand, the weirdness of the world not worth taking for granted anymore.

We soon came to her street, and then her house, climbing the handful of steps up to her front door, where she fumbled her keys out. She rushed inside, shouting for her mother. I followed her in, Spot dashing from room to room as I closed the front door and moved into the hallway cautiously. The house was a three story one, narrow, with high ceilings and a staircase taking up most of the right side of each floor A living room and kitchen composed the lower floor, both empty. The next floor up had a pair of small bedrooms and a small bathroom, followed by the top floor of a single master bedroom and a large family bathroom.

I found Amy crying in the master bedroom, and I knew her mother hadn't been home. I did the only thing I could and knelt next to her, taking her in my arms while she sobbed. As I held her, I looked out of the large bay windows, seeing the tall trees in the distance at the end of the road.

She was probably still there, trapped, I assumed, as no mother I knew worth the title would abandon their child, especially for days at a time when the world had basically ended.

I sighed as I accepted the choice I'd already had rattling around in the back of my head. I was going to have to go get her out.

SIXTEEN

IT TOOK ME the better part of an hour to calm Amy down, and considerably longer to convince her that she needed to wait at home while I went out to find her mother. Thankfully, there were dozens of photos of her around the rooms. One entire wall was plastered in smiling pictures of her and a big buff-looking fucker cradling a baby, her and her friends on nights out, and right in the center, a picture of a soldier in full dress uniform.

I didn't want to, but I had to.

"Amy, is this your dad?" I asked quietly. She nodded proudly and pointed to several photos of them together. "Where is he?"

"He's on the base, down south. He's going away again, so they made him go down there…" she said with tears in her eyes.

"He's going away, but he's not gone yet?" I asked pointedly.

"No, he's supposed to be flying tomorrow, or the day after?" she said, unsure, and I released a worried breath.

"That's great news," I said, smiling at her reassuringly. That meant he was probably waiting for a flight. If this really was the same across the world, he'd be making his way back home, meaning that if I could get her mom free, they'd be all right; hell, with a soldier with as many combat ribbons as he was wearing in the photos, he'd probably kick the hell out of the gypsies on his own…

I pulled a photo of her mom free from the wall, examining it and burning the face into my memory before slipping it into my back pocket. 'Alyssa Jefferson, 2017, The Lakeside Lodge.' was written on the back, and I nodded to myself, glad I at least had a name now.

She had dark hair, cut in a pixie bob, high cheek bones, and a narrow chin, with a smile that looked like it was always on display; great figure, too. Overall, she was beautiful, and that gave me a little hope that if these murdering scumbags had taken her prisoner, she'd be kept, rather than fed to a lion or whatever.

I left the medical bag in the lounge, eating some of the food I'd looted… there wasn't much that was quick and easy, but dried jerky washed down with energy drinks would do. I made Amy promise to stay inside, safe, and I set off walking to the park.

I jogged down the street, hiding in a garden and waiting for ten minutes. I watched her front door intently until I was sure she'd actually listened and stayed behind, before I relaxed and moved on. Crossing the road and weaving between parked cars, it took a few blocks of scurrying along before getting my first good look at the park in the daylight.

Someone had clearly looted the hardware store nearby, as the high metal fence that ringed the park had been supplemented with wooden boards, and there were the clear signs of a wall being built as I moved closer.

The usual arched gates that allowed entry into the park had been sealed up tight, and a platform had been constructed over and behind them. A bored-looking sentry sat atop it, calling out as people walked up.

"If you want food, you have to work! No more free handouts. Move to the main gate and see Mickey. If he gives you a job, you'll get fed at the end of the day…" he repeated the information in a careless drawl and ignored the questions people called up to him. He glanced over at me, then frowned, standing up. "Hey, you!"

I stopped, looking up at him, still unsure what my play was going to be here. I'd been thinking I'd try to sneak in, search for Amy's mom, and then escape with her, but even for me, that was a half-assed plan. I'd been planning on a circuit of the park first to see what it looked like.

"What?" I called up.

"Where'd you get the swords?" He grinned down at me.

"From my house," I said, unsure of him.

"Chuck them up, let me have a look," he ordered.

"No," I said flatly, knowing I'd never get them back.

"Hey, asshole, I told you to toss them up," he growled, his attitude changing immediately.

"And I told you 'no,'" I replied. "Why the hell would I give you my swords?"

"It's like that, is it?" he said, glaring at me. "Fine. Whoever gets me his swords gets a bag of food." He called out loud, pointing at me. I froze as the dozen or so hungry-looking people up and down the street turned their focus from him to me. One man started moving straight for me, grim-faced.

"Sorry, pal, but I got kids to feed," he explained, cracking his knuckles threateningly.

"You don't want to do this..." I warned him, drawing the wooden sword and pointing it at him.

"Maybe not, but I'm gonna do it anyway..." He set his jaw, spat on the ground, and lifted his fists in a boxer's stance.

"Go on, there!" the asshole guard called down, grinning at the rapidly unfurling tableau. Two other men and a woman were hurrying over towards me, and I swore. This plan had gone to shit even faster than my normal ones did, and that was saying something.

"Oh, fuck this," I said, shaking my head. I could try to run, I could fight, or I could win. The last option required doing what nobody expected and going balls to the wall.

I started to spin the sword in my right hand, rolling my wrist to keep the blade in constant movement as I reached into my top, wrapping my left hand around the grip of the gun. I flicked the safety off as I pulled it free, slashing the sword hard across the closing man's braced forearms and drawing a grunt of pain from him. He started to crouch, readying himself to jump at me, when his eyes widened at the sight of the handgun, and he quickly started backpedaling.

I turned, looking up at the guard, who, until now, had been grinning down at me. The distance between us was less than ten feet, but considering my inexplicably amazing shots so far, I paused as I lined the gun up, just long enough to see the shock and horror on his face as I pulled the trigger once.

The bullet took him high in the chest, sending him staggering back. An old rifle dropped from nerveless fingers as he fell out of sight, and I spun round, making sure. Those nearby were backing away as quickly as they could, and I nodded to myself in satisfaction, even as my stomach roiled at killing another person...again.

I flicked the safety on, sheathed my sword, and ran at the barrier. Jumping and kicking off it, I grabbed onto the ornamental scroll work of the arch and pulled myself up, then clambered quickly over the top and onto the guard post.

The man I'd shot was lying on the grass behind the gate, ten feet or so away from where I crouched. He'd landed badly and was coughing up blood, the hole in his chest spurting out even more as he tried to cover it with both hands. Glancing to either side, I couldn't see anyone else, but I discovered a bag full of groceries up here where he'd been, and a bottle of whisky. I grabbed the groceries and dumped them over the far side, where people could get to them, and hefted the rifle warningly as I called down to them.

"I'm going to be here for a while. Any of you fuckers try to climb the fence, or go warn the other guards, and you die, got it? Behave, and that food down there is yours..." There was a long moment of silence, before the man who'd attacked me came out from behind a car.

"I can have the food?" he asked cautiously.

"Yeah, you can have the food," I replied, then grinned as a thought occurred to me. "And if you'll guard the gate from anyone else trying to climb over, I'll give you another bag when I leave. One-time offer."

"Deal," he growled, shouting across the street toward a second man hiding behind another car. "Carl! Take this back to yer mom. Tell her there'll be more, and I'll be back soon." He strolled over to the gate and took up station, glaring at anyone who came near, as his companion ran over, grabbed the bag, and ran off down the street. I noticed two other men set off in pursuit of Carl, but I dismissed it. I couldn't help everyone, and he'd either be okay, or he wouldn't. I'd agreed to help a little girl, and that was enough stress for me.

I checked the area again, made sure I wasn't getting snuck up on, and pulled up the flashing notifications.

Congratulations!
You have defeated two opponents classed as 'Lesser Ghast'
Lesser Ghast level: 1
Your level: 4
XP awarded: 300 ((XP awarded on second kill has been halved due to Dungeon creatures killing it at your direction.))
*

Congratulations!
You have defeated two opponents classed as 'Looter'
Looter level: 0
Your level: 4
XP awarded: 50
*

Quest!
'A Daring Rescue…'
You have agreed to not only find Amy's mother, but also rescue her. Remember, words have consequences! Rescue Alyssa and return her to her daughter.

- +1 to top three Attributes used.
- +1 Skill point to allocate
- 400 XP

***Note**: Rewards have been increased on this quest, due to level of difficulty.*
You have reached Level Five!

You receive five Stat points to invest in your attributes and gain access to your first Choice!

'Who will you be?'

You have reached your first Choice! You must choose a path to follow. Many creatures have chosen the safest path, but among those neglected are opportunities denied to many...choose wisely, as this Choice cannot be undone.

Due to your actions so far, three Standard and one Rare path have been unlocked:

Adventurer:

The Adventurer is ubiquitous across the Multiverse. Every evolved world has a name for these brave and excessively foolhardy individuals, but they all boil down to the same: Idiots for hire.

Adventurers make a living delving the dungeons, exploring the unknown, and facing the creatures of the night. As such, they gain the following one-off bonuses:

- + 2 to Strength
- + 2 to Constitution
- + 1 Stat of your choice
- + 1 Class Skill Point

Arcanist:

Arcanists are the wielders of Mana and knowledge in the Multiverse, searching out power wherever it can be found and seeking to grow their knowledge above all else...they gain the following one-off bonuses:

- + 2 to Intelligence
- + 2 to Wisdom
- + 1 Spell
- + 1 Class Skill Point

Healer:

Healers are everyone's favorite people. No matter where you go, they are in demand, and the Multiverse is no different. Healers gain the following one-off bonuses:

- + 2 to Intelligence
- + 2 to Dexterity
- + 2 Class Skill Points

Rare Class:

Dungeon Lord:

Dungeon Lords are whispered of, rumored and often legendary figures, as much revered as reviled, depending on who is speaking. This class controls the vitally important Dungeons of the Multiverse, and depending on their choices, they rise to either slaughter millions, or uplift entire civilizations. Dungeon Lords gain the following one-off bonuses:

- + 2 Spells
- + 2 Class Skill Points
- + 1 Personal Pet

I read and reread the details, before shrugging and selecting the bloody obvious choice of Dungeon Lord. As soon as I chose it, I was greeted with another series of screens.

Congratulations, Dungeon Lord!
You have 2x Spells to select and 3x Class Skill points to assign, along with a Personal Pet to select. You have gained your first Dungeon Power: Forced Evolution.

Forced Evolution: You may forcibly 'evolve' a Dungeon Species of your choice. Depending on the mana invested, this species could evolve in new and interesting ways. Beware: this will evolve the base species in a new direction, removing the original version until a new one is scanned and made available to the Dungeon. Not all evolutions are worthy of continuation.

Do you wish to select your choices now?
Yes/No

Not even a slight hesitation. I wanted them right-goddamn-now, for sure.

Spells:
Summon Familiar/Pet: Summon your Familiar or Pet directly to your side, regardless of your location.

Incinerate: Cast a blast of terrible heat at a target, achieving up to 1000 degrees of heat in a single location.
Note: This spell has lessening effects, depending on the area covered, and ranks from 0 (10cm) to 5 (1000cm).

Winter's Heart: Cast a blast of terrible cold at a target, achieving up to -200 degrees of cold in a single location.
Note: This spell has lessening effects, depending on the area covered, and ranks from 0 (10cm) to 5 (1000cm).

Tame: Tame a creature, adding it to your Dungeon lists.

Intimidate: You fix your target with your terrible glare and demand they agree to your terms. This spell ranks in levels from 0 (Weird) to 5 (Nightmare).

Examine: This spell allows the nascent Dungeon Lord to divine details about a target that are hidden from the eyes of most mortals. This skill ranks in levels from 0 (Curious) to 5 (All-Knowing).

Summon Golem: Summon an Earthen Golem to do your bidding.
Note: This spell will summon a Golem depending on your ability, and ranks from 0 (100cm high) to 5 (10,000cm high).

Lightning Bolt: Cast a blast of Lightning at your target, stunning and possibly frying them with the power of electricity.
Note: This spell has lessening effects, depending on the area traveled, and ranks from 0 (50,000v) to 5 (150,000mv).

Class Skills:
Imbue: You may choose to give freely of your own manapool to imbue an item or creature of the Dungeon with magic. This ability can fail, and spectacularly so; however, creations of wondrous might can also be brought into being. Be wary.

Monster Master: No longer do the creatures of the Dungeon view you with apathy or irritation when you pass by. Now they are devoted to you! This skill ranks in levels from 0 (Interested) to 5 (Worshipful).

Breeder: Your breeding dens are no longer the exclusive places they were. Want Gnolls and Goblins to 'get it on'? This is how that happens, as well as all the craziness that will ensue.

Crafter's Potential: Random sentient Dungeon creatures will now have a chance to be struck by inspiration, driving them to learn to create. These crafters will be capable of designing items in very specific ways, Leatherworkers will, for example, be far less useful if only permitted to work with metal and may rebel. This skill ranks in levels from 0 (Botched) to 5 (Legendary).

Pets: Your sentient Dungeon inhabitants can gather and breed pets. Beware: certain species choices of 'pets' are not for the fainthearted! This skill ranks in levels from 0 (Vermin) to 5 (Magical Creatures).

Insatiable Curiosity: Random Sentient Dungeon Creatures will now have the chance to be spawned with an insatiable curiosity. These creatures can be put to work in your Research Nodes to increase Research by a staggering degree. This skill ranks in levels from 0 (Incompetent) to 5 (Genius).

Manafield: Your Dungeon's Manafield will now passively expand at 10% more than the previous rate, enabling greater growth in a shorter period of time. This skill ranks in levels from 0 (Restricted) to 5 (Expansive).

Reach Out and Touch Me: Your Dungeon is no longer only controllable when you are within its own environs. Now you can interact with it at increasing distances. This skill ranks in levels from 0 (Local) to 5 (Interstellar).

Personal Pet:
You may select a pet to assist you in and out of your dungeon. Four variations of pet are available due to your skill level, location, and inclinations:

Canine:
Canines are often referred to as 'Man's best friend' due to their long-standing relationships with humanity. While not outstanding in any area, they are the pet 'average,' with abilities that are useful in many areas.

Dragonkin:
Dragons are the most fearsome creatures to naturally reproduce in the Multiverse, and as such, are almost impossible to tame. They are also, however, almost uncontrollably horny, and as such, many tens of thousands of versions of Dragonkin exist.

Insectoids:
Insectoids are the evolutionary winners on many planets, their wide variety of forms finding niches to survive that many would find unbelievable. Sentient Insectoids are often considered blasphemy by many races, mainly because they react differently to other, weaker life forms.

Automata:
Automata are creatures that are created from inorganic materials and imbued with a basic level of sentience. Instead of gaining strength through leveling, they are upgraded, and can rank in sizes from 0 (Small) to 5 (Continental).

I remained crouching on the platform for long minutes, reading over and over the options, before I blinked and remembered what I was doing, and more importantly, where I was. These options were vital to me, but I needed them all, and god damn it, I needed them all NOW.

"Okay, spells. I've got two, Let's sort that now, really quick..." I muttered to myself. Summoning a pet was out. As cool as it was, it'd only be a case of re-summoning it if it died, right? Well, regardless, I needed something that would be useful now, so I left that. A Golem would be cool, but at a meter high, it would be too big to be stealthy, and too small to be useful at the moment, so... nope. 'Examine'...yeah. Yeah, that, I was gonna need. There was too much going on right now that I had no clue about, so something that would make things clearer was needed. I selected that and continued on. 'Intimidate' was a no, if it just started off making them think I was weird. I was already weird enough. That left me with three fighting options, and...Tame. Normally, I'd have ignored Tame as well, but after that incident with the tiger in that cage, I had a new appreciation for just how fucking terrifying they were. If I could reach the cages and tame one, or more, then set them free?

Alternatively, the three 'attack' spells were all awesome for different reasons. Heat? Yup. Cook some fucker; that'd be useful. Cold? Yeah, I could see that. Freeze people in place with that kind of cold, and then I can just stroll on by...These two were AOE, or Area of Effect spells, so I could scale the target area up or down, depending on need, while Lightning Bolt…that was a single target affair. On the upside, I was willing to bet it was more useful, as I vaguely remembered that police tasers were around the fifty-thousand-volt mark. That meant even from first getting it, I could stun someone, making it a more silent and targeted approach.

I considered it for a long minute, watching the area to make sure nobody was sneaking up on me, before finally deciding that I needed to be as effective as possible. Tame was cool, but if I couldn't reach the animals, it didn't matter.

I picked Incinerate, guessing that I'd have more use for that, mainly because a smaller area reaching insane temperatures would be easier to hide than an arc of lightning shooting from my fingers like I was a withered old Emperor kicking ass. Shame, though. Hopefully I'd be able to pick more later on.

I moved onto the Dungeon Class Skills, I had three, and it was an easier choice all around. I dismissed Breeder, Pets, and Reach Out and Touch Me straight away. They'd be useful, but not as much as others. Imbue was a given; hell to the yes. I chose that and dismissed Manafield. I needed that, but again, not as much as others. Insatiable Curiosity was a yes, even though I only really had the dumbest creatures for now. That meant that I needed Monster Master as well, as there was no point in creating the creatures if they'd ignore my commands.

Again, I hoped I'd get another chance later on to choose more.

Pets was a no-brainer. As much as I loved dogs, and Dragonkin would be cool, Automata sounded friggin' awesome. Insectoids didn't get a look in.

I choose the Automata and was offered the chance to disassemble something to provide the base components for my pet. Looking around, I couldn't see anything useful, so I just left the option available, and dismissed the prompts for the moment, gripping the edge of the wooden barrier next to me in white-knuckled hands as a terrible burning filled my veins. The sensation passed as quickly as it had come, leaving me gasping as I sagged to all fours.

I could 'feel' the knowledge of the spells in my mind now, like I'd always known them, having only locked them away. I knew that Incinerate was simply exciting the atoms of my target, causing them to vibrate in ways new and unusual; the vibration would generate energy in the form of heat, energy that wanted to escape…all I had to do was designate the target and reach out with my mana, sinking it into the elementary particles of said target, and watch the world *burn*.

Examine was different. While, once again, I sank my mana into whatever I was looking at, as it permeated the target, I would gain an insight, learning more the longer I held it. If I maintained it for prolonged periods, I would slowly gain insights into its past, its present, and its potential.

My mana was easy to use, I suddenly found, simple patterns being all I needed to follow to have the required effects come to pass. Releasing the mana was like relaxing my butthole after a particularly nasty curry; what was held inside just wanted to get out.

I reached out to the plank of wood under my right hand and poured mana into it, twisting my fingers in a pattern that directed the flow unconsciously.

Wooden Plank	Item
This wooden plank has been hammered and nailed into part of a rough structure. Unseasoned and soft as it is, it is likely to fail before the end of the year.	
Durability 7/10	Special Features: 0/0

"Cool," I murmured, then checked my mana. It was currently at one hundred and eighty of two hundred, so that small use had cost me twenty mana. Feck.

I shrugged and looked around a final time before climbing down and heading into the woods that surrounded the path, I planned to find a chance to test the Incinerate spell as well, but for now, I needed to get hidden.

I crept through the bushes, thankful that, at this time of the year, they were thick enough to cover me without being full of fallen leaves. I worked my way from shrub, to tree, to bush, until I reached the edge of the small boating lake and checked the area. The park had changed dramatically from the way I'd last seen it in daylight a few months ago, and in the dark the other night, I'd been unable to make anything out.

The gypsies, and what looked like others, had set up a large tent in the middle of the main field, surrounding it with their caravans and bigger vehicles. Even now, a handful of people were visible, hammering sheets of wood into rough walls to surround the impromptu structure. Even as large as their camp was, it wasn't big enough to take up the majority of the field, as the space was over three hundred meters in length. As I watched, I noticed that there were another twenty or thirty people working in a fenced-off area adjacent to the camp, planting and digging…

"They're setting up to grow crops…" I muttered to myself, nodding in grudging admiration. The area they'd fenced in could conceivably feed hundreds, depending on what they chose to grow. For a second, I wondered if it'd all been a mistake, or…

Then I saw a man walking past the edge of the water, a shotgun in his hand, and a tired, bedraggled group of men following him, staggering as they went. I swore silently as I saw the state of the other men, and I set off, following them easily through the trees.

The entire group was clearly physically exhausted, and judging from the way they walked, heads lowered, feet not lifting from the ground, shoulders slumped, they were mentally broken as well.

We went maybe a hundred meters, with me sprinting from cover when need be, before they reached a large building which I vaguely remembered had been a petting zoo, or something of the sort, for kids. Now, it'd been heavily altered, and the large cages at the back were suddenly holding people. People who were clearly filthy, dispirited, and hungry.

There was a canteen line, and as I continued to watch, the group I'd been following was led up, bowls were handed out, and a thin gruel portioned into each, before the men were locked away in the cages.

The man who'd been directing them sneered as he walked away, spitting into the cauldron of gruel as he passed, much to the laughter of another man who sat nearby. I noticed they ate from a much smaller, but clearly better-quality pot, and I felt my anger simmering higher.

I'd not been mistaken, and my worst fears were coming true. Not only did I now know they were actively slaving, but they were also transforming the park into an armed camp! Amy's missing mother wasn't in sight, but that wasn't saying much. There were easily dozens of people in the cages, eating what I assumed was their midday meal.

I'd passed areas where the trees had been cut down, where the playpark was in the process of being torn up, and bowling greens had been turned into grazing areas for their horses, so I could only assume that this wasn't a short-term plan developing before my eyes.

These people were here to stay, and they were clearly not going to be good for the area. I had a rifle with three bullets, two handguns with a total of sixteen bullets between them, two swords that were deliberately blunted, and an Incinerate Spell, which I had no idea how much it cost to cast…

"Well, let's find out," I growled under my breath as I watched another man walk up and say something to a woman in the cage. She looked shocked and disgusted, and he laughed and walked away, calling over his shoulder to her.

"You'll soon change your mind!"

"Not fucking likely, pal," I muttered, setting the rifle down and concentrating. I held out my right hand, aiming carefully, and focusing on the power of the spell as much as I could. I felt my fingers twisting, the knowledge of the spell flowing through me as I focused on exciting the atoms of a particular area to shift, then to vibrate and shake.

The guard staggered, his hands going to his crotch, before screaming, his cry rising from a surprised grunt to a high-pitched wail that lasted seconds as everything around the area suddenly charred black, the center glowing with ruby red light.

He collapsed to the floor, dead, as his clothes burst into flames. The body curled up as muscles contracted, fats hissing and popping, and the sickeningly sweet smell of burning meat filled the air.

There was silence for a handful of seconds as the other two men slowly, cautiously, rose to their feet, looking shocked.

"Did…did you see that?" The man who'd led the slaves up asked the other hesitantly, lifting his shotgun and hunting around. I swallowed hard, trying not to be sick where I crouched in the bushes. A powerful headache was flaring, and I checked my mana, groaning softly when I saw that it sat at ninety-three of two hundred. Given my regeneration of a hundred points an hour, that gave me a cost of a hundred per casting, and I'd just emptied my mana pool by half with a single spell.

I suddenly wished I'd chosen the lightning bolt, as I guessed it might have had a lower cost, or at least a less gruesome outcome than the greasy, burnt smell that was filling the clearing.

"What did you do?" The man who'd been guarding the slaves snapped at the woman in the cage, stalking forward, lifting a handgun and pointing it at her. "What did you do to him?!?" he bellowed in fury, and I blanched, realizing I had no time to reconsider. I lifted the rifle, aiming at his back and closing one eye, and sighting down the barrel.

He grabbed the bars of the makeshift cage and shoved the gun through them, pointing it at her face as the other three in her cage backed away quickly.

"Don't be stupid, Sam!" the other man called to him, facing out instead and searching the area. "It's got to be one of those creatures!" he snarled, his shotgun up and braced against his shoulder as he searched, the twin barrels flicked from side to side, while he shouted out as loud as he could in the direction of the old gothic mansion in the center of the park.

"Help! We're under…urk!" His scream was cut off as I switched my aim, pulling the trigger as soon as I had it lined up on him, desperate to not to let him shout anymore. The bullet took him in the stomach, knocking him from his feet and sending him rolling. His shotgun discharged wildly into the air, and the twin gunshots sent birds bursting from nearby trees.

"What the…?" the other man screamed in surprise, twisting around and lining his handgun up on the approximate area he'd heard my gunshot come from. He squeezed off two shots, one missing completely, the second tearing a branch from the bush I was hidden in. I jerked the rifle toward him, pulling the charging lever back and forward before firing at him, my shot flying wide, slamming into the head of a man standing up behind him in a cage.

"Fuck!" I cursed, dropping the rifle. It was just too unwieldy in the tight confines of the bush. I drew both handguns and fired with them both, realizing as my intended target dove to the side and I completely missed…that it was true what they said.

Two-gun mojo was bullshit.

Adjusting my very impromptu plan, I pointed with the right, fired, and hit him in the chest. The bullet impacted high on his left side, slamming him back into the floor. I wasted no time in shooting him again with the left gun, this time in the head as I marched out of the forest, making sure he was dead. I moved to the other man, doing the same again, clamping down hard on my stomach as brains and blood splattered across the pavement.

The people in the cages were screaming, a mixture of panic and hope, as some begged me to let them free, and others cursed at me for my mis-aimed shot, or cried in fear that the unknown would be worse than their current lot in life.

"Shut it!" I snapped at them, gesturing in anger. As I was holding a gun in either hand, they complied quickly, and I cursed again as I heard shouts in the distance. I rushed forward, roughly searching the nearest corpse, grabbing the shotgun and two shells for it—buckshot, I guessed. I pocketed one, after snapping the shotgun open and reloading the other barrel.

I grabbed the other handgun from the floor, ejected the clip and found four bullets. Since it was identical to one of mine, I dumped the gun and pocketed the clip for later. Knowing I didn't have much time left, I rushed to the nearest cage, searching the group, then moved to the next, and the next. Panic started to rise at the incoming shouts and running feet that drew closer, before I checked the final cage, finding plenty of desperate faces, but no sign of Amy's mom, despite me taking the time to be sure she hadn't just been out of sight, as I'd been hoping.

I swore, ducking into the narrow gap between the nearest cage and a large tree trunk as two more guards appeared. The first missed me crouching there, but the second didn't, aided by one of the dead slave's friends pointing frantically at me.

He twisted, firing his shotgun roughly in my direction from the hip, spraying the caged slaves more than me. Cursing, I ducked, grunting as hot pain tore through my left cheek when a single pellet ricocheted to find my flesh.

I thrust my left gun out, firing twice in rapid succession, missing entirely, but making them dive aside as I sprinted free, heading back the way they had come, toward the big house.

"This is such a stupid idea!" I growled to myself, the sound of running feet alerting me to the next thug as he rounded the corner just in time to take a bullet to the face.

He hurtled backwards, blood spraying, dead before he hit the floor, even as I fired blindly behind me, trying to keep the other two back.

I had the shotgun in my right hand now, handgun in the left, swords on either shoulder, a handgun in my belt, two half-filled clips, and a building, desperate fury to *do something* about all this shit. The man I'd just shot had been carrying a baseball bat, and I ignored it as I ran around the corner he'd so recently cleared.

I barely noticed the short, well-maintained borders of the flower beds on either side of the path leading up to the house, my attention arrested by the man standing stock still in the middle of the path. A much more expensive and clearly better quality rifle was being aimed steadily at my face.

I dove to the side. His first shot tore through the air an inch from my face, his second slamming into the hilt of my wooden sword as I hit the ground and rolled. The pommel shattered, splinters flying, but it deflected the bullet enough that the projectile hit pavement rather than me, and I rolled again, firing the shotgun one-handed in his direction.

His gun was a weapon of precision death; mine was more of 'to whom it may concern,' as I'd clearly caught my finger on both triggers, rather than just one. The cloud of buckshot in the left barrel sprayed outwards, while the birdshot in the right turned the air into what I imagined a tiny claymore might when triggered.

The angle, distance, and my rolling saved my target from being entirely shredded, but his left leg was blown apart, sending him screaming to the floor, a third bullet tearing into the trees to my left.

I scrambled to my feet, dropping the shotgun and rushing forwards, I shot him in the back as he rolled on the floor, reaching for his injured leg, then ripped the rifle free of his grasping hand. Before I could search for any ammo, though, I staggered to the right, a bullet slamming into my left shoulder and spinning me around to see the other two had cleared the corner.

Two more bullets flew after me as I dodged, zigging and zagging, heading straight for the house, until the door opened wide a man walked out with a second rifle similar to the one I now held, pointed at my chest.

"Stop right there!" he snarled, and I hesitated, swearing and lowering the rifle at another man's gesture as two more, then three, stepped out of the house, taking up places on a small balcony and a veranda to the right.

The hoarse panting and low growling coming from behind me let me know the other two had closed the distance as well, and my FPS experience had come to an end.

Damn; good run, though. I thought as I dropped the rifle to the floor.

SEVENTEEN

"JUST WHO THE ever-living fuck do you think you are?" the man who I'd tentatively named 'Mr. Moustache' in my head growled at me, punching me in the gut.

I coughed and wheezed, hunching over as best I could. Blood dripped from my broken lips and nose to join the mess of blood that covered me now. I'd been dragged into the house, stripped of all my weapons, and tied to a low, old chair that I vaguely recognized as a period piece from the Victorian era, from the one time an ex had dragged me around the building. I had no idea why that detail had stuck with me, beyond the fact that I'd probably been considering screwing her in it at some point.

I tried to pull my arms free again, and for easily the tenth time, the handcuffs rattled as the ancient oak of the chair resisted me easily. No easy escape for me this time, I knew. As the owner of possibly the most untrustworthy facial hair in the world screamed in my ear at drum-rupturing volumes again, I jerked my head back up sharply, feeling his nose crunch as he staggered backwards.

"Modder-fuk..." He cried, staggering back and bringing both hands to his face, as the other two men started forward to grab me. One, seeing his friend reeling, punched me in the face, while the other swung his cricket bat at my left leg.

I grunted, then screamed, as first one, then both hits landed, before being kicked in the face and falling backwards, still chained to the chair, by Mr. Moustache. My head slammed into the stone slab floor with a resounding crack, and I lost consciousness, my last sight being the incoming steel toecaps of one of the men.

I came to a few minutes later when a bucket of cold water, presumably from the lake, was poured over me, and I blinked and looked around in confusion. My right eye had swollen shut, and my lips felt like a filler job had gone very, very wrong.

"Whu..." I managed to get out before Moustache grabbed my head and yanked it back, glaring into my eyes.

"You're gonna tell me everything, boy. Who you are, why you're here, all of it. Because when the King gets back, he's gonna want to know, and I'm not gonna be the one who couldn't tell him..." He stepped back and gestured to his friend, who stood off to one side, blowing into the holes on the side of a charcoal brazier.

The glow of the charcoal grew steadily brighter as I watched with rising horror, and when I looked back at Moustache, he was grinning at me.

"I've always wanted an excuse to do this, so thanks for that," He pointed to a metal wastepaper bin and a pair of small white rats in a cage nearby. "You see those?" he asked, waiting until I looked back at him. "Normally, we'd use the bigger, really feral kind, but I want you to last long enough to actually answer, so here's what we're going to do..."

"Oh, this is gonna be fun..." his friend chortled, and I looked from him to Moustache in confusion.

"We're gonna put you on your back again. Then we're gonna put the rats in the metal bin and strap it to your chest. Then the coals go on the top, and we keep piling them on until the bin glows red. The rats have two choices then, you see? The open end of the bin is against your skin, so they can either stay there and cook to death, or..."

"Or they can eat me..." I finished thickly through bloody lips, as I realized what he was saying.

"Well, you're a bright one, aint ya!" He smirked, leaning in and stroking the tips of his fucking stupid looking moustache. The damn thing looked like he'd gone for a full beard, then forgot and shaved the bottom half off, styling the remainder into a cross between a handlebar style and the 'Fu Manchu'. It screamed 'kiddie fiddler' as soon as I saw it, and he really wasn't doing anything to disabuse me of the notion.

"I'm gonna kill you, just so you know that..." I whispered, staring coldly at him. "And generations of little kiddies will say my name in their prayers because of it."

He punched me in the face, then tipped me over again, my head banging off the stone. Snarling, he spat on me before roughly tearing my top open. He dumped the pair of small white rats into the metal bucket then upturned it and slammed it down on my chest, making me wheeze in pain as broken ribs shifted.

"You think you're funny, pal?" he growled to me, while his friend started using duct-tape to attach the bin to my chest. I could feel the tiny paws rushing around inside the bin, and I glared at him, ready to cast my Incinerate spell, and just hoping it'd work fine, when one of the other two stepped up and said something to Moustache quietly.

"Here? What's she…fine!" he snapped back at the lackey, before turning to the other one. "Stay here. Watch the fucker and make sure he doesn't do anything. One coal, that's it!" He held a finger up in warning, storming from the room, the man who'd spoken following him out.

I waited on my back for an indeterminate length of time before the final man in the room slowly walked over, waving a glowing red coal in front of my eyes with some tongs.

"Let's just give ya a little taste, eh?" he whispered, drawing it slowly across my cheek.

I screamed as it burned the skin, a hissing noise filling my head. I glared furiously at him as he stepped back. I'd been planning on holding the spell until I could get Moustache, hopefully when there was just him and me in the room, but fuck that.

"You look like you want to tell me something?" he whispered, letting out a little giggle and reaching out with the coal again.

"Oh, I fucking do…" I snarled. "INCINERATE!" I didn't need to say it, but it really, really helped, as I poured mana into the spellform I wanted. My eyes blazed as I focused the spell on his head.

He blinked, his mouth dropping open slightly, before steam burst from his eye sockets, and popping and crackling noises filling the room. His corpse collapsed to the floor, twitching and thrashing, the hair blazing like a torch as smoke billowed up, making me cough again.

He'd knocked the brazier over at some point as he'd fallen from my sight. I looked around frantically, trying to figure a way out of the restraints.

The room was clearly an impromptu storage area; dozens of computers, copper pans, and random stuff which I guessed had once decorated the walls filled the room, but I could see nothing useful. I checked my mana, finding I had regenerated sixty points, giving me a total of fifty-three now that I'd used another hundred, and I wracked my brain, trying to figure a way out…I checked my flashing notifications, skimming past the deaths I'd meted out, and realized that I had five points left to assign!

Maybe I could up my strength enough that I…I froze, seeing the prompt I'd left for later…

Do you wish to create your Automata Pet now?
Yes/No

"Oh, yes. Yes, I fucking do…" I whispered to myself, a feral grin spreading across my lips in the darkness. Immediately, a wireframe box appeared in my vision, and I found I could manipulate it, shrinking and growing it in size to cover different items in the room. I dragged it to its biggest size with my mind and placed it over the pile of computers, pots and pans, and random junk. It flashed for a few seconds before more text appeared.

Assessing...please wait...
Technology limited to Bronze: Stone, Wood, Unrefined materials, and Bronze amalgamations are the current limit for your Automata. *Scanning...* Copper, Zinc, Tin, Wood, Stone found at acceptable levels. Neural pathway potential examined and found acceptable.
Do you wish to Proceed?
Yes/No

"Well, let's see. I'm strapped to a chair, about to be tortured to death. Maybe I should wait..." I muttered sarcastically. "Proceed!"

Please choose Automata physical form from the following:
Avian
Canine
Insectoid
R...

"Canine!" I snapped before it could finish listing all the options. I could hear the sound of footsteps echoing in the distance as people started walking down the stairs and into the corridor, presumably heading towards me.

Canine form accepted. Commencing build...

Piles of random gear was ripped from the walls by a localized gravitational field, dragging parts into the darkness and melting, restructuring, and redesigning with a cracking, hissing noise. Sounds like bones being broken echoed around the room, then electrical shorting and fizzing, before the pile of random components started compressing down, plastics being discarded as the Automata steadily built itself.

I was staring at the shifting pile, frantically hoping it'd be done in time, when the door opened with a boom, and a barrage of noise assaulted me. I tried to look towards the door, laid on my back and strapped to the chair as I was, but couldn't see anything. There was a collective intake of air as they saw the state of my thoroughly cooked captor, before snarling questions were hurled at me.

"What the hell happened?!?" demanded Moustache, the first to move into my field of vision, and I glared up at him. Looking back into the darkness, I couldn't see my Automata at all anymore, just a jumble of discarded parts, and I felt a spike of fear that it may have abandoned me.

"I said, what happened!" Moustache cried again, kicking me in the side of the head. I grunted, and a second voice called out. One that was much more familiar.

"Stop it, please. There be no need for this, there musta bin a reason he attacked us…" Hannah interrupted softly, looking down at me. I felt hands pull my chair upright, and she crouched before me, smiling sadly and reaching out to stroke my cheek. "Please, mate, we don't want to hurt ye. We just need to know what happened to our friend, an' why you attacked us. Are there more o' yer out there? Please, dinna make me leave yer with these men, I'd rather help ye, but…"

"mumble mumble mumble" I said, hanging my head low.

"Eh?" She asked, lifting my chin gently and moving closer, as Moustache started to speak up.

"I wouldn't get too close…" he started to say, just as I yanked my head back and nutted her.

She fell to the floor with a cry, swearing and clutching at her nose as blood leaked out between her fingers.

"I said 'Get fucked, Hannah!'" I snarled at her, and her eyes widened as she finally saw past the new swelling and injuries to recognize me.

"Matt?" she asked incredulously. "Be that you?" She pulled her hand back, staring at the blood on her fingers, then snorted and spat a bloody wad onto the floor, before glaring at me. "Fine. So playin' nice dinna work. That's all right; nasty's more fun anyway!" she snarled, hauling herself up and punching me in the face. "Now, where the fuck did ye go, what are yer doin' here, and where's Keith?" She didn't even wait for an answer before punching me again.

A light started to flash in my vision, and I selected it, grinning as I read the text that was clear as day, despite the rest of my vision being blurry now.

Automata construction is at 76%. Systems online.
Designation?

"Jack." I said with a grin, thinking of a dog I'd loved as a kid.

"What's that?" She asked, and I ignored her, reading the next line.

Designation 'Jack' accepted…
Primary combat systems are now being prioritized due to situation.
Current status:
Mobility: 74%
Internals: 96%
Combat: 58%
Estimated time to completion: 4m58s

"You really want to know?" I asked her, figuring I needed to buy all the time I could while I pulled up my stats quickly, allocating my remaining five points. I wanted to up my Agility, but that was useless when strapped to a chair. Only three things could help right now: Strength, to pull myself free, Charisma, to charm my way out, or Wisdom, to boost my mana regeneration, and maybe let me pull another Incinerate out of the bag. I tested the chair, finding it was too solid, with not even a creak in response as I pulled, so I dismissed Strength. I didn't like relying on Charisma; if it was just one on one, maybe, but there were four of them...

With no other logical choice, I put all five points into Wisdom, stiffening as the changes took effect, then shaking my head from side to side as new connections were made, my brain feeling like it'd been stabbed with hot needles. I started to relax as a punch hit me in the jaw, stunning me again.

"Yer think this is a wee game? Is that it?" Hannah snarled at me. "I remember yer pissin' yerself in the cage with Simo. Yer wanna go back? Be that it?"

"A deal..." I offered, glaring up at her through swollen eyes and lips. "I'll do you a deal...in my back pocket, there's a photo of Alyssa. She's here somewhere. Bring her here, and I'll tell you everything."

She roughly searched me, pulling the picture out and shrugging as she looked it over.

"Never seen her before," she said, passing the photo to another of the group. It wasn't until it reached Moustache that he nodded in recognition.

"North field...She didn't want to warm any man's bed, she said, so she was sent there 'til she learns her place."

"Her place?" Hannah growled, backhanding Moustache, hard. Her rings tore three lines in his cheek as he staggered backwards. "Her place is wherever she wants it to be, and don't ye forget it! A woman ain't just useful to yer fer sex, you fuckin' ejit. I'm twice the shot ye are, I lead half the huntin' parties, but yer sayin' I'm just good fer a tumble? That what yer sayin'?" She snarled at him, and he frantically shook his head.

"No...NO! No, I just meant...she didn't have any other skills, she wasn't one of us, we couldn't trust her..." he babbled, and she made as if to hit him again, making him flinch back.

"She a free worker?" she asked, and he shook his head. "A slave, then? Ah, fuck it. Go get her, an' be quick!" He rushed out of the room as she turned to me, arching her eyebrow as I sagged in relief. "Who's she to yer?" she asked.

"Nobody; I've never met her before." I said, and she glared at me.

"Eh? So what, ye thought she looked pretty, and ye'd come free her?" She scoffed, and I grinned at her, before coughing and spitting blood onto the floor to join the mess.

"Nope, her daughter was starving and roaming the streets, looking for her. You fucking animals abandoned a child to die because you wanted a pretty slave! Kinda proves all your talk about helping people is bullshit, doesn't it?"

There was a pause in the room as she glared at me, before she looked at the others, then back to me, then shrugged.

"Shame an' all, but we don't need kids here. Only so much food te go round, ye see? Now, she's bein' brought here, so talk. Where's Keith, and what the fuck happened to this asshole?" she asked, kicking the corpse on the floor.

"Well, 'Mr Toasty' there was a victim of spontaneous combustion. Weirdest thing I ever saw. Seems he was gonna try to cook the rats in here…" I said, arcing my back a bit to lift the bin upright and shaking it slightly, making the residents squeak in protest, "in the hope that they'd eat me, and I'd give up all my secrets. Thing is, it seems the gods disapproved…" I grinned, checking my mana.

Since I'd dropped the five points into it, the regeneration rate had gone up to one hundred and fifty points an hour. A quick bit of mental math gave me two and a half points per minute. I'd had fifty-three points left, and in the minutes since I'd cooked that fool, it had risen to sixty; then I'd upped my Wisdom, and it was now at sixty-five.

Fourteen minutes was all I needed, and my Automata, Jack, was nearly complete. I caught a faint movement in the darkness of the room behind them to the side of the door, and knew it was him.

"Bullshit," Hannah said, eyeing the brazier. "So yer sayin' that if I try that, I'll die?" She quirked one eyebrow in question.

"Oh, you'll die," I said, smiling. "Believe me on that if not anything else, Hannah. You're fucking dead meat, and so are the rest of your cocksucking friends, but not straight away. I need to find her, after all."

She smiled back at me sweetly, then reached out and placed her foot on my crotch, slowly increasing her weight as she stared into my eyes.

"That's nice…now, where the fuck is Keith!" she asked me coldly.

"Bitch!" I groaned, glaring up at her. "Keith's dead…so's his friend, fatso…" I grunted out, and she leaned in closer, applying more pressure.

"I don't believe yer," she said flatly. "Ain't no way a little pissant like yer would beat Keith inna fight…"

"Gun…" I hissed out through gritted teeth, and she let up the pressure slightly. "I brought his gun in my pocket…"

She turned to scan the room, clearly not finding it anywhere, then called to one of the men she'd brought with her. "Steve, go see who swiped his gear, an' bring it down. Tell 'em I want it all, not just fuckin' some of it, right?"

"Aye Hannah, give me a minute," he grumbled, turning and lumbering out of the door, leaving me with only her and one companion. I checked my mana, letting out another groan when I saw it'd only reached seventy-five.

I could risk it, use the 'Examine' spell, see if I could find out something useful, or save it, and maybe be able to cook one of them, intimidate the other, but I still needed twenty-five points, and that was ten damn minutes…I'd lose a ball long before then, at this rate.

"Let's try again, all right?" Hannah said grimly. "So far, ye've claimed yer killed me favorite fuck toy, said ye know nowt about the crispy asshole in the corner, an' I bet yer got nowt to say about the dead men outside either? Yer see why I'm thinkin' it's time to just off yer now…"

"Outside? Oh, you meant the incompetent assholes I shot on the way in?" I hissed out, and she leaned back, releasing the pressure on my balls again so that I could speak. "One of your lackeys tried to pick a fight with me, so I killed him, then more came running, and I killed them, then I got surrounded, and long story short…" There was a long pause as she looked me over.

"Bullshit. Ye were shittin' yerself in that cage with Simo. Ain't no way you did that; there's just no way," she said eventually, and I grinned at her. "What?" she asked skeptically.

"I killed them, because the thing you fucking assholes seem to have forgotten is that hiding and only fighting when you outnumber someone isn't the only way. There's a better one…"

"And that is?" she asked slowly.

"There's two actually; I misspoke…" I said, forcing a smile. "First, there's the ballsy way, the way I did that out there. I sniped your assholes, then just fucking ran at them, grabbed their guns, and used them. Think FPS…"

"FPS?" She frowned, confused.

"Yeah, First Person Shooter. Ever wonder why the characters survive? Why they kick everyone's ass? Because if you take the risks, you fucking win. You win every time, until you don't, and then it doesn't matter, because you're dead. Get it?"

"Yer mean ye just ran at 'em an' relied on blind luck? That's a dumb shit's way of doin' it. Ye'll die quick…"

"Yeah, maybe. That's where option two comes in, but I'll only tell you that one when I see Alyssa…"

"Yer'll do what I…" She started to say when a sound from outside the room distracted her, and Steve walked back in, a long sports bag in one hand. He set it down on a nearby table and opened it, showing her the guns inside. She moved back, finally removing all the pressure from my balls, and I let out a sigh of relief, checking the time I needed. Six minutes more. Thank god she liked to gloat.

She rummaged through the guns until she picked up the one I'd taken from Keith, holding it up to the meager light and swearing as she saw details she clearly recognized. She checked through the rest, then pulled a clip out of her pocket and slotted it into the gun, loading it and stepping forward to face me.

"You really killed 'im?" she demanded in a low growl.

"I really did. He was in my flat, eating my food, and he'd stolen my fairy."

"The fairy?" she asked, confused. "The thing in the crystal?"

"You've got it?" I asked her, and she snorted.

"I had it; lost it in a card game. What's it worth?"

"You better be shitting me right now!" I snapped at her.

"Nope, lost it two nights ago, Martin won it." I glared at her.

"And am I supposed to guess who that is?" I snarled, eliciting a grin from her.

"The man whose friend yer cooked there," she said, kicking the corpse's foot before gesturing towards the door. "Martin went for yer girl…"

"Ah, Moustache!" I said suddenly, relief filling me. "Well, that's something at least. I was always going to kill the ugly bastard, so that's a relief."

"Yer gonna kill him too, are ye? How you gonna do that?" she asked me, toying with the gun. "Considerin' yer all tied to the chair there, and we've got yer guns…"

"See, that's another thing you assholes don't get…" I said, forcing a smile. "I saw it years ago on a movie, can't remember which one it was, but it's so true, it's insane. Guns? They're tools…not weapons."

"Right?" she said, looking down at the gun in her hand, then back up at me.

"They're tools." I repeated. "Like a shovel is, or a carving knife. It's not a weapon, until it's used as one by an idiot. And you're an idiot, because you use it as a weapon. It's not."

"So what is it then, smart arse?" she retorted, and I heard echoing feet stomping down the corridor towards us. I checked the counter, seeing I had less than a minute left before I would have enough mana. It was time.

"It's a tool," I repeated. "The reason it's a tool is because ***I*** am the weapon."

Martin walked into the room, pausing as Hannah burst into laughter, and looked from her to me and back again, before shoving Alyssa forward. She staggered and almost fell before moving to stand with her back to the wall, staring at the ground. She was clearly terrified, on the ragged edge of physical and emotional exhaustion, and barely decent, considering how wet she was, and the way her ragged clothing stuck to her. Almost every inch was liberally coated in mud, and her hands, elbows, and probably half her body was covered in bruises and blisters. She was barefoot, and her hair was in a filthy ponytail, rather than the pixie bob in my photo. Despite her disheveled state, she was still clearly beautiful, and I saw the way Martin was staring at her.

"So, she's here," Hannah said, waving the gun from her to me. "Now spill it."

"Alyssa?" I called to her, and she flinched, staring down even harder. "Alyssa, I found Amy. She's safe. She and Spot are waiting for you, and I made sure she had food and rest."

There was a long pause after I spoke, then she seemed to make sense of the words through her exhaustion, and her head lifted fractionally. She tried to speak, then coughed, and tried again.

"Amy…my Amy? She's…okay?" She asked me, meeting my eyes hesitantly.

"She is," I insisted firmly. "Now, you don't need to see this, so do me a favor. Turn around and face the wall, okay? Close your eyes, and keep them closed until I say you can look…"

"O…okay…" she said, turning and pressing her forehead against the wall.

"Now what yer gonna…" Hannah started to say, and I glared at Martin.

"Right, fuckface. Time to come clean. The fairy you won from Hannah; where is it?" I growled and he started, then sneered at me.

"You want to trade for it? Not like yer got anything…?" He sneered before I cut him off.

"Just your life, Martin. Just your life." I closed my eyes, drew in a deep breath, and straightened up, looking around the room and concentrating. I could feel Jack waiting for a command, and I mentally designated everyone in the room, excluding only myself and Alyssa, as enemies.

Then I fixed my glare on Hannah.

EIGHTEEN

"SO, HANNAH, THE other way you win, is you make sure you have a backup plan," I stated slowly and clearly. "Pick one of your assholes," I ordered, and she frowned at me, then shrugged.

"Steve," she said, nodding to the man she'd sent to get the guns.

"Say goodbye, Steve, and remember…she picked you." I glared at him and activated 'Incinerate'. The mana flooded out of me, pouring into him as his chest erupted in flames, clothes burning, hair blackening, and orifices leaking steam. His corpse crashed to the floor, not even a scream escaping him, and at the same time, Jack struck.

My automata leapt from the darkness, teeth flashing in the reflected candlelight, and bit down hard on Hannah's outstretched arm. The sound of the bone crunching filled the air for a split second before his teeth met, and the hand, still holding Keith's gun, fell to the floor, severed.

Both men froze, fear on their faces, as Hannah staggered back, shoved aside by Jack as he raced for me. I yanked both hands up as high as I could, and his teeth sank into the wood below them, biting and ripping.

The wood was oak, ancient and well-seasoned, but against jaws made of bronze that could cut through bone with ease, it didn't last long. Hannah collapsed into her other goon's arms, and was dragged free of the room as I threw myself sideways, tilting the chair over and falling to the floor.

Martin yanked a pistol out of his pocket, the hammer catching on the thin material and snagging long enough that by the time he managed to fire, Jack was moving again. He'd freed my right hand, and then dove at the asshole. The bullet Martin had intended for me was intercepted, ricocheting off into the darkness to thud into something, and then Jack hit him, a menacing growl reverberating through him as he sank his teeth into Martin's most prized possession and froze.

I managed to shift the chair enough for my freed arm to reach the gun that Hannah had dropped, prying it from her severed hand before pointing it at the still-open doorway. Hannah's screams receded down the hall as she was dragged away by her friend. I changed my aim to Martin, who had also frozen and was whimpering, as red started to stain the crotch of his jeans, all around Jack's muzzle.

"Now, Martin," I said into the sudden ringing silence of the room. "This is what's going to happen. You're going to free me, very carefully, and you're going to tell me where the fairy is. If anything happens to me, Jack there is going to bite down. You see the gleam of metal on him?" He nodded slightly, still whimpering. "That's because he's not a dog. He's a…robot…or near enough. That means you shooting him is only going to piss him off. The only, and I mean *only*, way you live through this, is to make damn sure I do. His orders are to literally tear you apart. Slowly. Nod if you understand."

He nodded slowly; his eyes screwed tightly shut.

"Good boy. Now where are the keys?" I asked, and he started to move his hand to his pocket, freezing when Jack growled louder. "Jack's just letting you know he's watching you." I said, smiling slowly as I pointed my gun at the door again. "Go ahead, get the keys out and move over to me, carefully. You can give me your gun and free me."

"O…okay…" he whispered, his hand moving again. He pulled the keys free, then whimpering, he moved towards me, Jack moving slowly with him so as to not tear any further wounds without orders to do so.

The gun was pressed into my left hand, and he unlocked my handcuffs on both hands.

"I…I can't reach the ankles…" He whispered, and I looked down, then nodded.

"A fair point," I conceded. "Jack, release his cock, but if he makes any moves I don't like, tear his throat out."

Jack released him immediately, stepping back and growling metallically as Martin sank to his knees, moaning through gritted teeth as the wounds Jack's teeth had left tore open wider. He quickly released me, and I stood up, stretching and throwing the bucket of rats off to the side before moving to the door and sticking my head out. I couldn't see anything, but judging from the shouting upstairs, the corridor wouldn't be clear for long. I turned back to the room and called out to Alyssa.

"Alyssa, I'm Matt, and Amy asked me to rescue you, so if you give me a minute, we'll be on our way, okay?" She nodded slowly, sneaking a peek at me. "Oh, and you can look around if you want. I just thought you might not want to see all of that unpleasantness, that's all!" I said, forcing a chuckle.

I ached everywhere, but I knew I'd be all right. My wildly accelerated healing was already at work, and I could feel my body fixing itself. My mana was climbing steadily, despite the developing migraine trying to spread, and I had a fairly defensible location to get started with.

I went to sort through the bag of guns, checking them over and finding that not only was the rifle I'd grabbed in the bag, but so was the shotgun, three other handguns, some brass knuckles, my diving knife, which I didn't even remember I'd had until now, so hadn't missed, and my intact training sword.

"So, where's my fairy, Martin?" I asked, and Jack growled, the sound rumbling from deep inside somewhere.

"I…in my room…" he whimpered.

"And that is…?" I asked, leaning closer.

"Upstairs…second floor…"

"Good boy!" I said, smiling. "Right, then; can you shoot a gun, Alyssa?" I asked her. She started to shake her head, then stopped.

"I…I've never done it before, but I will," she said, determination filling her voice as she turned from the wall, glaring at Martin.

"Glad to hear it," I said, offering her a handgun that I'd just checked. "This is the safety…" I said, pointing to it. "You have this in this position when you don't want to hurt anyone, and here…when you do," I said, demonstrating. "Beyond that, point and pull the trigger. Nice and simple. For now, that's all you need to know, and hopefully you won't need to use it." I slipped my sword back over my shoulder, stuffing a pair of handguns into my belt with only a momentary fear of blowing my cock off.

I reattached the knife to my right ankle and took up the rifle. It was the most modern one I'd ever seen, and I looked it over, checking to make sure I could work it before calling to Martin. "Where'd you get this?" I asked, knowing that it would have been nigh-on impossible to get before the end of the world, gun laws being what they were in England.

"Armed police," he said shortly.

"And?"

"And what?"

"And where the fuck are they, and how did you get your hands on their guns?" I growled.

"They're dead," he said bluntly. "There's a couple of normal coppers in the slave gang, but the armed ones were too dangerous, so we killed them."

"Right," I said grimly, I'd always intended to kill Martin when his usefulness was over, but he'd just made sure Jack was going to be the one to do it. "How many of you are there?"

"Of who?"

"You, you gypsy prick," I snarled.

"I'm no gypsy!" he retorted, then whimpered as he shifted and bled heavier. "I need bandages, please…"

"How many are there!" I snarled, and he gulped before answering.

"About fifty. There were a lot more gypsies, but most wouldn't follow the King, and they left. About twenty of them stayed here, and then we all joined them, made a new gang, and agreed to follow the King."

"Fair enough. How many in here?" I asked, gesturing upwards.

"Usually about five of us; we were having lunch when you attacked."

"Where's the rest of you?"

"Spread out. Look…we make sure they don't know how few of us there are, okay? There are two groups of five out hunting for food, raiding the shops an' shit. Then five of us here normally, and ten with the King. the rest are spread out around the park, keeping people workin.'"

"And there's no warning sign, no alarms?" I asked.

"What would we use? There's a bell that we ring for lunch, but it's a tiny thing. The walkie talkies don't work, so we just shout…"

"Better and better," I said. "Now, all you have to do is take me to the fairy." I shot a warning glance at him, before turning to Alyssa. "Could you carry that bag, please?" I asked her, having stripped the corpses of their guns and chucked them inside. "We're going to be filling it as we go."

She nodded to me, glaring at Martin again, and edged around Jack to pick it up and sling it over her shoulder.

"Want some good news, Martin?" I asked him, smiling grimly as he glared at me through tear-filled eyes. "You get to lead the way!"

"I'm bleeding to death here!" he snarled, and I smiled at him coldly.

"Then we'd better hurry, hadn't we? Unless you're saying you're of no more use to me?" I asked, and on cue, Jack moved closer to him, his shining teeth gleaming in the dim light as he rumbled.

"I…I'll lead!" Martin hurriedly said, forcing himself to his feet with a moan of pain. He staggered past me, glaring at me, before looking away quickly, and leading the way out into the corridor.

I went next, and Alyssa followed, obviously unsure but determined to get back to her daughter. She tried to ask me questions, but I shook my head.

"I'm sorry Alyssa, but we've got no time. I'll explain everything later. Just know that she's safe, and I'll take you to her." I said, reaching out to Jack mentally, I ordered him to follow along behind us, watching Alyssa, just in case, and to make sure we weren't jumped on. Then I added that if Martin tried to run, he was to hamstring him.

We followed Martin along the corridor to the next floor, moving up from the old stone slabs and crumbling brick lower floors into the customer-facing and obviously recently renovated main floors. Here, it was all burnished wood, clean cream walls, and glass meeting rooms, with a decent-sized café and a private area to conduct weddings…covered in marks everywhere from muddy boots, blood splatters on the walls, and filth already starting to build up.

We took a side passage, then another, and left the customer friendly areas, still encountering nobody, but when we climbed the next set of stairs, we paused at the entrance to the next floor when we heard voices in the distance.

"You go!"

"I'm not going! You think I'm fucking crazy? It's another one of those *things*; it's gotta be!"

"You think the King's gonna just shrug when he finds out we hid? That's his fucking daughter that they carried out! If we don't kill it, he'll kill us!" I turned to Martin and looked at him questioningly.

"They must have seen Hannah get carried out. There'll be more coming," he whispered sullenly.

"What creatures?" I asked him, and he blinked.

"You've not seen them? Weird things. Some are just rats with freaky tails or teeth, but some are…I don't know what. A thing like a fucking dinosaur killed a kid yesterday in the park, just swooped in and grabbed him; tore his head off as it flew away."

"Okay, how many are likely to be in there?" I gestured with my head to the door where we could hear the low voices.

"Probably just the two of them. Sounds like Adam and Petey, both cowards, but they're fast enough to try to get the spoils when newbies join us…"

"I don't even want to fucking know what kinda shit you're hinting at," I said, glaring at him. "Lead the way and call them out, now."

He winced, straightening up and pushing the doors open to walk into a corridor with a dozen rooms on either side.

"Who's up here?" he called out in a strained voice. Silence met him, and he growled. "I heard you talking, you fuck nuggets! Get out here!"

"Martin?" a voice answered, and a greasy mop of hair peered around the corner of a door, then ducked back when he saw me keeping my gun pointed downwards, with enough space away from Martin that I was confident I could get him if I needed to. Just in case, I pulled the handgun out of my belt with my left and flicked the safety off, holding it out of sight.

"Who else is it going to be, you idiots!" Martin snarled, then staggered, grabbing at the wall. "Get out here!" First the greasy one stepped out; a knife held loosely in his fist. A long green hooded coat almost covered him from head to ankles, clearly meant for someone much larger, while his friend, a spotty, half-grown beard covering his face and enormous hair styled into a collection of spikes, reluctantly joined him.

The pair of them looked ridiculous. Their clothes would have been called hand-me-downs, they fitted that badly, but they were clearly brand-new and looted. They appeared to have the muscle tone of over-stretched elastic bands and the kind of personal hygiene that peasants in the dark ages would have been offended by. The only reason I didn't dismiss them both entirely was that the first one's knife hand and that side of his clothes showed speckles of dried blood, while the other twitched incessantly and stared fixedly at Alyssa, as though the rest of us didn't exist.

"You…" he whispered, pointing at her. "You're her…I remember you. Too pretty, don't wanna talk to the likes of us; oh no, not 'til the new world comes! I caught you, I brought you in, but they took you…you were supposed to be mine…" he said, practically drooling at the sight of her. "M…Martin, you wanna trade for her? Or can I just…"

The boom of the handgun I'd given Alyssa going off right next to me sent me flinching away, as the first bullet slammed into him, taking him from his feet. She fired again, and again, until the clip was empty and both assholes were on the floor, blood splattered everywhere. She collapsed, dropping the gun to the floor and pulling her arms and legs in tight as she sobbed uncontrollably.

Martin tried to run, shoving me where I stood. Stunned by the sudden attack, I fell backwards, hitting the doors and crashing through them into a room full of junk and stolen random gear.

I hit the ground, twisted, and tried to get to my feet by grabbing a box to help me up. The case promptly shifted, covering me in hundreds of packets of condoms. I swore, frantically thrashing, just in time to hear a horrific scream from Martin as Jack carried out the orders I'd given him earlier. I made my way out just in time to see him tearing out the back of Martins lower legs and leaving him on the floor, thrashing and screaming.

"Motherfucker!" I snarled, moving back out into the hallway and taking in the scene of chaos. Martin hadn't even made it a dozen feet before Jack got to him, and now he was screaming, blood spraying all over as he tried to drag himself over the corpses of the pair of idiots Alyssa had shot.

"Jack, kill him," I snarled, grabbing the other handgun from my belt and discarding the rifle for now. I moved quickly, ignoring the bodies and the sobbing woman, kicking open the nearest door and staring inside. Nothing, just a pile of gear and a single mattress in the corner.

"Jack, search this floor. Anyone attacks you, kill them. Anyone you find unarmed, bring them to me." I sensed the hesitation from the Automata for the first time. Clearly, my orders were too vague. "Dammit; fine! Find any live humans on this floor," I commanded, and he spun around, racing from room to room. I moved slower, searching them quickly after him. The first five rooms had nothing in them, the sixth had three bullets on a counter, but none would fit my guns, judging by the size, so I pocketed them and moved on.

The next two rooms held nothing of use, but the ninth contained a pile of plain black long-sleeved tops on the desk. I quickly grabbed an XL and pulled it on, searching the room and finding little else. The remaining rooms were disappointingly empty, until I reached the last one. A small desk and bed furnished it, with an ornate cabinet full of china dolls that just freaked me the hell out.

They'd all been stripped of whatever outfits they'd worn, painted with lipstick, then dressed in tiny kid's clothes. I shuddered at the mind that would do that, then let out a sigh of relief when I saw, tucked away in the corner of the cabinet, the crystal case for the fairy. I pulled it out and checked it over, noting the obvious attempts to open it from the scratches and chips that marred the surface, but it was still safe inside, if looking even more battered.

"Thank fuck." I whispered to myself, turning and exiting the room, before pausing to step back inside and pick up a long trench coat I'd seen hanging up. It wasn't the weather for it yet, but damn if it wasn't cool looking.

I pulled the coat on and took advantage of the multiple pockets, stuffing guns and ammo into them from the bag, leaving Alyssa to deal with for last. Finally, when most of the guns were secured and I looked like either a total badass or a complete nutjob, I moved to her. Jack had returned to the top of the stairs as soon as he'd completed his sweep and was standing guard, watching the next level up and the way down with equal fervor.

"Alyssa…" I said quietly, reaching out to touch her shoulder. She flinched away, turning to face the wall more fully and pulling her legs up as close as they'd go. "Alyssa, Amy needs you." I hesitated, unsure of what else I could say to her. At first, it didn't seem to get through to her, so I went on. "Amy's all alone with Spot. She's in your house, and she's already been out searching the streets; first for that dumb dog, and then for you. You don't want her out there, do you? Not with the creatures…not with assholes like these walking around?"

She shifted slightly but didn't respond, and I was about to try again, when a warning growl came from the stairwell.

"Shit!" I cursed, moving quickly to grab the rifle, the handguns slotted away safe in my new coat as I moved to a position where I could see Jack. He was facing downstairs, a low steady rumble of warning filling the stairwell, as he'd clearly heard something I couldn't yet.

I looked down, then back at Alyssa and up to the next floor, before darting back inside and grabbing her under one arm. I dragged her to her feet and out into the stairwell, ignoring the mumbled pleas to just leave her there.

"Amy needs you, so pull yourself together!" I snarled at her, pointing her up the stairs to the next floor. "Jack! Make sure there's nobody else in the higher floors." I ordered, and he tore off, running past us and nearly taking the doors off their hinges as he went.

I struggled up the stairs, half carrying, half dragging Alyssa with me.

"I…I…" she mumbled, rubbing her hands frantically. "I killed them! I…"

"Yeah, well, they're no loss to the world. Frankly, you probably cleaned the gene pool up a bit…" I muttered, looking over the side of the railing to verify that nobody was following us. I had started to hear sounds from downstairs, but nothing I could identify.

The next floor was split down the middle; half had clearly been in the process of refurbishment, with plastic sheeting hanging in places, while the other side was open plan, with desks and tables stacked against the wall.

There was also a hell of a lot of food stacked inside; hundreds, probably thousands of tins, crates of random stuff…It looked like they'd looted the back room of a supermarket and dumped it all here. It was easily enough food to supply a hundred people for a week, I guessed, and then as we went in further, I revised my estimates.

There had to be enough food for at least a month, if not longer, for hundreds of people, if they were sensible about it. Cases of pasta, boxes of sauces, crates of drinks, crisps, long-life dairy goods, and around one corner, I even saw piles of nappies and books. The main floor had been converted into a warehouse, and yet, just outside, people were starving.

It made my blood boil, even though I knew that there was a need for control. Just killing the assholes and leaving wouldn't end well. People would grab what they could, fight over the rest, and then starve in a few weeks' time.

"Shit!" I repeated, looking around and letting go of Alyssa. She slumped to the floor, rubbing at her hands again, and I ignored her, moving between aisles of stacked food to reach the front windows and look out.

There were two people waiting out front, with a half dozen more coming out of the trees and heading towards us now. Each one was armed, and in the center of the group was the asshole, self-styled King. He was stomping along, clearly furious, with blood on the front of his clothes, carrying a rifle that looked to be a match for the one I held.

Doing a quick count, I saw that there were six rifles, at least ten handguns, and three shotguns spread out among the eight outside. Even so, one guy had a single handgun, while others had shotguns or rifles strapped to their backs, indicating that they were unwilling to share or be under tight control.

"Okay…" I muttered quietly, looking my new rifle over again and moving to a low stack of tinned spaghetti nearby. I rested the barrel of the rifle on top and flicked off the safety, sighting along it. Focusing, I began drawing in a slow breath and holding it, as I remembered hearing it was done from TV.

I tracked the King, watching as he waved his hands in the air, giving orders, and then backhanding someone that came running up to tell him something he didn't like.

I let my breath out, took in another…held it…and squeezed the trigger gently. It seemed to take much longer than I thought, bending back further and further as I slowly shifted my point of aim, before it finally fired, the bullet flashing across the distance between us…to totally miss him. Instead, it took the man he'd just backhanded in the ass, making him squeal and jump, as the rest of the group froze.

I swore. Having never fired the rifle before, I'd completely buggered it, and instead of taking advantage of the shock, I'd frozen as well. They scattered, and I started firing at any of them I could, missing four out of the next six shots I managed to get off. One man got taken down with a lucky headshot, and I somehow got another high in the thigh, spinning him from sight with a scream of pain.

I spun around and raced for the stairs. Hoping there was only the one way onto this floor, but seriously doubting it, I grabbed the first slab of cans I could reach and started piling them up, making an impromptu barrier I could hide behind. I managed to get it a dozen slabs high, two wide, and three long in an inverted 'L' shape before the first of them cleared the stairwell, and I dove into cover.

He was a big man, pale as milk, with a massive beard that was missing the chin, and his first shot slammed into the tins an inch from my head, the second going past so close I could have sworn I felt it pass.

I ducked down, then rammed the rifle through a small gap I'd left accidentally and shot him in the chest, sending him flailing his arms as he fell down the stairs, his gun clattering to the floor at the top.

Jack came tearing down the stairs from above and leaped at a second man just as he came into view, bearing him down the stairs with a quickly cut-off scream as he started savaging the thug's throat.

I used the chance to grab another few slabs of cans and start work on the second leg of my impromptu fort, aiming to make the 'L' into a 'U' as quickly as possible, when I noticed Alyssa frantically crawling deeper into the room, away from the door. I silently wished her good luck, figuring that if she managed to escape in all this mess, then at least she knew where her daughter was.

I felt a pain in my side, and looked down, then another, and one in my left arm, but there was no visible injury…when I realized what it had to be. Nobody else had come up the stairs yet, since Jack had descended into a frenzy. I had to guess it was him I was feeling, from the echoing gunshots.

"Jack, get your shiny arse up here!" I bellowed, before looking around and swearing. I couldn't see the gun bag. I'd brought it upstairs, I knew I had, but I just didn't know where I'd left it in all the confusion!

Fuck it.

I had three handguns on me now, all fully loaded, and the rifle had at least another twenty bullets in it. The clip had held twenty-eight when I'd grabbed it, and while I'd fired a few rounds, there were more loose bullets in my pockets, so I could reload it a little, at least. I scanned the room again, wishing I'd had time to search it properly.

"Alyssa!" I called, getting no response. "They're coming, Alyssa! They're gonna come up here any minute, and you can either fight, or you can pray they won't kill you, but you'll never be free, you know that! You need to pick a side!" Again, no response, but I heard another burst of fire from below and a clattering sound as Jack came into view.

He looked like shit. I'd barely had time to look at him when he'd first been finished, briefly registering a mess of coppery bones and armor, wiring and wood, but where before he'd looked like a polished and lovingly made steampunk dog, now he looked like he'd gone through the washing machine on a spin cycle with a ton of rubble.

He was missing one eye, had a hole in the side of his skull, and his front left leg was dangling uselessly, connected only by a few trailing wires. He was scratched, scuffed, and covered in blood, but he was functional still, even if only barely. He hobbled to my side and froze, awaiting further orders.

I looked him over quickly, and a prompt popped up. I almost dismissed it, but took the time to read and understand the state of him in all its damning glory.

Jack	Automata
This Automata has been named Jack, and is a level 0 Dungeon Lord Pet. It is built along the 'Canine' design, maximized at 'Bronze,' with serrated teeth and sharpened claws. The present design has space for five upgrades but is currently heavily damaged.	
Durability 5/20	Special Features: 0/0

"Shit, sorry, buddy," I said, reaching out and awkwardly patting him on the head. "I've really not looked after you very well, have I? Welcome to the world, I guess, considering you're less than an hour old…"

I shook my head and glanced back at the stairs. I could hear voices from below, swearing and shouting for help, but I had no idea how many were left.

"Jack, I need you to go find out if there's another way to this floor, beyond the stairwell…" I said to him, but he just stood there. "Dammit! Jack go, uh, search? Find another way down?" I ordered him, and again he stood still, but after a handful of seconds, he turned and started limping off into the aisles.

I watched him go, then shook my head, just hoping he didn't find one. They needed the food, so their only real option was to charge me. If there wasn't another way to this floor, I could slaughter them, but…

There was a boom of a shotgun from deeper in the aisles and I swore, a clatter of running feet on the stairs announcing another two men rushing up. I shot at them frantically, even as they fired back, bullets slamming into the tins around me. I got the first in the knee, then the top of the head as he fell forwards. The second managed to dive aside, and I missed him entirely, but he was still in the stairwell, with only up, down, or this floor as an option.

I looked around again worriedly before focusing on the stairs again.

"Alyssa, I really hope you got away!" I said aloud as two more ran up into view, and before I could shoot at them, a rifle appeared around the corner, the man who'd survived spraying bullets wildly.

I ducked reflexively, then growled at myself, as the bullets hit the tins and either bounced off or were stopped. I forced myself to be calm, looking down the barrel of my rifle and holding my fire, ignoring the scream of bullets hitting into metal things all around me.

It felt like a million shots hit too close to me as I lined up and pulled the trigger, but as I took the first in the face, sending him cartwheeling backward, and the second in the shoulder, I felt an odd acceptance come over me. I knew I was probably going to die soon. Hell, I'd been living on borrowed time since all this began, but while I was here, I'd make sure these assholes died first.

As the second spun around, the force of the bullet practically tearing him from his feet, the one that was hiding stepped out and frantically fired at my cover. I ducked aside as a lucky bullet passed down the gap I was using to fire from. Then I pulled the trigger again and again, firing blindly back until their gunfire stopped, and I heard more screaming start up.

I risked a quick look, seeing the pair of them were down, one of them writhing on their back with hands pressed around their stomach, the other unmoving, and then I felt a phantom pain rip through my head, stunning me for a few seconds.

By the time I could see again, another man was advancing cautiously up the stairs, and when I grabbed my gun and took aim, he panicked and started firing his shotgun at the tins. The birdshot slammed into my makeshift wall twice, until his finger clicked on an empty barrel. I moved quickly, sliding back behind the rifle and fired at him, three shots, hitting him in the chest twice. The third hit his shotgun, sending it flying from his hands.

Then I heard a click behind me.

"Nice to see you again, Matt..." a familiar voice said grimly, and I froze. I shifted slightly, and he spoke again. "Ah, ah...don't be movin' now...wouldn't want my men to be makin' a mistake, now would we?"

I felt the barrel of a gun pressed to the back of my head, and then a new voice whispered to me.

"Move slowly, stand up, arms out to the sides..." I did as I was ordered, straightening and feeling a hand pat me over, grabbing my guns and throwing them aside. I left the rifle hanging half out of the gap I'd been firing through as I turned and looked at the three of them standing there.

The self-styled King stood in the middle, waiting at the back while one man stood to my left and one to the right. 'Lefty' had a handgun pointed at my forehead from a few inches back and had clearly been the one to search me, while 'Righty' was a half dozen feet back, and moved to lean his rifle on a stack of tinned peaches, keeping it trained on me.

"You're a fuckin' cockroach, you know that?" King said, sneering at me. "Three times, we've tried to dispose of you now, and they do say the third's the charm, don't they?"

"How's Hannah?" I asked, glaring at him.

"She's fuckin' dead!" he spat, fury clear on his face. "Whatever your 'dog' was, it tore her arm clean through. She bled out before I could even get to her! Believe me, boy, I'm gonna make your death slow for that. So, so slow..."

"Yeah, she tried that kinda shit too; see how well that worked out for her?" I shifted my gaze to Lefty. "What did you hear? You hear how I killed her guards? Hmmm?" I turned and looked at Righty, recognizing him at last as the man who'd dragged Hannah away. "You know what I'm capable of, don't you…" I said to him, and concentrated. I hadn't regained much mana yet, just under forty points, but maybe…

I focused on his left hand where he held the rifle and tried to use the 'Incinerate' spell…nothing happened, aside from a sudden flare of pain in my head. I switched to my other spell, hoping and praying it would work.

Arnold James Wester	Human
Arnold James Wester was born on the 23/11/1972, has one sister, has been married twice and has three children, none of which are in contact with him. He has a deep and abiding hatred for all foreigners and steadily believes that if he was given 'his due' it would all be different. HP: 97/100 Stamina: 45/80 Mana: 0/0 Fear: 7/10 Level: 0	
HP 97/100	Special Abilities: 0/0

"Well, Arnold?" I pressed him. "Not gonna tell the others what you saw? The way I burned your friend to death with a fucking word? Tell you what; let's see if you're as lucky a second time around, shall we?" I turned to King and spoke directly to him, noting the uncertain glare he was giving Arnold now. "Hey 'King,' pick one of your two friends here for me…" I said, forcing a grin as I desperately tried to come up with a plan beyond bullshitting my way out.

"Don't!" Arnold snapped desperately. "Don't let him talk!"

"What's up? Afraid of what I might say?" I asked, continuing to grin.

"I told you, King…he killed Steve with a fucking word!" He glared at me. "I don't care what anyone says; one more word and I'll shoot…" he warned me, and I turned back to King, quirking an eyebrow at him.

"I'll get the truth out of yer later…" King growled at Arnold, before fixing me with a glare. "Seems like every'un believes in magic these days, don't it… well, shit on that. You speak, you die. See if you can still do it with your head blown off, eh?" He pulled a filthy handkerchief from a pocket and waved it at the guy with the handgun. "Here, ball that up and stick it in his mouth; should shut him up."

I saw the filthy thing and felt my bile rise along with my fear, as my attempts at contacting Jack had totally failed. They'd blatantly killed him when they came onto this floor, and now…

Prompts! I thought desperately, pulling them up and scouring through them.

Congratulations!
You have defeated Fourteen opponents classed as 'Gypsy Thug'
Thug level: 0
Your level: 5
XP awarded: 350
*
Congratulations!
Your Bonded Automata has defeated four opponents classed as 'Gypsy Thug'
Thug level: 0
Automata level: 0
XP awarded: 100
*
Congratulations!
A member of your party has defeated two opponents classed as 'Gypsy Thug'
Thug level: 0
Party member level: 0
XP awarded: 25
Current XP to next level: 500/600…

I swore internally. I needed four more of them, four! After all of this, I still needed four! I glared at King as I dismissed the screen, but then I couldn't help it…I started to smile, the faint uplift of the corners of my mouth quickly progressing from a little smile, to full-on amusement.

"Now what the fuck are you grinnin' about?" King asked rhetorically, when he heard the click from behind of a safety being flicked off. He froze as Alyssa pressed a shotgun firmly into the back of his skull.

NINETEEN

I NODDED TO HIM and then slowly reached up and pointed to the pair at the back of the group, first Arnold, then the other man, flicking their gazes over to see what had stopped their boss mid-conversation.

As soon as the man closest to me looked the other way, I moved, my boosted Strength and Dexterity enhancing my moves enough that when I slapped the handgun aside, I was fast enough to grab him by the throat and drag him between Arnold and I, who fired, shooting his friend in the back.

I dropped to the floor, the tins protecting me enough from sight that I managed to get my nearest handgun back into my grip as I called out, King remaining frozen at the end of Alyssa's shotgun.

"So, how about we all stay exactly where we are, eh?" I said, slowly straightening up, the handgun aimed between Arnold's eyes. "Now, Arnold, you put the gun down, and we can make a deal, because you already know I don't die easily…can you say the same?"

"What deal?" he asked, and King growled in fury.

"No deal! Shut yer mouth, Arnold…"

"Get fucked," Arnold retorted, still glaring at me, but the barrel of his rifle was visibly trembling. "What deal?" he asked again.

"A nice, simple one," I offered. "You put the rifle down there, back up, and fuck off. If I don't see you ever again, it'll be too soon. You go live your best life, and I'll forget I ever saw you, or we shoot each other now, you die, and I get annoyed. Then I'll piss on your grave and go looking for your ex-wives, your three kids, and your sister, make sure they understand why I've come for them." I bluffed, having no idea who they were or what they looked like. Hell, they could be great people for all I knew. I just needed to scare him further.

It was enough.

His eyes widened even further, and he swallowed hard, shaking his head as he started to slowly back up.

"I'll go, but you leave me and mine alone; and I'm taking the gun…"

"You try to take it, and I'll make your balls explode," I growled. "The gun stays here." He froze, then slowly shook his head.

"I don't know what you are, but if you could have done that, I'd already be dead…" He said slowly, licking his lips and looking around. "No, me and my gun are going…you do whatever you have to here. I want none of this shit…" He took another step back, then turned and ran, disappearing into the aisles as I turned to Alyssa and King.

I walked over to them, smiling to King as I passed him, before making damn sure I was out of the line of fire.

"Thank you, Alyssa," I said gratefully, and she nodded, looking suddenly unsure of herself. "Want me to take over?" She swallowed hard, before nodding slightly. "That's fine. Thank you again for your help, okay? Now, do me a favor and go have a look out the windows, see if Arnold is out there…"

"Why?" she asked me, lowering her gun as my own handgun took up station pressed to his forehead.

"Well, is he a man you'd trust walking around with a rifle?" I asked her, and she shook her head, before pausing.

"But you made a deal with him?" she said, doubt in her voice.

"Nope. I offered a deal to him. He was to leave the gun, and then he could fuck off safely. Instead, he just left, refusing the deal." King snorted at me, before speaking to Alyssa.

"A real trustworthy man, this; sure you picked the right side, girl?"

"At least he's not tried to rape or kidnap me!" she snarled at him, storming off.

"She's got a point there, you know," I said before using 'Examine' on him and snorting at the results.

Louis Briccant	Human
Louis Briccant, or Lou, as he hates to be known, has spent a lifetime living down the name his uncaring parents saddled him with. He has one wife, Esmerelda, and no living children. The driving tenet of his personality is a low-lying paranoia that has cost him any real chances at authority or healthy relationships for his entire life. He rules by fear, as any kind of loyalty shown to him is acknowledged simply as his due, while any possible disagreement must be a sign of betrayal. HP: 100/100 Stamina: 38/70 Mana: 0/0 Fear: 7/10 Level: 0	
HP 100/100	Special Abilities: 0/0

"Lou Briccant?" I chortled, unable to help myself, and his eyes flashed in fury at the response he'd presumably had all his life.

"It's King Louis!" he snapped, and I snorted again, shaking my head.

"No, it's dickhead. That's the name you've earnt Lou. I'll make this easy. Where are the prisoners, the guns, and your stash? Because we both know a fuck-head like you always has a stash set up somewhere, ready to run when it all goes tits up."

"I'm telling you nothing!" he hissed, and I cocked my head to one side as I looked him in the eyes.

"You sure about that? Because that means you're pretty useless to me; you know that, right?" I said, and he glared at me.

"He's there, crossing the path downstairs." Alyssa called to me, and I shrugged to Lou.

"Sorry, Lou, you're clearly useless, and I've got things to do. Bye!" I pulled the trigger as he tried to dodge. He'd barely moved an inch when the bullet slammed into his skull, and he fell in a shower of gore as I hurried over to the window, putting my handgun away and taking my rifle in hand.

Sure enough, Arnold was hurrying away across the main path, gun clutched in both hands and head practically spinning, he was trying to look in all directions so much.

I took a deep breath, leaning on the windowsill, and Alyssa opened the window for me as I sighted along the barrel.

"Thanks, Alyssa," I murmured, stroking the trigger once. A hole appeared in the hurrying man's back a half second later. He was thrown forward by the hit, his gun tumbling to the dirt, and he tried to cry out, only able to release a pained gasp as he died, half of his heart torn apart by the bullet's passage.

I straightened up and looked at Alyssa, who was resolutely facing away from the window.

"I know I probably don't seem like it right now, but I try to be a good man, and I keep my word, Alyssa. I told Amy I would see you home to her, and I'll damn well do that, or die trying. That man would have tried to set up again somewhere else with a weapon like that, I've no doubt, and I won't allow that. I hope you understand."

She just nodded once but refused to look at me.

"That's fine," I said, a touch sadly. "Look, what we're going to do is this: you grab as much food as you can carry, and I'll escort you out and make sure you get home. Then I'm going to go free the others, and make sure this gang is taken down, okay?" She nodded, but she still wouldn't look my way. "Okay, go get whatever food you want to take."

I watched her go before hurrying to the bodies strewn about the room, stripping them of their guns and any ammo. Beyond that, I ignored them and started searching the outer edges of the room. It didn't take long to find Jack's remains. His body was damaged, but the head was almost completely gone, blown apart by that asshole Lou.

I grunted as I picked him up, carrying him back to the main area, where I found a small hand cart. Alyssa had selected a few bags of food and that was it, so, sighing, I loaded up the hand cart with slabs of tins and bags of food, remembering at the last minute to grab one for the guy outside the park, before setting Jack and my bag of guns on the top. It was awkward getting it all down to the ground floor, especially with the blood everywhere, but it only took a few minutes, all told. I asked Alyssa to pull it, while I led the way with my guns at the ready. When I passed Arnold's corpse, I relieved him of the rifle, putting it and the three clips he'd been carrying into the bag after replacing the empty one in my gun.

We followed much the same path as I had on the way in, pausing at the slave cages to free the captives and directing them to leave the park for now.

"There's food in the mansion," Alyssa spoke up suddenly, and the entire group fixated on her and the hand cart she was pulling, making me swear in frustration.

"There is," I confirmed. "However, I've just had to fight dozens of people for that food, and there are still more of them roaming around, so you can go looking, or you can leave the park, as I said. Then once I've killed the rest of them, you can go eat what you want."

"Why should we believe you?" one man demanded, glaring at me.

"About what?" I asked.

"That there's more food there; there's food right here…" His ravenous gaze ran over Alyssa and the food she was pulling along, and she went, if possible, even paler, realizing what she'd just done in drawing their attention to their stomachs.

"Because I'm the man that's just killed over a dozen men and freed you. You can believe what the hell you want, as long as you fuck off, but let me make this clear: you try to take *this* food, and I'll kill you," I said coldly, pointing the rifle at his forehead.

"O…okay.." He threw his hands up in acquiescence, backing up quickly.

"Good boy." I sighed, looking around the rest of the haggard faces. "Look, I don't give a shit who you are or what you've done to get here. I'm leaving the park now with Alyssa, here. You can come or stay; just don't try anything, as I'm not in the mood, right?" The group all looked at each other, but they moved back in deference to the obvious threat I was posing with my rifle. "Alyssa, let's go," I said and stalked onwards, making it clear I was pissed off and not to mess with me right now.

We moved down the paths, and the trip to the gate where I'd entered was thankfully uneventful. When we arrived, I could hear arguing from outside, as the man I'd bribed to guard the gate kept people back. I climbed the structure quickly and moved to the edge where I could see what was going on but stayed as low and quiet as possible.

"...I don't give a shit! I said nobody goes in, so you can fuck off somewhere else, or I'll smash your teeth in...right?" My man growled at the small group before him. He had a single guy on his side, and nine men were facing them now, two of which had picked up golf clubs and were obviously building up to using them.

"We need food, Barry! I don't care what you promised. You move, or I swear I'll..." one man said, lifting the club threateningly.

"You'll what, exactly?" I asked, deciding it'd gone far enough and standing up in plain sight. I leveled the rifle at him and waited, watching the irritation turn to shock, and then fear, as he started to back up. "You think you get to threaten a man I've hired to do a job, do you? Threaten him with a fucking club? That makes you a bully in my eyes, and I hate bullies..." I let my voice trail off at the end, and I made a point of sighting down the rifle at him. He started to wave his hands, clearly trying to show that he wasn't a threat, then realized what he was holding and dropped the golf club like it was on fire.

"No! It.... It's not what it looks like, okay?!" We're just hungry!" he called, and I snorted, shaking my head.

"And you think getting in here would help that? Look at these people!" I said, gesturing down to where the structure shook as people pulled the bracing free and opened the barrier. Their efforts exposed a way through that was braced from the inside, making it almost impossible to force, but easy to open, when you could see the structure.

As the last sections were pulled free and people started filing out into the street, they were greeted by gasps of shock. The men that had been so desperate to get in began to back away quickly, seeing faces they recognized, now gaunt and worn after only a few days of exceedingly hard work and little food.

"What the hell..." Barry muttered, dumbfounded, before seeing Alyssa, who stumbled out next, pulling the small handcart of food, the body of my dog Jack laid atop it.

"They've been lying to you all," I said, moving down from the upper structure and clambering out of the exit as well. "The gang in here is half gypsy assholes, half local regular assholes, and they've been slaving, starving the people they want, and they probably only take new ones in when they kill older ones. There's a lot of food, but not enough for everyone forever. They had fields being planted, so there'll be crops, if people put the effort in, and the food that's here could feed a lot more, if there's a tight control on it, a community working together, rather than just feeding themselves." I looked around at the men and women staring at me, the slaves and those that were desperate to break inside.

"There's still a load of scumbags in there, and they're armed…" I said, gesturing over my shoulder with a thumb. "I'm going to go free the rest. They've got a load more people held captive, and then I'm moving on, but I could do with some volunteers?"

"You got my food?" Barry asked me gruffly, and I nodded to him, pulling the bag of food I'd prepared from Alyssa's cart. I threw it to him, and he grunted, looking inside before passing it to the other man who stood with him, a man I realized I'd seen before when he'd sent him off with the first bag of food. "Take that home and stay there, Carl. I'll be home soon." The younger man nodded, then took off, sprinting out of sight as Barry turned back to me.

"You kept your word, so I'm in. I get guns…right? And they're mine to keep!" he said firmly, and I nodded in agreement.

"I'll lend you a gun for now, and when you kill an asshole with one, that gun becomes yours, and mine goes back in the bag. But let me make this clear: you try to fuck me over, you'll regret it."

"I keep my word," Barry growled, and I nodded to him.

"And that's why I'll give you a gun, Barry. I'm Matt, by the way…" I pulled the other rifle from the bag and passed it to him, along with a handgun and two clips for each. "Now, I need to get Alyssa home, and then I'm going back in. We clear the scum out, and you all get to put a community together to maintain what they've started, just without the slavery and shitbags. Deal?"

"Deal." He checked the gun and freed the clip before slamming it back in with a practiced hand.

"Army?" I asked him, observing the casual competence he displayed.

"Bite your tongue," he snorted, smiling for the first time since I'd met him. "Marines."

"Then I was luckier than I thought when we first faced off," I acknowledged, nodding in respect to him. "Stay here and keep things under control; I'll be back in ten."

"Aye, sir," he said, straightening and almost saluting, before he caught himself.

I grinned and led Alyssa away, waiting until we turned the next corner and moved out of sight before stepping into a garden to hang back as she carried on down the path. Sure enough, a handful of seconds later, I heard two voices approaching the corner, arguing over what to do.

"…and I'm telling you, we wait till he fucks off, and then we grab the food!" The first said, a whiny, nasally voice that made my fists itch to hear.

"What about the girl?" asked a second man, in a much deeper, more gravelly voice.

"What about her? She can go complain to his grave if she wants. The gypsies'll kill him. You don't know them like I do, and we need the food more than she does!" The first voice said fervently. I waited patiently, hearing the quick steps reach the corner, pause, and then the second voice began muttering in confusion.

"Where's he gone?"

"He's probably run off and left her already. Come on, this is our chance…" the first voice said, and I steeled myself in grim certainty, stepping out just as the pair of hurrying feet scurried closer.

They drew alongside my hiding place inside the overgrown hedges of a garden, and I struck out with the butt of the rifle, catching the nearest in the temple and sending him sprawling. Before he'd even hit the ground, I snapped the gun around to level it between the eyes of the second man.

The man I'd hit was the bigger of the two, blond, with a scraggly beard. He'd clearly been heavyset going to fat before the fall, and looked generally scruffy, while his friend was thin, and the combination of filthy clothes, the strong smell of body odor and greasy hair, combined with the thick bristle of an unkempt beard and a huge nose on a narrow face made it clear who'd been which voice.

"What you doing, rat?" I asked him, and he froze, his mouth hanging loose and exposing crooked, yellow teeth.

"Why'd you do that?" he whined. "We didn't do anything to you…"

"Because you were going to," I said, cutting him off. "I heard everything you said, you little shit, and now I'm just trying to decide if it's worth leaving you alive, rather than killing you outright."

"We weren't gonna do nothin'…" he tried again, then attempted to smile ingratiatingly. "We were just going for a walk to look after our family…that's all…"

"Bullshit. You were going to attack the girl and steal her food, at the very least, and I doubt you'd have stopped there…" I growled. The man on the pavement groaned, squinting up at me and clutching his head.

"We'd not have hurt her; we just wanted the food," he mumbled, as Rat snapped at him.

"Quiet, you fool!"

"He heard us…" the bigger man mumbled, pulling his hand from his temple and inspecting the smear of blood on it. "Why'd you do that?" he asked, looking up at me reproachfully. "You could'a just told us to fuck off…"

"Because this was always going to turn into more," I said as calmly as I could. "Scum like you would have just denied everything, walked off and waited for me to leave before going back for her. Fuck no."

"Look, you can't prove anything," Rat said, smiling nastily. "It's all hearsay."

"Do I look like I'm going to drag you to the police station?" I asked conversationally, and he frowned before turning an even pastier shade of white.

"You gotta, though. We didn't do nothin'…so…what? You're just gonna let us go…right?"

"You know what you were going to do, and so do I. So why would I leave you alive?" I asked, making a snap decision. I didn't want to kill any more than was necessary, but scum like this wouldn't just leave people alone, I knew with absolute certainty. I kept the rifle pointed at his forehead, while pulling the handgun out and shooting him in the knee. Lowering the gun, I turned and met the horrified gaze of the bigger man as Rat collapsed, screaming.

"We both know he's the brains here…so let's make this clear: he's a twisted little fuck, and you're dumb but honest, I'd guess. Do better than this, or I'll kill you. Understood?" I asked, and he nodded quickly. "Good. Now, take your friend and fuck off. If I see you again, it'll be five million years too soon, and I'll kill you both."

Leaving him to collect his mangled companion, I pocketed the handgun, flicking the safety on and hurrying after Alyssa. I managed to catch her at the end of the street and took up station walking alongside her, rifle at the ready.

"What happened?" she asked, her voice harsh and uncertain.

"Two assholes were following us. They were apparently going to rob you once I'd left you."

"And will you?" she asked, making me blink in surprise.

"Will I what?" I repeated.

"Leave us," she replied shortly.

"Uh, yeah?" I switched from scanning the surrounding area to face her, confused by the look on her face. "What am I missing here?" I asked.

"I want to know what this will cost me," she said grimly, coming to a halt, her house nearly in sight.

"What?" I asked her, dumbfounded.

"You know what!" she snarled, suddenly furious. "All of this! The world's gone fucking mad, everyone with any power is suddenly murdering and raping, and you come out of nowhere, rescue my baby girl, then me, and feed us, give me a gun, and say you're gonna leave us alone, let us live how we want…I want to know what this is costing me!"

"I…I…"

"Sex; is that it?" she spat harshly. "If I let you fuck me, will you leave us alone?" I heard the hard fury in her voice, mixed with the fear and desperation, and I realized that she really didn't believe that I was going to go without any compensation. She didn't know if Amy was in the house or not, and she was terrified to upset me, just in case, but she clearly had to know.

"No," I said, shaking my head and lifting my left hand in a 'just wait' gesture as I saw the tightening around her eyes. "No, I'm not after anything from you." I clarified. "Do I want to fuck you? I admit you're pretty, and in the photos on your wall, you have a great figure, which isn't exactly hidden here, either…" I gestured to the coat she'd looted from one of the corpses in the house. It'd fallen open and her physique was clear even in her ruined clothes. "But seriously," I went on quickly, "I'm not a fucking asshole. You're married, and I don't want shit that's not given freely. I wouldn't want to fuck you, unless you wanted to fuck me. Ah, crap…look, I'm not saying this well. Long story short, no. There's no cost to you. You don't have to fuck me and hope I leave you alone after, or slit my throat when I sleep or…" I paused, catching her flinch, and blinked as I realized that she'd been planning on doing just that. I felt anger flooding through me at all the shit I'd had to wade through, and the fact that everyone always seemed to think I was out to get them, to pull a fast one.

"Look," I said firmly, my voice harsher than it had been. "I saw a little girl in trouble, so I made sure she was safe. Then I brought her home, found out you were prisoner at the park, and she begged me to help you. I'm not such an asshole that I'd leave a fucking child in need, right?" I glared at her, unable to keep my frustration in check. "I was going to ask you to look after Jack, to keep him with you until I could come get him, but now? Hell, no." Fuming, I reached over, pulled my gun bag off the top of the cart and slung it over my shoulder, then picked Jack's body up with a grunt, heaving him into a shoulder carry and ignoring her attempts to talk to me.

I stalked off, crossing the street to a concealed area where I could see her house, and sure enough, there was Amy, perched in the upstairs window, staring out with desperate hope in her eyes. She saw me, and then saw her mother hesitantly walking to her door, pulling the cart, her gaze following where I pointed.

Alyssa stopped dead, abandoning the cart and running towards the house, Amy vanishing from the window with a cry. The pair of them came together on the stairs of the house, a mess of sobbing, shouting, and cuddles. Satisfied that I'd kept my promise, I turned, walking away from them.

Pride at managing the quest, the knowledge of doing the right thing, warred with my anger and irritation over Alyssa's behavior—even though I understood it, to some degree—and fury with myself. When she'd offered herself to me, for a second, just a second, I'd been tempted to say yes. To claim what she offered as a reward, after all I'd been through.

I hated that I'd even considered it, and my mood turned blacker as I stomped along the road back in the direction of the park entrance where I'd left Barry.

I needed to go fucking kill someone.

"Matt!" a small voice rang out from behind, and I half-turned, before Amy slammed into me, nearly knocking me from my feet. The small girl wrapped her arms around me and buried her face into my coat, barely able speak for sobbing.

"Tha…thank you, Matt! You…saved my…momma!" She wailed, hugging me tight, and I could hear Spot going apeshit with excitement somewhere out of sight. As I looked up from the top of her head, Alyssa ran into view. Tears had cut clear paths through the grime on her cheeks as she hurried over to me as well, slamming into me right beside her daughter, and sobbing about how sorry she was.

I froze up, then really awkwardly patted her on the back and gruffly told her it was okay.

"No, it isn't!" she insisted, tears streaming, her face going red and blotchy as she could barely speak. "You did all that, and I accused you of…You're a good man, Matt, better than any I've ever known…You'd never do that, and I'm so, so, sorry…I…"

"It doesn't matter!" I snapped, shaking free of her, and gently but firmly pushing Amy back as well, my anger only rising because of the thought I'd had. I felt sickened, dirty, as though I was no better than the others, the ones I'd killed.

My heart clenched at the expressions of pain on the girls' faces, and I forced myself to take a deep, calming breath before I spoke again.

"Look, it's okay, and Alyssa, I'm not a good man. I'm just trying not to be a bad man. There's a hell of a difference, all right?" I dropped my gaze, afraid to look at her in case she saw the truth in my eyes. "Amy, go home with your momma. Eat some food, but store as much as you can. There's not going to be more coming to the shops, after all. Alyssa, give it a day or so, then go check out the park, okay? But be careful. I've got that Barry guy to help me, and I'll tell him to help you. Once the park is cleared, help him and whoever else to make it into a community farm, and secure it. You'll have all the shit they had; I don't need it. Seriously…plan for the long haul, here. The power isn't coming back on." I said firmly, shaking my head as I accepted the truth in a way I hadn't until now.

She nodded to me, holding Amy, and mouthed 'Thank you' to me. I nodded in acknowledgement, then looked down at Amy again. Dropping to one knee, I set Jack on the ground as I looked her in the eye.

"If you need me, Amy, you remember where I am, right?" I asked her. She sniffed and nodded soberly. "Good girl." I smiled, reaching out to stroke her cheek. "Take care of your family for me, and remember, stay the hell away from the cathedral, okay?" I said seriously, fixing her with a glare. She nodded gravely, and I straightened up, pulling the weapons bag around. I pulled a case of shotgun ammo out, and a handgun with two clips, passing them to Alyssa with a nod.

Then I set my bag right, lifted Jack back onto my shoulder, and turned from them, hurrying back to the park. Oddly, I found myself feeling simultaneously lighter and more disgusted with myself than ever before in my life.

TWENTY

I IGNORED THE FLASHING notification light and kept stomping along until I heard gunfire coming from the gate. Jolted from my thoughts, I swore, stopping and looking around cautiously. I had maybe a hundred meters left along the street before I'd be in sight of the gate I wanted, but I couldn't use the rifle properly with Jack on my back. I glanced around again, confirming that there was nobody in sight, then edged close to a badly overgrown thorn bush in the front of the nearest garden.

"Sorry, boy," I muttered apologetically, dumping Jack's mangled body into the bushes in the hopes that I'd be able to get him back later.

Once I was satisfied that he couldn't be seen from the road, I set off running to the end of the street, looking left and finding Barry crouched down behind a car. Three thugs from the park had taken stations up on the structure over the gate and were firing at him.

I also saw Carl's body, the young man who I'd assumed to be his son.

The boy had clearly been one of the first casualties, and his body still in the middle of the road. A pool of blood slowly spread around him as Barry screamed in incoherent rage and fired over and over at the thugs, demolishing the barrier they hid behind, even as they fired back.

I pulled the rifle around, bracing it against the wall and aiming carefully, conscious that I wouldn't t get another chance to surprise them. I sighted carefully, picking one out and leading the target as he moved. He stuck his head up and shouted something at Barry, and as he raised his weapon, I fired.

The shot was a lucky one, hammering high into his chest between his left arm and neck. The spray of blood and surprised grunt as he fell from sight was worth the wait, and I quickly moved my aim, firing shot after shot into the soft wood that I knew the remaining two were crouching behind. I was rewarded with another scream as someone appeared, splinters of wood having shredded their way into his face.

As he popped into view, Barry fired, taking the top of his head off, and then fired again, keeping the final one pinned down. I rushed forward, rifle kept upright and ready, and when Barry ran out of bullets and the last scumbag lifted his head into view to take advantage of that, I was ready. I fired twice in fast succession, hitting him in the head and shoulder, sending his corpse falling from sight.

"Motherfuckers!" Barry screamed at them and rushed forward, the handgun in his hand as he vanished from view. I heard the sound of him emptying his clip into the survivor, before he staggered back into the street and rushed to Carl's side, falling to his knees and reaching out.

I crept over to him, keeping my rifle ready, just in case. I kept my eyes up, trying to look everywhere as the big man began to cry, a low keening sound that shouldn't have ever come from a man that size. Or any size at all. It tore at my heart as he clutched the body to his chest, whispering over and over to it.

"...son, my poor son. I'm sorry. I *failed* you. it should have been *me*...I..."

I swallowed hard, blinking away unbidden tears and left him to weep as I crept into the park. Searching quickly, I set to finding all three corpses and relieving them of the weapons and ammo they'd had before hurrying through the bushes to a spot where I could see more of the park.

The central area, where all the caravans and the tent city had sprung up, had gone from an ordered little campsite into a kicked anthill. Everyone was streaming back to the area from seemingly all over the park. Groups of slaves were being pulled in from their jobs by men and women on horseback, forced to stand in a circle around the outside.

"Holy shit...human shields..." I hissed angrily, looking them over and spitting on the floor in disgust. Doing my best to move stealthily, I headed back through the bushes toward the gate, and approached Barry, who still laid on the ground, holding his son.

"Barry..." I said quietly, crouching down next to him. "I'm sorry for your loss, mate...I..."

"They took my son!" he snarled wildly, glaring at me with red, tear-filled eyes.

"And they've fallen back to their camp now. They're making the slaves stand around them. They're using people as human shields, mate..."

"You think I care?" he said, his voice flat and dismissive. "Leave me. Leave me with my boy..."

"They killed him, Barry!" I said firmly. "They starved you, and they tried to kill me, then they opened fire on you all, and now? They're using others as shields to save themselves! Are you going to let them get away with this?"

"I don't care!" He shoved me back furiously. I fell on my ass, catching myself as best as I could, before shaking my head and picking myself up. The others I'd already brought out of the park had evidently joined the locals in peering around, but all were keeping their distance.

"Fine," I spat. "I'll just fucking do it myself, as usual." I stalked off, sweeping up the spare clip Barry hadn't used yet. Clearly, he didn't need it.

I strode into the park again, storming into the trees and ducking out of sight before stopping and leaning against a tree, swearing sulfurously. I needed a plan, as 'run at them screaming and shooting' was clearly not going to work and a half-assed berserker rescue attempt would only succeed in getting more of innocents killed than anything else.

I calmed myself as best I could and edged through the trees. I watched out carefully, seeing no movement yet. I crept up to the trees at the edge of the small lake and stared intently at the now-fortified camp on the far side.

There were maybe thirty caravans, cars, trailers, and smaller tents making it up, as a rough estimate, with the 'Big Top' tent rising from the center. Judging from the figures in view, at least a hundred people surrounded it, standing listlessly and looking sightlessly outward.

They were too far to make out great details from where I stood, but they were clearly the slaves and prisoners, all filthy, exhausted, and barely decent in ragged clothing. They swayed gently as the wind blew, but every time one tried to sit, they'd be shouted at and hit by one of the assholes who patrolled behind them.

I swallowed my anger and wracked my brain for a plan. There was no way I was going to get them from here. I skirted the lake to the left, scouting quickly through the trees and heading to the far end of the park. I moved carefully, avoiding as many of the fallen branches and general underbrush as I could. It was slower moving so carefully, but it was worth it to stay alive, I figured.

It took me nearly ten minutes to cover what would have taken me less than five strolling along normally, but when I reached the edge of the path through the trees, I could see two men standing on top of the nearby gate. They held their rifles at the ready, staring out over the road outside, while two more sat below, hidden from sight, clearly ready to jump up and join in the shooting if they were needed.

Fools didn't seem to have considered that there could be someone inside already, though, I thought, slowly approaching and running from bush to bush, before lying down fully and bracing the rifle like I'd seen it done in the movies. I pulled out two extra clips and laid them down as well, aiming carefully, before checking my surroundings one more time, just to be sure.

There was nobody visible nearby, but as dense as the woods were, heavy underbrush surrounding the outside of the park and obscuring the space where I laid, I couldn't see particularly far. I just damn well hoped no one would stumble over me anytime soon. I sighted back along the rifle, slowing my breathing as much as I could, then opened fire.

My first shot took the man on the top left, who had been leaning against the barrier. It blasted through his shoulder blade, high on the right side, sending him spinning out over the edge to fall from view. Unwilling to waste the precious seconds before they started firing back, I shifted, locking in on the man on the top right and firing again. He'd just started to turn, following the sound of the gunshots, and my shot was incredibly lucky, taking him in the throat and sending him staggering. He dropped his rifle, backed into a post, then fell forwards, dropping face first to the ground on the inside of the wall. His descent barely registered in my peripheral vision as I changed my aim again, lining up on the two men who'd been stationed below.

They'd both scrambled for their guns, and the first on the left, had opened fire indiscriminately into the trees, thankfully firing over my head. He had a pair of handguns and was firing them both at the same time, while his friend had produced a shotgun and pumped it while looking in my general direction.

I switched from targeting Handgun, and locked in on Shotgun, figuring his spray had a better chance of hitting me. I fired once, twice, and then a third time, and he rushed to the left, trying to make it to the tree line and cover.

The third hit him high in the thigh, knocking him from his feet, even though the first and second missed completely. As soon as he fell from sight in the bushes, I turned back to Handgun. He'd tried to do the same, barreling into the hedges on his side of the path, but they were thick and springy, and he barely got halfway into one before bouncing back out. My first bullet slammed into the hedge and tore through it, the second caught him in the left arm as he raised his gun, twisting him sideways, while the fourth took him in the back, sending him staggering a few steps before crashing to the forest floor. The third bullet, which had missed completely, had torn a hole in the barricade and out into the street, eliciting a scream from someone outside.

I jumped to my feet and ran to my right, trying to flank the shotgun wielder, when he fired from cover, sending me diving to the ground as buckshot tore the bushes around me to shreds.

I rolled, forced myself to my feet, and dove behind a nearby tree, gritting my teeth as pain flared in my right shoulder. I clutched at it and looked down, frowning at the tear in my shirt and the shallow wound I'd completely missed taking in the adrenaline-fueled exchange.

Annoyed at yet another shirt being ruined, I growled and leaned around the edge of the tree to fire back, aiming for the approximate position I'd last spotted the shotgunner. I risked my exposure long enough to send two shots slamming into the bushes before pulling back. A second later, a boom echoed again, and the tree I was hiding behind shuddered. Bark flew everywhere as the far side was smashed by the buckshot. I was suddenly glad that I'd managed to get behind an old oak tree, rather than a much smaller one.

I fired back, only once this time, figuring if I couldn't see him, I was just wasting ammo, and hid again, waiting.

There was a tense pause as we both waited for the other to make a move, and then he was up, sprinting from the cover of the bushes, racing toward the corpse of his friend, diving for the rifle…

I stood, firing four shots at him and missing twice. The third and fourth took him in the side and leg, knocking him sideways as I sprinted toward him. He reached out desperately, hands scrabbling for the gun that was just out of reach, but I pulled the trigger twice more, finishing him off.

I stood there for a few seconds, chest heaving, heart hammering, before I heard the shouting and running feet incoming.

"Shit!" I snarled, diving back into the bushes, near to the space where he'd been hiding. The shotgun had been abandoned nearby with the chamber open; clearly, he'd run out of ammo before I did.

I forced my way deeper into the hedge, burying myself as much as possible from sight, and checked my rifle. I still had nearly half a clip and sighted carefully in the direction the voices were coming from, hoping that there'd only be a few of them.

I'd barely stopped moving when the first two rounded the corner One carried a rifle, older than the one I had acquired, clearly a single shot hunting model, while the second brandished something that looked as though he'd looted it from a World War One reject bin, a handgun that just screamed lethality…though if it was lethal to the operator or the victim, I wasn't sure…

I could hear more coming behind them, and I paused, trying to decide if it was better to pick these off, then wait for more, or not. Once again, I cursed my lack of real-world tactical training before falling back on my 'Call of Duty' skills.

It was all I knew.

I fired at the rifle wielder first, taking him in the leg, then the stomach as he ran closer. Quickly switching to Reject Bin, I fired at him more carefully, getting my adrenaline slightly more under control. One bullet hit him in the chest, more blind luck, as he'd jinked to the side, right into the oncoming shot, and I resolved to either put more points into Luck in the future, or to get some training time in. Preferably both.

I was suddenly reminded of the flashing notifications and wondered for a split second if I had enough to level yet, cursing furiously as the screen popped up and obscured my vision. I dismissed it, but in the two seconds of blindness, another man had taken the corner, and my motion had clearly attracted his attention.

I ducked, bullets hammering into the wood and hedges around me, and he began shouting to others. Soon, a barrage of bullets hammered through my hiding place, and I screamed as one tore through my left calf, then my right earlobe, then the outside of my right hip…

"Hold your fire!" a voice rang out, and after a few more shots, they complied. I huddled in the dirt, panting, pain radiating through me. "Throw out your gun, or we open fire!" the same voice called to me, and I laid beneath the leafy canopy, frantically trying to figure a way out.

I was injured, essentially stuck under a bush, as I now realized my cover wasn't just protective. When they hadn't known where I was, it had been great, but now that they did, it was awful, as the same thickness that provided excellent camouflage was also dense enough that it'd be a nightmare to try to quickly break free of. A vision of the shotgunner had attempted to burst free came to mind, along with how easily I'd hit him.

"Last chance!" the voice rang out again, and I reached out very slowly, my hand shaking, and grabbed the shotgun by its stock. Leaning my arm as far to the left as I could, I threw it clear, hoping they'd fall for it and also think that I was slightly further over than I was.

"You think I'm fucking stupid?" the voice roared. "Take aim!"

"Fuck, fuck, fuck…" I muttered to myself, peering through the brush at them. Five of them had arrived, all standing close to each other in the open as they moved forward, and…

There were only five of them, all within a space of maybe three meters… Incinerate could take two down. I'd literally only gotten my mana back to full a few minutes ago, and I could get one at least with the rifle…

I cast the spell before I could think better of it, hitting the outer right, who had a pair of handguns, and the outer left, who had a hunting rifle. As they screamed and dropped, I opened fire with the rifle, not taking the time to aim, just pulling the trigger as fast as I could. Somehow, I managed to hit the center man in the face, also taking the man next to him in the shoulder as they tried to scatter.

Three down. One wounded, and one totally fine. I could do this, I could…

Click I heard from behind, and I froze as something hard pressed against the back of my head.

"Drop the rifle, hold your hands out to the sides, and do nothing else. Face down, you fucker," a voice said firmly.

"Okay…" I replied quietly, slowly moving the rifle out to my right and dropping it, as another voice behind me and to the left called out to the others.

"Don't shoot! We've got 'im!"

"He killed Terry, and Mike, and…"

"They were fucking idiots anyway," the voice from behind me cut him off. "Should have thought and stalked their prey, not run in guns blazing, should they?" I stayed still and silent, thoughts racing as I came up with and discarded a thousand possible plans. Almost all of them revolved around the single point that I'd been a complete idiot to use up both of my spells at once. They were my trump card, the only weapons that couldn't be seen, and I'd lost them for almost another hour.

"Okay, shitbag, get up, and do it damn slowly…" he said, and I heard him moving through the bushes next to me, stepping out to where he could be seen clearly. "Mark, search him." he ordered someone else, and I ever so slowly started to crawl out from under the hedge I'd been hiding in.

I pushed myself to my feet, biting down on a scream as the multiple wounds started to screech for my attention. As I turned to look at the group, I realized three men surrounded me, with two more moving in from further down the path.

"Who are you?" the first man asked gruffly, walking around to face me as I raised my hands above my head, while a second man stepped in and started to pull my handguns free.

"Just a man…" I said, glaring at him.

"Well, 'just a man,' why'd you attack us? How many more are there?" he pressed me, rapid-fire style, still staring down the barrel of his shotgun.

"You attacked me first, tried to kill me, make me a slave; you want me to go on, dickless?" I snarled back at him, glaring furiously.

"He unarmed now?" he asked the man who'd just been frisking me, and when he got the nod, he stepped in and slammed the butt of the shotgun into my face, sending me sprawling to the floor, nose broken and head ringing.

I laid there for a few seconds, the world spinning, before I realized he was talking again.

"…well? Last chance, you asshole! Where's it gone!"

"Wha…?" I mumbled, shaking my head.

"Oh, great, you've scrambled his friggin' brains, you idiot!" someone else cut in. "Give him a minute, or you'll never get anything…"

"Who do you think you are, callin' me an idiot you prick…wait…who??!" he started, before a cacophony of gunshots rang out. I flinched, instinctively rolling into a ball, arms over my head as I tried to protect myself.

After a handful of shots, silence returned to the park. Only the screaming of birds in the distance and the occasional shouted question in the distance filled the air as I slowly lowered my hands, looking around. My ears were ringing; all the gunfire had been so close in that last exchange, but as I blinked away the confusion as best I could, I focused in on the man who stepped forward out of the tree line to my right, strolling onto the path and advancing toward me, pulling the trigger once over each body to make sure they were dead.

It was Barry, and he looked seriously pissed.

"B…Barry?" I croaked out, and he glared down at me then nodded sharply and whistled to some others, who moved in and grabbed guns and ammo before vanishing silently into the trees again.

"You shouldn't have gone off on your own," he said to me matter-of-factly.

"I thought you weren't coming…" I replied, confused.

"They killed my son." His eyes were sorrowful, his voice grim. "I told you I'd help you, and I will. I'll kill each and every fucking one of them," he promised fervently, scowling down at me. "How badly are you hurt?"

"Not bad…" I muttered, checking myself over and wincing as my hands came away bloody each time. I'd taken over a dozen minor wounds now, all little, but the mounting pain and blood loss was going to be a problem.

"You look like shit," he said bluntly. "Pete! Get your lazy arse in here." A few seconds later, another man appeared nearby, crouching down and checking me over.

"Okay, mate, you just lie still…" the man said, looking me over quickly. "You've been in the wars, haven't you?" Shock was clear in his voice as he counted all the injuries. "Normally, I'd be saying you need to stay calm, and I'd be driving you to hospital, if not calling in a Heli-med, but I guess that's not an option anymore, is it?" He checked me over thoroughly, his expression sober. "Right; we need to strip you and get some bandages on, stop the bleeding and…"

"Just stop the worst of the bleeding and get me back on my feet," I growled at him as he probed a shoulder wound. "Believe me, I'll be fine."

"You're not gonna be fine at all," he shot back, pulling a bag around from his back and taking a handful of bandages and needles out as he got to work.

"Army doc?" I asked him, and he shook his head.

"RAF medic," he corrected me shortly. "You've lost a lot of blood, mate, and…Jesus…" He stopped suddenly, staring at my chest. He'd used some scissors to cut my top away, exposing the scars that seemed to be everywhere already. "What the hell did all of this?" he asked. I distractedly started to list them, gesturing as I pulled the prompts up.

"Rats, knives, gunshot, a gang of assholes, fire, a Ghast, a…"

"What the hell's a Ghast?" I heard him ask, but I ignored him.

Congratulations!
You have defeated nine opponents classed as 'Gypsy Thug'
Thug level: 0
Your level: 5
XP awarded: 225
*

Congratulations!
Members of your party have defeated five opponents classed as 'Gypsy Thug'
Thug level: 0
Party members level: 0
XP awarded: 62
*

Quest Complete!
'A Daring Rescue'
You have succeeded in not only finding Amy's mother, but you managed to rescue her. You receive the following rewards:
+1 to top three Attributes used
+1 Skill point to allocate
400 XP
Note: *Rewards have been increased on this quest due to level of difficulty.*

I quickly pulled up my character sheet and grinned with excitement as I saw the details. I'd managed to boost my Perception by two points, one with the excessive firearms practice, and one as a reward for using it so frequently. My Constitution had risen by one for that reason, as well, and it was about to level on its own from all the injuries I'd taken. The third stat to be boosted as a reward was Dexterity, and honestly, I wasn't complaining about any of those.

Name: Unnamed				
Modifiers: None				
Species: Human		Bonus: None		
Level: 5		Progress to next level: 1187/600		
Assimilation: 0%		Dungeon Level: 0		
Control: 12.5		Dungeon Capacity: 10		
Host Powers: 1		Dungeon Spells: 1		
Stat	Current points	Description	Effect	Progress to next level
Agility	7	Governs dodge and movement.		82/100
Charisma	8	Governs likely success to charm seduce or threaten		33/100
Constitution	11	Governs Health and Health Regeneration	HP: 11x20 = 220	92/100
Dexterity	15	Governs ability with weapons and crafting	+10% Increased chance of improved result	62/100
Endurance	7	Governs Stamina and Stamina Regeneration	Stamina: 7x10	25/100
Intelligence	10	Governs base manapool, standard intellectual capacity plus Control when combined with Wisdom and divided by 2	Mana: 10x20=200 Control: (10+15)/2 = 12.5	23/100
Luck	9	Governs overall chance of bonuses and critical hits		47/100
Perception	10	Governs ranged damage and chance to spot hidden items/traps	+0 to all ranged attacks	3/100

Strength	11	Governs damage with melee weapons and carrying capacity	+1 to all damage with Melee weapons	38/100
Wisdom	15	Governs mana regeneration and Control, when combined with Intelligence and divided by two	150 mana regenerated per hour Control: (10+15)/2 = 12.5	19/100

I concentrated and changed something that'd been annoying me for a while, which I'd just never gotten around to fixing, and a second later, my name changed from 'Unnamed' to 'Matt.' It was a stupid detail, but I'd kept dismissing it, and it was time.

I moved on, seeing I was at one thousand, one hundred, and eighty-seven XP out of the required six hundred, and the next prompt, sure enough, was informing me of my leveling.

You have reached Level Six!

You receive five Stat points to invest in your attributes, plus one Skill point.

I looked over the details quickly, delighted that I now had four skill points to allocate. I'd somehow turned the notifications for the skill levelling off before, but with a thought, it popped back up, this time codified into a handy template. I glanced at it, then glared as seemingly hundreds, if not thousands of skills were listed, ranging from 'Mixology' to 'Seduction' to 'Tracking' to 'Stealth' and more. I concentrated, and again, the lists blurred, trimming down until it was a manageable size, displaying only the relevant skills .

Skill	Subskill	Level	Effect
Blades		5	25% chance of familiarity with unknown bladed weapons operation
	Small Blades	4	8% increase in chance to inflict critical damage
	Longsword	4	8% increase in chance to inflict critical damage
Dodge		9	9% chance to dodge attacks, 9% increased chance to mitigate damage inflicted to lower tier

Firearms	General	7	7% chance of familiarity with unknown Firearms operation, 7% increased chance to hit your target
	Rifles	6	12% increase in chance to inflict critical damage, 6% increased chance to hit your target
	Close Range	3	6% increase in chance to inflict critical damage
	Handguns	5	10% increase in chance to inflict critical damage, 5% increased chance to hit your target
First Aid	Generalist	5	*See attached table for chances of wound mitigation…*
Stealth		3	9% chance to avoid detection
	Ambush	3	15% increase in damaged done when undetected
Unarmed		5	10% chance to inflict critical damage

I looked it over quickly, not having the time for details, and saw that once skills reached level five, they seemed to grow considerably, so on a hunch, I put one of my available skill points into 'Dodge'.

Congratulations!

You have increased your 'Dodge' skill to level 10!

At level Ten, you gain an increased chance to dodge attacks and to mitigate your damage to a lower tier. 9% chance to dodge attacks becomes 10%. 9% chance to mitigate damage downwards one tier becomes 10%. Now your 'sixth sense' of impending doom has increased to include a 10% chance to sense the kind of threat posed!

I nodded to myself; that was useful. I quickly put the remaining three points into Firearms (General), boosting that to ten.

Congratulations!

You have increased your 'Firearms' skill to level 10!

At level Ten, you gain an increased chance to hit your target by 10%. This stacks with the class of firearms, such as a 5% chance to hit with energy weapons becoming a combined 15%. 10% chance of familiarity with unknown firearms, and now you gain a 10% chance to intuit methods of repair and maintenance for any firearms in your possession. Increased familiarity with said Firearm will increase this chance.

I nodded to myself again, happy with my choices, and drew in a deep breath. It was leveling time. I had so many areas I needed to improve, it wasn't funny, but right now, the areas I needed to focus on were clear. I needed to *survive.*

That was down to three things in my mind right now. Don't get shot, shoot the enemy first, and survive if I did get shot. All those things were covered directly by Agility, Constitution, Luck, and Perception. One point into each wouldn't really help, and, seeing as ten seemed to be an important threshold, I dismissed Perception straight away. That left Agility at seven, Constitution at eleven, and Luck at Nine. I put three points into Agility, two into Luck, and just hoped I wasn't making a huge mistake that would kill me later.

I was essentially betting that I wouldn't get hurt, as opposed to playing it safe and doubling my health.

I accepted the changes and groaned as my body shifted, tendons and muscles, nerves and more all changing in minute ways. It felt like someone was tearing them loose then stitching them back on, tiny white-hot needles being used, and my own cells instead of thread. It took less than a minute, but when it was over, I laid there panting as Pete mumbled on about how it wasn't that bad and that I'd have to learn to put up with having stitches done like this if I insisted on the life I was living these days.

"What?" I asked him, panting. "What're you talking about?"

"Look, mate, the way you were squirming there when I cleaned out that little cut..." He started and I snorted, shaking my head as I pushed him back and stood.

"Pete, right?" I asked him and he nodded. "Well, if you ever get to level, you'll understand..." I shook myself slightly and inspected my wounds. I could feel them itching like crazy, and I just hoped whatever he'd put on them didn't interfere with the crazy speed healing I'd been doing of late. I glanced over the new notification and dismissed it with a shrug as soon as I saw it wasn't useful yet.

Congratulations!

You have unlocked 'Luck's Favor'!

When all you need is a single chance, just a little push on the scales of cosmic balance, remember this Ability! Activating 'Luck's Favor' will boost your luck by the original amount plus your luck modifier for ten seconds once per day. Note: 'Luck's Favor' is unlocked at +20% but as you are now classed as 'of above average luck', you have become aware of this ability early...

"Who're your friends?" I asked Barry, and he grunted, gesturing to the right at a tall dark-skinned man.

"That's John, ex-Military Police, but he's all right, really; not a total dick, despite that," he said as he checked his rifle.

"John," I said nodding to him, and he nodded back at me. He was easily three or four inches taller than me, topping out at around six four, six five, and had a build I could only describe as 'rangy'. Big boned and stringy muscle, with barely an ounce of fat on him, he was wearing a set of desert camo pants with a plain green top. A shaved head and deep, sunken eyes combined to make his gaze unnerving, until he smiled, and then you couldn't help but smile back.

"That's Ken," Barry continued, pointing to the trees on the other side of the path, where a small, dark-haired man crouched, one of the dead men's rifles in his hands as he stripped it, checked it, and reassembled it with terrifying speed. He was pale-skinned, tired-looking and scruffy, with torn jeans and a top that was too big for him, but the way his hands moved as he examined the surrounding area was scary…

"You've met Pete…" I nodded to Pete as he went on. "He's a medic, good lad, for all he cheats at cards…" Pete tried to deny it, but the wide 'honest' smile and the way he tried to look hurt made me snort at the attempt.

"And the last one is Jimmy; he's out there, keeping an eye on the rest of them…" he concluded, nodding further up the path. "Jimmy's a scout sniper, or he was back in the day. We all met at the local veteran's group. Good lads, except Pete; he just crawls the bar, trying to get someone to play with him."

"Typical shitbag card player then, got it," I said, making a point of checking that I still had my wallet.

"Hey, come on, no need for…" Pete started to say before a low whistle carried from the trees deeper into the park, and Barry snarled at him to shut up.

"Let's move," Barry ordered quietly, and his group set off in the direction of the whistle. I hesitated for a second, then ran in the other direction, finding my bag of guns. A quick detour allowed me to grab my rifle and handguns on the way back, and then I hurried to catch up.

I jogged back along the path, the big bag over my shoulder throwing off my balance and making me stagger slightly, even as I swapped a clip out and slotted a new one into my gun.

"Hssst!" I heard from the left. Pausing, I looked around, confused, before Ken seemed to appear out of nowhere, waving to me to make sure he had my attention, then vanishing again.

I changed direction and set off following him, and less than a minute later, I was crouching next to the group in a small clearing surrounded by thick bushes.

The wooden planks on the ground suggested that a group of kids had been making a den here at some point, but what everyone was fixated on was the small group of men facing off a few hundred feet away, where the edge of an enclosed area held the horses that the group had brought, and the others that they'd stolen, bought, or scavenged since arrival.

Six men faced four; the four were trying to calm things down, but the six were adamant they were leaving, and taking the horses with them.

"Think you could hit them from here with that?" Barry asked the man I assumed was Jimmy. He was laid out flat, a long hunting rifle in his arms and a sight glued to his eye.

"Barry, *you* could hit them from here. Well, maybe not *you*…but a child could…" Jimmy said slowly, never moving from his position.

"Yeah, well, get fucked," Barry retorted, still staring at the group. "How many could you take down?"

"Three, maybe four, before they get down. If they try to run, I could get more, and if they charge us? Probably six before you manage to hit one," he listed calmly, utter confidence in his voice.

"Hold your fire, then," Barry ordered. "Wait to see if they want to do the job for us; if not, then we take them. Targets are John, far left, Ken, far right. Matt, go for the center. Pete, stay down and stay quiet; Jimmy, take down as many as you can once it starts. Confirm."

The others all said something in the affirmative, ranging from 'Yessir,' to 'yup,' to 'aye.' Barry turned to look at me after a few seconds, one eyebrow raised.

"Oh! Uh…yeah, sorry. Fine with that…" I said, shaking myself. I dropped the bag of guns down and let out a groan of relief as the weight no longer pulled on me. "Anyone need a handgun or some ammo?" I asked, and Barry opened the bag, grunting as he passed a few clips and handguns out.

By the time he was done, the bag was pretty empty compared to how full it'd started when I'd returned to the park, but there were a lot more dead bodies around, and I was feeling better about our chances.

The groups by the horses continued to argue, until one of the four said something to the others, who gripped their two guns and a knife nervously, and he took off, storming past the group of six toward the tent city.

He got two steps before one of the six shouted something and stabbed him. Dropping, he screamed and shot the man who'd stabbed him, and it degenerated into a free-for-all, guns booming, knives flashing, and one of the idiots in the group of six actually fired his shotgun at one of the four, taking not only him out, but his comrade who'd been about to attack him as well.

When it was all over, only two men stood still: one was the shotgunner, who looked horrified and was shaking his head, and the other was a tall Asian man with a bloody knife in one hand who was holding his stomach as blood leaked out around his tightly-pressed fist.

"Well, that's made our job easier…" Ken muttered, and the others mumbled an agreement, before two more figures, a man and a woman, who I was startled to recognize as Esme, sprinted out of the tents, heavily armed. They ran as fast as they could, two big backpacks bouncing on their shoulders and snapping orders at the two survivors, who immediately turned their weapons on them, before the two groups moved around each other, grabbing at the horses. The beasts were pulling on their lead ropes, clearly spooked by the noise.

"Do we let them go?" Jimmy asked, and I spoke before Barry could.

"No, they die. If we let them go, they'll just do the same as they've already done, it'll just be somewhere else…" Jimmy finally looked up from his scope and then from me to Barry, who stared at me for what felt like a long time.

"They die," Barry finally said flatly, nodding once to me. Jimmy turned back around and shifted, getting comfortable around the rifle, before saying quietly.

"Firing…"

With a blink, he shifted smoothly, his rifle barking four times, and four bodies fell. The fourth, the woman, had made it to horseback and had been frantically digging her heels in while firing over her shoulder aimlessly in the direction of the trees.

"Is that it?" I asked the group at large, and they all regarded each other uncertainly, before we looked as one at the tent city, where the slaves were all splitting up. Some were rushing inside, desperately looking for food. Others were running for the gates. Still more had simply sat down, too exhausted to do anything but rest.

"I think so…but we need to be careful…there should be at least two more gates, and…" Barry said, as we left the cover of the trees, guns at the ready as we headed for the tent city. We spent the next two hours sweeping the entire park, checking the area over as best as we could. It seemed that the guards at the eastern gate had fled, and another group of vigilantes had killed the single guard on the remaining gate. Three of them had died in the act, but the rest were flooding in and demanding food as I turned to Barry and his squad.

The sun was setting as I shook their hands and gathered up my guns again. They had well over a dozen firearms now, as well as knives, clubs, two crossbows, and a longbow and arrow that I was muzzily convinced was mine from when I'd come to the park first. I was too tired to care, though, and wasn't even a hundred percent sure I'd actually brought it from the gang in the first place.

I gathered my gear, took a decent supply of food and one packet of every medicine they had that I didn't already have. I turned down my portion of the spoils after that, insisting that Barry, who'd now become the de facto leader of the park, give that share to Alyssa and Amy instead.

"All I need is a horse to get me and my gear home…" I maintained, shaking my head again. "Hell, I don't even need the horse once I make it back; nowhere to keep it, so I'll have to set it free…"

"Jimmy!" Barry called, and the scout-sniper sauntered over from the cooking pot he'd been supervising. Lines of hungry people had been seated around the tents now, eating or waiting their turn, with children running about and laughing for the first time in god knew how long.

"What's up, boss?" he asked simply.

"You're going for a ride with Matt. Make sure he gets home, then bring the horses back here. Keep him safe; he made this all possible." Barry gestured around the inside of the 'Big Top,' especially at the families of the small group, who sat together, safe and well-fed at last.

"Aye, boss," Jimmy said, saluting. "You ready, Matt?" I nodded tiredly. The adrenaline crash had hit me hard, and all I wanted to do was sleep now, but I needed to be home, back in my Dungeon, not messing about here, playing 'happy families'.

"One last thing, Barry…" I said, drawing him aside as Jimmy went to sort out our horses.

"What's up?" he asked.

"Look, I can't explain what I know or how, since it'll never make sense to you. Hell, it makes no sense to me…just, you need to know…the power isn't coming back on, mate. And things are going to get worse. Creatures are coming. I've fought some already. They appear more in high mana areas, like in the city center. Out here, they'll appear less frequently, but they'll still come. You need to be ready."

"What kind of creatures?" he asked gruffly, eyeing me with concern.

"Oh, fuck, man, I don't know! All the creatures you don't want to see, believe me. I've seen giant rats, goblins, and a few Ghasts, not to mention some kind of ghoul…thing…" I shook my head apologetically. "I don't expect you to believe me, but plan for it. Hell, you better plan for assaults by hungry people. Build walls, grow crops, protect yourselves here. Just don't be dicks like the gang was; they were doing the right thing with the food, they were just doing it totally wrong. Last of all, if you need me, like really fucking need me, go to the Tokyo Bar in Newcastle. You know it?" I asked, and he nodded, even more confused.

"Well, go there and wait, and I'll find you. And stay the hell away from the cathedral!!" I shook my finger at him. "Seriously, man, promise me you'll stay the fuck away from there!"

"What do you know, Matt? What the hell is a 'high mana area'...radiation or something?" he growled suspiciously at me, but I just lifted my hands placatingly.

"I don't know, not really. I just get...hints, flashes of insight...call it whatever you want; just remember what I told you!" I insisted, and he grunted in hesitant acknowledgement, reaching out and shaking my hand.

"Whatever. We'll talk about this properly when I don't have a million things to do first," he said, waving someone else to wait as they rushed up. I took his proffered hand and clasped the back of his hand with my second, then turned, leaving the tent and heading over to where Jimmy waited, already astride one of the horses.

We didn't talk much. Jimmy didn't ask, and I didn't offer, but we took a quick detour to retrieve Jack, strapping his body to the back of the horse I rode, then stopping off at Alyssa and Amy's, so I could give them the news.

Alyssa seemed upset and embarrassed, but I did what I'd gone to do, and I rode away after telling her it didn't matter. Amy had tried to get me to stay, but I'd simply reminded her where I'd be, and while I needed her to keep it to herself, to come to me if she needed help. She'd been all right about it, only shedding a few tears over the bloody state of my bandages and damaged clothing.

Two hours of cautious riding later, and we were in the city, close by the Tokyo bar, and only one street over from my Dungeon, when I slid down and passed the reins to Jimmy.

"Thanks for the escort," I said quietly to him, and he nodded, reaching down to briefly grip my hand and give me the ghost of a smile.

"Not a problem. Thanks for back there...we needed the kick to start it all off."

"You'd have done it yourself soon enough..." I said, giving a nod to him and stepping back, clearly waiting for him to leave.

He nodded distractedly, taking in the darkened buildings around us, and the skittering noises in the dark alleys, then shifting his gaze back to me, and around again, before taking the hint. He turned, heading away silently, his rifle in one hand as he watched for anything coming out of the darkness.

I waited until he was out of sight before hurrying along to the end of the street, crossing over and turning down the alley that led to my home. The door opened with a thought as I stumbled along, then closed behind me, and five minutes later, I was slumped across my sofa, gear discarded around the room. Taking a long swig from a bottle of rum and glaring at my now silent and lonely room, I pulled up the flashing notification, saw the minor gains, and dismissed it with a shrug, too tired to care.

Congratulations!
Members of your party have defeated four opponents classed as 'Gypsy Thug'
Thug level: 0
Party members level: 0
XP awarded: 50

Amy had been a distraction, and a pain in the ass, but it'd been a good reminder that I needed company.

No man was an island.

With that thought, I let my drooping eyes shut completely, and a few seconds later, the sound of my snores started to fill the Core chamber, as I finally rested after what seemed like a month of nonstop action.

TWENTY-ONE

WHEN I AWOKE, it was with a fuzzy head, a bladder filled to bursting, and a now-familiar warning tingle that was growing stronger by the second. I sat up, looking curiously around the room, and swallowed hard. The foul taste in my mouth made me almost retch as I remembered eating the first thing I could find before washing it down with rum.

Clearly biltong for supper wasn't the way to go. I practically fell from the sofa in reaching for my gun bag, but I managed to right myself, picking up a handgun, my rifle, and the shotgun, chucking a few boxes of ammo onto one side of the sofa and sitting back. Comfortable with my defensive situation, I began relaxing my mind's eye and practically pouring my consciousness into the Dungeon for the first time in ages.

Instantly, my mind was clearer, and I felt as though I hovered in the middle of the room, with a sense of the claimed locations all around me. I turned my attention up and behind the room I was in, orienting from where my body slumped on the sofa, and I started moving my consciousness in that direction, floating upwards, passing into the next floor up to find that the bar had been even further looted.

Someone had smashed the front windows in and broken the locks on the metal grates that covered the front, then they'd clearly stripped the bar of all the booze they could carry and legged it. There were still several crates of various beers, spirits, and mixers strewn around the storeroom, with some piled closer to the front door for easy retrieval, but a significant portion of it was gone.

The security grates had been pulled down and made to look like they were closed and secure, but I could see straight away that they weren't. The warning tingle had come from the presence of a group of men gathering outside, with a damn trolley they'd clearly stolen from a supermarket.

They all carried what looked like baseball or cricket bats, and they were leaning against the grates, talking, and judging from the looks they gave the two passers-by on the far side of the road, they were waiting for them to be out of sight before looting again.

"Oh, I don't think so, boys," I declared to myself, reaching out. I could see them clearly in my Dungeon sense, and in the day or so since I'd left, the Dungeon territory had grown enough that they were only about six feet from being inside of it, so I went to work, pushing and prodding the field, slowly, ever so slowly, expanding it outwards and claiming the space between my position and the grates.

It seemed to take forever; I knew it was faster than it had been last time, when I'd first hidden the way down to the dungeon from the looters, but it really didn't feel like it, as I anxiously watched them shifting and looking around.

I pushed another foot closer to them, then one more, the Dungeon aura claiming the room gradually, permeating the wooden floor and the shattered glass of the windows.

"Okay, they're outta sight…move it!" hissed one of the men, and I growled mentally as they started for the grate, grabbing it and yanking it up. I was so close! Literally less than six damn inches before I'd have reached the grates, and then it would have been simple to repair them, locking the bastards out!

Four men streamed in, three with bats and one dragging the trolley, before a fifth followed behind, pulling the grates back down and taking up a watch position.

"What do we get this time?" one of the men asked, and the man who was on watch called back to them straight away.

"Stick to the plan. Get the champagne, if there's any left, big bottles only, and grab as many as you can. Once those gone, named whisky, rum, or vodka; none of that cheap house shit. Get them all in the trolley, and we go. We can come back as many times as we have to, so don't rush it. We're just to not get caught. then when all this blows over, we sell it. Nice, easy money."

"Better than the jeweler's…" one of the group muttered, and the guard merely flicked him the finger.

"What happened with the jeweler's?" one of the others asked the man who'd spoken.

"We did them over two days ago. Nicked a shit load of sparklies, and now what? Can't get them on the internet, ain't nobody local interested in them. Just left them all in the house. Damn waste of a night."

"You thought it was worth it at the time, Jake," the man on guard snapped. "Just get going, and grab what you can!"

I watched them as they split up and fumed at hearing their plans. They were clearly moving from business to business, cleaning them out, and now it was my turn. It didn't sit well with me that they were essentially robbing people. Technically, so was I, in stealing the entire building, and eventually the street, but still.

I started pushing out again, spreading my influence around. The Dungeon aura sank into the floor and windows, the walls, and ever so slowly, the ceiling, until almost the entire front of the room was claimed. The only exception was the section where the guard was standing.

I had twenty-three mana left at that point, so I started going around absorbing things. The broken glass was first; again, leaving as much as possible around him, but getting the rest that had gone from sight, sliding under chairs and tables.

I slid into the walls, leaving the structure intact—I didn't want it to collapse, after all—but absorbing the wiring and electrical bits, the alarms, sensors, all of it. Up to thirty-eight mana now, I glared at the looters roaming free in my building; no, in my dungeon, but there wasn't much I could do…

Or is there? I wondered.

I had claimed the room, and they *were* stealing from me…I shrugged and decided that maybe I could scare them off. They were looters, which meant they were literally out to gain by ruining other people's lives…

I summoned a goblin into the shadows at the back of the room, getting a shock as the little bugger manifested. First, because it was no surprise at all, the creation process actually generated a lot of light as tiny motes 'built' the creature, and I'd totally forgotten that.

Secondly, I was astonished because it appeared with a stick in its hand. The upgrade I'd queued for it had taught it to use a weapon! It was a terrible weapon; it was only a stick after all, but still! My little beasties were getting stronger!

By the time it'd finished appearing the guard had screamed, and three of the four men inside had come running. The fourth tripped and dropped a case of vodka, cutting himself on the glass, but it was only a minor wound.

"What the hell is that?" The first shouted, pointing a shaking bat at the little goblin's head, who immediately hissed in anger and leapt at him, teeth bared and stick clutched in hand. It managed to get a single hit in, before being smashed to the floor by a bat, and then the entire group started smashing their weapons down, breaking the poor little goblin's body into a bloody mush.

Strangely, it didn't dissipate this time, as they always had before, and instead, a tiny triangular box appeared rotating above its corpse.

"Hold it!" one of the men said, pointing at the box. "Don't anyone do anything!" He reached out slowly and touched the box with the tip of his finger, then started to laugh as he seemed to reach inside, his hand vanishing for a second into an altered space of some kind. When he pulled his hand back, he was holding a pristine packet of crisps.

The box and corpse vanished, disappearing into motes of light, and the laughing man froze temporarily before tearing the bag open and trying a crisp, then starting to laugh even more.

"Lads, we've hit the fucking jackpot! It's a Dungeon!"

"A what?" one of the others asked him, confusion clear in his voice.

"It's a Dungeon! No idea how or why, but it's a Dungeon, a real one! Look…" he said, gesturing and getting excited. "It's a place that will spawn creatures like that, well…that *goblin*…we kill them, and we get 'loot'. No idea why it's a packet of crisps, but it is! Hopefully, it'll give us more worthwhile shit once it gets bigger and stronger…"

"Whadda ya mean, creatures?" one of the others asked.

"Creatures!" the knowledgeable one declared, shrugging. "Could be anything, but the Dungeon'll be making them appear like that, then we kill them, and see what happens. What we got to lose?" he asked, clearly excited by the turn of events.

"Why?" asked another man.

"Because we get free shit! If it gets stronger, it'll start dropping better loot, shit like weapons and armor. Hell, who knows? Gold, diamonds; there's no limits to this kinda thing in the games. No idea why it's here, though…fuck it. 'Don't ask too many questions.' That's what my old man used to say. You see a door that's unlocked, or a purse that ain't been watched, you grab chance by the titties, and you go for it!"

"No, you idiot," the man who'd been on guard interrupted him, speaking over the others who were talking as well. "Why the hell does it do that? Why make creatures, then reward us for killing them?"

"I don't know…in the games, it was always because the Dungeons were evil, and they were trying to kill people. Maybe this one's just a baby or something?"

"So, the Dungeon's what? Alive?" he asked and the other man shrugged.

"Usually they have like a fairy or something. The Dungeon Core is like a crystal, and it just grows and makes things, makes creatures to kill people, then rewards the people who don't die with cool shit like armor and weapons. No idea why…"

"Hey Dungeon!" the guard shouted out, looking around. "You hear me? I wanna make a deal…" Silence fell, and I watched them until they started to grow uncomfortable. "Can it hear me, Greg?"

"How would I know? Seriously, Kyle, I don't know what's going on any more than you do!"

"Bullshit. You think it's a Dungeon, right? And it has what? A crystal that controls it?"

"They do in the games…" Greg said, and Kyle nodded.

"That's good enough for me. Let's go get some gear. That little bastard looked like it'd give a nasty bite, so get your bike gear on, thickest you've got. We come back and search this place top to bottom. I want that Crystal. If it's here, we find it, and we can control the place, maybe make some decent shit we can use, like money!"

"Right!" A few of the others nodded, and they piled the booze into the trolley, but left it against the wall, exiting the building quickly and heading up the street.

"Well, shit," I muttered to myself, well aware that I'd gotten my first set of Dungeon divers incoming, Adventurers, I supposed I should call them, and not only was I totally unprepared, but I had practically nothing to work with.

"Okay, first things first, I need to make sure they can't find their way down to me…" I muttered to myself, gliding through the wall into the room next door, where I'd hidden the stairs down several days ago.

I examined it with a critical eye, seeing things like missing skirting boards, a sign that pointed to the wall, and more, and I spent the next five minutes fixing those discrepancies. Then I moved into the main room where they'd been and absorbed as much as I could in a few minutes, moving back to the window they'd smashed to get in. I didn't like that they'd smashed their way in, but if I blocked it off when they were so excited to explore, it might make them go looking for another way in. They might accidentally find my entrance, and I didn't want that.

I resolved that the first room was going to be left as the Adventurer's entrance, just emptied. The next room it led into, my Aura had already partially absorbed, so I pressed the Aura out as quickly as I could. I stopped suddenly, frowning as I realized I'd never have enough of a charge of pure mana to accomplish what I needed, not in the time I had…unless I took a risk. I turned and flew to the front of the building, and pushed outwards in that direction again, but this time, I finished claiming the entire room, including the smashed windows and the broken security grates. I didn't stop there, though, turning and searching quickly. Finally, I found what I needed just over ten feet out into the middle of the road, twelve to the right, along the front of the building on the path…

I paused for a handful of seconds, then firmly chose the path to the right. There were others in the other direction, but if I chose them I'd be getting towards the cathedral, and I didn't want that.

I pushed out a section of the Dungeon Aura along the path, only a handful of centimeters wide, just enough to carry me and my influence cleanly as I pushed along. It took me nearly fifteen minutes, sliding along and pushing steadily, sinking the mana into the path, but after what seemed like forever, I did it. I was floating directly over another sewer grate, and I began sinking the Aura into it, claiming it as fast as I could.

Minutes passed like hours, but eventually, after almost long enough that I'd started to grow truly desperate, fearing the group would return at any minute, the sewer grate was accepted as part of the Dungeon, and I was pleased that I could open and close it with a thought.

I had seventeen mana left. Seventeen! That was enough for a goblin, or almost a pack of three kobolds…I was tempted by the kobolds, but…Dammit! I'd not looked at the cost of the goblins since I did the upgrade! They'd gone from five to seven mana to summon each, meaning I'd only get one, and it had been crap with its stick weapon…but…. I summoned the goblin, remembering the abilities I'd gained as a Dungeon Lord.

"Okay, then, let's see what we have here…" I muttered, mentally cracking my knuckles and reaching out as soon as the goblin was spawned. It stood idly in the narrow space I'd claimed, literally standing atop the grate to the sewer and blinking around, clearly disliking the sunlight.

Since I was out of the Dungeon's mana, I checked my personal manapool, seeing it was full at two hundred, and I slowly, ever so slowly reached out and visualized mana pouring out of me and into the stick the goblin held.

Nothing happened.

I tried again, and again, and again, and…

Eventually, I gave up. I didn't have the time to waste screwing around with this, and I'd finally gotten enough mana for either a second Goblin or the kobolds, so I summoned the three kobolds, then sent the goblin and two of the three kobolds down into the sewer with the express orders to kill absolutely everything they could find, then closed it after them.

The remaining kobold I ordered inside, prodding its simple brain along as it got distracted by shiny glass and bottles. Once it was safely indoors, I had thankfully gained enough control over the grates that I could lift and lower them when I'd absorbed them into the Dungeon. I moved the kobold to the second room and ordered it to start making traps.

It set to with a will, stripping items nearby and using some personal Dungeon power the creatures evidently possessed to break them down into usable parts of string, wood, and other crap.

While it worked, and my mana slowly started to refill, I examined the little kobold. It was weird seeing the 'real' version of the creature after years of reading about them in books and killing them in games. It stood maybe two feet tall and three feet long from snout to tail. The small creature was clearly a lizard, for all that it was a humanoid version of one, and had three-fingered hands and feet, tipped with stubby black nails. Its long snout, short, upswept ears, and knees that bent backwards made me think of the old pictures of satyrs. I inspected him closely from several angles, deciding that one of the first upgrades I needed to do to the species would result in clothes, as the little sod was butt naked. At least he was covered with wiry muscle, and his grey scales were patterned in black, making him at least look the part of a Dungeon creature.

I felt a surprising amount of satisfaction, then mentally grinned as a sudden burst of mana trickled into me. They'd found something in the darkness to hunt.

A few seconds more, and a second, then third kill fed me more mana, and I went back to work. The layout of the bar was simple. If I closed off the door in the wall to the left, leading to the room that would bring them down to me, I could make a collection of four rooms in a square, starting in the bottom left, moving forward to the next room, then right into the third, and back toward the front, finishing in the fourth room.

None of them were particularly big, but that was fine. I checked over the Dungeon Capacity details I'd seen on my character sheet, and with my level of control, I had twenty-five points to spend. A little concentration told me that these simple creatures, goblins and kobolds and rats, were all worth one point. The Lesser Ghast was worth five points, but I couldn't make them yet anyway.

I summoned three more kobolds and ordered them to help the first, slightly surprised at seeing them dive into their job with glee while I moved into the third room. The space held a collection of tables, chairs, and fake plants in pots, all covered by tarpaulins, and I absorbed half of them eagerly, bringing me back up to sixty points.

"Okay, time to take a risk..." I muttered to myself, summoning two goblins. The first, I ordered to stay put, while the second, I told to hide and be ready if I needed it.

Pulling up the ability 'Forced Evolution,' I found that I had a twenty-four hour cooldown, and a single charge, so I just had to hope those points I put into Luck paid off as I focused on the goblin standing before me, and triggered the ability.

A new screen appeared, showing the outline of the goblin, but this was immobile, and positioned in the classic 'Vitruvian Man' pose, with bones, teeth, claws, and internal organs, including the brain, plus senses, each individually selectable. There was also the simple option of 'Generalized Boost' available.

I considered both the individual and general options over, then chose the general one. I wanted to really drill down and experiment with it, but I just didn't have the time.

General Evolution:
You have selected 'Generalized Boost' for the first time.
Do you wish an explanation?
Yes/No

"Come on, man! I can't wait any longer!" a voice called out from outside, and I swore. They were back already, and I just didn't have the time! I selected no, and a pop-up appeared with the four basic elements of Fire, Earth, Air, and Water, and a sliding scale sat next to each of them. I could seemingly pour mana into one or more of the elements and force an elemental evolution.

I didn't have time to think, so I selected 'Earth', set it to twenty-five percent, which was apparently the maximum I could manage at this point and mentally hit 'Accept'.

The goblin started to shake immediately, then screamed as its bones lengthened and straightened. The little creature surged upwards in height to almost four feet and grew thick, armored skin. It began to hunch over, its arms growing much more heavily muscled, but it apparently also lost a huge amount of mobility, as it staggered from the changes and fell over.

I quickly examined it and found that it was barely an improvement.

Unnamed Goblin Smasher	Goblin, Dungeon Creature
This Goblin Smasher has evolved from the most basic form through a forced Earthen Evolution. HP: 70/70 Stamina: 80/80 Mana: 0/0 Speed 3/10 Level: 1	
HP 60/60	Special Abilities: *Smash!*

"Okay…so you've got some potential, but…" I checked my personal mana and decided I had enough, taking the time to examine the second half-hidden

Goblin as the group outside argued over how they were going to do their first Dungeon run.

Unnamed Goblin	Goblin, Dungeon Creature
This is the second most basic form of the lowly goblin, evolved to use simple tools, and designed to be primarily used as fodder for more advanced creatures. HP: 30/30 Stamina: 20/20 Mana: 0/0 Speed 5/10 Level: 0	
HP 30/30	Special Abilities: 0/0

"Ah, okay…so normal goblins are shit, but they're faster than the Smasher. Right," I said to myself, looking into the next room. Realizing it was bare, with no hiding places or anything, I set the Smasher to hide by the door and summoned five more standard goblins to wait around the edges of the room, with a pair of sacrificial goblins ordered to stand in the center in clear view.

I now had a goblin and two kobolds out in the sewers, happily killing anything they could, four kobolds in the next room making traps, and eight standard goblins and one Smasher in this room. The Smasher had cost two points, so that took me up to seventeen points, leaving me with eight for the final room. I summoned two more Smashers, putting them in the corners to the right and left to offer a challenge as soon as someone stepped through the door, and found that until the 'sewer squad,' as I'd tentatively named them, made some more kills, that was all I could do.

The security grate was yanked up and the looters moved back inside, helpfully closing the grate behind them, and I settled back to watch the fight, content that I'd done all I could in the few hours I'd had.

It was time to see what my little Dungeon could do.

TWENTY-TWO

THE GROUP THAT stepped inside was very different to the one that had arrived earlier. For a start they were all decked out in what appeared to be motorbike leathers, and that annoyed me no end. They had goddamn armor already! Then I remembered that they were doing this in the hope of loot, and that all the creatures of my dungeon were set to 'Cheese and Onion' crisp mode currently. I grinned darkly.

I'd planned on changing that, but just hadn't had the time yet, so as far as I was concerned, this was now their punishment, unless they really pissed me off, and I'd change it to tomato sauce flavor. Or worse, even…MARMITE.

They were all still set to drop a magical Spellbook, Skillbook, or artifact as well, but as there was only a 1% chance of that dropping, and if necessary, I'd just spawn more monsters to get it, I wasn't that concerned about it. I shook myself mentally, ignoring the urge to laugh maniacally, and instead settled in to watch as they stood about nervously in the first room. As they were choosing to do a Dungeon dive, and as they were looters, they were fair game. If they died in the Dungeon, then it was their fault.

"So where is the Dungeon, then?" a man dressed all in red leathers asked one with what looked like a cross between military armor and a kinky leather weekend get-up.

"They usually have like a neutral zone at the beginning, somewhere you can rest, then the remainder is split up between normal low-level bad guys and a higher strength boss," the second man explained, and I mentally tagged him as 'Greg'.

"Well, we were in and out all day yesterday, and there wasn't anything then…" another spoke up, dressed in black and white body armor with the full kit: gloves, helmet, everything covering him, and he carried a cricket bat in either hand.

"Yeah, well, we weren't looking for the Dungeon then, were we?" Greg scowled at his friend. He wore just a balaclava on his head instead of a helmet, and I resolved to get him as soon as possible. He knew too much. "Seriously, it's probably below us, deeper underground. That's where I'd want to be as a Dungeon, after all, but…"

He was cut off by a choked scream as he idly walked forward into the next room, peering about, and was yanked from his feet by a noose that was dropped over his head by a kobold hidden on a small ledge over the door. The other three kobolds to the side of the door hauled back on a small pulley, lifting him higher and higher as he kicked and struggled.

"Greg!" someone screamed, rushing forward and grabbing at the hanging man's legs, lifting him and relieving the pressure on his neck somewhat. Another member of the group rushed in and grabbed his other leg, lifting as well, hard and fast, thinking he was helping.

"Wait…noooo…." Greg managed to croak out, before there was a sickening crunch. The kobold hopped off his little platform, landing on another and running for it, the three that had held the ropes doing the same.

"Wha…" I heard the leader, who I'd labeled as 'Kyle,' say, looking up sharply as Greg started twitching and spasming. They pulled him down, much more gently than they'd lifted him, feeling the resistance as his head stuck for a second, before the poorly-attached spike of stone snapped off the platform, and Greg's corpse fell bonelessly into their arms.

"Fuck, he's dead!" one of the group screamed, backing right up.

"Greg, no…mate, you…" another of the group started to say, shaking his head in refusal of the evidence. They'd actually driven Greg's head up into the spike the kobolds had attached to the bottom of the platform, killing him themselves, instead of saving him.

"Motherfuckers!" Kyle screamed, dropping Greg's corpse and sweeping up the bat he'd dropped in his shock. "That's it! They did this!" he screamed, pointing at the disappearing kobolds as they dived through the door into the next room. "Kill them!"

He and the remaining three others started running forward, some more hesitantly than others, but they all complied.

The second room was maybe thirty feet across, but the kobolds hadn't had much time. They'd done their best, but the only visible trap was a spike trap. Kyle's leading foot caught on the tripwire, but he was too fast, and the rest of the group too slow, the spikes dropping down from a cunningly concealed false panel in the ceiling. Only one of the eight actually hit anyone, and that was the third man's shoulder, bouncing off the reinforced biker leathers without leaving so much as a scratch.

"What the hell!" the man screamed, jumping aside and landing on the only other trap that the creatures had managed to build in the time allotted. It was a pressure plate, and it failed to activate, simply cracking and letting out a pathetic clunk.

"There are traps everywhere!" he screamed, turning and sprinting for the door, leaping over Greg's body, and slamming into the security grate as he yanked on it furiously. As soon as it had lifted a few feet, he dove under it and vanished. Kyle paused in the doorway, glaring at the running man, and then snapped at the remaining two, who looked unsure. They gathered in the doorway, glaring in at the piles of boxes that were covered by tarpaulins.

"Boss, I don't think..." one said to Kyle, and Kyle silenced him by grabbing his face and yanking him in close.

"I don't care what you think, Ricky..." Kyle snarled at him. "This fucking Dungeon just killed Greg, and we're gonna find out what the hell is going on. If even half the shit he was talking about is true, then we need to take it over. It's that, or we're back to grubbing around. You want to spend your life like that?"

"I wanna *live,* Kyle!" he responded quickly, fear obvious in his voice.

"SO DID GREG!" Kyle screamed at him.

The shout was all that was needed, and the five standard goblins, led by the Smasher, erupted from hiding and raced towards the little group.

The Smasher tripped over a box and fell full length, smacking its head into the floor and stunning itself, while the five smaller goblins sprinted forward with abandon.

"Look out!" the third and final man screamed, swinging hard at the nearest goblin, who'd appeared only a half-dozen feet from him. The cricket bat smashed the stick that the goblin was carrying and sent it hurtling through the air, the broken body of the goblin following it, killed by a single panicked swing.

"What?!" Kyle swore, spinning around and noticing the group of goblins rushing them. "Kill 'em all!" he cried, swinging his baseball bat at a second goblin. He missed in his excitement, but the greater reach of the bat over the goblin's stick meant that he got a second chance, and he smashed the goblin's skull with the back swing, sending it staggering sideways before it collapsed, blood and brains leaking out of its tiny skull.

Ricky backed up, first one, then a few feet. Abruptly, he turned and ran as well, heading for the door, and I dismissed him as a coward. That brought me down to two thugs now. Kyle and whoever the final man was remained unaware that Ricky had left them, and they battled on, frantically swinging. The goblins fell easily, leaving only the Smasher, who'd clambered back to his feet and rushed forward at the pair in the doorway. They both stood ready, winding up, and swung for him, obviously thinking he'd be as easy to kill as the others, until their blows landed and he screeched in pain. Enraged, the goblin glowed red briefly, ignoring the wounds and smashing the unnamed man into the doorframe with a terrific force.

The sound of bones breaking echoed in the small room, and the unnamed man coughed blood, spattering it across Smasher's back. The smaller figure of the goblin backed up, clearly about to try the attack again.

Kyle brought his bat around, slamming it hard into the side of Smasher's head. The blow sent it staggering, and then Kyle hit it again, and again, screaming in incoherent rage as he battered the poor goblin to death, continuing until his bat broke.

Unnamed dude slowly slid down the doorframe, collapsing onto the floor and coughing blood as he started to shake, clearly choking on it as Kyle stood there panting, unsure what to do.

The pair of Smashers from the next room made a noise, as one stepped close enough to the doorframe to be seen. The small group of kobolds could be seen moving around inside as well, and that was too much for Kyle.

He screamed a curse at them, then turned and ran, jumping over the fallen body of his friend, who laid there choking, watching his supposed friend leave him.

I hovered in place for a few seconds, unsure what to do, as Kyle, screaming swearwords and imprecations, fled the building. I stared down at the dying man, knowing I had no way of healing him.

I'd been defending myself against a gang of thieves and looters, a group that would no doubt have attacked me once they'd found out who I was, and that I was in charge of the Dungeon, but still. Watching the man slowly drown in his own blood was a bit too callous for me.

With a thought, I ordered a Smasher forward, and I turned aside as he ended the struggling man's life. I felt somewhat sickened by the whole thing. I pulled up the notifications in an attempt to distract myself, and started to swear.

Dungeon Update				
Adventurer Deaths	Level	Corrupted Mana	Purified Mana	Dungeon Mana Total
1	0	80	40	113
1	0	50	25	125

Congratulations!

Two Adventurers have made the ultimate sacrifice in your Dungeon. 10% of their accumulated experience has been siphoned into you.

Adventurer level: 0

Accumulated Experience: 8
Received Experience: 0 XP (partial XP is lost to the ether…)
Adventurer level: 0
Accumulated Experience: 9
Received Experience: 0 XP (partial XP is lost to the ether…)
Your current XP stands at 587/700 to Level 7

Looking the prompt over again, a few things became clear. First, thanks to the industriousness of the goblins and kobolds in the sewers, I had more mana available than I'd thought. Second, the assholes who'd died had been filled with corrupted mana, and from what I could remember, the entire purpose of the Dungeon was to get that mana and purify it, using it to improve the world. Lastly, and most annoyingly, once the Dungeon's mana reserves were full, any excess was lost.

The rate of corrupted mana to pure was about half, it seemed, so I'd need to find some way to store the mana to be able to do things with it. I moved my consciousness to the security grates, which flapped in the wind, and with a thought, I slammed them back down, locking them, now that I had control over them.

I repaired the windows as I worried about the two who'd escaped. I didn't have any way to know where they'd gone, or what they'd do now, so clearly my time to slowly expand and explore was coming to an end. I wanted to expand the Dungeon; yeah, of course I did, but before now, it had been my plan to make it into a way to help people, grow food and medicine, make a safe bastion against the creatures and changes that were coming.

That plan would have to be shelved for now, I accepted grimly. If those survivors decided they wanted to get revenge, they might burn the buildings down, or hell, lead a mob back here. They might throw Molotov cocktails, or explosives in from outside. They could do anything, and they might end up disturbing the creature in the cathedral.

I wasn't ready for that, not by a long shot. I needed to level up, I needed to be stronger, and I needed my Dungeon to be a lot stronger. I clearly needed to get the place fortified and ready for an assault no matter what, because eventually, it'd come, one way or another.

I repaired the security grates, then absorbed the broken lock that had sealed them shut, instead growing a thin layer of stone over the bottom of the grates. I smiled to myself as I imagined the looks on the faces of the next group to attempt to break in.

I was losing mana every second that I wasted, since the mana was flickering at the maximum. I ignored the remaining notification, quickly pushing the Dungeon Aura out. As I went, floating through the walls, I followed the front of the building, heading west along the street. I was both pleased with how big this series of buildings were when combined into one, and close to panic at the work ahead of me to secure it all. I claimed the windows, doors and pavement-facing walls, making sure they were secure.

For the moment, I ignored the rest of the rooms, concentrating on getting as much done at once as I could. I also checked the Research, remembering that it had completed while I was gone. I paused, looking over the options to work on while subconsciously continuing to expand the Dungeon Aura. Luckily, it wasn't exactly mentally taxing, once I knew how to do it.

I had five 'greater' options to work on, and then as I went into each, I had 'lesser' or more specific options to select within Core Upgrades, Dungeon Upgrades, Monsters, Loot, and Research Nodes. I chose Loot first, after reading it over, then set it to switch straight to Research afterwards, simply because I'd already taken the Insatiable Curiosity perk, and once I had a Node available, I could summon and kill goblins until I managed to generate one that had it, then assign it to work in the Node and boost research that way.

The Loot option came first because I'd finally noticed a really cool little mechanic I could take advantage of. It seemed that when a Dungeon-born creature died, the Dungeon then had to immediately spawn the loot that it was set to provide, using the current stores of mana. There was another way, however, and that was the Reliquary. Reliquaries were powered by the creature themselves from a tiny magical 'seed', and once they were made, they absorbed a small amount of the mana that the creature gained, then used that instead to spawn the loot drop. This meant that the longer a particular creature lived, the better a chance it would drop a bigger or more powerful loot item, and it would cost me nothing beyond the original 'seed'. The best bit for me right now was that the crisps were classed as 'Common' drops, meaning they cost virtually nothing, so the cost of swapping to a 'Common' Reliquary seed was the same. That meant that once the research was done, nothing would have changed, save that over time I would have a better chance of a drop I wanted. The final, and arguably the best bit, was that if a Reliquary was unclaimed after ten minutes, it'd collapse in on itself and revert to mana, and that mana would return to me. So, for the same investment I always made without realizing…a single point…I had a chance to get a load more back, rather than leaving little packets of crisps everywhere.

Hell, it'd probably even look cool!

The problem was that there was so much I needed to get, and possibly so little time. If I knew, for example, that the group would be back in a day, I'd concentrate very differently than if I knew I had a week, or an hour. I needed to secure the building and its surrounding linked buildings; that was my first priority.

The fact it was a series of bars downstairs, with offices above, meant that I'd gain a lot of items that I could break down into mana, powering the expansion, but it was a finite resource, and it took time, time I just didn't think I had.

As soon as I managed to get to the end of the row of buildings, I'd make sure they were all sealed, returning along the back of the alley, securing each entrance as I went. The higher floors, thankfully, all had railings and nails hammered into the outer walls, pointing down to discourage burglars, so I didn't need to waste time on them…for now. I resolved to simply seal the stairwells off as I acquired each building.

It seemed like a mammoth task at first, but a simple series of orders to the kobolds ensured they were back on the job of making the second room into a series of traps, then they were ordered to start to secure the entrance the group had used, just in case. To hell with the safe zone.

As soon as I had made the choice on the research and confirmed it, I allocated half the incoming mana to it, reducing the mana I had to work with significantly. However, as each step I took to convert to Dungeon Territory only took a few points, and the 'sewer-side squad,' as I'd come to think of them, were still merrily slaughtering their way through the surrounding area, I could stay just ahead of the usage.

I paused after two hours or so, my brain feeling wrung out, and a sharply building feeling of discomfort let me know that my physical body had needs, so I flew back to myself and groaned as I shifted muscles that had frozen after hours of inactivity.

I really needed a La-Z-Boy or something.

I dragged myself to my feet and rushed to the loo, relieving the most pressing urges, and got a drink. Then I spread the looted items I'd gathered out around the sofa, taking the time to absorb them all, one by one, mentally filing the items away as 'food,' 'medical,' and 'weapons,' depending on the item. I tried to file some Aspirin as 'food,' in the hope that I'd be able to 'game' the system and have it as a food drop, but it apparently used my own mind as the filter, and I knew it wasn't.

That meant there was no easy way to produce drugs and other materials, unfortunately. I briefly looked into the things I'd need to do to be able to use it as a drop, and found I'd need to create an Uncommon Loot Node somewhere in the Dungeon. That didn't seem too big a deal, until I found that I'd need to research and then build a Common Loot Node first, and then upgrade that. The Loot Nodes needed space and a supply of their own level of mana, so unless I allowed them to just absorb the required ambient mana from the surroundings, which would mean that the Dungeon overall would absorb less, I'd have to make a set of 'Accumulation Crystals' first. Those, in turn, needed to be researched and built, they had different tiers, depending on what kind of mana I needed…

I pulled my brain away from that forcibly. I loved that side of things in games, all the strategy of Infrastructure versus Research and Production, but I was rapidly finding that I hated it in real life.

I kept promising myself I'd work on it later, but I just couldn't deal with it right now.

I finally gave in and ate some food I'd quickly prepared, again acknowledging I really needed to make some living quarters, mainly because until I had a way to make, then absorb hot food, I was stuck with eating whatever it was out of tins, and cold beans really didn't do it for me.

I really needed to find a chef to produce a hundred different cooked meals, absorb them all, and then I'd be able to reproduce them and live nicely.

I shrugged, dismissing the idle thought, and instead looked over the list of recently absorbed items, seeing that I'd at least managed to snag the armor, clothing, and bats from the guys who'd died, as well as a surprising amount of jewelry and, disturbingly, a lacy red thong.

I pulled up the last few notifications, more to distract me from wondering who'd been wearing that, and to stop the flash, than anything else, as the flashing had become almost commonplace by now.

Congratulations!

Your Dungeon Creature: 'Unnamed Goblin Smasher' has killed an Adventurer!

As 'Unnamed Goblin Smasher' is the First Dungeon Creature to do so, he has gained a perk!

'Cunning' Perk has been assigned, gaining this Dungeon Creature a 10% boost to intellect, and a higher chance to use dirty tricks in fights.

*

Congratulations!

Your Dungeon Creature: 'Unnamed Goblin' has killed 100 rats!

As 'Unnamed Goblin' is the First Dungeon Creature to do so, he has gained a perk!

'Rat's Bane' Perk has been assigned, gaining this Dungeon Creature a 10% boost to damage against rats.

"Well, fuck…" I muttered, stunned. I'd not really considered that the creatures could grow on their own, and I quickly pulled up the goblin options, finding that I only had 'Smasher' now. I was confused for a few minutes, until

I remembered that I'd used the Evolution option, and the warning that came with it.

When I evolved a creature, the basic version was replaced with the new one, probably so you didn't end up with a million different goblin designs, but it also meant that I only had the option to summon Smashers now, unless…I reread the details, then summoned my 'Rat Killer' goblin back to the Dungeon.

This was a bit of a risk, but I thought it should work…

It took him nearly ten minutes to return, and I quickly summoned two more Smashers, sending them out in his place, giving them the orders to go and kill whatever they could, leaving only humans, cats, and dogs alone…unless they were attacked first.

Contrary bastard that I was, it just felt wrong to let my creatures hurt a cat or a dog, and if they found some kid hiding somewhere…I just didn't need that on my conscience.

Once the goblin returned to the Dungeon, I opened the door and locked it again once he was inside. My mind went back to floating around, while my body laid sprawled on the sofa. I quickly examined the Goblin, finding its details had been upgraded, as had its HP from the standard.

Unnamed Goblin	Goblin, Dungeon Creature
This is the second most basic form of the lowly goblin, evolved to use simple tools and to be primarily used as fodder for more advanced creatures. This goblin has gained the Perk 'Rat Killer' and does 10% more damage to rats. HP: 40/40 Stamina: 7/20 Mana: 0/0 Speed 5/10 Level: 0	
HP 40/40	Special Abilities: 0/0

I mentally changed 'Unnamed Goblin' to 'Rat Hunter Goblin', then took a deep breath and reabsorbed him. It took a few seconds, and I actually felt guilty, as he'd done a great job, and I was essentially rewarding competence with death…but shit happened. The other corpses of the standard goblins had despawned after ten minutes and hadn't left the loot, so clearly there were also rules to how long Adventurers had to claim loot before it was lost.

I pulled up the goblin interface and cheered mentally when I saw that alongside the Smasher design, I now had the Rat Killer variant. I quickly absorbed the Cunning Smasher and replaced the standard version with the Rat Killer, pleased with the upgrade.

For whatever reason, the kobolds hadn't gotten a kill accredited to them, possibly because the Adventurers had killed their friend, rather than the kobolds' traps actually doing it, but hell, I still liked the little guys.

I re-summoned the Rat Killer goblin, two of them in fact, keeping the standard to one side for reabsorption so that I would have the design to keep if I didn't like the new one. I sank the fifty mana into him, this time guiding the evolution as much as I could, concentrating on his eyes and claws specifically using fire mana.

It worked great, for about three seconds. Then the poor creature screamed and fell to the floor, twitching. Apparently twenty-five percent fire mana was waaaaay too much for the little guy.

Unnamed Blinded Goblin	Goblin, Dungeon Creature
This is the second most basic form of the lowly goblin, evolved to use simple tools, and to be primarily used as fodder for more advanced creatures. This Goblin has gained the Perk 'Rat Killer' and does 10% more damage to rats. *Disabled*: Through an excess of Fire mana, this goblin has been blinded, and internal damage has lowered all attributes HP: 12/12 Stamina: 10/10 Mana: 0/0 Speed 1/10 Level: 0	
HP 12/12	Special Abilities: 0/0

I reabsorbed the original Goblin, and deleted the 'blinded' variant, swearing to myself. I could see that the mana was coming in steadily, but I'd just used a huge portion of my reserves, and I couldn't afford to continue to 'play' for now.

I was about to return to the expansion project, when I remembered Jack.

TWENTY-THREE

I FLEW BACK TO the Core room, finding his body in the corner, covered with a coat where I'd left him. I scanned him, and tried to absorb him into the Dungeon, thinking how effective a dozen of him would be, before getting a warning.

Warning!
Automata designated as 'Jack' is a personal pet and is therefore too advanced to be absorbed into the Dungeon and reproduced.
Do you wish to continue?

Warning!
Continuing to absorb 'Jack' will result in removal of your Pet.
Yes/No

"No!" I blurted, and the screen vanished, making me let out a relived sigh. "Okay, can't reproduce you, but can I fix you…?" I wondered, reaching out and focusing on him. Much to my delight, a screen popped up easily.

Damaged Automata Discovered!
Do you wish to repair your Pet?
Yes/No

I selected yes, of course, and got a counter flashing before me, with a slide bar to allocate how much mana was required to repair him, clearly it was a lot more than I had available.

Please assign mana to repair project.
Current condition 23/100 AP (Automata Points)
17/1000 mana allocated to repair.

I assigned a further ten percent of the mana coming in to Jack, knowing that it wasn't much from the hourly intake, but the killing of the creatures in the surrounding area was helping that to climb…even if my goblins and Smashers were having to travel further afield to find rats.

It couldn't give me an estimate on Jack's repair eta, mainly because if they found creatures to kill or not, it changed so drastically, so I just left him in the back of my mind for now, and went back to claiming the building. After another hour, the Reliquary research was completed, and I grinned to myself as I locked it onto all my creatures and saw that the change over to the Research Node had gone flawlessly.

Three more hours passed with me expanding the boundary a foot or so at a time, deliberately pushing out as I moved. Occasionally, I absorbed things. When I claimed the bar area of the 'Revolution Bar' and I absorbed all the booze remaining, that jumped the mana charge considerably. Most of it was siphoned away into repairing Jack and the research project, admittedly, but it still gave me enough that I felt better about things, just in case. I paused at the three hour mark, mainly because I was back up to almost my full charge now, and I summoned four more 'Rat Killers', sending them up the drain pipes in the alley, with orders to start hunting the hundreds of thousands of wild pigeons that filled the city. Planning for the future, and hoping to make the goblins considerably more efficient killers, I went searching through the Research tabs, until after a bit of poking and prodding, I found a 'manual' option.

I couldn't help it; I started grinning to myself once I found it, and I took the time to satisfy my physical needs, then settled in, pulling up the facility.

Warning!

To access the 'Manual Research Design' option, you must have a working and manned Research Node.

"God damn it!" I roared; my hopes dashed again. I jumped to my feet, stomping around and swearing at the top of my voice. I kept the tirade up for at least ten minutes, until I finally calmed down and slumped into my seat, simmering with resentment and anger.

I sat staring at the far wall, grumbling away to myself, until I finally shook off the black mood, and decided it was time to try to get my home back on track. I needed to get things sorted, I needed to eat a real goddamn meal, get a real night's sleep, and by all that was sodding holy, I needed a shower that wasn't icy cold.

I'd managed to get most of the building to the West of my own claimed, or at least, I'd managed to claim the outer walls, sealing up the doors and windows as I went. Internally, the building to the East of mine was fairly secure, now that I'd claimed up to the adjoining walls, as it was an office block, and they'd done some sort of government work upstairs, meaning that the doors and windows were all pretty damn secure. I decided that enough was enough, and that the outer wall of the Dungeon was set for now. I could concentrate on them as they were, instead of claiming all the way to the end of the street.

With that thought in mind, I turned to the Research screen and assigned all but ten percent of the incoming mana to it. The indicator jumped repeatedly as my little army of goblins and kobolds slaughtered the vermin surrounding my home.

While they cleaned up the surrounding streets and sewers, I sent my mental self winging back into the Revolution Bar and began to strip it of anything I could, continuing the cycle of jumping the Dungeon charge, even though only ten percent was making it through the filters now.

After twenty minutes, I set the Research to work on the next level of Living Quarters, once the Node was completed, and just hoped that I wasn't making a mistake by going down this route. I just knew that I'd be far happier and more likely to think properly if I wasn't on the brink of exhaustion and constantly starving.

Not to mention stinking.

With nothing better to do, I returned to the mind-numbing task of stripping the bar, taking everything, from the railings, to the seats, to the marble-inlaid seating booths and the chipped and damaged back bar.

Another hour passed as I worked, before the research on the most basic of Research Nodes was completed.

Congratulations!
Research Node: Common has been unlocked!
Your 'Common' grade Research Node will enable you to increase research by 25% when unmanned, with increasing levels of productivity, the more appropriate the researcher assigned is.

Optional Research Project Unlocked!
Manual Research
Manual Research is directed research, such as disassembling an unknown item and producing a blueprint that can then be easily upgraded or altered to produce different effects.

Do you wish to add 'Manual Research Project' to your research list?
0/1000 Mana charge invested
Yes/No

The prompt triggered another ten minutes or so of solid swearing from me as I realized that the research, which I thought I'd just finished, now required an additional step. As soon as I finished and calmed down, I selected 'Yes' and moved it to the front of the list, ignoring the progress that had been made on the Living Quarters.

Instead, I subsumed myself into the Dungeon sense and moved down to the area around the Core, slowly mapping it out in my mind. Solid stone walls sat on two sides, both with ten and fifteen feet or so to go before they opened out again the surrounding sewer systems, while the other two directions, in this case, east and west, led into basements that adjoined my territory. They'd both been slowly annexed by the spreading Dungeon Aura, and were mostly under my control, with a few rooms extending just beyond the outer edge of the 'bubble' of the growing Aura.

I flew through to the west side, noting that it was all storerooms, and started pushing the Aura outwards, steadily growing it, while watching to make sure I didn't get too 'full' yet. It took maybe twenty minutes to finish claiming the sections of rooms in that direction, and I immediately pulled up the Research Node specifications, creating an overlap in the rooms of the Node. The way the basement rooms were set out, one large main room was central, with three smaller storerooms leading off it, and it contained a great deal of old machinery that had probably been heating or aircon at some point; now, it was just rusting crap.

That suited me just fine, though, as it was mostly metal, with a load of plastic and rubber, meaning I'd have a nice boost in mana once I had the time to absorb everything.

I checked the design for the Node, thinking that it looked like a weird combination of a small office and a dentist's surgery once it was completed. Seats and desks were stationed around the outside of the room for up to four people, with a single reclining chair in the middle, while each of the desks appeared to have their own specialty.

The first desk, working from the entrance and circling from left to right, was woodworking, with strips of various wood and tools I vaguely recognized set into holders around the desk. The next was cloth, then mechanisms and blacksmithing. I perused the mental image and shrugged, figuring there were times when you wanted to build with your hands, and times that you didn't, and that this room was built with that theory in mind.

A dozen different layouts were possible for the room, ranging from being blank with a single seat at a wooden desk, to ones that were set up like sweatshops, but having workshop-style desks stationed around the central chair room was the one I chose, and as soon as I confirmed the design, I was given the option to build it using the generic or manual interface.

Checking it over, I found that the generic interface actually cost more than the manual option, and as it wasn't the exact size of the room, just close to it, it'd actually end up summoning walls where they didn't belong.

I decided to do the setup manually, and pushed the design aside. Starting with the walls, I smoothed them back, absorbing the crumbling mortar and bricks, then replacing them with fresh stonework and an arced ceiling. I set a 'Glowstone' in the center of the ceiling, a device I hadn't encountered until using this part of the system, and when it absorbed a tiny amount of mana and let off a bright, welcoming glow like the sun at noon, I almost smacked myself.

I'd been struggling underground for days, getting used to the dim light, and here was a great light that cost practically nothing and used ambient mana that wasn't being taken in by the Dungeon anyway? Idiot!

I resolved to start again on the building once I completed the Research Node, considering the fact that actually creating the stone, rather than altering the stones and materials that were present, and then creating mana-infused magical frigging Glowstones cost me a huge four points of pure mana in total.

That was it. And the little lights absorbed the ambient mana from the area to charge themselves at a rate of 0.01 mana per damn day. Considering the fact that my Core wasn't even able to reach out this far yet? Madness!

I forced myself to be calm and got back to work. Once the walls were smoothed back, and the ceiling reinforced and well-lit, I absorbed a handful of the abandoned items in the corner of the room, clearing a space that was roughly three feet deep by six long. All that junk had taken me back to full, even losing a little over the top, but it meant I had the space to work. Smoothing the floor, I coated it in a thin layer of white marble speckled with quartz from a pattern I'd gained when absorbing the Revolution Bar's marble counters. Once it was finished, I made a single long desk that folded down from the wall on hinges, which could be placed back up when not needed. I made boxes next, running from the floor to ceiling at either end of the bench, and left them ready for whatever tools would be needed.

Then I repeated the process, clearing a space, smoothing and coating the floor, then building another set of desks and boxes, working until all three sides of the room were done, leaving only the middle and the doorway. The middle of the room then was cleared and fixed, followed by a handful of chairs, and just in case, I left a pile of blankets in one corner.

I couldn't help but feel pleased when I stepped back mentally and reviewed the room, receiving a popup relating to the work I'd done.

Congratulations!

You have completed your first Dungeon Facility: Research Node (Common Grade)

Current design allows up to four researchers to work concurrently. Do you wish to save this design as a blueprint for easier production in the future?

Yes/No

I selected 'yes,' of course, and relaxed a little as I looked the room over. It had been easier than I'd expected to make it, and it made me feel a lot better about the next stage, as the massive amount of mana that had come from stripping the room and the happily murdering goblins was enough to bring the manual research option that much closer to existence.

I decided a little exercise and relaxation was in order, fleeing back to my body while I waited for it to be completed. I got up, cleared things back so that I had plenty of room, and changed the assigned loot for the 'Cunning Smasher' goblin to magical drops only.

That meant there was a one in a thousand chance of me managing to drop a magical item, Spellbook or Skillbook, but it also meant that at least I wouldn't be wading through a pile of cheese and onion crisps by the end.

I resolved to keep going for as long as I could keep the mana charge over half. As the Cunning Smashers currently cost me ten points of mana to summon, and I was getting, on average, two hundred mana an hour now, with eight per hour from ambient absorption, and the rest from the murder squads, with the Research Node and Jack's repairs set at ninety percent, that meant…. I quickly started working the math out.

My maximum charge was set at one hundred and twenty-five; at present, I was gaining two hundred and eight mana per hour. Ninety percent was going into research, which meant that the total would rise by around twenty-eight points per hour. The number fluctuated, depending on how the goblins were doing, but it meant I could summon probably three to fight every hour, or thereabouts.

That worked out as thirteen days of constant fighting around the clock to find something magical, and there was no guarantee it'd be useful, but I needed to up my skill level, and more importantly, I needed to spawn a goblin with the 'Insatiable Curiosity' trait.

I gathered up my sword and started warming up a little, jumping from foot to foot, running on the spot and performing star jumps, until after thirty seconds, I gave it up as ridiculous. With nothing else to do in preparation, I summoned the first goblin.

The tell-tale motes of light flooded the area like the world's weirdest 3D printer, and the creature steadily formed from the ground up. When it was done, it blinked, looked at me, then started looking around the room, totally unconcerned.

I stopped in confusion, my sword drawn back, and tried to work out what had happened. Every time I'd summoned them before, they'd attacked me, and…

And this time I had the Dungeon Master Perk, so they now saw me as their lord, not their damn enemy!

I considered killing it anyway, I really did, especially when it turned away from me and started to sniff around the room, evidently hunting for food. I huffed and shook my head. I couldn't do it. It just felt 'wrong' to summon a creature that apparently bore me no ill will, and murder it, again and again.

I decided if I couldn't use it for fighting, I'd use it for experimentation. Instead of attacking it, I 'Examined' it, finding the exact same stats as I'd gotten before. I didn't have access to the Forced Evolution ability when in my own body, and as much as it seemed fine with me, I wasn't going to leave my body defenseless while it wandered around.

I tried to figure out what to do, how I could achieve something with the little bastard, when I realized something. The normal goblins spawned with the stick as their weapon. It was crap, but it was still a weapon. The Smashers didn't, and that meant that they either needed their hands for their ability, or they just didn't need the stick. I decided that would be a useful test and sent it to the far side of the room to wait, just in case. Quickly pulling up the menu, I set to making a sword for it to use.

While the sword was forming, I checked the Research tree, pleased to find that the Node was maybe an hour or so from being completed. Once I had that room available, I hoped I would be able to make changes to existing designs, such as scaling down the size of the sword, and making it in other materials, like metal!

As soon as I had the sword, I made another, giving me three identical wooden swords, counting the one I'd had already, and I closed the system, blinking as the screen cleared from my vision. I got up from the couch and walked over to the goblin, which was sniffing at a section of wall.

"Oi!" I called, and it jumped, spinning around and dropping low to growl at me. I backed up, sword in either hand, and glared at it as I saw the exposed pointed teeth, but as soon as it recognized me, it broke off with a sound like a puppy, all confused as it cocked its head to one side and stared at me with glistening black eyes.

"Okay…this is for you…" I said, awkwardly, straightening and flipping the new sword over and offering it to him, hilt first.

He made a sound halfway between a chirp and a bark and took the sword, sniffing it and looking it over. He tried to bite it, then licked it, then seemed to lose interest, dropping the sword on the floor and going back to examining the wall.

"Well, that's just great," I grumbled, shaking my head. Admittedly, the sword was literally larger and almost heavier than the goblin, which was only three and a half to four foot tall, at the very most, but still…

I shook my head and moved back to my couch, sitting with the second wooden sword across my knees and a handgun ready, just in case the goblin turned feral. More than it was already, I mean.

I started to examine the sword, pulling up the 'Imbue' option again. The description really didn't give much of a helping hand, simply saying I could give freely of my own mana pool to change an item or creature from standard to magical.

I tried all sorts of tests over the next few minutes: visualizing fire, talking to the sword, trying mumbo-jumbo made-up words that I guessed sounded magical. Hell, I even tried to somehow compress the mana I could feel in the air around me into the damn thing. Nothing.

It wasn't until I just relaxed, blowing out a deep breath, and placed one hand on either end of the sword, that I felt something…a resonance of sorts.

I froze, and the feeling vanished, making me wonder if I'd imagined it.

I tried again, shifting my hands, blowing on the sword, and getting more and more annoyed with myself, until I finally realized what I'd done differently. I'd relaxed. Taking a deep breath, I imagined that I was loosening the floodgates in my hands, letting the energy I now knew to be mana flow out and into the sword I held.

Immediately, it became to give off a faint shudder as mana flowed into it, and a counter appeared in my vision, slowly ticking upwards.

1/500…2/500…3/500…

My mana slowly poured into the wood, and as it did, I could feel something changing. The resonance slowly seemed to shift back and forth inside the sword, as though looking for something. I hadn't a clue what it was looking for, but I tried to clear my mind, just concentrating on pouring the mana in.

Minutes passed, and all too soon, my mana was almost totally exhausted, a headache building, and I still had nothing to show for it, just a counter that now read one hundred and ninety out of two hundred.

I grudgingly released the sword, leaning back and looking around the room. The goblin had evidently finished its investigation of the wall and had curled up in the corner, appearing to be fast asleep. I got up, taking the time to use the loo and get a drink and snack. The goblin, roused by my activity, perked up at the sight of food, and I threw him a trail bar as well, facepalming when he proceeded to eat it, wrapper and all.

I'd gotten used to the creature now. It was still fugly as all hell, but it seemed to be content to just chill out, and I didn't feel there was any kind of threat from it…so I shrugged and settled back down, sinking my mind into the Dungeon senses and fleeing my body, which slowly slumped to one side on the couch.

I watched the goblin carefully for a minute, then when I was sure it was asleep again, I addressed the notifications that were still flashing.

Congratulations!

Manual Research has been unlocked!

Your 'Common' grade Research Node will now be able to integrate a design and assessment facility, enabling you to increase research by up to 50% when unmanned, with increasing levels of productivity based proportionally on the appropriateness of the assigned researcher.

Optional Research Project Unlocked!

Uncommon Research Node is now available for research. This Node will increase the base research level of the Dungeon by a minimum of 25% over the 'Common' grade node while unmanned, with increasing levels of productivity based proportionally on the appropriateness of the assigned researcher.

Do you wish to add 'Uncommon Research Node' to your research list?

0/10,000 mana

Yes/No

I selected 'no' for now, instead boosting the Living Quarters research back up and mentally moving to the Research Node I'd built already. I pulled up the manual research option, and found three options available for building: a simple desk with various weird tools and what looked like crayons and paper on it, a dry erase board like the ones my teachers wrote on in school when I was a kid, and finally, the most expensive option.

The first two were fifty and seventy-five mana charge in cost, respectively, while the third option was five hundred, but as soon as I saw it, I knew it was exactly what I needed. It was composed of a seat that reclined and actually looked comfortable, with a screen that hovered in mid-air. I knew it was a totally different level to the first two, and that I could do amazing things with that.

I selected it, unsurprised when it warned me that I needed more mana charge after rapidly depleting the stored amount I had. I moved to the next storeroom, stripping it as fast as I could, seeing the familiar jump in charge, followed by the dip, and repeating the process again and again as the chair was built. I managed to completely empty the second room and was about to start on the third when I got a pair of new notifications almost in tandem.

Congratulations!

Common Living Quarters has been unlocked!

Your 'Common' grade Living Quarters are now available for construction.
Each set of quarters now comes with access to clean water and a bedchamber.

Optional Research Project Unlocked!

Uncommon Living Quarters are now available for research. These quarters will provide a degree of personal space not usually found in the Dungeon, including personal bathing facilities, cooking and eating areas, and an optional climate differential facility.

Do you wish to add 'Uncommon Living Quarters' to your research list?

0/10,000 mana charge invested.

Yes/No

I swore viciously. Again.

I just god damn knew I should have ignored the Quarters. I'd wasted all this god damn time! I glared at the notifications, before moving to the Research Node and angrily summoning a 'Cunning Smasher'. The ugly little creature appeared and looked about dully.

Do you wish to assign 'Cunning Smasher' to a research position in this Node?

Yes/No

I looked from it to the node and back, observing the dull, uninterested look it was giving the room, and I growled in annoyance before trying to activate 'Forced Evolution,' only to be reminded yet again that it had a twenty-four hour cooldown.

"Fuck it!" I screamed in my mind, and selected yes, sending it inside to work.

Warning!

Assigned researcher does not meet minimum Intelligence requirements.

Research speed will be lowered by 20%.

Accept?

Yes/No

I roared in fury, the general frustrations of the last few days getting to me, and I struck out, my spectral hands passing through the goblin, which panicked and started running, frantically trying to find somewhere to hide as the 'Spirit of the Dungeon' screamed abuse at it.

I finally selected no, when I calmed down somewhat, then led the Smasher out, setting it free into the sewers to hunt.

I flowed back to my Core room where the other goblin slept, finding that the little bastard had nicked a handful of tarpaulins and made a nest in the corner. I glared at it for a few minutes, before forcibly reminding myself that none of this was its fault. Sighing, I mentally prodded at it, leading it upstairs and dumping it with the others that roamed the upper floor.

With that done, and the kobolds still industriously working away on traps, I ordered them to move up to the roof when they were done and set traps for the pigeons, while I retreated and went to bed.

I was a *thousand* percent done with this shitty day.

TWENTY-FOUR

THE NEXT DAY, I awoke slowly and naturally, no sense of danger waking me for a change, or dogs wanting to be let out. So I basked in the stillness, calm at last, where yesterday I'd felt like I was back to running from fire to fire.

I laid on my back on the bed, gazing up at the remains of the pipes and ducting that I'd half-stripped to feed the Core, and I considered where I was and what I'd managed. I vaguely remembered that I'd assigned the research to work on the kobolds as I'd been falling asleep, queuing up three levels of it, just in case, and I remembered the flashing notifications I'd dismissed in a huff when I'd gone to bed.

I thought about the building I now lived in, and the things that my friends and the good people I'd known out there would be living through right now, while I was having a hissy fit in here, and I felt overwhelming shame.

I needed to do more. I needed help, and I needed to grow up.

I took a long, hard look at myself, getting up and wandering over to the remains of the back bar, where a single mirror still remained on the wall. I was tall, reasonably good looking, and physically fit, especially after I'd began to invest points in my characteristics, but my self-control was terrible.

I'd literally run from job to job yesterday, achieving little and probably wasting a huge amount of time, time I really didn't have to spare.

I locked eyes on the man in the mirror and I swore to myself that I would do better. I turned, moving back to my couch, and pulled up the notifications.

Congratulations!

Your Dungeon Creature: 'Unnamed Goblin' has killed 100 Pigeons!

As 'Unnamed Goblin' is the First Dungeon Creature to do so,

he has gained a perk!

'Flying-Rat Killer' Perk has been assigned, gaining this Dungeon Creature a

10% boost to damage against Pigeons.

*

Congratulations!

Your Dungeon Creature: 'Unnamed Kobold' has killed 150 rats using self-constructed traps!

As 'Unnamed Kobold' is the First Dungeon Creature to do so, he has gained a perk!

'Creative' Perk has been assigned, gaining this Dungeon Creature a 10% boost to creative endeavors.

*

Congratulations!

'Pathetic Kobold' has been upgraded to 'Common Kobold'!

Common Kobolds are slightly larger, stronger, and more cunning than the base creature, with increased chances to develop complimentary skills beyond
the racial trait 'Trap-maker.'

Optional Research Project Unlocked!

'Uncommon Kobold' evolution has been unlocked. Uncommon Kobolds are bigger than their more bestial and stupider cousins, with considerably higher mental capabilities. Along with the physical changes, these creatures can now begin to truly 'think' as a species, considering life beyond their immediate needs.

Do you wish to add 'Uncommon Kobold' to your research list?

0/10,000 mana charge invested.

Yes/No

*

Uncommon Kobold Research currently stands at 1198/10,000

*

Warning!

Cunning Goblin Smasher has reached the outer limit of your control radius and has begun to explore above ground.

*

Warning!

Cunning Goblin Smasher has been killed.

"Wait, what?" I asked in surprise, wondering what had happened. There was no timestamp or location or anything, so I had no clue where or how it had happened, either. I sat wondering for a few seconds, until I shook myself out of my funk. I'd gotten a load of research done, thanks to the killing the little groups had performed, and…

"The cathedral!" I blurted, suddenly remembering the orders I'd given it last night. I'd been so annoyed, I'd practically turned it out on its ear. I certainly hadn't bothered with the usual orders to maintain a good distance from it! "Shit!" I growled under my breath, and I jumped to my feet, quickly grabbing my weapons, my sword, rifle, and handgun, determined to get upstairs and figure out what I could see from one of the upper windows. I sprinted across the Core room and up the stairs, reaching the fire doors that served as the entrance and exit to my home just in time to sense someone outside.

I froze, my Dungeon senses telling me that a human—no, a pair of humans—had slipped into the alley and were making their way along it now. I stood there, hand half reaching for the door, and waited, hoping frantically that they'd go quickly, that they'd just pass on by and…and I felt it…something… *wrong* had entered the alley as well.

As I waited, hoping against hope that whoever the pair were, they'd just fuck off and leave my territory, I could feel the thing coming closer and closer. Each step seemed to radiate evil, a sapping cold pulling at my Dungeon Aura, pulling mana and energy away from me…

"Matt!" I heard a little voice squeak weakly, and a faint thump sounded on the door, inches from my hand.

"We have to go!" a second voice said, and I closed my eyes, hearing the fear in that familiar voice. Alyssa and Amy. Not only were they here, in my goddamn alley, but they'd apparently woken up whatever lived in the cathedral.

I paused for a long breath, my desire to have peace and quiet, to not be involved, warring with the need to protect that child, and to a lesser degree, her ass of a mother.

"Matt…please…" I heard Amy whimper from outside, and I growled to myself as I ordered the door to open, knowing I was exposing my sanctuary to that creature by doing it.

The doors swung out, Amy and Alyssa being pushed backwards by their trajectory, and I stepped out into the alley, recognizing the terror and desperation on their faces as I approached them.

"Get inside!" I ordered, looking past them and fixing my attention on the creature that was peering at me hungrily from the darkness ahead. It waited, hunched over under the shadowy overhang of the end of the alley, where a separate building joined my long stretch of claimed buildings with the ones on the other side of the alley. Watching me intently, it stood, its arms and legs seemingly far too long and thin. The face was that of a little girl, but horrifically stretched and thin, with tears in the skin where the jaws had grown, pointed teeth and dried blood marring the remnants of the childlike face.

She reached out and casually climbed up the wall to her right like a spider, passing out of the shadows and drawing closer in all her terrible glory. Forcing myself to hold my ground, I frantically activated 'Examine.'

<table>
<tr><td>Eidolon</td><td>Undead Ghoul</td></tr>
<tr><td colspan="2">The Eidolon is a creature of nightmare, born of a twisted desire to help a child pass back through the veil. This abomination is formed when a Ghoul's spirit has struck an unholy bargain with a grieving relative, granting a form of half-life to the child, even as it uses the relative's life-force to pass itself through to this side of the veil.

Once released, the Eidolon grows in strength, consuming the bodies of the living and the dead alike, raising its own protectors in the form of Lesser Ghasts. The Eidolon will continue to grow, tearing apart the form it has inhabited while feeding on the child's soul, until the relative dies. At that point, the loss of the primary source of sustenance, as well as the only source of emotional support for the child's soul, will set the Eidolon free to spread its curse, feeding and converting those it encounters to serve it.

Lure: The Eidolon can sacrifice fifty points of stamina to mesmerize a target and draw it closer against its will. Eye contact must be maintained and once broken, cannot be used against that target again for 3 minutes.

HP: 1200/1200
Stamina: 500/500
Mana: 0/0
Speed 7/10
Level: 4</td></tr>
<tr><td>HP 1200/1200</td><td>Special Abilities: 1/1</td></tr>
</table>

"Oh, fuck…" I whispered as the creature clambered up the wall, arms and legs spread out around it like some monstrous spider. Its flesh was bone white, dark red muscles and sinews showing through rents where the stretched skin had split. Maggots writhed in the broken flesh and fell in droves as it moved. The stench of death grew unbearable as it approached, while its broken, claw-tipped fingers clicked on the stone. A tiny foot fell free, tumbling to the cobbles, exposing a spiked, webbed foot that slowly flexed and unfurled from its former constrained position.

We both looked down at the lost appendage; the Eidolon, curious, me, absolutely fucking terrified. Then it seemed to dismiss the freshly released body part and turned its focus back to me, trying to smile. The light brown hair of the girl still held the remains of the headdress I'd previously seen on her, now filthy with matted blood. Then the eyes met mine. I'd been so absorbed with looking over the entire creature, I'd managed to not look into those glowing blue orbs until now, and when I did, I felt myself start to shake.

She smiled again, a long, segmented tongue flickering out as her mouth distended, opening far wider than it should have been able to. She inhaled deeply, sucking in the purified mana the Dungeon had produced.

Her twisted form started to shake as if in ecstasy, and she continued to climb along the wall, closer to me...when she suddenly screamed in pain and surprise, falling from the wall. She clutched at one hand, where a tiny metal trap had gone off, biting deep into the fingers. I blinked, shaking myself free of the hypnosis and saw, for just a second, a kobold on the roof.

The damn anti-pigeon traps I'd ordered them to make!

They'd made a tiny bear-trap of some kind, and it'd just bitten into the Eidolon's hand. She'd tried to grab onto a section of guttering where the pigeons must have been nesting!

She crashed to the ground nearby and I dove back inside, ordering the doors to close, frantically spamming the order over and over as she lifted her head and hissed at me in anger, scuttling forward on all fours as fast as she could. The metal of the trap clanged against the cobbles as she advanced hungrily.

I had the rifle slung over my shoulder, sword in the right hand, and handgun in the left, and yet I froze for a second, my mind screaming that the rifle would do more damage, but the time that I needed to get it into position...I ignored my brain and lifted the handgun, going on instinct, and fired over and over at the Eidolon, slamming bullets into it and knocking it back, but doing little else.

She hissed in fury, then tried to smile at me, the little girl's face rearranging to look more or less intact, despite the increased size of the skull causing it to look like something was wearing her face like a mask over its own...

Which it literally was.

I pulled the trigger finally on an empty chamber and swore, throwing the gun back behind me to clatter down the metal fire escape stairs as I held out the sword warningly and tried to get the rifle off my back. It wasn't working; the strap that someone had attached to it at some point just wouldn't come free...I was starting to panic as it came closer, grabbing the doors in either hand and pulling back on them, making the magic that controlled them shudder and strain.

It pushed its head forward, cocking it from side to side jerkily to look at me. The three feet between us was nowhere near far away enough for me, and it started to smile again, the mouth slowly widening, a look of hunger twisting its face.

I gave up on the rifle and stabbed out with the sword, the blunted tip smacking into the Eidolon's forehead and making it pull back with a hiss of anger, if not pain. As soon as it came close enough again, I twisted, slashing the sword in a rising arc from low left to high right, aimed not at its head, but its fingers.

I heard the crack of bones breaking as it impacted, and the creature released the door on that side with an inhuman shriek. I swung again as fast as I could, aiming for the fingers on the other side. I missed as it jerked the fingers free, but that was fine; all I'd needed was to free the doors.

As soon as they started closing again, I focused and yelled "Incinerate!" at it, desperately pouring my mana into the pattern needed. The magic flared to life and made the creature scream in pain as it backed away, slapping at itself as my spell battled with its own unholy constitution.

Had it been alive, I was sure it would have died, but as it was dead already? Animated by some combination of dark magic, unearthly hunger, and sheer bloody evilness? It merely screeched at me and fled from sight. The doors finally closed, and I sagged back against the back wall, dropping my sword and finally managing to free my damn rifle.

"Motherfucker!" I managed to get out at last, my mind filled with terror at encountering that goddamn thing all over again.

I dove my mind into the Dungeon Sense, just fast enough to 'see' the creature fleeing the end of the alley and heading back in the direction of the cathedral.

"'I'm gonna need a bigger boat…'" I muttered to myself, the bastardized line from an old favorite film coming to mind. "Hell, I need a bigger door! And a goddamn army; why the hell didn't I ever station some of the goblins out there?!" I immediately reached out to spawn a few, when a prompt sprang up.

Warning!

Control limit reached!

To increase summoned Dungeon Creatures past this point, you must do one of the following:

Increase your personal Control score.

Increase the level of your Dungeon Core

Increase the efficiency of the Dungeon Control system

Carry out further Monster/Dungeon Research

"What?!" I sputtered in disbelief, glaring at the screen. Dismissing it until I could figure out what to do, I pulled up the other waiting notifications.

Congratulations!
Your Dungeon Creature: 'Unnamed Kobold' has injured an Eidolon!
As 'Unnamed Kobold' is the First Dungeon Creature to do so,
he has gained a perk!
'Cunning Trapsmith' Perk has been assigned, gaining this Dungeon Creature
an increased chance to damage larger prey with his creations.
*
Your Kobold: 'Unnamed Kobold' has levelled up!
As this is the first Dungeon-born creature to level up, you may choose to
assign points for the creature, or allow it to assign the points as it chooses.
Assign points?
Yes/No

I selected 'yes,' mainly out of curiosity as to what the little bugger's stats would be, and I was both disappointed and elated when a stat screen bloomed to life before my eyes.

Name: Unnamed Kobold				
Species: Kobold		Bonus: Trapsmith		
Level: 1		Progress to next level 17/100		
Available points: 2		Perk: Cunning Trapsmith		
Stat	Current points	Description	Effect	Progress to next level
Agility	***2***	Governs dodge and movement.		17/100
Charisma	***2***	Governs likely success to charm seduce or threaten		0/100
Constitution	***2***	Governs Health and Health Regeneration	HP: 2x10 = 20	1/100
Dexterity	***5***	Governs ability with weapons and crafting		39/100
Endurance	***2***	Governs Stamina and Stamina Regeneration	Stamina: 2x10 = 20	11/100
Intelligence	***2***	Governs base manapool and standard intellectual	Mana: 2x10 – 20	4/100
Luck	***2***	Governs overall chance of bonuses and critical hits		12/100

Perception	*2*	Governs ranged damage and chance to spot hidden items/ traps		7/100
Strength	*2*	Governs damage with melee weapons and carrying capacity		1/100
Wisdom	*2*	Governs mana regeneration and memory	20 mana regenerated per hour	16/100

I looked the details over, seeing that kobolds were essentially thick as mince, and identical in every area except Dexterity, where instead of the standard two points, they had five. They received two points to allocate with each level up, and as such, I knew exactly what I was going to do with this.

I paused for a second, wondering if it would work, but decided the possible payoff was worth it. Once I assigned the two points to Intelligence, I ordered him back to the doors. It took several minutes; the creature was small, after all, and climbing down a set of iron rungs on the far side of the alley meant for adult humans took longer, but soon enough, he was standing outside the doors. I focused on him with the Dungeon sense, absorbing and killing the poor little guy. I felt bad about it, but as soon as I had the pattern with the newly increased intelligence, I respawned him inside the Research Node next door.

As soon as he arrived, I got a prompt.

Do you wish to assign 'Unnamed Kobold' to a research position in this Node?
Yes/No

I chose 'Yes,' obviously, and let out a relieved sigh when the system accepted him.

Congratulations!
You have assigned a researcher to your first Research Node! As this is your first, there is a corresponding boost to research. Please choose one of the following areas of research to receive this boost…
Kobold Pattern Upgrade
Research Node Upgrade
Living Quarters Upgrade

I paused for several seconds, watching the little kobold slowly examine his surroundings, and I swallowed hard, the various options spinning through my mind. In the end, there was only one option to take, really, and as much as I hoped it would boost the research significantly, it wasn't the Node. I assigned it to the Kobold Pattern, seeing the progress jump significantly to nearly halfway.

I grimaced at realizing how long it would still take to make it, as the little kobold was adding a whole three points per hour to the existing research. The total was boosted all the way up to one hundred and ninety points an hour, assuming my little team of vermin murderers kept going as they were, of course, though I knew that wasn't going to last forever.

That being said, if their hunting benefits lasted long enough to finish the Kobold Upgrade, I'd be pleased, as the kobold I'd just dumped into the Research Node was still only the 'Pathetic' variant, not the 'Common' ones I'd just unlocked. It'd take just over twenty-six hours to make the 'Common' into 'Uncommon,' and that, I had to hope, would be a significant jump.

I was about to compare the differences between the two standard versions and my level one Research kobold, when I felt something tugging at me.

I blanched and immediately pushed myself out of the Dungeon Sense and into my own body, which was slumped against the wall, with Amy and Alyssa on either side of me.

"…up!" Alyssa hissed at me, yanking on my arm, hard, even as Amy tugged on my chest.

"What?" I grunted, shaking myself. Alyssa and Amy immediately released me and backed away, glaring at me.

"I said, get up, you idiot!" Alyssa snapped at me, and I saw the handgun in her hand. It was held casually, but still ready to be used. She saw the direction of my attention, and she shook her head quickly. "It's not for you, but with that thing out there, what if it gets in here? We have to go!"

"Put the gun away," I growled at her, pushing myself up and collecting my thoughts as I spotted my own weapons and scooped them up. Once everything was secured, I made my way to the pair of them and nodded to the stairwell behind them. "Well? Are you going to go down, or are you leaving?" Alyssa's face colored, but she wordlessly turned Amy around and pushed her ahead, walking down the stairs.

"What is this place?" Alyssa asked over her shoulder.

"It's my home," I grumbled. "What are you two doing here, and what the hell did I tell you about the cathedral, Amy? What happened to get that thing's attention?" I snapped at her, anger bleeding into my voice.

"It wasn't my fault!" Amy replied, a whine raising her pitch. "Momma made us come past it!"

"It was the quickest way…" Alyssa interrupted, swallowing hard. "…I didn't know…"

"I told you!" Amy cried at her, stopping on the stairs and turning to point an accusatory finger at her mother. "I told you Matt said not to! You wouldn't listen!"

"I didn't know it was real! How was I…" Alyssa started to argue with her daughter, until I cut in, speaking over the pair of them.

"I don't give a shit!" I snapped. "You disturbed it and brought it to my goddamn door, and now it knows I'm here!"

"Well, I'm sorry!" Alyssa snapped back at me. "We didn't have a lot of options, okay? We had to go somewhere, and Amy said you had a safe place…" She trailed off as she peered around the dim fire escape, abruptly realizing that she'd probably just ruined that.

"Yeah…thanks for that," I grumbled, pushing past the pair of them and heading in to the Core room. Unceremoniously dumping my weapons on the floor, I sat on the couch, pulling the ammo bag over and sorting through it.

I had sixteen bullets left for the handguns, three shells for the shotgun, and ninety-two bullets for the rifle, stored in two clips of thirty-five each and the remains of the clip already in it. The swords were blunt and good for whacking things with force, but that was it. Last but not least, I still had my diving knife, which left me with a good arsenal, if all I needed was to scare some humans, or kill some goblins.

I was afraid it would be bugger-all use against that Eidolon, though.

Alyssa and Amy eased into the room slowly. Alyssa's attention at first was drawn to the glowing, spinning Core, before she looked down at the guns. Amy, on the other hand, was completely fixated on the collection and had reached out slowly to pick up the shotgun.

I snorted and pulled it out of reach, setting it down on the other side of the sofa from the pair as I worked, ignoring them and trying to get my annoyance down.

"Look, I'm sorry," Alyssa said finally, after the silence had stretched on long enough to make her uncomfortable. "Amy said you had a safe place, and, well…you're the only person so far that hasn't tried to either screw me or screw me over."

"What? What did Barry…" I scowled, my anger starting to boil again. If that asshole had taken the park and the community back down into the same kind of shit they'd been doing before…

"No!" Alyssa said quickly, holding her hands up and shaking her head. "He didn't do anything like that, and he's trying to help people, don't worry. It's just that he's gotten a load of local Army types to run things. They've taken over the park and brought some order; everyone works, and all the food has been taken in and rationed. They're getting things sorted out, but…"

"But what?" I asked, in a low growl.

"But they're the Army; they're all about control. You have curfew, you get the same thing to eat, you can't leave the area without a pass, the park itself is off limits unless you're working in it, and everyone works all day to tear the abandoned houses down. They're making roadblocks and…and…"

"Alyssa, it's a fucking warzone out there!" I snapped, cutting her off. "You've seen that creature! Well, there's gonna be more; lots more! They're breeding! Hell, they're killing and eating people, and you're complaining about being told you have to contribute?" I asked her incredulously.

"No! It's…it's not like that. I gave up most of the food. They took the shotgun you gave me, said it was for the armory, and they'd have taken the handgun as well, if I hadn't hidden it. I don't mind helping. I *want* to help… but I'm nobody, I've got no skills they can use, so I'm back to digging in the soil, and I hate it. I want more than that, especially for Amy! There's no school or anything; the kids just work with their parents. That means it's never going to get better, don't you see? I tried to talk to Barry; he saw me once, said he'd make sure we were looked after, and he tried. He gave us more food and everything, said he'd make sure I got a good, safe place to sleep for the two of us once the defenses were up, but every time I tried to talk to him after that, his 'helpers' just turned me away."

"So he's ignoring you?" I asked, confused.

"No! Honestly, I don't think he even knew I tried to reach him. He was getting pestered every minute of the day by people, so he put a team together to keep things going, and to keep him from being bothered; that's all."

"Look, I'm really trying here, but I don't know why the hell you're here, okay? It sounds like it was harder there than it used to be, but it's safe, right?" I asked, and she nodded. "And you were fed, and nobody tried…anything?" She indicated that everything I'd said was correct, looking crestfallen all the same. "Then why the hell are you here?" I couldn't hide my confused irritation.

"Because of you!" she finally snapped.

"Me?" I asked, even more dumbfounded.

"You!" she insisted, shaking her hair out and running her fingers through it. "Look, Matt, I don't know what's going to happen…" She met my eyes with firm determination. "I don't know why the power is off, or why the creatures are showing up, but you know something, don't you?" she asked, and I nodded slowly. "I thought so. Barry said when we talked that you'd warned him the power wasn't coming back, and he believed you enough to turn the park into an armed camp. He's organizing the area, making sure everyone's fed, making sure they all survive as best they can."

"But I don't want to survive, Matt…I want to live! I want to grow, to learn; that's what I've always done. I've got two degrees and I was studying for my Master's; now, I plant crops and dig up weeds. I get the same as everyone else, and that's fine, but I want more. More for myself, more for the future, and definitely more for Amy! I'm not letting her grow up just like this to become a goddamn farmer!"

I started to open my mouth, and she shook her head to forestall me.

"I'm not saying there's anything wrong with being a farmer. Seriously, there isn't. Fuck, we all need food, so they're gonna be seriously important from now on, but I. Don't. Want. To. Be. One."

"And you think I'm the answer to that?" I asked her bemusedly.

"I *know* you are!" she insisted. "You saw a little girl alone, so you took her home. You fought people along the way just to help out victims you didn't even know. You stormed a goddamn armed camp and freed me, because my little girl needed me, a girl you'd only just met, even when I treated you like shit, and you made sure we were fed, safe, and secure. Then you went out and killed everything that was a threat in the area, setting up a goddamn miniature kingdom to support and save the people in the area. You did it in a *day,* Matt. You. It doesn't matter that you turned over control to Barry and his friends. It doesn't matter that you might be here all alone. You know something, and someone who can do all of that in a fucking day and then walk away with hardly anything as a reward is someone that has a goddamn plan! I want in!"

"Okay, look, that sounds amazing when you put it like that, but seriously, I'm not that guy. I'm no hero, I just…"

"Really? You stormed the enemy 'castle,' slaughtered the bad guys, and rescued me. Then you turned down the role of boss or lord or whatever and walked off into the sunset. What the hell does that make you, if not the hero?" she asked me, one eyebrow raised and a sardonic smile touching her lips.

"I don't know…an idiot?" I shrugged, my cheeks turning red at the way she was looking at me. "I didn't set out to do all that, all right? I just wanted to do the right thing."

"Exactly. And what does that make him, Amy?" Alyssa asked her daughter, smiling.

"The hero!" Amy said, grinning at me.

"Seriously…I'm not." I shook my head, drawing in a deep breath and searching aimlessly around the room, before looking back at the pair of them.

"Look, I do…maybe…have a plan, and yeah…I know some shit. Not much, and most of it doesn't make sense, but I know something. And my plan isn't to just sort myself out; I'm trying to get things organized so that I can help everyone, but its gonna take time. There's so much to do, and with those creatures out there…"

"Then let us help," Alyssa said simply, and Amy nodded in enthusiastic agreement. I paused, momentarily surprised at the offer.

"You said you left the group because…" I started to say.

"Because that wasn't a life. There, I was basically going to spend my life grubbing in the soil, and so was Amy. Here, with you? We can make a difference. I don't care if I have to do exactly the same work here as I was out there, or wherever we go…as long as there's a chance for more for her, I'll do it. And you're gonna need more from me than just working to keep some food coming. You say you've got a plan? Let me help. My degrees are in social studies and history, and my thesis is in the industrial revolution. I know they don't sound like much, but they mean I understand people! That's why I knew I couldn't stay there. It'll take years to set up the basic systems for the community to stabilize, the way they're doing it, and once you're in a job, especially one that's desperately needed, like being a farmer, they can't afford to let you better yourself. That's nothing bad against them; they're acting as a group for the greater good of the community, but it means the individual just gets ignored. I need more. I can *be* more! And so can Amy. She's smart, she's resourceful… please, Matt, just give us a chance!"

"You gave up on them after, what, a few days?" I asked her skeptically, and she tilted her head at me in confusion.

"It's been nearly a week since you left us?" she replied slowly, and I blinked in shock.

"No. No, it couldn't be…" I started to say, shaking my head.

"It's been six days, Matt," Amy insisted sadly. "It's been horrible. All we do is work until we pass out, then work some more. The food's horrible, and…"

"No…" I muttered, thinking rapidly. I'd been underground, true, so I hadn't seen the sun or sky, and yeah, I tended to lose track of the time, especially with the mind-numbing tasks, like pushing out the Dungeon Aura, but it couldn't have been more than three days, right? I tried to count up the meals and toilet breaks, as well as the amount of times I'd actually slept, and found that I really couldn't. I'd thought it was a few hours, here and there, but last night, or when I'd gone to sleep at least, I'd passed out, and I had no way of knowing how long I'd actually slept. I had my grandfather's watch, but I'd never figured out what time it was in order to wind it back up and reset it, so I'd just been wearing it as a keepsake…

I shook myself, cutting off the random train of thought, and I focused on the pair, realizing they'd been waiting on me. I yawned suddenly, and for the first time in what seemed like days, I paid attention to myself, to my body. I ached, mainly from lying around for hours at a time. I was filthy, hungry, and thirsty, and yeah, I needed the loo. I was a mess, and as I regarded myself and the now-filthy Core room, noticing the discarded food wrappers, the empty cans, and other careless debris, I nodded in understanding, believing at last that, even if it hadn't been six days—and they had no reason to lie about that—it'd definitely been more than the two I thought it had been.

"Okay, you want in? Fine." I said. "I need help, and yeah, there's definitely more interesting shit to do than planting crops and weeding. I don't know how the hell I can integrate you into all of this, but I could really do with the help. I'll warn you now, though, there's not much in the way of luxuries in here, and I've got too much to do to make the living quarters better at the moment, especially with that fucker out there…"

"We're staying here?" Alyssa asked me, surprised. "I thought we'd leave; maybe go, well…somewhere safer?"

"No," I said firmly. "Believe me, there's nowhere safer right now than here. Even with that fucker prowling around outside. What happened to get its attention?" I asked suddenly, remembering that they hadn't mentioned it.

"Spot…" Amy said, and I saw tears welling up as her shoulders shook. Alyssa moved to her, pulling her close and speaking quietly.

"Shush, Amy, it's all right. It's not your fault. Spot died to give us the chance to get away, to escape, and find Matt…" Alyssa looked up at me sadly, her hair falling to the sides of her face as she obviously tried to fight back tears. "The daft bugger, he started sniffing around, and all of a sudden, he tried to run to the cathedral. Amy pulled him back, but the lead snapped, and he ran off, barking at something…next thing we know, that thing was there, waving to us from the window, and more of them, smaller bony things, came running out, chasing us. There were three of them, and when we ran, they…they caught Spot. The big one came out after us, ignored the others and…what they were doing…"

"I remembered where you lived!" Amy said suddenly, speaking up, pushing her mother back and smiling at me. "I saw the street, and I remembered you were down it, and I knew you'd be here, and you'd kill it!" Her words grew fiercer as she continued. "I want you to get it! Kill it for what it did to Spot!"

"Amy, no…" Alyssa said quietly, sadly, shaking her head. "Baby, no, I'm sorry, but that thing, it's too big, too strong. Matt can't kill it…" She started to explain, when I cut her off.

"Don't worry, Amy. I'm going to kill it, all right," I said grimly, locking gazes with her. "As long as that thing's out there, we're not safe in here, and neither is anyone walking past. I've needed to do other things first, and there are things I still need to do, but don't worry. I *will* kill that fucker," I promised, determination filling my voice.

"Matt, that thing…" Alyssa started again, and I cut her off.

"Alyssa, believe me, that thing is going down. Now, before you panic, I think we need to talk about a few things, and I need to bring you up to date with what I know. But be warned, you're not gonna like it…" I said, clearing some space on the sofa and settling back. Alyssa took the hint and took a seat, picking Amy up and holding her in her arms. I made a mental note to make something for them to relax on soon, and then I started to tell my story.

I told them the entire thing, glossing over certain details out of deference for Amy, as I didn't want to give her nightmares.

TWENTY-FIVE

"BULLSHIT," ALYSSA SAID firmly, sometime later, lifting Amy to her feet and shaking her head as she got off the couch. "I'm sorry, honey. I made a mistake. Matt's got some kind of problem, and we're not going to be safe here…" She said, starting to pull Amy to the stairwell.

"Wait!" I said, holding my hands up in the air. Alyssa glared at me and kept trying to get Amy moving. "Seriously, will you just fucking wait a minute?! I can prove it!" I insisted, and she paused before glaring darkly at me.

"Fine. Prove it. Make me believe you're not just a delusional nutjob who's broken into my favorite bar to drink it dry," She said sarcastically, and I forcibly stopped myself from glancing at the empty bottles in the corners, and the general mess I'd left the place in. It wasn't like I'd been expecting visitors, after all!

"Okay, look…just sit down and wait a minute, okay? I need to concentrate here…" I waited until I got the slightest of nods from Alyssa before diving into the Dungeon sense and…finding that I was still at my maximum control limit. I couldn't just summon another creature out of thin air. *God dammit!* I thought, scouting around. The majority of the goblins upstairs were just wandering aimlessly. Thankfully, due to being Dungeon creatures, they could survive on the mana that they were created with, but they were looking a bit lean…I paused for a second, considering if I should set up some kind of vending machine for them. I had crisps and so on, after all, but I dismissed the thought as stupid and reached out, picking a goblin at random and reabsorbing him. He'd been one of the most basic, stick-wielding ones, which meant I only made a single point available. The new upgraded Kobold took two points to summon and control, so I reached out and absorbed a second goblin, all the while, hoping that I didn't regret reducing the force upstairs for this.

As soon as I had the points available, I returned to the Core Room, finding Alyssa pushing Amy towards the exit. I growled and reached out in concentration, summoning the little creature into existence. I placed it next to the door, on the far side from Alyssa and Amy, and as soon as the motes of light started to stream toward it, literally printing it into life, Alyssa screamed and pulled out her handgun, shooting at the rapidly appearing creature.

"Whoa! Fuck's sake, stop it!" I shouted, diving into my body again. I tried to get up and found that I was still sluggish from the speed at which I'd dived back in. I staggered and fell to the floor, shaking my head as the room spun around me.

"Get back!" Alyssa screamed at Amy as the creature finished. It slowly opened its eyes, blinking, and the third bullet hit it dead center in its chest, making it screech and clutch at itself. The fourth and fifth bullets made sure it was dead. The last four bullets before her clip was empty were totally wasted, as had been the first two that had simply buzzed through the gathering form.

"Fucking stop it!" I roared at her, having finally gotten to my feet and made it over to them. I grabbed the gun from her and pinned her to the wall, staring into her frightened baby-blue eyes and glaring down at her. "Alyssa, stop! It's dead, for fuck's sake." I scowled at her and she struggled to get free of me. In the end, I had to pin her, spinning her around and wrapping my arms around her from behind to hold her arms tight against her sides. As I lifted her feet from the floor with a grunt, I turned around, making her face the corpse that was leaking blood on the floor. "See?" I asked her. "It's dead! You just killed it you, stupid sod!"

"It's a monster…" she gasped out, struggling against me. "It's one of those creatures!"

"It's one of MY creatures!" I ground out, squeezing her harder against me as she struggled. "You just killed one of my Dungeon Creatures. I had control of it, and you just wasted the damn thing's life…" I shook her from side to side to try to get her attention, before giving up and waddling awkwardly over to drop her onto the sofa. She bounced—the damn thing was hard—and twisted around to look at me, her eyes still wild.

"What was that?" she asked fearfully, reaching unconsciously for the nearest weapon, which was one of mine, a shotgun. I stepped on the barrel, pinning it to the floor as she glared wildly at me.

"I told you Alyssa, I'm a Dungeon Lord. It's one of my minions, and they cost resources and effort to make. You just killed it and weakened us if that creature comes back!" I growled, before rubbing my face and relenting. "Look, how about we just calm down, okay? I told you I'd prove to you that the Dungeon was real. I mean, you've already seen the damn flashy Core there…" I gestured offhandedly towards the Core where it slowly rotated and pulsed with light. "I can summon creatures. They do as I say, and they protect my Dungeon, both from creatures like the Eidolon, and human looters and criminals."

"I thought you were lying…" she mumbled sullenly, still unable to take her eyes off the corpse.

"Yeah, I know, and now you've wasted not only my resources and time, and cost him his life, but you've wasted a full damn clip of bullets!" I said, shaking my head in disgust.

"You should have warned me…" she started to protest, still glaring up at me as I shook my head.

"You didn't give me time, did you?" I retorted. "You agreed to let me prove it, then as soon as I was in the Dungeon Sense, you started trying to run out of here…" As I scolded her, I frowned, looking at the shotgun and the rifle where they lay. Something wasn't right here… "Wait…where's my handgun?" I asked, looking around.

"Um…it wasn't my bullets that I used…" she admitted slowly, and I turned to look at the gun I'd pulled out of her hands. It had fallen to one side on the floor, and as I went to inspect it, I started to swear. She'd taken my gun, clearly planning on stealing it, and then she'd fired a full clip into my poor sodding Kobold!

"Oh, hell no!" I lifted the gun and glared back at her. "Where's *your* gun?" I asked through gritted teeth, and she stood up, lifting her top slightly and pulling it out of the waistband of her pants. I was distracted for a second by the flash of red, lacy underwear, and then her jumper dropped back down, cutting off the sight. I ground my teeth even harder as she ejected the clip and showed it to me.

Empty.

"Are you kidding me?!" I asked, anger and disbelief staining my voice. "I left you two full spare clips, and the gun was full. I left you a shotgun that I could have sodding used, and all that ammo, and you've used it all?!"

"You don't know what it's like out there…" she started to argue, and I cut her off.

"No, YOU don't know what it's like!" I snapped. "I had to kill dozens of men for those weapons, and not only did you fucking waste them, but now you've wasted mine!" I shook my head, ready to tell her to get out, when Amy stepped between us, waving her hands.

"Stop it, both of you!" she cried, peering up at us with wide eyes. "Just stop, okay? You're both in the wrong." I started to glare at her until she leveled a finger at my nose and went on. "You could have warned us exactly what you were going to do before you did it, and you…" she said, pointing at her mother, "you need to stop it! Every time you see Matt, you just shout at him! Remember what you said when we were coming here?

That we needed to help him, and you wanted to make up for the way you treated him? You're just making it worse!" The sound of unshed tears in her voice made it clear just how upset she was, even though she was clearly fighting them back. It got through to me in a way that other things hadn't, and I stepped back, taking a deep breath and nodding to Amy.

"You're right, Amy. I'm sorry," I said, and I heard Alyssa muttering something similar to her daughter. "Look, everything I told you is true, okay?" I insisted to the pair of them, and Amy spoke up quickly.

"All of it? So, you could make us somewhere to sleep, rather than on the floor or the sofa? And you can make whatever food we want?" She fired the questions at me excitedly, making me smile sadly.

"Yes, and no. Sorry, Amy, but while I can make 'Common' class quarters, I can't make the good ones yet. They'll take days of research time, and, well, I've got too many other things to worry about to invest that kind of time in them. The food, though…yeah, I can summon whatever food I've absorbed into the Dungeon, like the crisps and the chocolate and so on. Those, I can make again and again," I admitted, shrugging.

"You could make us 'Common' Quarters, though?" Alyssa piped up, and I nodded to her, meeting her gaze earnestly.

"Yeah, I can, and I will, just not right now. Thanks to that creature outside, I need to consider my next move, and that's going to take a load of resources…"

"Okay…do you think you can kill it?" she asked me frankly. "And if you do, what then?"

"Yeah, at least, I hope so," I said. "As time goes on, it's getting stronger, and it sounds like it's making minions as well. I'd hoped for a few more days at least to make some weapons, and the time to teach my creatures to use them, but I don't see me having that time now…"

"It's a race, then," Alyssa said firmly, and I nodded.

"What?" Amy asked, confused, and Alyssa smiled at her, hugging her tight.

"It's a race, honey. Matt is racing the creature that followed us. If he wins, he can create enough creatures to overwhelm it, or strong enough creatures to help fight it, so that he can kill it, and then we can rest…"

"What if he loses?" she asked hesitantly.

"Then we lose. Momma's gonna make sure that doesn't happen though, honey, don't you worry." With that she kissed the top of Amy's head and glared at me. "We're staying, if that offer's still open?" She asked, with more than a hint of challenge.

"It is…" I said, meeting her eyes grimly. "But this is the last chance, Alyssa. If you go off in a mood and try to steal from me again, you won't be welcome back; understand?"

"I do, and I'm sorry. We've gotten off on a bad foot, and I keep making it worse; I know that. I have to think about Amy first, though. Everything else is secondary, and when you told me all this…"

"I know," I replied shortly. "Well, I guess some quarters were overdue to be built, and it's not like it's for many people…" I started to acquiesce when I caught a change of expression on her face. "What am I missing, Alyssa?" I probed warily, and she shrugged.

"It's just…look, you're handsome and all, but I *am* married, and…"

"I *know* that, and I haven't…" I sputtered, my irritation rising, when she cut me off with a raised hand.

"I know, I know!" she said quickly. "What I'm saying…is that my husband might come, and then we'd need some more space, that's all…"

"I thought he was deployed?" I asked, then remembered. "No, he was down south, ready for deployment, wasn't he?" I said.

"Exactly." She sagged, hope and fear warring across her features. "He'll come for us. Even if he's got to fight everyone between here and there, he'll be on his way…"

"How the hell will he find us, though?"

"I left him a map!" Amy chimed in, smiling proudly at me. I closed my eyes, swearing internally.

"A map? You left a map where anyone could find it, one that shows where we are?" I asked slowly, trying to stay calm.

"Yeah! And I told him that we'd be here, and that there was food, and it was safe!" She said proudly as I turned to glare at Alyssa.

"I didn't know about the map!" She held her hands up defensively. "This is the first I've heard about it! I left word with Kelly, my sister-in-law, where we were going. She's smart, and I told her not to tell anyone but Mike. She swore she wouldn't…"

"Fuck's sake!" I groaned, pinching the bridge of my nose.

"She's going to give it a few more days there, she said, to see if it gets better, and then she said she'd come here…" Alyssa admitted softly, wincing at the look of fury on my face.

"Are you for fucking real?" I asked her, throwing my hands up. "I've spent all this time and effort to build this up, and you're going around telling people where I am?! You know what people will do for this, don't you? For a safe, secure facility with the potential to produce anything we need as a society, when the whole world's going to shit?"

"I do…" She swallowed hard and lifted her chin. "But I'm not sorry, Matt. To do all that, you need people. You need a community, and until now, there's just been you. We can help! You know you need help! Mike's a soldier, special forces. Kelly works for the courts, advising the judge on what sentences are appropriate, and she used to work as a medic. I know history, and I know how things used to be done. You say you need to build your way through tech levels? Mike can make things safe, protect us all, and train people. Kelly can write laws that are actually fair and make sure we can keep society going. I can help on the research side. I can teach your…minions…how to do things. I also know the basics of the industrial revolution better than anyone I know. Crop rotation, steam power, mass production, all of it, and if we recruit more like us? We can make a real society, and we can actually help people!" She spoke passionately, her voice rising until it rang with fervor.

"Yeah, that's all good…" I said cautiously. "We just have to survive long enough to do it!" I turned away from her and walked across the room towards the Core, staring into its glowing depths and thinking. Long minutes passed before I shook my head and gave in, admitting to myself that we…*I* needed this…I just didn't like the feeling of losing control, that was all. "Okay, this is how it's going to work for now…" I started, looking back at the pair of them. "Amy, you're responsible for our living space, since this is where we all live for now. It'll get better, but for the moment, this is all there is, okay? I need you to clean the place up. gather all the rubbish in one spot, and I'll have the Dungeon absorb it. I'll get some more sofas or whatever brought down so we all have somewhere to sleep, but once they're here, you take care of them, and you're in charge of food, okay? We need meals, regular, proper meals. Can you do that?" I asked seriously, and she proudly agreed.

"We're all going to be living on chocolate and tinned spaghetti hoops now; you know that, right?" Alyssa asked me, a faint smile on her face as she ruffled her daughter's hair.

"I know how to make more than that!" Amy protested, shoving her mother playfully and grinning at me.

"I hope so, because for now, there's not even a cooker, so we'll have to figure something out. Luckily, there's bread and fillings, so for now, it's sandwiches and cold tins. Sorry," I said apologetically as Amy looked less certain. "As for you, Alyssa, please don't kill the kobold this time?" I asked her, receiving a nod before I closed my eyes, summoning a second kobold.

Once it was completed, Alyssa and Amy simply stepped back, ready to defend themselves, but not acting as frightened. I reached out to the Kobold's mind, which I instinctively knew how to do, thankfully, and imprinted Amy and Alyssa onto its consciousness as friendly fellow Dungeon Creatures. As I felt the change take hold, the building fear and alarm that had filled the tiny creature's mind was wiped away in an instant. At first, it squinted at them curiously, then it seemed to dismiss them, and it started looking around the room, scuttling to one side and picking up a discarded wrapper.

I examined it in the Dungeon Sense and couldn't help but grin.

Unnamed Kobold	Kobold, Dungeon Creature
This is the second most basic form of the lowly kobold, evolved to use simple tools and create basic and common traps. This kobold has spawned with the Perk 'Insatiable Curiosity' and has a 5% chance per hour of activating its special ability 'Burst of Inspiration'. This ability may lead to significant breakthroughs in whatever the kobold is working on at the time. HP: 30/30 Stamina: 30/30 Mana: 30/30 Speed 5/10 Level: 0	
HP 30/30	Special Abilities: 'Burst of Inspiration'

Okay, so this one was clearly not as smart as the last one, which I'd invested two points into its Intelligence, but it was slightly bigger and had more stamina than the standard, previous version, so that was good. More importantly, it had the Perk!

I frowned for a second, considering my options and comparing the two designs for kobolds that I had available now: this new 'baseline' version, and the upgraded, but lower starting level version. I could delete the old version, despite the increased Intelligence and its Trapsmith skill, but decided against it. It cost the same to summon as this new version though, so sooner or later I'd have to decide if I needed both. I also reminded myself that the 'Uncommon' variant was currently being researched as well.

I set the matter aside for the time being, opening my eyes and joining the girls, who stood watching the kobold.

"What do you think?" I asked them, and Amy looked up at me, eyes shining.

"He's awesome!" she said, then tried to run forward before being pulled back by her mother.

"Is it safe?" Alyssa asked me anxiously, and I nodded, smiling.

"It is. He views you both as fellow inhabitants of the Dungeon, so while I'd like you to be careful, he's got no reason to hurt you. If you attack him, or do something he doesn't like, though, it's your own fault," I warned the pair of them.

"Like what?" Alyssa asked, and I shrugged.

"Like hit him, or steal his guns and waste bullets; that's sure to piss someone off…" I forced myself to wink at her as she snorted and shook her head.

"I'm never going to live that down, am I?" she asked and I grinned mischievously.

"Nope. Anyway, the reason I summoned him is that kobolds are slightly brighter, at a basic level, than goblins are, not to mention more personable. Goblins are, well…fugly, basically. He's simply weird, and given the choice of the two, I know what I'd rather work with…" I explained and Alyssa nodded in understanding.

"Yeah, I agree. Can you run through the Research side of things again?" I obliged, briefly describing how the Node increased the output of the dungeon overall by up to fifty percent, provided all the stations were manned and the creatures working there had the minimum required Intelligence. "Okay, and what do you want me to do?" Alyssa asked when I'd finished.

"Simple; I want you to make sure my troops survive. We'll leave them working on the current research, upgrading the 'Common' Kobolds to 'Uncommon', as that'll give them a much wider utility, not to mention making their traps better. While they do that, I want you to work in the free design chair. It'll let you take existing designs and rework them, altering them or starting from scratch. I need ranged weapons, armor, and god, I need a proper sword! Take the design for mine, but make it metal and sharp!"

"Then what?" She persisted, and I nodded upwards.

"Then me and 'the boys' go to pay our neighbor a visit…"

TWENTY-SIX

THE NEXT DAY was long, and hard, and to my great displeasure, it wasn't a euphemism. I'd found through the day that Alyssa jumped into my mind at odd times, and I chalked it up to the combination of it being a while since I'd engaged in any 'horizontal jogging', the fact that she was very beautiful, and the close proximity we worked in, as well as the sure knowledge that nothing could happen between us, as she was married, and I had strict rules about not shitting where I ate.

While she was working in the Research Node, and Amy was cleaning around, I'd flown through the building above us and searched the rooms one by one, finding a pull-out futon in a very expensive-looking managers office on the top floor. I'd directed the goblins to bring it down, dropping it off at the bottom of the stairs in the Core room and leaving quickly. Even though I'd taken the time to 'Imprint' the girls on the minds of all my Dungeon Creatures, the goblins were just weird and ugly enough at this stage that I didn't want them around Amy too much, just in case.

I wasn't so concerned about Alyssa, figuring she'd probably tear them a new asshole, now that she was over the original scare, but still. No need for more minions to die.

Once the futon was down, I'd gone back to expanding the Dungeon Aura, working my way steadily up once the lower floors were secure. I'd replaced the windows with bricks and built a solid wall directly behind each door. I left them in place, in case someone came past and noticed, but I'd filled the keyholes as well, just to be doubly sure.

I'd also noticed that there were far less people roaming the streets now, and I guessed that the inquisitive had died, and with everything else here supposedly closed and left secure, there was just no reason to come looking.

I absorbed the rest of the goblins in the building, leaving only two 'Cunning Smashers.' I left a single 'Goblin Rat Killer' out in the sewers, and kept five of the most basic kobolds, one out in the sewers and three around the building, continuing to gradually kill anything they could. I set the last 'Common' kobold to work in the research node with Alyssa and the other level one Kobold. That gave me ten points to use, so I summoned a pair of Goblin Rat Killers, one to keep on hand for the pattern, and one to experiment on, just in case it was a failure like the blind one had ended up.

I did my experimenting well away from the girls, just in case, and as I activated 'Forced Evolution,' I decided to make a complete change from the generalized plan I'd used for the 'Cunning Smasher.' Rather than choosing to let the automated system do its work with just one of the elemental forms of mana, I chose to mix them.

I pulled up the design screen, seeing the goblin stretched out in the same ring as last time, the muscles, bones, skin, and organs somehow all clear, despite the reality of them being layered the way they were.

Once I could see everything, I made small alterations. I used five percent of Water Mana, sinking it into the joints, five percent Earth, smoothing it into bones and skin, five percent Air into its brain and muscles, and then five percent of Fire, guiding it into the nerves and brain.

When I was done, I paused, looking it over, then decided to go for broke, and as the maximum mana was twenty-five, I sank the remaining five percent of Pure Mana into the goblin as a whole. Then hit accept.

The new creature writhed and whimpered, the skin shifting as though something was moving beneath it. Cracking, hissing sounds escaped its mouth as it shook, blood starting to seep from its orifices. I raised my hand, sighing, about to put the creature out of its misery, when it stilled, drawing in a deep breath and straightening, standing taller than I'd seen a goblin do until now. I hastily hit 'Examine' and looked over the details.

<table>
<tr><td>Unnamed Goblin</td><td>Goblin, Dungeon Creature</td></tr>
<tr><td colspan="2">This is the second most basic form of the simple goblin, evolved to use simple tools and weapons. It has been further augmented by the use of 'Forced Evolution.' The newly created goblin has greater Speed, Strength, and Intelligence than the standard variant, and has been gifted with a new Ability: 'Rush'

Rush enables the user to cross short distances in a flash, consuming Stamina to do so.

HP: 60/60
Stamina: 30/30
Mana: 20/20
Speed 8/10
Level: 0</td></tr>
<tr><td>HP 60/60</td><td>Special Abilities: 'Rush'</td></tr>
</table>

I examined the creature, grinning to myself with the realization that I now had a viable foot soldier, even if it was weak and it had little Stamina. I absorbed it and the other, more boring version back into the Dungeon, making sure I still had access to both designs before summoning two copies of the new version. One, 'just in case'.

The other, I was going to work on personally…

I returned to my body and headed up to where the goblins waited, finding a comfy perch and ordering the nearest one to come to me.

It wandered over and stared up at me, its coal black eyes glittering as it weaved slightly in time with each breath. Looking at it, it really made me wonder about the 'High Goblins' I'd seen referenced before, considering that the little sod looked barely able to stand on his own. Yet I knew from the overview, and from commanding them, that they were vicious creatures, the sharp teeth and nails making a hell of a difference when they attacked something…I took its stick and tossed it aside, putting both hands on its head and closing my eyes, concentrating and trying to ignore the throbbing feeling of the creature's blood just beneath the skin.

It reminded me of how thin a newborn baby's skin was, and that just freaked me out for a second before I relaxed and concentrated again.

Do you wish to activate 'Imbue' at this time?
Yes/No

I chose 'yes,' and I felt my mana slowly leeching out of me into the Goblin.

1/350…2/350…3/350…4/350…

I kept at it, both relieved that it was less than the sword I'd tried before, and slightly worried, as I really had no idea what would happen when the counter was full. I kept at it until I was down to a hundred points, the minimum I needed to 'Incinerate', as I wanted to keep that spell in reserve, just in case. I rested for forty minutes or so, and then went again, and again.

The time passed slowly, but after several hours, I satisfied the limit, and as soon as I hit the three hundred and fifty mark, I was greeted with a new prompt.

Congratulations!
You have successfully Imbued a creature of your Dungeon: 'Goblin Footsoldier' with your mana!
'Goblin Footsoldier' has been altered at a fundamental level.
Two paths are now available to the Footsoldier:

Mageling:
Goblin Magelings are the most basic of all magic users. Scrawny and weak, they sacrifice their own meager health pool to power their spells, often resulting in their deaths.

Spells:
Flamedart:
Fires a flaming dart that burrows into the target's flesh and ignites, causing both fire and bleeding damage. Damage: 1 point of damage as long as the dart is embedded. Removing the dart results in 5 points of flame damage.
Cost: 5 HP per dart

Disgust:
Few creatures find anything as annoying or irritating as an unevolved goblin. This spell takes that feeling to another degree, focusing all an enemy's attention on the caster.
Disgust lasts for a maximum of ten seconds, draining the caster's lifeforce at a rate of three points per second.
Cost: 3 HP per second
Summoning Cost: 15 mana to summon, 5 mana per day, 3 control points.

Goblin Wretch:
The Wretch is both the most despised and the lowest skilled of the goblin-class castes. Even other goblins bear a well-earned hatred and suspicion towards them. Wretches steal, murder, and plunder, and typically fulfill the role of 'Scout' in goblin society. Members of this caste can be relied upon to attack weakness without mercy, but will flee from any strong opponent.
Wretches gain the innate ability to manipulate mana, but instead of external effects, the Wretch instead directs all effects inward, quietening footfalls, increasing their senses, speeding their feet when fleeing. The greatest ability of a Wretch is 'Shadow'.

Spells:
Shadow:
Wretches are physically weak creatures. Their only saving grace in combat is their ability to deal terrific damage through 'Backstab' or 'Bleed' attacks. To get close enough to use such attacks, the wretch has to be hidden. Shadow grants 1 second of blending into the shadows per point of mana invested, and each level of skill in this ability gains 5% additional stealth until at level 20 the Wretch becomes fully invisible…for so long as their mana holds out…
Summoning Cost: 8 mana to summon, 3 mana per day, 1 control point

I contemplated both options, knowing I couldn't keep them both yet. I had to choose one and just hope I could do this again in the future to get the other option…I wavered between the two, knowing that they were the weakest variants, and tried to decide what would be more useful. They were both 'Squishy' classes and would be slaughtered in combat, but that was fine. They were both weak as hell at this point, but, I got the feeling that they'd both be awesome in the future if I could level them.

An invisible rogue that could strike with impunity? Hell yes, that would be seriously useful for the Dungeon. It would take down any trespassers easily, I'd bet, but a Mage? Or Mageling, I guess? The spells drained their health instead of mana, which was a bit weird, but that was fine. If I could build up their health a bit, then four or five of them could seriously fuck up someone's day. That Flamedart Spell cast by four of them at once? It'd do four points of damage a second, and a further twenty when they were pulled free. That was if they only cast one at a time. If they cast, say…five? Twenty points of damage a second, and a hundred once they were pulled out? Hell yes.

I could kite a big enemy around, and they could bleed it…

I sat staring at the goblin for several moments before making my decision. I needed them both, I really did, especially as I could see the rogue being awesome at killing things and feeding the Dungeon, hunting down pigeons and rats, especially…

However, I knew I'd already made the decision, as I was thinking about how useful the rogue would be in the future, and how much I'd have to get it. The Mageling, though? I'd already accepted that I *needed* that one now.

The Mageling could hide behind the footsoldiers and pepper the enemy with Flamedarts. When it was nearly dead, it could use its 'Taunt' skill, Disgust, and draw enemies from me when I was getting swamped, or entice creatures into the kobolds' traps…

I didn't think about it any longer. I just accepted it and watched the effect my choices had on the creature before me.

Where the Footsoldier had piled a bit more muscle on, morphing from a starving child with big feet and hands into a reasonably healthy looking, if still fugly, child, the Mageling reversed that change.

Muscle mass seemed to slough off it and the head grew in size, the weak neck appearing too small to hold it properly, and it bobbed around like a bobblehead. It still wore only a loincloth, and its arms and legs looked like they were wasting away. I pulled up its details, wishing I had been able to see them before.

<table>
<tr><td>Unnamed Goblin Mageling</td><td>Goblin, Dungeon Creature</td></tr>
<tr><td colspan="2">This is the second most basic form of the simple goblin, further enhanced through both a standard Forced Evolution and an Imbuing of the Dungeon Lord's personal mana. This goblin has evolved to a level that allows it to use simple tools and basic magic, though it requires its own health to cast any spells at this stage. Each spell consumes HP instead of the standard mana.

Spells:
Flamedart: Cast a flaming, barbed dart at a target inside of 25m. Target loses 1 point of health per every second the dart is embedded and five points when the dart is removed.
Cost: 5 HP per dart

Disgust: Makes the target creature aware of the Mageling in a new and horrific way, instilling a feeling of utter disgust, hatred, and a need to rid the universe of such a creation before all else.
Cost: 3 HP per second for a maximum of 10 seconds.

HP: 25/25
Stamina: 10/10
Mana: 20/20
Speed 4/10
Level: 0</td></tr>
<tr><td>HP 25/25</td><td>Spells: 2/2</td></tr>
</table>

"Okay, so you're weak as hell and unfit. We can fix that." I said to myself, having noted before that the level-up ability of the kobold had allowed me to learn that, in addition to the stats, we shared another detail: they could improve their stats though hard work.

I was going to make a drill sergeant somehow soon and have it make the goblins' lives a misery until they were up to a reasonable level of health and fitness. I grinned evilly, having visions of dozens of goblins being chased around the Dungeon by a staff sergeant screaming at them about how his dead mother could do better.

I shook myself out of my daydream and straightened, hoping that Alyssa had made good use of the time she'd had as well. Tomorrow, when the sun rose,

I was intent on attacking the cathedral. That meant I needed to make the most of the time I had left.

I pulled up the screens that showed me what I had and where, and I pulled everyone back in, except the research Kobolds, the 'sewer-side squad,' and the two Smashers that were patrolling the ground floor of the building.

I quickly absorbed the remaining kobolds and goblins into the Dungeon, making sure I had the patterns saved for my latest creations, and then started my summoning.

The Footsoldiers required seven mana to summon and two control points, while the Mageling cost me three points. I absorbed one of the 'Cunning Smashers', then summoned six Footsoldiers and two Magelings, taking me up to my maximum of twenty five points. Then I spread them out around the building. The Footsoldiers were still armed with only a stick; surprisingly, even the mages had spawned with one, but I'd fix that later. I designated three of the Footsoldiers as a team, sending them into the sewers and directing them to head north and to kill any vermin they could, as for whatever reason, that direction seemed almost as poorly explored almost as the south-east, toward the cathedral.

I decided that there was no time like the present and used some of the mana I still had left to create a doorway in the wall between the Core room and next door's basement, where I'd set up the Research Node. I quickly walked down and checked on Amy, finding her fast asleep on the futon.

I continued through the open doorway to the Node where Alyssa lay half-slumped on the Research chair on the far side. She was totally focused on what she was working on, and for the first time, it let me observe her when she wasn't expecting me.

I saw the beauty that the pictures had captured, the glaring eyes and suspicious hardness gone as she relaxed and worked, and I smiled without realizing it. She was a hard woman, harsh even, with me at least, but I'd come to realize that it wasn't intentional. It didn't seem to be who she was normally, but since everything had gone tits-up, it'd been who she'd had to be. The trust had been hammered out of her, leaving only the fierce need to protect Amy, and to survive for her sake.

I took in a deep breath, half wishing she was single, and half glad she wasn't, as with her looks, I had to admit I was very attracted to her, even if only to myself. The problem, or good thing, depending on how you looked at it, was that she was actually a good match for me in some ways.

She was intelligent; hell, I thought she was considerably smarter than me, actually. She was focused, and I really wasn't. I tended to run from fire to fire, never fully dealing with anything, and most of all, she had a real, iron-clad reason to make things work here. The reason I was glad she wasn't single, was that if she had been, and things went down that route, I'd probably end up risking everything in a relationship with her. Or we'd kill each other. We were that kind of a match.

I just hoped her husband was all right, and I resolved to keep my distance, despite the fun I was sure we could have had, as it just wasn't worth the cost.

I coughed and she jumped, the guarded, wary look coming back into her eyes, and the pair of kobolds froze, panicking slightly as they saw me, before relaxing and returning to work.

"How's it going?" I asked her, and she stretched, hopping out of the chair and cracking her back.

"Good, actually…" she said, then yawned and rubbed her eyes. "I got the sword sorted out first; I used that wooden one you gave me, and the Node picked up something weird, or at least different. So, I included that in the metal one. Want to see?" I grinned, nodding excitedly.

"Damn right, I do! What have you got for me?" I moved forward, sharing a smile with her as she spun the screen around, tapping at it and bringing up a beautiful sight.

Bronze Longsword	Item
This Bronze Longsword has been designed with a combination of ancient and modern knowledge, resulting in a slightly more deadly weapon than your ancestors used to wield. This blade incorporates a fuller and is sharpened on both sides, coming to a razor's edge at the tip. *Special ability:* This sword has been partially imbued with mana using a Dungeon Lord's ability, but not fully, resulting a slight improvement over the standard weapon, plus ???? Damage: 10-25	
Durability 15/15	Special Features: 1/1

"You see?" Alyssa inquired, pointing to the words 'Special Ability'. "I've got no idea what it actually does. It says it has an ability, but not what it is."

"Yeah, that is weird. I mean, I started to imbue the wooden one, but not this?" I said slowly.

"I guessed that, so it looks like if you can unlock its ability, we'll be able to use this system to copy it and make more. The problem is, I have no idea how to do that, or how to imbue it further. I mean, can you do more with it? Imbue it some more?" she asked, and I shrugged, closing my eyes and checking the interface over.

I had thirty-seven points available, and the sword would cost me forty, so I explained I couldn't materialize one for testing yet. She looked mildly depressed until I promised to summon it as soon as I could.

"While we wait for enough of a mana charge, what else did you do?" I asked her, and she smiled, swiping the longsword aside and pulling up another design.

"I considered the creature out there, and the things that killed Spot…" she said, trailing off darkly and glaring at the screen momentarily, before shaking herself. "So I made these, rather than smaller swords like yours." She gestured to the screen.

Bronze-clad club	Item
This bronze-clad club has been designed to be extra effective against the undead. The grip is wrapped in leather and a strap added to ensure the wielder retains the weapon. Damage: 5-15	
Durability 12/12	Special Features: 0/0

"How's it 'extra effective'?" I asked her, looking it over. It was a pretty plain design, literally just a larger, heavier stick, with a head that looked like it'd been dipped in liquid bronze and hardened, with small knobby bits all over it.

"It's essentially a basic mace, and they were always supposed to be good against the undead in the movies…makes sense, really, as they're bags of bones, and a heavy club would smash them…"

"Uh…okay?" I said, unsure, before shrugging in acceptance. It kinda made sense, I supposed. I just hoped we weren't falling into the trap of believing what the movies made us see.

"Just trust me, it should work. And if it doesn't, well, you won't have to worry about anything anymore," she said, earning an annoyed glare before I snorted and shook my head.

"Yeah, okay, I guess," I said, seeing her point. "Anything else?"

"Yeah, a basic crossbow." She pulled up the next screen and expanded the description.

Simple crossbow	Item
This simple crossbow has been built to be easily repaired or replaced and will fire a bolt up to 100m with some accuracy. It is a lightweight design, suitable for smaller minions. Damage: 7-35	
Durability 9/9	Special Features: 0/0

"Sweet!" I grew excited, noting that resizing it was literally as simple as using a slider bar to make it smaller or bigger. That was an amazing advantage, as I realized we could make large cogs and mechanisms, then simply shrink them down to any size we needed.

"So, we could…" I started, having zoomed in on the mechanism, and Alyssa laughed as she read my mind.

"Exactly!" She beamed. "We can make some amazing weapons, like repeating crossbows. It's just a case of figuring them out. Maybe a trip to the library across town, and we can loot some textbooks? It'll make a hell of a difference, I promise; not to mention, things like steam-power. You ever read any steampunk?" she asked me, and I shook my head. "Well, considering the way things are looking these days, you might want to start. It's all about modern ideas with Victorian-age technology, like airships and mechs…"

"Could we actually build mechs?" I asked, a sudden vision of me inside a Timber Wolf, stamping on the cathedral and squashing the Eidolon flat under one insanely well-armed foot.

"Not like you're thinking, I bet. Well, not yet, but at some point…hell yes."

"Oh yeah…" I muttered; my thoughts lost in visions of chrome-plated insanity.

"Where's Amy?" Alyssa suddenly asked me, and I gestured back over my shoulder towards the Core room.

"She's asleep in there," I answered distractedly, still focused on her work. "Anything else you managed to design?" She held her hand flat, dipping it from side to side in doubt.

"Yes and no; I found the designs for the motorbike armor you 'absorbed'. They're good; hell, they're great, even, but they'd stop you from moving much, and you said you like to be able to dive and dodge. I made another two versions, one for the goblins, which is small, obviously. It still costs seventy-five mana charge, and yours costs more…a lot more."

"How much?" I asked hesitantly, and she grimaced.

"Four hundred and seventy."

"Seriously?" I groaned. "That's days', maybe weeks' worth, not counting the sewer-side squad…"

"The what?"

"Oh…just my name for the goblins in the sewers…sorry…"

"You're such a geek," she grinned, shaking her head.

"Yeah, well, shit happens."

"Look, the armor I've designed is worth it, seriously." She swiped through several designs, searching for a particular one. "Not that one…no…nope…ah! Here it is."

She pulled up the suit of armor, making it fill the screen.

"You see the differences from this and normal armor, right?" She asked, gesturing to the screen that hovered before me. "I had to make a lot of changes from the motorbike design, mainly because we don't have access to those types of fibers, but the ones we do? Leather, metals, stone, and bone, amongst others have actually made me seriously surprised by the comparisons. Especially because we can design something and then scale them up or down. Look here…" She said, zooming in on the chest. "I made a dozen small scales, each the size of my fingernail, rounded them out into a real 'scale' design so they could overlap better, and then I made an oblong section with several attached. they're thin enough that they're not too heavy, but strong enough to stop a bullet!"

"Seriously?" I asked, surprised.

"I mean it, Matt. The force is spread across the entire surface area of the panel. They won't stand up to repeated fire, and it'd sting like a bitch, but a bullet would *not* get through. Once I was sure the design would work, I overlapped the sections to make a breastplate of sorts. It's more expensive than if we just made a solid slab of bronze, but it's much lighter and more flexible."

"Why make it into panels, then?" I asked and she smiled wryly.

"You're welcome to try designing them a better way. But seriously, a panel in the design system can be cut or joined, and it can be copied and pasted over and over, which is much faster to make a variety of pieces. Add to that, you don't want this all over your body. You're not strong enough by far. As scale mail, though, a little here, a little there, then some rubber it which fortunately is a mostly natural substance, so we can get away with that it, add some leather, and wow. Suddenly, you've got armor, and it's some strong stuff. I wouldn't want to go up against someone with a stockpile of heavy ammo, but in a fight with something like that creature? It'd be a hell of a help, as it should deflect most strikes, even if it doesn't last long."

"That's all I need it for. Thank you, Alyssa." I nodded back to the designs. "Anything else you want to show me?"

"Just a few knives and a hammer, in case you didn't like the clubs," she said, shrugging and pulling up the files. They were simple, basic, even, but they didn't need to be more than that. I looked the last of the options over and noted a prompt that pulsed gently in the corner.

Add inventions to Dungeon system?
Yes/No

I selected 'Yes' and was pleased to find that I could access them from the main system now. Selecting the Goblin Footsoldier, I found they now came with options of knives, club, hammer, or crossbow, as well as armor. The cost was drastically higher, though, considering I could summon a living, if dumb as a rock, Footsoldier for seven points; summoning the same creature with armor and the bronze club would cost me one hundred and one points.

"I'm going to go get something to eat and see Amy. Shout if you need me." Alyssa said after waiting a few minutes as I examined the details, I nodded absently and said something back to her, but I had no idea what it was.

Curious, I went looking and found that the exorbitant comparative cost was simply because we didn't have the facilities for the constructions yet. If I were to build a Manufacturing Node, it would drop significantly, and, once staffed, I'd be looking at the overall cost being around twenty to thirty points. It was clear, the Manufacturing Node would have to be researched, and then built, which meant that it went on the list to be done, but it wasn't an option for now.

I checked the cost of the weapons again, finding the bronze-clad club was probably the best weapon for the goblins, with a dagger, if I was feeling generous later. The clubs cost twenty points to summon individually, with the armor costing seventy-five points. I considered holding back, maybe sending the entire team out on a murder spree, but I shook my head after a minute. I couldn't risk the time. If things were spawning in the cathedral, the difference of a day could be the difference between life and death.

I had the guns as a force multiplier, and if I could get all of the goblins a weapon that would really work, that'd hopefully make enough of a difference.

I checked the charge now, seeing that it'd crept up a bit again and now stood at forty-eight, so I sank my consciousness into the system and flew deeper into the building. I summoned two clubs for the goblins roaming the building, dropping them before the little creatures as they walked along. I had to admit, I enjoyed the surprise on their faces and the guttural shouts of triumph from them as they grabbed at the weapons, snarling at each other and waving their new tools around excitedly.

I returned to my own body, smiling to myself, and walked through to the Core room. Alyssa tiredly stared at a sandwich and picked at a packet of crisps, a beer in one hand.

"You okay?" I asked her, and she forced a thin smile.

"I am, sorry; I'm just tired, that's all. It's been a long day, and it seems like forever since I got to really work like that. Using my brain, I mean, rather than my hands."

"Oh, no worries, I know what you mean. The way the system works, it's a bit exhausting and weird at first," I reassured her, remembering how much I'd had to concentrate at first to use it.

"Doesn't help that there's no manual," she said, knuckling her back and stifling a yawn. "If there was even a basic 'how to,' it'd help, rather than making it up as I go. I kept finding things that were shortcuts…*after* I did it the long way each time…"

"Sod's law," I agreed, nodding to her. "I keep doing it that way myself; I guess the fairy that came with the system was trained and knew what it was doing, but we're just stumbling around in the dark."

"Yeah; wish it'd survived…" Alyssa murmured, and I froze, my eyes going wide. "What's up?" she asked me, sensing the change in mood.

"The fairy!" I said, stunned. "I'd totally forgotten about it! We've got its corpse. Maybe we can make it in the Dungeon. Hell, maybe we can resurrect it!" I hurried over to the gun bag and tipped the crystal out onto the floor. The Dungeon immediately picked up on the item, as everything seemed to pause.

Dungeon Fairy 112 detected, mana is being diverted.
Do you wish to cede control of the Dungeon to: Dungeon Fairy 112?
Yes/No

"Fuck no!" I cursed, grabbing the crystal and lifting it away from contact with the floor.

Do you wish to repair: Dungeon Fairy 112?
Yes/No

"Nope. Absorb," I said flatly.

"Absorb? I thought we were going to…"

"It just tried to take control of the Dungeon," I explained grimly, keeping my focus on the Dungeon.

"What?!?" Alyssa practically screamed, waking Amy as she dove for a gun.

"Relax. I'm in control here, and I'd have to agree to it, it seems," I said, hoping like hell I was right. I looked at the fairy, still slumped, broken in death within the crystal, then shook my head, cursing myself for a fool as I used 'Examine'.

Dungeon Fairy 112	Fairy, Dungeon Master
This is a deceased fairy. The remains are highly damaged, and the organic parts are beyond repair. However, the nanite sections are stable and deemed repairable, although currently unpowered. HP: 0/1000 Stamina: N/A Mana: N/A Speed 10/10 Level: 37	
HP 0/1000	Special Abilities: 0/35

"Oh, hell no." I wasn't about to risk an unknown entity taking over all of my hard work and destroying my home and plans. "Dungeon, absorb this *NOW*." I ordered, reaching out and forcing it manually, surprised to feel a strange reluctance from the Dungeon. After several seconds of resistance, it seemed to break through a barrier, and the Dungeon Sense flooded into the remains, examining, cataloging, and then absorbing it.

"But…but…" Alyssa sputtered. "We could have learned so much! We might never know now…"

"Or it might have taken control and killed us all. The 'organic' bits were dead, leaving only the nanites intact, apparently. I'm gonna bet that if it was able to be repaired, its first act would be to take control. With us here, in the most secure area of the Dungeon, and not under its control? It wouldn't have ended well. We can try to make mobs with the details later, but I'm not having that thing boot us out and go back to whatever its orders were…"

"But…"

"For all we know, it was to kill all of humanity, okay?" I stated baldly.

"What's going on?" Amy asked in a low, scared voice, eyes wide at the sight of her mother with the shotgun in her hand and the glares on our faces.

"It's nothing, sweetie. It's all right." Alyssa forcibly smoothed her face and eased the gun down. Her fingers stayed close to it, though, I noted as I let out a long breath and sat down on the edge of the sofa.

"Seriously, Alyssa…" I said, dropping my head into my hands. "We just don't know enough. We're stumbling around in the dark here. That was too close…"

"I know," Alyssa replied, her voice low as she stroked Amy's hair and tucked her back into the makeshift bed. "We need to be careful, Matt; seriously careful."

"I need to kill that Eidolon," I stated flatly. "Tomorrow. Once it's dead, we seal the entrances and go into lockdown for a few days to get the basics worked out, learn the rules, and start to get some defenses in place. We also desperately need to make some living quarters and fresh food."

"We need more people first," Alyssa countered, shaking her head. "We need to get Kelly and Mike, at least. With them here, we'll all be safer. Kelly can help me do the research, Mike can keep us all safe, and then you can concentrate on the Dungeon itself. Please, Matt, don't lock them out…we need them."

"There's never going to be a perfect time to do it, Alyssa," I said slowly. "Look, we'll talk about it all tomorrow; afterwards…if we win, then maybe we can monitor the area or something, but if not…well." I met her eyes apologetically. "No offense, but your husband and your sister-in-law aren't people I've even met. I'll give them a chance, and even if we seal the whole place up, we can watch out for them, but we need to try to get this place sorted."

"What if you die?" Alyssa asked me suddenly.

"What?" I replied, cocking my head to the side.

"I'm serious. What if you die out there? Are we trapped inside? Will the Dungeon kick us out, or lock us in? Will it let me take your place?" she pressed, studying me intently.

"I've…no idea, to be honest." I considered the possibility for a moment. "I'll order it to let you out, but I don't know if it can accept anyone else. It's literally a part of me now, so…" I shrugged, trying to hide the sudden worry that she might try to smother me in my sleep if I made her my heir.

I checked the mana charge and found that I had just enough to summon another bronze club, and I grinned delightedly, sinking my mind into the system and flying up to search for a goblin…only to find a scene of furious growling and spitting as the goblins all faced off against each other.

TWENTY-SEVEN

"WHAT THE HELL?" I muttered in surprise, swearing as the Smasher jumped forward and slammed its fist into one of the Footsoldiers, killing it instantly and grabbing its club.

The room descended into a panicked brawl as the Smasher laid waste to the others. The Magelings started casting, and the Footsoldiers bunched up, surrounding the Smasher.

"Stop!" I bellowed, projecting the order with my mind hard enough that the goblins all collapsed to the ground, spasming. The two Magelings writhed in agony as their spells dissipated without being fired, the cost in blood apparently increasing when they lost concentration.

"What the hell are you all doing?" I roared at them and watched them flinch in terror, scuttling under boxes and tables, like cockroaches running from the light. I also saw three goblin Footsoldiers push past their terror to start fighting over the other club, effectively trying to mug the one who had it.

"Oh, shit," I muttered, suddenly realizing what was happening. The goblins had ignored each other when none of them had anything, but now, they had just enough Intelligence to know they wanted more, and nowhere near enough Wisdom to wait. I'd essentially taken away the reason for them all getting along away and dropped temptation into the middle of the room.

"Dammit!" I snarled and reached out, mentally tearing the clubs free from the struggling goblins. I had to shake the Smasher up and down in the air before he let go, but I had to admit, at least to myself, that the sight of the Smasher bouncing around amused me and made me feel slightly calmer.

I could reabsorb and reproduce the club later, I knew, but it'd have a cost. Creating was around a third to half again as expensive as absorbing an item, if not more, so I didn't want to do that.

Instead, I instilled an instinctive need in all of them to stay away from the doors to my Core room, and I ordered the Smasher to take the clubs down to the door of the room and wait. Then once I returned to my body, I took them from the little bastard and ordered him back into the main section of the Dungeon. I heard him grumbling and whining under his breath as he stomped away, but at least it was done.

I started summoning the clubs I could afford to produce, two of them by now, and then I dumped them at the top of the stairs, inside the closed doors and went back down, exhausted and still annoyed with the goblins. It seemed I couldn't just arm some of them, or that if I did, I needed to make the others Intelligent enough to not fight their brethren.

And I had absolutely no idea how to do that.

I shook my head in disgust, ate a quick sandwich, had a beer, and stretched out on the floor, studiously ignoring the shapely length of bare leg that had fallen out of the blankets on my sofa, where Alyssa snored gently.

I'd kind of thought that they'd share the futon, considering it folded out into a full double bed, but clearly I'd been wrong.

As I laid back, trying to ignore the pulsing light coming from the Core, I made a rough plan for the next few days.

I'd summon all the gear and weapons I could. Once the entire Dungeon, except the researchers, were armed, I'd storm the Cathedral. We'd go as far as we could, killing anything inside—hopefully all of them—then return to the Dungeon, re-summon and re-arm, if we hadn't killed them all, and then go again.

I'd keep going until we cleaned the place out, then lock up the Dungeon, make the living quarters and a kitchen, then set up a Manufacturing Node and start working on leveling the inhabitants. Ideally, we'd make them some decent weapons and armor so they lived long enough, and see about making them into real guards, or, if they were too dumb, keep them as monsters.

I made another club, seeing the charge jump suddenly just as I was dropping off to sleep, and then let the darkness take me, sleeping steadily until the Dungeon awoke me. I'd ordered it to give me a little buzz when it reached full on the charge, but evidently, I needed to tone it down. When it hit me, I jolted out of the blanket with a hiss, body stiff and feeling like I'd just had a live power cable rammed up my arse.

"Motherfucker!" I hissed in shock, staggering around as my left leg chose that exact time to go into a cramp. Crippled, I collapsed to the floor, frantically rubbing at my calf. A few seconds later, I felt hands grab my leg, and I twisted around, shocked.

"Be quiet!" Alyssa hissed at me, digging her fingers into my leg and working the knotted muscle. "You'll wake Amy!" She went back to massaging it as I tried to stay quiet. Between the steel pins I was starting to believe she had in place of fingers, and the nightdress she was wearing, which exposed a generous amount of cleavage and a *lot* of leg, mainly thanks to the angle she was at, I suddenly became aware that I was in only my boxers, and that a certain… part…was stirring reflexively.

I panicked, shoving my mind into the Dungeon Sense and frantically trying to think of anything else as my body sagged backwards, the muscles relaxing. I saw the hundred and twenty-five points that we'd reached in the Dungeon charge, and I paused, then grabbed the nearest available option, a saved design for the Goblin Footsoldier in full armor with a club. I hit it and ordered it to spawn, recalling that I hadn't replaced the other Footsoldier who'd died yet. I spawned him in the corner of the Core room in my desperation for a distraction, and I had to reach out, assuming control and directing him up the stairs, opening the doors, and shoving him out into the night.

I gave him orders to patrol the local area, and immediately, if somewhat sheepishly, slipped back into my body. Alyssa was straddling me when I opened my eyes, and the first thing I saw, thanks to the way she was moving, was straight down her top. My eyes opened wider, and the part of my body I had the least control of popped back to attention, to my everlasting embarrassment.

Alyssa, it turned out, had panicked when I suddenly went limp, or at least most of me, and had been putting me into the recovery position, while trying to decide if I needed mouth to mouth. My eyes suddenly popping open right when they did, the flagpole in my trousers, and the direction of my gaze, all sparked her sudden realization of how little she was wearing, and how we were positioned.

We both panicked, trying to look anywhere else but where we both wanted to most. Alyssa jumped back and rushed to her blanket, and I grabbed at mine and pulled it over to ball it up, poorly concealing the effect her scantily clad figure and closeness had on me.

"I…"

"Sorry!"

"I shouldn't…"

"I should…"

We both paused, staring at each other in the dim light. The gentle snoring of Amy was the only sound in the room as we both breathed quickly, severing our shared gaze and trying not to look at each other. Eventually Alyssa spoke up, breaking the awkward silence.

"Look, it's not that I'm not interested, or attracted to you. I sort of am, honestly, but I think we both know it's down to the situation, and the way things are now, as much as…anything else…" She hesitated, shrugging. "But I love Mike, and I have to hope he's okay. I have to pray he's coming home to me…"

"I understand..." I said quickly, forcing a smile as twinned elation and annoyance tore through me. Elation, because she was stunning, and yes, god yes, I wanted to jump on her, or better yet, have her jumping on me. Annoyance at myself because I knew, I just *knew* it'd be a mistake, but the little head didn't want to hear it. Also, as she'd said, she was married, for god's sake. "I'm, well... you know I'm attracted to you as well..." I muttered, a rueful smile playing at the edge of my lips as I gestured down at the balled-up blanket. "I didn't mean to get an eyeful; honestly, I didn't..." I said, recognizing the truth of what she'd said. The situation, with all the uncertainty, the adrenaline, the fear; it was sending my natural urges into overdrive every time I saw her bare leg, let alone accidentally down her top. I resolved to avoid looking as much as I could.

"What happened to you?" she asked, latching onto any distraction.

"I set the Dungeon to give me a little shock to wake me up once the charge was full, so we wouldn't waste any, only it felt like getting a wake-up call from a car battery. Then my leg went into a massive cramp, then..."

"Then I tried to help you, and...well..." she said sheepishly, brushing her hair back from her face and stifling a quiet laugh.

"Yeah. And I tried to distract myself, so I dove into the Dungeon Sense and spawned the goblin. By the time I thought it'd be safe to return to my body..."

"I was checking to make sure you were okay...and..." Alyssa gestured to her top, giving a little laugh and hiking it back up, then lifting her blanket to cover two...points of interest...

"Sorry!" she apologized again, wrapping the blanket around herself and coughing, her face red with embarrassment. "I didn't want to bring too much in the way of baggage, so I only have these and a set that's...well...for Mike's eyes only, okay?" She said, swallowing hard and looking away.

"Ah...!" I said, cutting myself off before the little head could ask to see it. "How about we try to get some sleep?" I suggested quickly. "Then once things are a bit safer, I'll take you and Amy to the nearest clothes shops, see if we can loot you something a bit less provocative? Not that I don't appreciate..."

"Stop!" she waved furiously, trying not to laugh. "Okay, look, we'll chalk this up to experience, and yeah, let's go to sleep, okay?" I grinned back at her, relieved that we'd not just ruined our working relationship. "And tomorrow, I'll just sleep in my jeans and a top or something..." she promised, shaking her head and wrapping the blanket around her more securely.

"Shame..." I heard myself say before I could think better of it, the words slipping out of my treacherous mouth. A snorted giggle from the direction of the sofa let me know she'd heard.

I lay there for a long time, deliberately slowing my heart rate as I intentionally relaxed and wiped the memories and the sights I'd accidentally just experienced from the hard drive of my brain, while setting the entire allocation of mana to outfitting my small squad. I'd managed to organize, after trying to distract myself for a while, a queuing system. I'd immediately set it to produce the remaining six clubs I needed, my sword, then a suit of armor for me—the more basic of the two that Alyssa had designed—and then several sets of armor for the goblins.

The next morning when I awoke, Alyssa was already up. Thankfully, she was dressed and quietly eating breakfast. Amy was collecting a pile of random bits and bobs into a pile in the middle of the room, and I had a series of notifications waiting for me.

'Unnamed Goblin Footsoldier' has leveled up!
As this is a Dungeon-born creature, you may choose to assign points for the creature, or allow it to assign the points as it chooses
Assign points?
Yes/No

I checked the next notification, and found it was the same, for the same Footsoldier. He'd apparently been busy, and I found that not only had the clubs been finished, but the armor for me was about three hours away, unless something drastically changed.

I ordered the system to shift it, as it was only ten minutes into this production run, and reordered the list, specifying armor for the goblins and a pair of the knives for the Magelings, as I couldn't justify the expense now. It'd been a vain hope that I'd wake in the morning and find it all ready for me, almost as vain as the dream of Amy going for a walk, and Alyssa…

I shook my head, getting out of bed and exchanging an embarrassed nod with Alyssa. Last night's flirtatious behavior seemed far less innocent and fun, now that we were properly awake.

I pulled my dirty clothes on quickly, grabbing a bite of dried biltong and a beer, drinking half of it and letting out a belch that echoed off the walls.

"Classy…" Alyssa arched an eyebrow, shaking her head.

"Well, I'm just a classy guy," I said, then grinned and took another swig, bit down on some more dried meat, and walked over to one of the closed side rooms.

I'd started dumping odds and ends in the space, my spare clothes, everything. I sorted through it, stripping off entirely and redressing in the best gear I had, from boxers to my Under Armor sports top. I strapped the scabbard for the sword to my back and hunted around. After a bit of rummaging and rearranging, I succeeded in finding my rifle and all the ammo I had left for it, and slotted the clips, loading it with a full one, instead of the half empty one I had in it originally.

I strapped the diving knife to my right calf, and while I really wanted to, I just couldn't justify taking the shotgun or the handgun, so I resolved to leave both with Alyssa. Finally, I grabbed some food and hung a canteen of water on my hip, thankful that some of the things the idiot Adventurers had brought were survival supplies. I also grabbed a packet of matches, a small first aid kit, and a dozen small bottles of vodka, partially because I thought I could use them to clean wounds, and partially because I just knew I was going to need a serious drink at some point.

I'd checked the research and found it steadily plugging away, the next level of kobold only a dozen hours away, now that I'd reverted the allocation to fifty-fifty. I looked in the mirror on the wall and snorted, using the small sink on the back wall and washing my face and hands, then working a little water into my hair and styling it as best I could.

The Eidolon might not appreciate the effort I was going to…but fuck it. Might be my last day, after all, and I resolved to make it a good one. I strode out of the small room, having taken the time at the end to put a little aftershave on as well, and for the first time in days, I felt almost human.

"Very pretty," Alyssa commented, trying to summon a smile. She jumped to her feet and I paused as she moved between me and the pile of weapons. "Look, I'm sorry! I just…do you really have to do this now?" She gazed anxiously up at me.

"What do you mean?" I asked.

"I mean, why go now? Why not wait a few days; a week, maybe? Or we could go and get Barry. He'd come and help you if you asked. You know he would…" she said quickly.

"We've been over this, Alyssa." I shook my head, crossing my arms

"If I stay, if I wait, we just give it more time to prepare. We just give it a chance to grow stronger, and we can't risk that. Look, you know what I said about the leveling?" I asked, and she nodded. "Well, I know now that Dungeon creatures can level, and the thugs we fought? They were marked as 'Level 0' thugs…what if that thing can level too? It's got to have been growing stronger… Actually, I'm pretty sure the Lesser Ghasts I fought before and killed with the goblins were level one…That means the creatures can level as well. More time means they grow stronger, faster, smarter." I sighed heavily. "Do you really want to face that thing with human Intelligence? Hell, it could be smarter than us, and then we really are fucked."

"Smarter than you, maybe…" Alyssa said, forcing a smile before dropping her eyes to the floor. "I'm just worried; that's all."

"I know." I said, putting one hand on her shoulder and squeezing gently. "Look, I've left orders for the Dungeon to let you out if you want to go. Either it doesn't understand, or it won't allow me to set you up as a successor, so that's out, I'm afraid…" I lied, having decided that I didn't trust her that far…yet. I might yet get smothered in my sleep, even if I won after all. "…so for now, that's the best I can do, but at least you're both safe."

"Thanks, Matt," she said quietly. "Look, I'm sorry for being a bitch. I'm…"

"Just worried about Amy and the future. I know, it's okay." I reassured her. "Well, no time like the present, I guess. Want to help me carry this gear upstairs?" I gestured to the piled-up goblin weapons, sweeping up my sword and sheathing it awkwardly.

"Yeah, of course…" she said, forcing a smile. I smiled back at her and gave Amy a hug. The small girl smiled up at me, clearly worried, but doing her best not to show it until she grabbed onto me and hugged me again, much harder.

"Good luck Matt," she whispered into my ear. "You can do it…"

"Thanks, Amy…" I whispered back, giving her a squeeze. "You look after your momma, okay?" she nodded soberly, and I let her go, straightening up. Alyssa and I gathered up the clubs and carried them upstairs, me resolving, once again, to put some damn lighting in the fire escape so that it wasn't black as pitch down there. Once we were at street level, I summoned the goblins to the alleyway and paused.

"Remember, they're under my control, and they think of you as fellow members of the Dungeon, so don't bloody attack them!" I ordered, mock-glaring at Alyssa in the darkness, who snorted out a low laugh and promised to behave.

I took a deep breath and ordered the doors to open, smiling reflexively at the gathered motley group waiting for us.

I'd summoned a wide variety of several different shapes and sizes, from the most basic version, enhanced to a Cunning Smasher, to the Goblin Footsoldiers, to the Kobold Trapsmith, and the two Magelings, who skulked at the back. Their skin was green and brown, mottled with hairs sprouting at odd places, and none were higher than four feet, giving the impression that I was about to be mugged by a gang of fugly kids. I looked them over, shaking my head in amusement, then focused on the armed and armored one, the goblin I'd created fully geared in my panic last night.

He stepped forward when I gestured to him to do so, and I mentally prodded at him, slipping my mind partially into the Dungeon Sense and seeing his stat screen pop up. I grinned to myself as I looked over his stats and the marker of two levels, and therefore four points to invest.

Name: Unnamed Goblin Footsoldier				
Species: Goblin		Bonus:		
Level: 2		Progress to next level 95/200		
Available points: 4		Perk: Rat Killer 10% damage to Vermin		
Stat	Current points	Description	Effect	Progress to next level
Agility	***3***	Governs dodge and movement.		19/100
Charisma	***1***	Governs likely success to charm seduce or threaten		0/100
Constitution	***3***	Governs Health and Health Regeneration	HP:3x10= 30	78/100
Dexterity	***2***	Governs ability with weapons and crafting		83/100
Endurance	***4***	Governs Stamina and Stamina Regeneration	Stamina: 4x10 = 10	76/100
Intelligence	***2***	Governs base manapool and standard intellectual capacity	Mana:2x10 = 20	3/100
Luck	***3***	Governs overall chance of bonuses and critical hits		41/100
Perception	***2***	Governs ranged damage and chance to spot hidden items/traps		11/100
Strength	***3***	Governs damage with melee weapons and carrying capacity		53/100
Wisdom	***1***	Governs mana regeneration and memory	1x10=10 mana regenerated per hour	7/100

I weighed the options, thinking for several seconds…I could choose to spread the points out, or I could assign them all in one area; then I had to decide if I was going to kill him—well, absorb him. If I did, it meant that the next generation of Footsoldiers would be much more deadly, but I didn't have the mana charge to summon him again, and it'd take the entire day to gain it back, as we weren't going to be killing the usual vermin all day long.

I decided to play it safe and dropped two points into Constitution, giving him a better chance of surviving injuries, and the other two points, I dumped into Agility. I wanted him to do more damage—hell, I wanted him to be much better in every way—but that wasn't possible. Instead, I'd settle for him having a better chance at survival, and if he did survive, I'd add the points where they'd do the most good.

I got him to hand out the clubs, watching as he snarled at the others, showing he was in charge, and noting the way the Smasher glared at him in hatred. I quickly reached out and changed the 'Unnamed Cunning Smasher' to just being called 'Smasher,' as I'd already decided if he fell today, I was going to cut out that line of minions, recreating them instead by evolving the 'Common' goblin form.

It's a pain in the ass that I have to do it that way, but it is what it is, I thought to myself. The majority of the goblins were scrawny, at best. Honestly, the two Magelings looked like they wouldn't be able to stand upright when pissing, they were that emaciated and weak-looking, but the Smasher and the Footsoldier that I'd just upgraded were starting to look much more dangerous, and I imagined the effect a hundred upgraded Footsoldiers would have. If I had that many, I could just send them out to clear out the area!

And then the mental image caught up, me in my secure Dungeon, sending goblins out to wreck the area. All I needed was a cat to stroke as I laughed maniacally, and I could be an evil overlord.

I shrugged, thinking 'If the boot fits…' and straightened up, aware that I'd been silent for several minutes while I made the needed upgrades, and that the way the goblin had screeched and writhed when I applied them had clearly made both the girls concerned. I quickly renamed the upgraded, armored goblin as 'Bob' for convenience, then dismissed the interface and turned to the girls.

"It's okay, sorry; I was making some upgrades to him," I explained quickly. "Well, wish me luck!" The girls sent me off with a quick last minute hug before I gestured to the goblins and ordered them to 'follow me'.

I walked out, hearing the door closing behind me, and I let out a long breath, both concerned and relieved at once. I was scared shitless about this; I was literally going to go face that creature in its den, and with hardly anything in the way of real weapons. I had a rifle, a bronze longsword, and a knife, along with a gaggle of mismatched minions, but that was pretty much it. That thing had scared the living shit out of me when I'd seen it every single time, but at last, it was started, and there was a kind of mad relief to knowing that it'd be over soon, one way or another.

We moved to the eastern end of the alleyway, and I peeked around the corner, making sure there was nobody to see us. There'd been fewer people around by the day, and while some of the nearby buildings showed the inevitable signs of looters, nobody was in sight now. Relieved, I took a deep breath, turning to the south and sending the goblins straight to the cathedral.

I ran slightly behind the main group, Smasher and Bob keeping pace alongside me, while both Magelings huffed along behind us. It didn't take us long to cover the distance, but we paused. Besides a building feeling of terror and the certainty that we were being watched, everything was silent. As the Cathedral was in the middle of the city, there wasn't a huge graveyard or anything to walk past on this side, so I directed Smasher to open the door.

He waddled forward, hissing and grumbling at the other goblins he passed, and stretched up, barely able to reach the handle on the door. With a fair amount of tugging and pushing furiously, a rattling clank echoed into the building as the latch bounced around, until he finally let go and glared at the door. After several seconds, he tried it again, then gave up and plonked himself down on the floor, scratching at himself furiously.

"Are you fucking kidding me?" I growled from my position at the back of the group. I tried reaching out through the Dungeon Sense, but found it blocked, as I was beyond the outer edge of the Dungeon now. I swore, realizing that I was stuck with these idiots as my only help, and I couldn't rely on being able to direct them remotely anymore.

It was obvious, now that I thought about it, but I'd gotten used to having that control over the last few days. My mood darkening, I snapped at the rest of the group to 'get ready' before striding up the steps. Turning the old, blackened iron ring, I lifted the latch on the door with a loud 'clunk'.

Cautiously, I pushed the door open and immediately stood back, lifting my rifle to my shoulder and searching inside the shadowy entrance to the Cathedral. I vaguely remembered that it had been undergoing some kind of renovation recently, but I'd been busy with other things and hadn't really cared. However, I was pretty sure that what greeted my eyes wasn't what the church would have approved of.

Two small rooms sat on either side of the main entrance, both sets of doors slightly ajar, with the main hall as a long oblong heading toward the altar, leading away from at the main doors. Halfway down the length of the hall were two small wings leading north and south. The north side had held a handful of small rooms, as near as I could remember, while the south remained open. At the far end were two more sections; the one leading off to the north had been changing rooms, quarters, and general administration, if I remembered right, composed of a dozen or more rooms, while the south had been used for meeting and prayer rooms, only three or four, but again, it'd been a long time ago since I'd been inside, and I hadn't been that interested, even then.

Now, with the majority of the windows covered, the atmosphere was dim and dark inside, the air thick with the scent of rotting flesh and fresh shit. Water trickled steadily from somewhere high overhead, the sound of dripping echoing as I slipped inside. The ancient ornate oaken pews that had lined the middle of the hall were scattered, overturned, and damaged, with blood splatters across more than one. I swallowed hard as I continued to search around, ordering the goblins forward, and instructing the kobold to start making traps behind us that it could activate after we passed, if we needed to run.

In the middle of the cathedral, a mass of torn and shattered masonry had been dispersed indiscriminately. Huge blocks that had clearly been part of the floor were now scattered around a deep hole, and sounds of hissing and cracking echoed from within the pit.

I didn't want to turn my back on the hole, but equally, I couldn't trust the goblins to do anything significant. They were cannon fodder; that much was obvious to me now, so I moved to the first room to my left, on the north side of the cathedral, and I ordered Bob to open it.

He growled but shuffled forward, reaching out with the tip of his club and shoving the door hard with it. The sound of the bronze-clad wood hitting the ancient, iron-studded door echoed around the hall, and I swore internally as the sounds from the pit ramped up in volume.

I stepped inside, searching quickly. The room was maybe eight meters across and four deep, and it was thankfully empty, beyond blood splatters that coated the far wall. I spun and headed straight for the opposite, south-facing room, determined to make sure they were all clear before I turned my back on them.

Fortunately, it was the same; filthy, but empty, and as I made my way back into the main hall, I saw one of the goblin Footsoldiers approaching the edge of the pit. He walked on all fours as naturally as on two legs, his bronze-clad club dragging across the floor as he went. As soon as his head appeared over the edge of the pit, a long white hand snapped out and yanked him in.

The little goblin disappeared with a squeal. The sound of breaking bones, hissing, and growling echoing up from the pit made me freeze. The hand that had grabbed him had been at least a foot across, with three long bony fingers and a thumb. It'd also been a horrible shade of dead white, and as the goblins hissed and growled in response, moving forward as a pack, their own differences were forgotten in the light of a real enemy. Undeterred by their approach, the thing slowly levered its way out of the pit, almost making me soil myself as I saw it clearly.

It was the Eidolon I'd seen before, but it also wasn't. While I'd been concentrating on making my Dungeon into a home and preparing for the long term, evolving things gradually, this thing had clearly taken the opposite approach since we'd last locked eyes.

It had grown, practically exploded, and the blood that covered its face and hands explained how it'd managed that. As it hauled itself up, I backed away a few steps, impressed for the first time by the goblins as they ignored the foul thing's aura of fear and spread out, hissing and growling.

The Eidolon's ghastly frame straightened, rising to at least five meters in height and towering over us all. The flesh that had covered it previously hung torn and tattered, barely able to cover a third of the new shape. What shreds remained were stained black with filth and slowly dropped maggots. It still maintained the same basically humanoid shape, but where it differed was in the details. The long legs were jointed in three places now, and ended in wide, six-clawed, webbed pads. The arms too were longer than before; in fact, they seemed to extend as it shifted, bones cracking and clicking into place, with three-fingered hands that seemed far too huge. The claws were long and black, more talons than fingers, and there, too, the original flesh hung in strips. The thing's body was revolting and naked, although thankfully no reproductive organs were on display. A huge, protruding belly hung low, an apron of fat dangling from its middle, with…things…clearly writhing inside.

Its head sat atop a long prehensile neck, like a short, fat snake, easily half a meter long. It swayed slowly from side to side as the creature stared down at the intruders to its lair.

The head, though…that was the worst. Beyond the upper half of the face, it had clearly given up on the need to appear human. Its jaw had become canine in shape, long and triangular, with rows of sharp teeth that looked like they'd be more at home in a shark's mouth than anything with legs. The nose was gone; long twin vertical slits quivered, with mucous dripping from them as it scented the air. All that remained of the little girl's face had stretched hideously to cover the front of the skull. The small, bright blue eyes glowed eerily, while four more orbs sat several inches above them. These, however, were black as night and reflected the dim light wetly. Ragged, oily strands and clumps of hair and rotting skin covered a domed, bulbous skull, and short, fat spines protruded here and there, finishing off the appearance of a creature of the darkest pits.

I forced myself to use 'Examine,' and flinched when the creature immediately fixated on me, clearly sensing the use of mana…

Evolved Eidolon	Undead Ghoul Boss
This Eidolon has used the souls of dozens to force an unnatural evolution into its current form, growing stronger and far larger. It has sacrificed its meagre, though stable, feast of grieving souls, and instead has risked it all on a roll of the dice. This forced evolution has granted the Eidolon the following abilities: ***Soul Shear***: Killing and consuming the souls of creatures with even rudimentary souls grants a boost of 10% to the Eidolon, increasing it in Strength, Constitution, and Intelligence, if at full health, or repairing damage if not. ***Feast***: The Eidolon can feast on the bodies of the dead, repairing itself and absorbing the parts into itself. ***Unholy Terror***: Once per hour, for 1 minute and at a cost of 100 Stamina, the Eidolon can cast 'Unholy Terror', driving all creatures inside a 10m radius to a state of uncontrollable terror, forcing them to flee for the duration of the ability. ***Lure***: The Eidolon can sacrifice fifty points of stamina to mesmerize a target and draw it closer against its will. Eye contact must be maintained, for, once broken, it cannot be used against that target again for 3 minutes ***Spawn***: This creature has evolved the capacity to birth multiple 'live' young at a time, provided there is sufficient biomass and a high enough concentration of mana in the area. HP: 1900/1900 Stamina: 300/300 Mana: 0/0 Speed 5/10 Level: 7	
HP 1900/1900	Special Abilities: 4/4

"Well, fuck me gently with a running chainsaw…" I whimpered, gaping at the mass of data I was suddenly presented with. I glanced it over quickly before dismissing it and realizing that the godawful thing was still staring at me. It slowly shifted, its lips drawing back as it lowered its head. Its eyes remained locked on mine, and it forced a rictus of a smile onto its ghastly face.

"Hellll...oooo..." it warbled at me, coughing up a lump of bloody flesh that I recognized as part of the goblin that had been dragged into the pit. It grabbed the chunk and gobbled it down quickly, but the break in eye contact was all I needed. I didn't think it'd had the chance to use its ability on me, but I couldn't take the risk, and I shouted out into the still air.

"Attack! Kill that fucker!" I roared, and the room burst into motion, three smaller creatures running up out of the pit to join the big one. They looked like twisted skeletons of animals, with human skulls and fixated black eyes. Each of them paused for only a second, before launching themselves through the air at a different goblin, and I lifted my rifle, pulling the trigger frantically as soon as it was centered on the massive thing in the center. Bullets flew through the air, slamming into the chest of the nightmarish creature, staggering it briefly. It howled in rage and lunged forward, digging its hands into the pile of rubble and throwing itself at me.

I opened my eyes wide in shock as it hurtled across the church and frantically dove aside, rolling and coming to my feet in time to fire two more bullets into a massive hand that slammed down inches from me. I heard the bones breaking, saw the bullets smash their way through the hand and ricochet off the stone slabs beyond, yet doing little more than annoying the damn thing.

I cursed, backing up and aiming at the head, firing two more bullets quickly, before managing a rapid burst of five. Thanks to my shitty skills, low experience with firearms in the real world, and panic, I managed to hit it twice. One bullet took out a series of teeth as it ploughed along its jaw, and the other slammed into the outer edge of the eye socket next to the bright blue eye on its right. It screamed, flinching back and lifting a hand to cover that side of its face before hissing in rage and lunging at me again.

The goblins piled onto it as I dove aside, barely dodging the attack, and as I sprinted in the opposite direction, they started laying into it with their clubs. The sound of enraged shrieking filled the air, as did the sound of breaking bones. I dared a glance over to the left as I ran, seeing that two of the goblins had lost their fights with the bone minions, but the third had won, and that one was leaping onto the back of one of the two damaged survivors.

I heard pain-filled cursing in the warbling goblin tongue, and a flash of fiery light illuminated the room, swiftly followed by a second, as the two Magelings used their Flamedarts. I followed the projectiles' trajectory, watching them embed themselves into the chest of the massive creature, which howled in rage and backhanded one of them, smashing him into the far wall, where he slumped to the floor. The streak of blood that ran down from the point of impact told me he was dead before he'd hit the ground.

It whipped around, glaring at me again, and rose to its feet, kicking out and killing another goblin almost negligently. I had Bob and Smasher left, as well as the kobold, one Mageling, and two Footsoldiers. That was it. One of the Footsoldiers was badly injured, having won its battle against the second minion, and, despite its wounds, was doggedly stumbling after the third and final minion, which was equally damaged.

I spun to face the Eidolon, backing away into the south section of the Cathedral. I began fervently hoping that the lower roof here would slow it down, as I aimed and fired again and again. My bullets merely sparked off its head or sank in with no apparent damage beyond irritation, from what I could see.

I swore and tossed the rifle aside. It was clearly doing sod-all for me. Instead, I drew my sword, slipping into my fighting stance and glaring at the creature. I figured I still had two weapons to pull out that I needed to save for the right time.

The Eidolon screeched at me, rising up to its full height. Ignoring the attacking goblins, it took a deep breath. Opening its mouth wide enough to swallow me whole, the monster let loose a terrifying bellow.

I backed up a few feet, feeling somewhat scared, but the effect on the goblins was different. I suddenly knew what it'd done as they screamed and fled. It had used its 'Unholy Terror' ability, and while I was outside its range, the rest of my squad hadn't been. It saw them fleeing, fixed its eyes on me, and hissed in triumph. I quickly glanced to the right, breaking eye contact, and heard a hiss of fury before it struck out with one hand. I flinched, jumping to the side reflexively, but it wasn't me it had been reaching for.

The disturbingly white appendage plucked the broken, blood-dripping corpse of my goblin Mageling from the ground and brought it up to its mouth, glaring at me unblinkingly as it started to consume it, I froze, then paled as I saw the effect the meal was having. The clearly broken bones in its feet and legs that had, I guessed, been slowing it down, started to reform, and it paused in its grisly feast to hiss in triumph at me.

"Oh, fuck no!" I snarled, all fear gone as adrenaline and determination flooded through me. I rushed forward, sword held high in my right hand…as I tore loose the small bag from my hip with my left, hefting it in preparation.

The Eidolon lashed out, sweeping its right arm across my path from my left to right. I leapt over the deadly limb as the creature pushed more of the Mageling into its mouth, determined to finish its feast. I lashed out at its nearest leg, the bronze sword slicing through the outer layer of rotting skin, before cracking bone and making the beast choke as it tried to scream in pain around a mouthful of goblin.

I ducked under the right arm as it pulled back, swinging for me, and ran around its back, smashing the bag in my hand off a large piece of shattered masonry…just in time to be sent tumbling into the wall as it lashed out with its left leg in a vicious back heel kick.

I hit hard, feeling a rib or two break, and before I could get up, I screamed as I felt its foot come down hard on my right forearm, pinning it to the floor and bruising, if not breaking, the bone.

It had spun around faster than I'd been able to move, and now, it grabbed me around the waist, squeezing and lifting me as it dragged its foot from my arm. It hoisted me into the air, bringing me closer to face it. Leering hungrily, it hissed in pleasure, its thick tongue flicking out to taste my blood where it dripped from a cut on my right cheek.

I felt the thick mucus the appendage left behind, and I shuddered, trying to breathe through the pain and terror as it brought its rotting face closer to mine.

"Hellllloooooo…" it whined, the eyes searching mine for understanding as it tried again. *"Friennnnnnds? Foooooood?"* it warbled. I guessed it was picking words that had carried meaning in the memories of its host, but not understanding them fully itself. *"Looooove youuuu…"*

I fixed the abomination with a glare and raised my left hand, smashing it into its face. The malformed ghoul growled in rage, its right hand coming up and grabbing at my left. As soon as it opened its mouth, I threw my hand's contents, the bag flying true, and the fugly bastard took the bait, biting down on it, hard.

Suddenly, it howled, slamming me to the floor and releasing me as it clawed at its mouth. The broken glass from the ten tiny bottles of vodka had embedded deeply. The bag had already started to drip with the cracked bottles inside, but the thing's bite had truly broken them. Vodka filled its mouth, and I grinned up from where I lay broken on the floor beneath it, coughing up a bubble of blood that spattered across my lips and chin.

"Incinerate…motherfucker!" I wheezed, aiming the spell at its mouth, and sagging with relief at the flash of heat, as the spell ignited the vodka, spreading further and faster than it normally could. The flames exploded, the Eidolon screeching in pain and fury as it beat at its face, staggering away from me and falling as one foot snagged against a broken pew. It fell to the floor and writhed, frantically trying to beat the flames out.

I lay motionless on the floor, knowing I needed to finish it, but the pain…

A shadow suddenly fell across me. Light I hadn't even noticed streaming in through the doorway was suddenly obscured as first one, then another, then all of my remaining Dungeon creatures made a reappearance.

They ran past me, the goblins falling on the shrieking creature, clubs rising and falling to smash its arms and legs. Meanwhile, the kobold grabbed me, its little claws digging into my skin as it frantically started to drag me out of the cathedral. I caught a glimpse of Smasher jumping into the air, his arms glowing suddenly red as he brought them down, a club in each hand, to slam into the Eidolon's skull. A sick crunch echoed around the cavernous vaults of the ceiling as Bob lashed out repeatedly, working in less of a frenzy, and in more of a workman-like fashion, cracking bone after bone as he made his way steadily up the nearest arm.

The Eidolon screeched and fumbled, writhing around while desperately trying to protect itself, even as its arms and legs were broken and the flames consumed its head. The last sight I saw as I was dragged from the darkness of the cathedral and out into the gentle, early morning sun, was the look of hatred on its face as it turned its head, fixing me with a glare, only broken as the eye popped from the heat and shriveled away.

I cried out in pain as I was unceremoniously bounced down the stairs, the surviving Mageling appearing next to the Kobold and taking my other shoulder. My creatures tugged hard as they both dragged me up the street, away from the fight. I groaned in agony, broken ribs grinding against each other. My right knee had dislocated and was clattering and jouncing with every impact against the asphalt as the little guys worked desperately. A shout rose from the connecting street, echoing from the surrounding buildings. I managed to turn my head, unable to focus for several seconds as the Mageling yanked hard, and pain dug its red-hot claws into my brain.

Once I'd focused, I cried out, but it was too late, as a tall, dark-haired man slammed a hammer down, killing the Mageling with one blow.

"Die!" The man screamed. My kobold tugged frantically at me, fear making it whimper, but it still stayed, and I managed to lift my right arm enough to get the man's attention. "Don't panic, I'm here!" he roared, pulling back for another swing as a voice from behind called out.

"Look out! There's more!" I couldn't see who spoke, but I waved my arm frantically, managing to grab the man's leg as I called to the kobold.

"No! Run away! Get to the Dungeon!" It froze, desperate to help me, but my order gave its fear enough strength to drive it back, and the man's second blow missed, slamming into the road next to me. I tugged frantically, trying to stop him, and he paused, looking down as he stood over me, then looked away again.

"It's all right! I'm here. I'll save you," he growled. I slapped at his leg, my senses telling me that my Dungeon Creatures were closing in.

"No!" I cried out, then coughed, spattering my own face with blood. "Stop!" I managed to gurgle out just as a woman appeared, crouching next to me. She leaned in, grabbing my arm and looking into my eyes kindly as she tried to calm me.

"It's okay; we're here to help…" she said soothingly, then blinked in shock as she registered my features. "Matt?!" she asked, incredulity clear in her voice.

"No!" I snapped at her, desperation filing my words. "Not a threat…mine!" I managed to croak out before coughing up more blood.

"What?" she asked, confused.

"The…creatures…" I gasped. "Mine! Protecting ME!" I cried, sagging back and drawing in a deep breath, then calling out in as clear a voice as I could. "Stop!"

The sudden indrawn breath of the man above me indicated that my goblins had heard me. A second later, the woman was leaning in close again, her hair falling down, while the sun behind her obscured her face.

"What do you mean, they're yours?!" she asked quickly. "Are they friendly?"

"Yes…" I managed to get out, before choking on more of my own blood. My right lung deflated, making me gasp in pain and terror as I started to drown in the blood filling my airways.

"Mike! I need you!" the woman snapped, a knife appearing in her hand as she quickly cut away my top, turning me onto my side. "My bag! Get the needle!" I heard her say as I struggled for breath.

"Which one?" the man called, rummaging through the bag as the woman snapped directions at him.

"Inside pocket, under the flap! The canula!" I blinked, worn asphalt filling my vision as my lungs heaved and shuddered. The right had deflated, the left was filling with blood, and I blinked dazedly at the sight of the crimson blood that dripped from my lips onto the ground, trailing a dozen feet beyond it. I caught glimpses of Bob and Smasher, badly battered but staring at me fixedly.

"Those things are still there…" the man ground out, and the woman snapped at him, gesturing furiously.

"I don't care, Mike! Here, hold him still…" I felt rough hands grabbing me, pinning me, before a sharp pain flared in the side of my chest. With a hiss, the air that had been slowly crushing my lung was released, and I drew in half a lungful of sweet, sweet air as the world faded to black.

TWENTY-EIGHT

IT WAS HOURS later, though how many, I had no idea. I awoke on the futon, pain shooting through me. I blinked blearily, trying to focus. I could feel something quivering in my side and a thick tube rubbing my throat raw. I coughed, gagged, and shook as I tried not to be sick, retching before my hands could reach the tube and yank it out.

I coughed and spluttered, a thin bile spraying from my mouth to spatter across the blanket covering me, and then the floor, as shouting filled the air.

"Shit, he's awake! Mike, god damn it!" the same female voice from before shouted, as the male voice responded quickly.

"Fuck's sake! What does it take to knock him out!" he cried, exasperation filling his voice as the sound of running feet the room.

"Just do it properly!" the first voice snapped. "It's not that hard, Mike!"

"I did! I gave him the full goddamn needle!"

"Bullshit!" the female voice snapped, rolling me onto my back and bracing against my shoulders as I tried to get up, panicked and confused. "Matt! Matt, it's okay! It's okay! I need you to stop. Just stay still; I'm nearly done!" Her face finally clear to me, I stared into Kelly's eyes, confused to all hell.

I felt a jab of something in my left shoulder, followed by a cold sensation as the man injected me with something, and I blinked down at the needle, then back at Kelly.

"What the…" I managed muzzily, before she smiled at me. My mind froze, flashing back to that night in the bar, to her wrapping her arms around my neck and kissing me,: how beautiful she was, and now, here…somehow even more beautiful, even with her hair scraped back into a ponytail and no makeup on, dirt coating her cheeks. I blinked at her and managed to gasp out a few words before the world slipped away again.

"You're beautiful…" I murmured, and her eyes widened slightly, accompanied by the start of a smile, and the redness rising in her cheeks.

Untold hours passed once again. I awoke confused, feeling groggy as hell, but I was alone, at least for now. I stared at the ceiling, recognizing the familiar mess of pipes and brackets, as a little voice inside counseled me to absorb them sooner, rather than later…Absorb! The Dungeon Charge!

I dove into the Dungeon Senses with relief, feeling the grogginess, confusion, and discomfort all slip away as my mind seemed suddenly clear again. I hovered there, in the middle of the room, observing the sleeping forms of Amy, Alyssa, and Kelly, and the hunched over form of whom I assumed to be Alyssa's husband. I remembered hearing them call him Mike, so that made sense. He was seated on an office chair, clearly looted from upstairs and carried down. On the table before him, which had been secured the same way, I assumed, he had several guns spread out and was steadily cleaning them, all the while muttering the words to a song under his breath. I moved closer, listening carefully, until I mentally snorted in amusement.

"I'm a barbie girl, in a barbie world…life in plastic…is fantastic…" I couldn't wait to take the piss out of him for that. I left him then, deciding that I wasn't at any immediate risk, so I'd address the notifications and then either sleep some more, or try to figure out what the hell had happened. I quickly pulled up the interface and found that I had four surviving minions. The two kobolds, one of which had remained with Alyssa, doing research, sat miserably in the Dungeon above us. With him were the other kobold who'd dragged me out and stood up to Mike, clearly kicked out as well, and Smasher and Bob.

Where the Kobolds were depressed, kicked out of their places in the Node, the two Goblins wandered aimlessly, watching out of windows and generally keeping an eye on the building. I dismissed most of the notifications, finding them to be about the goblins who'd died, and finally reordered the system. Now it would only show me details of surviving creatures, which was a relief, because there was still a load of work to be done with just that information.

Congratulations!

You and your party of Dungeon Creatures have defeated five opponents. XP breakdown as follows:

- Matt: Party leader, 40%
- Bob, Smasher, Unnamed Kobold Trapsmith: 20% each
- Evolved Eidolon level: 7
- Your level: 6
- Bob level: 2
- Smasher level: 2
- Unnamed Kobold level: 1
- XP awarded: 2575
- Matt receives: 1030 XP
- Bob receives: 515 XP
- Smasher receives: 515 XP
- Unnamed Kobold Trapsmith receives: 515 XP

Bob has leveled up!

As this is a Dungeon-born creature, you may choose to assign points for the creature, or allow it to assign the points as it chooses.

Assign points?

Yes/No...

Smasher has leveled up!

As this is a Dungeon-born creature, you may choose to assign points for the creature, or allow it to assign the points as it chooses.

Assign points?

Yes/No...

'Unnamed Kobold Trapsmith' has leveled up!

As this is a Dungeon-born creature, you may choose to assign points for the creature, or allow it to assign the points as it chooses.

Assign points?

Yes/No...

I selected 'yes,' of course. Bob had hit level four, so I split the four points he'd gained, dropping them instantly into Intelligence and Wisdom. It might not have seemed like a good pairing for a Footsoldier, I reflected, not at first anyway, but they didn't need to be. This was part of my plan to improve the entire species, as the Footsoldier was now my 'standard' Goblin template. I felt satisfied, since he was now a solid 'all-rounder'. I did intend to improve the goblins, moving from 'common' to 'uncommon' at some point, but for the next little while, at least, I was going to keep them as they were.

Name: Bob				
Species: Goblin		Bonus:		
Level: 4		Progress to next level 10/500		
Available points: 0		Perk: Rat Killer 10% damage to Vermin		
Stat	Current points	Description	Effect	Progress to next level
Agility	*5*	Governs dodge and movement.		19/100
Charisma	*1*	Governs likely success to charm seduce or threaten		0/100

Constitution	***5***	Governs Health and Health Regeneration	HP:5x10= 50	78/100
Dexterity	***2***	Governs ability with weapons and crafting		83/100
Endurance	***4***	Governs Stamina and Stamina Regeneration	Stamina: 4x10 = 40	76/100
Intelligence	***4***	Governs base manapool and standard intellectual capacity	Mana: 4x10 = 40	3/100
Luck	***3***	Governs overall chance of bonuses and critical hits		41/100
Perception	***2***	Governs ranged damage and chance to spot hidden items/ traps		11/100
Strength	***3***	Governs damage with melee weapons and carrying capacity		53/100
Wisdom	***3***	Governs mana regeneration and memory	3x10 = 30 mana regenerated per hour	7/100

I assigned the points differently for Smasher, more as an experiment than anything else, since I'd decided to stick to the decision I'd made with him earlier, and I wouldn't be making more of his kind, not the basic ones anyway. I assigned all six of his points into Intelligence, figuring he could live out the rest of his days in the Research Node. He'd managed to reach level three, and that made a hell of a difference to him, going from an Intelligence of one point one, to a surprising seven point seven.

Name: Smasher				
Species: Goblin		Bonus: Cunning		
Level: 3		Progress to next level 285/400		
Available points: 0		Perk: 10% increase to Intelligence		
Stat	Current points	Description	Effect	Progress to next level
Agility	*3*	Governs dodge and movement.		19/100
Charisma	*1*	Governs likely success to charm seduce or threaten		0/100
Constitution	*3*	Governs Health and Health Regeneration	HP:3x20 = 60	78/100
Dexterity	*2*	Governs ability with weapons and crafting		83/100
Endurance	*6*	Governs Stamina and Stamina Regeneration	Stamina: 6x20 = 120	76/100
Intelligence	*7.7*	Governs base manapool and standard intellectual capacity	Mana: 7.7x10 = 77	3/100
Luck	*3*	Governs overall chance of bonuses and critical hits		41/100
Perception	*1*	Governs ranged damage and chance to spot hidden items/traps		11/100
Strength	*4*	Governs damage with melee weapons and carrying capacity		53/100
Wisdom	*1*	Governs mana regeneration and memory	10 mana regenerated per hour	7/100

Lastly I pulled up the kobold's stats. I was going to be replacing his kind soon, so while I'd make a few copies of him for the research node, I knew the research into the 'Uncommon' level of Kobold was nearly finished. Smiling, I put all six points into Intelligence, boosting him all the way to ten, then changed his name to Kenny. Just for shits and giggles.

Name: Kenny the Kobold Trapsmith				
Species: Kobold		Bonus:		
Level: 3		Progress to next level 232/400		
Available points: 0		Perk: Increased damage to larger prey		
Stat	Current points	Description	Effect	Progress to next level
Agility	***2***	Governs dodge and movement.		0/100
Charisma	***2***	Governs likely success to charm seduce or threaten		0/100
Constitution	***2***	Governs Health and Health Regeneration	HP: 2x10 = 20	0/100
Dexterity	***2***	Governs ability with weapons and crafting		0/100
Endurance	***2***	Governs Stamina and Stamina Regeneration	Stamina: 2x10= 20	0/100
Intelligence	***10***	Governs base manapool and standard intellectual	Mana: 10x10 = 100	0/100
Luck	***2***	Governs overall chance of bonuses and critical hits		0/100
Perception	***2***	Governs ranged damage and chance to spot hidden items/ traps		0/100
Strength	***2***	Governs damage with melee weapons and carrying capacity		0/100
Wisdom	***2***	Governs mana regeneration and memory	20 mana regenerated per hour	0/100

Once the changes had been accepted, I absorbed him, feeling a little shame, as I essentially killed the creature that had saved me. I paused, examining my feelings and wondering about whether I had acted callously. They were recreated, after all, once I re-summoned them. Was I essentially making them immortal, summoning them again and again? Or was I killing them and replacing them with a blank version each time?

I thought on it for a few minutes, before shaking myself out of it. It didn't matter. I had things to do, and my world to save. I'd ask Alyssa and the others; let them worry about it. Maybe.

I felt my focus shift, and I started to travel back to the Core room unthinkingly, the desire to see Kelly again strong in my mind. I halted myself, quickly diverting my path to the Research Node instead. Progress had dropped to a crawl since the changes, especially since the researchers had been kicked out and my 'sewer-side squad' had all been killed. With no mana coming in beyond the ambient absorption, I had to move quickly to get things running again.

I had a full charge of one hundred and twenty-five points. Summoning the upgraded Kobolds back was cheap enough, as previously I'd gotten three for five points, and even now, at their more advanced stage, they only cost me fifteen points for three. I assigned them all to the research node, along with Smasher, who merrily ambled upstairs to the door, where I let him in. I felt Mike moving, heading to the research area, no doubt drawn by the light of the summoning, and I swore, dipping back into my body.

"Mike..." I croaked, coughed, and forced myself to sit up, hearing the sound of feet as he quickly moved to me.

"You're Matt, right? Look..." He started, reaching a hand out to me, and I cut him off.

"We can talk in a minute. For now, just chill...the light, that's me. So, I need you to leave it alone...stay here, and for the love of god, don't pull an Alyssa and kill my creatures..." I said, cutting off as a memory surfaced. "...you already did, didn't you?" He coughed, scratching the back of his head.

"Yeah, sort of; when we found you in the road..."

"Right." I sighed, closing my eyes and ignoring the sounds of the other three starting to stir. "I'll be right back, just...just stay here, okay?" I dipped back into the Dungeon Sense, hovering next to him for a minute, just to make sure he would do as asked, and that he wasn't going to drug me again. When I was confident that he had settled down, I moved on.

Now that I had the research positions filled, I was ready to branch out, and I summoned another three kobolds for the roof, giving them the orders to make as many traps for vermin and anything else that might come exploring as they could. Finally, with those deployed, I had thirteen of my maximum control points in use, and ninety-five remaining points of mana available. I checked the upper floor, discovering that Smasher and Bob had brought back four clubs, two each, so I summoned four 'Bob's'.

They cost me two points of control each, leaving me with four points overall, and although the cost of the Footsoldiers' summoning had gone up, it was only to ten points apiece, so the forty spent there left me with fifty-five. I decided to take a punt on things, and used the last fifty-five points as well, creating a crossbow, costing fifty, and a few bushels of bolts, costing five more. I dropped the items at the feet of one of the kobolds stationed on the roof, ordering it to kill any flying creatures it could, and to come to the door downstairs if it ran out of bolts.

I planned to check on it regularly, but just in case…I mentally shrugged. With that, I slipped back into my body and blinked as I tried to readjust to the injuries and aches. I sat up again, slowly, and shook myself, flinching when I felt another pain in my side. Looking down, I saw I still had a drain embedded, leading down to a jury-rigged bucket and a canula in the back of my right hand, as well as…

"Okay, who the hell put a damn tube in my dick?" I asked loudly, my voice a cross between a manly growl and a girly squeal.

"I did," Kelly said matter-of-factly, and I turned to glare at her.

"Really?" I asked. "Why the hell…"

"Well we didn't know how long you'd be out, and rather than have you piss yourself repeatedly, I put in a catheter. It's kinda the thing to do." She got up and approached my bedside to check me over. She calmly took my pulse while I glared at her, before turning and fixing my attention onto Alyssa.

"I thought you said she worked at the court?!?" I snarled.

"I do," Kelly confirmed, dropping my wrist and folding her arms. "But I was also a nurse cadet, and our parents both work for the NHS. I've had all the basic training, as well as a fair bit of extra. I just don't like the assholes you have to deal with as a doctor."

"So, what, you trained to be a doctor, then went to work as a scribe instead?" I asked sarcastically.

"Not a scribe, a magistrate," she corrected me grimly.

"What?" I frowned in confusion, and she rolled her eyes.

"A magistrate!" she repeated. "I act as a volunteer, listening to cases and deciding which ones go to the Crown Court, as well as dealing with the minor stuff, like shoplifting. I also act as a legal advisor, helping the judge determine what's appropriate for different cases." She frowned in annoyance at me. "You know, you were a lot nicer when you were drunk or unconscious. Now you're just being an asshole."

"I literally woke up with a pipe in my dick!" I growled, gesturing down at my crotch, and somewhere in the room, I heard Amy start to giggle. "The last thing I remember is the man mountain there killing my only surviving Mageling, and then you were stabbing me with something, and I woke up like this!"

"Yeah..." Mike said, rubbing the back of his head self-consciously. "Sorry about that, mate. I thought the little guy was attacking you. You were a mess, if it's any consolation."

"Not so much." I snapped, before pausing, closing my eyes, and taking a deep breath, then letting it out. "Okay, stop," I said as Alyssa, Mike and Kelly all started to speak.

"I..."

"This is all..."

"Dick." That last comment was muttered just loud enough for everyone to hear, and I glared at Kelly as I opened my eyes.

"Right; let's start again," I said finally. "Mike, it's nice to meet you. Kelly, it's nice to see you again. Now, how about you help me to get this tube out, and I can get some pants on? Then we can all have a little chat, and I'll explain a few things," I asked as nicely as I could.

"I already told them everything," Alyssa spoke up helpfully.

"And I showed them the kobolds!" Amy called out as Kelly shifted my blankets to the side, uncovering my pride and joy but keeping me from flashing the rest of the world.

"Great...yowww!" I cried as Kelly 'accidentally' tugged on the pipe, the sticky tape that she'd used to secure it to my leg tearing out sections of hair. I noticed the quick jerk at the edges of her mouth as she tried to hide her smile, shooting a sharp frown her way in return.

She knelt on the floor, draining the catheter with a little syringe, and I tried to stay as still as possible.

"Okay, everyone!" Alyssa said suddenly, clapping her hands and making me jerk, then groan. I winced at her, catching the look of chagrin on her face as she went on. "I don't think Matt needs us here while this happens, Amy, Mike, let's go make breakfast..." She shooed the pair away, firmly turning Amy's head as the girl tried to see what Kelly was doing.

"So..." Kelly said to me as she emptied the syringe and repeated the process, draining the last of the liquid into the bucket.

"Yeah…so…look, I'm sorry for being an asshole…it wasn't intentional." I said, and she shrugged.

"Most assholes say that." She didn't look up, but I saw the edge of her lips quirk again as I gritted my teeth, trying not to swear as she pulled free the last of the medical tape that had held the tube against my leg, and removing a load of hair with it.

"Yeah, well, like most assholes, I was hoping to see you in this kind of position, just minus the tubing…although, if there was a nurse's outfit involved, maybe I'd be okay with it…" I murmured thoughtfully, and she snorted, shaking her head as she pulled the tubing free in a single smooth motion.

"Yeah, believe me, it's not how I intended for this to go, either. I'd hoped for dinner and some drinks before seeing you naked…" She smiled up at me, and I felt it coming. I tensed, up, trying with all my might to fight against an instinct as old as time.

She knelt before me, literally having just handled my manhood, if not in the best way, and she looked up at me, eyes widening at the look of strain on my face, and she froze.

It was not to be, though. No matter how hard I fought, I couldn't stop it, and it happened…

"While you're down there…"

The words just slipped out, straight past all the mental barriers I tried to erect to prevent them from escaping, following instincts that couldn't be denied.

"You ass!" Kelly laughed, flipping the blanket over me as she stood up, and I joined her, laughing quietly as well, and fixing her with a grin.

"Well, you can't blame me. You were literally at the right height and everything. Just a little closer, and…"

"And even though it's the end of the world, the power is gone, and creatures roam the streets, a man tries to get his dick sucked at any opportunity. Good to know some things never change!" She snorted, coiling the tubing up with practiced motions.

"Look, seriously, though…" I said, shifting uncomfortably and shrugging before making eye contact again. "I am sorry. It was just a bit of a shock, and I hadn't realized what you'd done until I was back in my body properly. It was a surprise."

"Well, it needed to be done," she said, waving off my apology. "I will say, you're healing well. I expected you to be out for another six hours or so at least, and…" She broke off when I tugged the tubing free of my side, then yanked the canula out." "Stop! What are you doing?" she snapped, grabbing my arms, swearing as she realized the damage was done.

"It's all right," I said, taking a deep breath and wincing at the pain. "I'd have done the same with the catheter, but I could feel something inside me; didn't want to rip my dick off." I winced slightly as she glared at me.

"And do you want to explain why you just undid all my hard work?" She crossed her arms, forcing a calm tone past her gritted teeth.

"Because I've had people try to kill me practically every day since all this began," I said mildly, and she flinched, looking at my scarred chest and up at the healed line that ran across my cheek and up into my hairline, where I knew that more scar tissue told a grim tale. "Yeah, I mean it." I insisted, meeting her eyes. "As part of surviving all that, somehow I started healing faster. Give me a second…" I said, closing my eyes and pulling up the notification I'd known had to be there.

You have reached Level Eight! You receive ten Stat points to invest in your attributes, plus one Skill point.

I took a deep breath, switching to my stats screen and looking it over. I'd improved in a few places through simple effort as well, which was awesome in its own right. I dismissed the screens identifying that information, as I could see it for myself straight away, knowing the stats that I had previously compared to now seemed to be etched into my soul.

Name: Matt				
Modifiers: None				
Species: Human	Bonus: None			
Level: 8	Progress to next level: 817/900			
Assimilation: 0%	Dungeon Level: 0			
Control: 12.5	Dungeon Capacity: 25 points			
Host Powers: 1	Dungeon Spells: 1			
Stat	Current points	Description	Effect	Progress to next level
Agility	11	Governs dodge and movement.	Heightened chance to dodge attacks 10%+10%= 20%	34/100
Charisma	8	Governs likely success to charm seduce or threaten		76/100

Constitution	13	Governs Health and Health Regeneration	HP: 13x20 = 260	11/100
Dexterity	16	Governs ability with weapons and crafting	+10% Increased chance of improved result	2/100
Endurance	8	Governs Stamina and Stamina Regeneration	Stamina: 7x10	82/100
Intelligence	10	Governs base manapool, standard intellectual capacity plus Control when combined with Wisdom and divided by 2	Mana: 10x20=200 Control: (10+15)/2 = 12.5	48/100
Luck	11	Governs overall chance of bonuses and critical hits	+1% chance to find a favorable outcome in any situation, 'Luck's Favor' unlocked at +10%	97/100
Perception	10	Governs ranged damage and chance to spot hidden items/traps	+0 to all ranged attacks	28/100
Strength	11	Governs damage with melee weapons and carrying capacity	+1 to all damage with Melee weapons	68/100
Wisdom	15	Governs mana regeneration and Control, when combined with Intelligence and divided by two	150 mana regenerated per hour Control: (10+15)/2 = 12.5	31/100

I put five points into Intelligence, upping my 'Control' stat to fifteen, my available mana to three hundred, and my summoning limit to thirty points. Two points each went into Luck and Endurance, bringing them up to ten and thirteen; my Endurance changed from eighty, or eight times ten, to two-hundred as the modifier kicked in at ten points, doubling it up to twenty points per point invested. Last of all, I slipped a single point into Charisma. Partially because I felt having any points below ten was unworthy of me, and I'd always thought I was a good-looking guy, but mainly, and I'd never admit this to anyone but myself…the sight of Kelly down on her knees had sparked a lot of thoughts, and I *needed* to do something about that. She'd been very interested the other night, and well…a man had needs. The rule of never shitting on your own doorstep was written up when the old world was still with us.

It wasn't anymore.

TWENTY-NINE

"WHAT THE HELL did you just do?" Kelly asked me with concern when I got control again. Hitting the 'Accept Changes' selection was always painful, and adding five solid points into Intelligence had felt like someone stitching sections of my brain together with white hot needles.

"I…I levelled up," I muttered, catching my breath.

"Wow, well, that explains so much. Thank you for that helpful and wise answer," She retorted sarcastically, and I growled under my breath, shaking my head in annoyance.

"Okay, levelling…I guess nobody else seems to be doing it yet, maybe it's the Dungeon that's letting me do it early or something? Have to have a think about that…" I pondered, before shaking my head. "Look, I need to have this conversation with everyone, so how about you give me a bit of privacy to get dressed?" I asked, and she raised a questioning eyebrow.

"Really? What have you suddenly got that I haven't seen before?" she asked, that damn smile quirking the edges of her lips, before she laughed outright. "Sorry! It was worth it for your face! It's okay, I'll go while you…"

"Meh, I was being polite. I don't mind if you don't…" I said, cutting her off and tossing the blanket aside. She'd literally seen everything; hell, she'd had to *handle* it to insert the catheter, but still, her eyes darted down, and I mentally awarded myself a point for that. "Gotcha!" I said, winking.

"Ass." She slapped my shoulder. "You sure you're okay?" she asked, doing her best not to look down as I stood up, towering over her and practically bouncing my love truncheon off her hand by accident

"I am, honestly," I said, shuffling past her as she stepped back. I quickly collected my boxers and jeans from a pile on the floor and went to pull them on, grimacing at the filth and dirt that coated them. I shrugged and made do with the boxers, instead hefting my jeans in my hands and closing my eyes. I had three points of Mana Charge available, and it showed as needing five. Typical. I hunted around, ignoring Kelly's wolf whistle as she walked away, heading into the next room to join the others, and I found a pair of comparatively clean pants to make do with for the moment. I took the badly soiled and damaged pair with me, though, as I followed her through the doorway.

"So, morning all," I said, forcing a smile.

"Hi, Matt!" Amy called, running across and hugging me.

"Hey Amy," I said, smiling and hugging her back. "You miss me, kid?"

"Momma said you looked like shit," Amy told me seriously.

"Amy!" Alyssa gasped, looking scandalized.

"You did!" Amy said, all childlike innocence. "You said he looked like he smelled!"

"I…I…" Alyssa spluttered helplessly, face going red, and I closed my eyes, nodding in amused acknowledgement.

"She's probably right, Amy. Thanks for that," I said calmly. "Don't worry, though; living quarters are on the list for today, and they'll include a shower, or bath, or something…so, hopefully, I'll stop smelling so bad."

"Okay! Thanks, Matt!" Amy chirped happily as Alyssa tried to avoid my eye.

"Well, looks like I'm the only one who hasn't really met you before…" Mike said, stepping forward and holding out his hand. "I'm Mike."

"Matt," I said, gripping his hand and shaking it, glad that he didn't go in for the whole 'manly dominance crush-your-hand' thing.

"I've got to thank you first…" Mike said, shaking his head as he let go of my hand. "Amy and Alyssa told me what you did for them. I'm just sorry I wasn't here for them when they needed me."

"No need, mate. You were getting ready to defend the county, and all of us. You weren't away on a stag do or something." I reassured him. "You'd have dealt with it faster than I did, no doubt, if you were here."

"Well, still, I wasn't, so thank you, Matt. Anything you ever need, I'm your man. I'll never be able to repay you for what you did." He reached out and pulled Alyssa to him, his arm around her shoulders as he kissed the top of her head and ruffled Amy's hair with his other hand.

"Daaaad!" Amy groused, pulling back and shaking her head, trying to smooth her hair back down.

"So…what's for breakfast?" I asked. "And when did we move all the food in here?"

"I did it yesterday," Amy said. "Momma helped, but it just seemed smarter to have it all in one spot."

"Works for me." I said, looking around. Where I'd had everything piled up randomly, she'd organized it; tins together, dried foods on one side, long-life milk on the other, beers and spirits at the back, bread and random bits in another section.

I reached out and picked up a box of cereal, pouring some into a bowl and adding milk. As I attacked it with the hunger of a starving man, I reflected how, in a few short weeks, I'd started to eat so much more healthily, it was insane. Before the end, I'd viewed breakfasts that weren't fried as a waste of everyone's time.

"God, what I wouldn't do for bacon…" I sighed after swallowing a mouthful of the tasteless cereal.

"You and me both, brother," Mike said, looking sadly at his bowl, while the three girls showed every sign of enjoyment as they ate it.

"I mean, surely there's as much taste in the packaging as this shit?" I asked the room at large, getting glares from Alyssa and Kelly, a giggle from Amy, and fervent nodding from Mike.

"We called this punishment breakfast in the army. It means you f…uh…made a mistake and had to make amends…" Mike said, hurriedly changing his phrasing just in time when he remembered who was present.

"You and me, Mike?" I said putting the bowl down on the floor and shaking my head. "We're going 'shopping' today." He grinned at me, dumping his as well.

"You think there's going to be much left in the area?" he asked, and I shrugged.

"We only need one of anything, and the Dungeon can make more."

"Really? Alyssa said it can make things, but…"

"Food is easy," I confirmed. "Whoever designed it, they set it up so that food was available easiest. Other, more complicated things have prerequisites. Like the clubs my goblins had outside? Alyssa helped to make them, and they took days of maneuvering bits into place before they could be made. But something as complicated as a packet of crisps?" I scoffed, displaying my own disbelief.

"They're cooked to perfection, evenly flavored, wrapped in a foil so thin, it'd never be reproducible by hand, and still, boom! I can set it to appear easily. A bullet? Might take months of work and some seriously expensive kits to be made first. Just be glad you guys missed all the really tedious bits."

"How bad?" Kelly asked, and I shrugged.

"Lift your right hand," I suggested, and she complied. "Now, imagine you're moving through thick honey, pressing against a bubble that might pop at any second if you touch it too hard, and slowly move your hand." She shifted it a few inches and looked at me in question. "Yup, well done. That's basically what it's like to expand the Dungeon Aura so that I can affect a greater area. It took a day or so to acquire this space. Almost a week got me the first floor of this building and along to the Revolution Bar on the corner. Mind-numbing," I asserted ,shaking my head. She winced, and Mike shook his head.

"Rather you than me, mate." he said, and I nodded.

"So, if you guys are going looting…sorry, '*shopping,*' today, we're coming with you." Alyssa said firmly. "We need clothes, sanitary products…"

"And if we leave men in charge of the food, we'll all die of gout…" Kelly cut in, getting a firm nod of agreement from Alyssa.

"…So anyway, we're coming." she finished, and I looked at Mike, raising one eyebrow.

"Don't look at me, mate, I just married her. You're in charge in here." He lifted his hands in mock fear.

"Thanks for that…" I said, shaking my head. "What about Amy?" I asked.

"I'm coming too!" she spoke up quickly, and Mike, Alyssa, and Kelly all jumped in straight away, telling her she wasn't. "But I want to!" she pouted, before smiling evilly. "Besides, I'll just follow if you don't let me go."

"And that's why someone has to stay here with her," I said, laughing and dumping it right back on the others. "I'll let you all decide who." With that, I walked out of the small 'kitchen' and back into the main room, sitting down on the sofa and concentrating.

I had eleven points available now, and I checked through the details quickly, finding that most had come from pigeons being killed. I relaxed and slipped into the Dungeon Senses, flying up to check on the kobolds. My little kobold archer was perched on the highest part of the roof he could find, tracking a starling. As I watched, he fired, totally missing it, and yipped in excitement, pulling up another bolt and struggling to reload. I checked and found he'd gone through two complete quivers of bolts, and I quickly made him another three, dropping them next to him and watching with amusement as he squeaked and danced, upon finding them. I mentally snorted at the little creature's excitement and slipped back to my body, smiling as I sat back upright.

"What's made you smile like that?" Alyssa asked me and I started, not having realized she had come through. I could still hear Kelly and Mike arguing over who was going to stay behind with Amy.

"Kobolds," I admitted, chuckling. "I gave one a crossbow; he's perched on the roof now, taking potshots at everything that flies past."

"They're so weird!" she said, shaking her head. "But I've gotta say, they're… well…nice as well. Well, no, 'nice' isn't the right word…cute? No…"

"They're like lizard puppies that can think," I offered.

"Yeah!" she agreed enthusiastically, laughing at the comparison, and I saw what I'd seen the other night when we'd flirted late on: a flash of her personality that was carefree and joyful. She smiled at me, then Mike's voice rang out as he said something to Kelly, and Alyssa suddenly went red-cheeked and looked away, clearly remembering the other night as well.

"Look…" She said, stepping closer and speaking quietly.

"Nothing happened, Alyssa," I said quietly but firmly, smiling gently at her.

"Thanks," she breathed, relief clear in her voice. "So, Kelly told me how you two met…what's happening there, then?" She smirked, changing the subject.

"I really don't know…" I said honestly. "She's beautiful; hell, she's amazing, and medical skill, as well as law? Perfect for me, especially here and now, but…"

"But?"

"But the world just ended, everything is going tits-up, and I don't know if I'll be alive tomorrow. Doesn't really seem like the right time for a relationship, you know?" I grimaced.

"Really?" Alyssa countered, looking at me intently. "Sounds like the perfect time for one, really. You see things changing anytime soon?"

"Well, no…" I admitted reluctantly.

"So, you think what Mike, Amy, and I want to see is you two staring at each other like lovestruck puppies, then? I saw the way you two look at each other." She bumped my shoulder, smiling mischievously.

"Ah, shut it," I grumbled, and she laughed at me.

"Look, all I'm saying is that Kelly doesn't like many people. With the things she's done and seen, she's used to seeing the worst in people. If she likes you…well…maybe you're not the complete fuckup I thought you were," Alyssa winked, and I snorted, returning at her smile.

"Wow, thanks for that ringing endorsement!" I scoffed, and we both turned as Kelly stormed out of the 'kitchen.'

"Right. Alyssa, she's your daughter, so either you or Mike can stay here with her. I *literally* have only the clothes on my back. I need more, and I need…other things. You sort this shit out." She frowned at her sister in law, ignoring Mike's protestations that, as his younger sister, she should stay behind. "Hey, Matt? I heard about this 'magic' you can do, but I haven't seen it. Want to show me?" I grinned cheekily at the opportunity she'd just handed me.

"*That's what she said…* "I said quickly, and she paused for a minute, closing her eyes and muttering.

"Give me strength…" Her eyes shot open. "Just to be clear, I mean…"

"It's okay…" I grinned. "I get it! Look…" I held up my torn, bloody, and completely filthy pants. I slipped my mind partially into the Dungeon Senses and selected them, then selected 'Repair' and accepted the mana cost of five points.

I heard Kelly gasp as my pants blurred in my hands, tears mending themselves, dirt and bloodstains vanishing, and in seconds, they looked brand-new.

"Now *that* is magic," she whispered, moving over and plucking my pants from my hands. She examined them closely, turning them over and over, and even sniffing at them cautiously, before smiling hugely. "Can you do this for my clothes?" she asked, gesturing down at herself. I noticed that she was wearing sturdy utilitarian black jeans, a baggy green top, and mismatching boots that looked more suited to the army than her outfit, but I nodded.

"I'd need to touch them, though, with the Dungeon senses, and you'd need to…not be wearing them?" I said carefully, trying not to smile.

"You're determined to get me naked, aren't you?" she retorted, trying to hide a tight smile. "All of my clothes?" she repeated, and I shrugged.

"Just the ones you want me to clean and repair…" I said.

"All of them," she agreed firmly. I closed my eyes, finding that the charge was back at seven points, so clearly the teams were doing well, steadily working away. I nodded to her in confirmation, opening my eyes.

"Depending on the items themselves, I can do some. I don't know what until I…touch them…though. It's not me being weird!" I clarified hastily, seeing Mike's glower. "I mean touch them with the Dungeon Sense. If I attempt it when you're wearing the clothes, it won't work, and I don't know what it'll cost until I've examined them. For example, my pants cost five points, and I have seven available right now."

"Right," Kelly said, determined. "I need clean clothes. Alyssa, you come with me; Matt, you can wait outside the door." She gestured to one of the side rooms. "I'll strip off, Alyssa passes you the clothes, so don't get any ideas about sneaking in, and you can clean what you can."

"Um, I'll be fine here. I need to be in the Dungeon Sense for this." I said. "You can literally just put them on the floor in there with you if you want…" I offered politely, and she looked at me skeptically.

"And when you're in this 'Dungeon Sense,' what do you see?" she asked slowly.

"Everything," I replied honestly. "It's like being a ghost, I guess. I can fly though the walls or floors to wherever I need to be inside the Dungeon's Aura. I don't 'see' the way I normally do; it's more of a mix of sight and wire drawings, like engineering outlines, but yeah." I shrugged nonchalantly.

"Okay, new house rule," Alyssa interjected quickly. "Anywhere we're getting changed and the loos are off limits. I don't need you floating through when I'm getting changed…" she said, frowning suspiciously at me.

"Whoa, nope!" I held up defensive hands, shaking my head. "I mean no to spying on you, not to the rule," I quickly clarified. "I've never spied on you, and never would…don't worry!" I said hastily, although a little voice inside lamented the missed opportunity. I squashed the voice harshly and went on. "Like I said, it's all outlines and wire frames anyway. It's about as exciting as a topographical map. Seriously, Kelly, you and Alyssa go get changed. Just put the clothes somewhere you feel safe, and then call and tell me where to look, okay?" I said, exasperated as the girls all scowled at me, and I caught Mike staring pointedly too, clearly wondering if I'd been watching his wife. "You all know the Dungeon is part of me, right?" I said, frowning back. "I can sort of sense everything in here, and it's weird enough, so let's just move on."

There were a few minutes of uncertainty, but the awkward moment was broken when Kelly shrugged and set off walking for the far end of the room, and Mike asked me loudly if I could do his clothes next.

I looked him over, observing his standard Army camo pants and olive-green top. I nodded to him in thanks, realizing what he'd not said: that he'd trust me to do it.

"I can, but it'll have to be a bit later, need time for the charge to build up, after all," I answered loudly enough for the others to hear.

"Fair enough," he said, grinning. A few seconds later, Alyssa shouted that Kelly's clothes were ready next to her in the main room, and as I slipped into the Dungeon Sense, I heard her call out that Kelly was in the room behind her, and I wasn't to go peeking.

Truthfully, until this awkward conversation, it had not really occurred to me, as I'd had too much else to worry about, but now, knowing Kelly was literally on the other side of a thin internal wall, stark naked, considering the items in the pile of clothes on the floor…I froze, considering if I should…well, I knew I shouldn't…but…

I mentally scolded myself and focused on the clothes, examining each item quickly. Her underwear was cheapest, at two points each, and then she'd apparently been wearing a small top under her green one, which was three more points. Her jeans, green top, and boots came in at five, three, and four, respectively. I checked my points and found that I had nine available, so I did her underwear and her jeans, then slipped out of the sense enough to call out that I was going to try and gather enough of a charge to do the rest, and that she could put those things on now. I quickly sent myself winging around the room, gathering up all the rubbish that Amy had been piling aside, absorbing it and more, before picking a crate of beer and absorbing that as well.

I quickly returned and did the last of her clothes before slipping back into my body and sitting up.

"Okay, all done!" I called, turning to Mike. "I broke down some rubbish, so I've got four points left; probably enough to clean that top, if you want?" I offered, and he grimaced down at the bloodstained top he was wearing. He'd clearly tried to wash it at some point, but he grinned at me as he pulled it off and dropped it onto the floor. Seconds later, I was sitting back up, and he was pulling a spotless top back on, sniffing it.

"Man, it even smells fresh! Thank you!" he said, shaking his head. "I don't care what else you can do; if you can clean clothes like this, can you cook? I don't know where I would go for a divorce these days, but I'll damn well marry you!" He grinned good-naturedly, his eyes twinkling with laughter.

"Ha! I know, man. Clean clothes; simplest pleasure in the world!" I agreed, grinning back at him. "And, in fact…" I lowered my voice conspiratorially. "If we can get some cooked food, I can absorb it, then reproduce it fully, piping hot and all!"

"Oh, hell yes!" he said happily. "Any limits?"

"Not that I know yet, but we'd need to test it…for the sake of science, of course…"

"Of course!" he repeated, mock seriously, as the girls walked back over to join us. Kelly smoothed her top, looking much more comfortable, even if her cheeks were red.

"Thanks, Matt," she said gratefully, looking around at Mike and Alyssa. "So, who's coming and who's staying?"

"Well, there's one more who's joining us…not counting our escort," I said, having just read a notification. The others blinked at me in surprise, and I called out clearly for all to hear, "Jack! Here boy!"

The pile of material I'd been using as a bed had been dumped in the corner atop his damaged form at some point, as Kelly and Mike had brought sleeping bags, and when it stirred, shaking and falling to the ground, everyone spun around. Jack struggled out of the cloth, shaking himself and smoothly moving forward. Stopping a foot in front of me, he totally ignored the others, even though both Alyssa and Mike had guns trained on him, and Kelly had pulled out what looked suspiciously like my diving knife, quickly placing herself between Jack and Amy.

"It's all right, everyone!" I said hastily, even as Alyssa blinked, recognizing him.

"I thought it was destroyed!" she said, amazed.

"What was?" Mike asked, confused as he saw her lower her gun.

"He…it? Nah, fuck it, *HE's* my dog; Jack," I explained, reaching out and awkwardly patting him on the head. Jack sat stoically, totally uninterested in the petting, and I shrugged. Dropping my hand, I turned and stared at them all before asking the obvious question. "Is that my fucking knife?" I shook my head as I met Kelly's eyes, who colored and relaxed slightly, after seeing that Alyssa had calmed down. She probably figured that a robot dog was one of the less weird things she'd seen recently.

"Well, you didn't need it at the time…" she stated, slipping the knife back into its sheath, and then having the gall to tuck it down the back of her pants to go on. "But it's a bit awkward to carry, so if you could sort out a hip sheath for me?"

"Seriously? What the hell is it with your family, dude?" I asked Mike with annoyance, noting that he had my shotgun, and Alyssa had my handgun. "Are you all thieving sods, or is Amy the black sheep of the family, as she doesn't grab my weapons at the first opportunity?" Mike snorted in amusement, then shrugged.

"I'd rather apologize for using a weapon that wasn't mine, than need one and not have it." he said earnestly, and I waited. "What's up?" he asked me after a few seconds of awkward silence.

"I give up," I sighed. Clearly the apology wasn't forthcoming, and neither was me being given my guns back, from the looks of things. I was more than a little annoyed, but I knew where I'd left my sword and rifle, so I decided it was time to make the rules clear. "Look, Alyssa, I need you to stay here, please…" I started, and she immediately began to complain, until I held up one hand and talked over her protestations.

"I don't care. I need you to stay here, as someone needs to both keep an eye on Amy, and keep the research going. That, unless you've forgotten, is your job here!" She subsided with a sullen glare as I went on. "Kelly, get a list of everything that Alyssa and Amy need or want, please. Mike, you get to be pack mule today, congratulations!" As everyone started to speak up, I slammed my palms together hard, the crack echoing around the small room. In the silence that followed, I pressed on.

"Look, I'm going to make this very clear. I want you all to stay. It's true that I need you, and you need me, not to mention, what I can eventually do with MY Dungeon, but let's get this laid out from the start. It is MY Dungeon. It's bonded to me. If I die, it dies." I doubted that was true, but I didn't need any power plays coming up in the future. "I intend to make a safe refuge for people here. I'll expand the Dungeon Aura out to cover the entirety of the city at some point, if I can, as it's the corrupted mana that spawns these creatures, like that fucking Eidolon. One of the Dungeon's primary purposes is to absorb that mana and alter it, releasing purified mana into the area in its place. A side effect of this is that those who have the most access to it will grow stronger, physically, mentally; the lot. You'll be able to 'level' and probably far more. If you can get to level five, you'll even get to choose a class, and that comes with a fuck-ton of perks and boosts and spells and shit. The point is, though, I need to work to reach that point. I need a team to support me, and you need somewhere safe to live, and a purpose, frankly."

I looked from one person to another, judging how my little speech was going down. "You all want to help people? This is how we do it. Once we've got the prerequisite structures in place, we can start to mass produce food, medicines, guns. and probably more. My 'Firearms' skill mentions energy weapons, after all. I already had to rescue Alyssa from one gang of scumbags, and we all know that in situations like this, the scum rises to the top."

I huffed out a breath, reading the looks, the way that Kelly watched me, Amy's look of concerned hope, Alyssa and Mike, who'd moved to hold hands as they listened to me.

"They're out there, and they're going to do what scum always does: take and take and take. They're going to hurt good people, starve them, and worse. With no power, no communication, and no leadership, the country—hell, the world—will break down into armed camps. There'll be raiders, Vikings, bandits, you name it. The army and police are fractured into gangs themselves. Hospitals will be raided by people who need drugs, and once they're all gone? We all know millions will have died already, possibly billions soon. The only chance we have?" I said fervently, lifting my arms out to gesture around us.

"It's this; this tiny Dungeon. In here, we can make everything we need for the future. We can secure ourselves, then start to grow, providing food and shelter, laws and goods, safety and leadership. What we can't do, though, is save everyone. We need to accept that and work to save ourselves and secure the Dungeon first. We have to keep this place safe. To do that, I need to know where you stand. Do you want to help me, knowing my intentions? No hard feelings if not, but I need to hear it from you." I waited as the silence spread.

"So, what? You want to be king?" Mike asked me slowly, eventually breaking the awkward silence.

"Hah, no. I'm not looking for a title!" I said, grinning. "Seriously, though, I *AM* the Dungeon, and as such, I will make the final decisions here. I want you to help me, though; talk me out of it if you think I'm doing wrong. I'll listen. I won't promise to change my mind every time, but I *will* listen."

"And if we say no?" Mike pressed suddenly, and I noted the way he stroked the butt of the shotgun with one finger.

"Then you can make a decision. Either you leave, if that's what you want to do, or if you want to stay, I'll assign you jobs each day, and I'll feed you, but you'll have no say in any of this Dungeon's growth or our policies."

"You'd not just kick us out?" He gazed at me intently.

"No," I said, sighing heavily. "Seriously, I didn't know Alyssa when I agreed to save her. I was going to leave the damn Ghast alone when Spot and Amy got its attention, and I had no choice but to fight it or leave it to kill her. I'm laying down the law, because I think it's better to do that now, so we all know where we stand, but I'm not a shit. I'd give you somewhere safe to live, either way."

"Alyssa told me what you did, and so did Amy." Mike admitted grudgingly. "I'll agree to a trial, if you will? We do what you say for, say, a week. Then we reconsider. If it's not working out, we go our separate ways. If it is, you give us real jobs, and we work together…with you at the top of the food chain."

"Thank you; I accept," I said appreciatively, and the others nodded slowly, before gathering together as I left the room. Making my way up the stairs, I reached out and summoned the four armed goblins, along with the kobold archer. I stood in the alleyway, deliberately not listening in on the conversation they were having downstairs. I gave the group orders to follow along with me, and to watch out, warning me of any threats, then waited for a few minutes.

Then longer.

After nearly twenty minutes, I'd nearly given in, preparing to sit down and sink into the Dungeon Sense in order to listen in and see what the hell was being said, when Kelly and Mike appeared, both armed. They walked up to the doorway and paused, eyeing me cautiously, and it felt like the world held its breath, until Kelly winked at me.

"Sorry, I had to fix my hair," she said, and I snorted, while I could tell that she had, in fact, taken the time to put some makeup on, while Mike shrugged as though it didn't matter. I gestured to the goblins and kobold and spoke quickly, holding my hands up in mock pleading.

"Don't shoot! Friendlies!" I insisted, and Kelly raised an eyebrow at me, as if to say '*Really, is that the best you can do?*'.

"So, first stop is the cathedral. Don't suppose either of you went in there when you found me?" I asked, and they both shook their heads.

"Okay then, I need to grab my gear, and we need to search the place, just in case. Then we're off to get food. There's a place a few streets over that has a load of army surplus; we'll check them out, then hit a supermarket a few streets past that, then loop back towards the Dungeon, calling in at a pair of clothes shops on the way, men's and women's…no prizes for guessing which one will take longer…"

"Yeah, you lot always take forever," Kelly quipped, smiling uncertainly at me before looking away.

"Damn right, we do. Got to look pretty for you, after all," I returned laughingly, leading the way. Pausing at the mouth of the alley, I felt very conscious of Mike walking only a few steps behind me with a loaded shotgun, and Kelly wielding a handgun and a knife, while I was unarmed.

They didn't know about my spell, but still.

The goblins and kobold seemed to have picked up on my mood and were jittery, spending as much time watching the pair of humans as they did everything else.

Once I was satisfied it was clear, we jogged across the empty streets to the cathedral entrance. The patches of blood and drag marks on the pavement indicated where I'd met the pair earlier.

"Be careful inside. I know we defeated it, but I don't know whether it's dead or not. I get rewarded as long as it's incapacitated, and death is not the only criteria. It's weird, but that's the way this works, for some reason," I explained quietly, sending the goblins in but keeping the kobold near to me, just in case.

We stepped inside carefully, easing past piles of debris smeared with bloody streaks. The doors had been left open, and one swung crazily on a hinge that I didn't remember being broken, but I quickly found what I'd been looking for first: my sword.

I swept it up, spinning it as I rolled my wrists and cut a figure of eight in the air. I reveled in the motion, feeling all manly and shit, until I heard Mike's whispered words, pitched to carry across the room.

"If you play with it too much, you'll go blind..."

Kelly started to snigger, and I felt my cheeks flush. That bastard! Ruining my moment like that!

"I'd throw you a beating...but we both know you'd like it," I growled back, shaking my head as I moved away from him. I made my way through the main area, clambering across more rubble and searching carefully as I went. It had to be here; I just knew it had been somewhere around here...there! I sheathed my sword and reached down, sweeping some debris aside and lifting my rifle.

I made sure the clip was still seated right and flicked the safety on, tipping the barrel down and giving it a shake, hoping that if anything had gotten inside, it'd fall out, when I heard a low whistle.

"Where the hell did you find that?" Mike asked, approaching quietly.

"I took it off an asshole in the park a while ago, then dropped it here during the fight." I shrugged noncommittally. "Now, try to keep quiet. The Eidolon was there..." I said, pointing with my rifle barrel at a big patch of blackened and dried blood, and the drag marks that led to the massive pit in the center of the cathedral.

"Think it's still alive?" Mike asked, hefting his shotgun.

"Damn well hope not," I muttered, moving closer to the shattered stone rim of the hole.

"Don't suppose you fancy swapping?" Mike offered, his voice still low. "I'm trained with a rifle, and even if it's not an SA80A3 like my usual, I'll bet I'm a lot better with it than you are…"

"First, you probably are; second, I nearly died to get these guns; and third, shut the fuck up, dude, we're sneaking here…" I muttered back to him, shooting him a glare that he totally ignored as he continued looking my rifle over lasciviously.

"Play nice, boys…" Kelly whispered, equally unaffected by the glare I shot her, although we all froze when the first goblin stood at the edge of the pit and looked in, barking something in its language.

I grimaced regretfully, figuring I needed them to learn English as well, and made my way over to it, carefully keeping my rifle trained on the pit, despite the way that the goblin, quickly joined by the others of its kind, and Jack, stared down dully.

Upon reaching the edge, I peered in, before straightening up and swearing.

Down at the bottom of the pit, easily thirty feet below us, was a nest. Piles of broken bones and rotting flesh, tufts of fur and hair, shattered stone, and torn coffins lined the center, with three small passages leading off into the darkness, seemingly into the sewers. Right in the middle lay the Eidolon.

It was clearly dead, bones jutted out at all sorts of impossible angles. Blood coated it, congealed and giving rise to clouds of flies, with a veritable horde of maggots working their way across the corpse, but the thing that got to me was its guts.

It'd been torn open and was deflated, with a trail from at least one, though probably two or three, creatures leading outwards and disappearing down into the tunnels.

THIRTY

I SWORE REPEATEDLY, STARING down into the pit and chewing on a knuckle as I tried to think.

"What's up?" Mike asked me, looking down himself. "Looks dead, whatever it was." He shrugged, clearly unphased.

"It is, but the fucking thing had…kids or something, I don't know! You just had to come and interrupt, didn't you?" I snapped at him as I vented my frustration.

"What?" He gaped at me in disbelief.

"Yesterday! If you hadn't fucking well attacked my Mageling, the others would have stayed in here, finishing it off, rather than leaving it to have to come defend me. For fuck's sake, man! Now I'm gonna have to go down there, go crawling around in the dark, and get murdered, all to fix your fuckup!" I snarled, knowing, even as the words left my mouth, that I was being unfair, and that knowledge was only driving my anger higher.

"Hey! Fuck you, asshole! We came to help, and you'd have fucking died if we hadn't!"

"Bullshit!" I snapped. "I had it all under control…"

"You were bleeding out and being dragged away by monsters," Kelly cut in calmly.

"MY monsters!" I clarified, and she shook her head.

"Look, Matt, Mike apologized for killing the goblin, and you said you understood, so either you lied, or he's not the one you're really mad at right now?" Her tone remained neutral, though her eyes gazed sharply around the cathedral.

"I…I…" I spluttered.

"Exactly. So, you want to explain what we need to do, or are you just going to rant at us for saving your life?" she demanded, and I glared at her.

"Don't look at her like that," Mike growled at me, and I glared at him instead, before turning away and drawing in a deep breath, rubbing my face with one hand as I tried to get control over myself. It took a long moment, filled with low grumbling and muttering coming from Mike that kept my irritation boiling over, even if my anger was simmering down.

"Look..." I said, sighing and turning back to the pair of them and my team. "I'm sorry. You're right. This isn't your fault, and shit happens. Basically, whatever that creature spawned is gonna be bad news for everyone, unless we get those offspring killed. Those tunnels are too dark for us all to go..." I huffed out a breath and shook my head regretfully. "I know this is a mistake...but here," I said, holding out the rifle to Mike.

"What's going on?" he asked, suspicion clear in his voice.

"Someone needs to go and finish this, and a rifle is going to be too big to use in there. Give me your shotgun, and..."

"Hell, no. If any of us are going down there, it's me! I've had training to clear rooms, so I stand a much better chance than you..."

"The goblins can see better than any of us. I can use them to scout; you can't. Plus, I've got the dog," I said simply.

"Then make me a torch!" Mike countered.

"And you think you alone, down there, will have better chances than me with a gang of goblins?" I asked. "When all I have to do to get more is find the section of the sewers nearest to the Dungeon and summon them?"

"Or, you could both stop measuring your dicks, and you could send the goblins and Jack in, because that's what they're for, and then we could go get what we need. You could make more goblins or whatever this afternoon, give them whatever gear will work best, and just keep sending them until they do the job, and nobody has to go down there." Kelly pointed out, adding her voice into the building argument.

We both stopped and looked at each other, then at her, then at each other again. It was clearly the best option, and neither of us really had wanted to go in anyway. It was just the best choice at the time.

"Okay...that sounds more sensible..." I admitted slowly, nodding gratefully to her. I ordered the goblins into the sewers, with instructions to track whatever was down there and to kill absolutely anything that wasn't human. Jack went along to hunt the damn mini Eidolons, or whatever they were. Then I told the kobold to get busy making traps all around the pit, just in case, and then to return to its vermin-killing post on the roof of the Dungeon.

"So..." I said quietly to Kelly, as we watched the goblins clambering down into the pit. There was a moment of concern as something moved, and the goblins all fixated on it, but when one jumped in, swinging its club, then shoved something with a long, hairy tail into its mouth, we all relaxed.

"Yeah?" Kelly prompted me, peering at me out of the corner of her eye as she clambered over some fractured slabs of paving.

"Umm, sorry about that…" I started sheepishly, and she snorted.

"Are you?"

"What?"

"Sorry for snarling at us, sorry for going all 'I'm-Billy-Big-Balls-and-this-is-all-my-shit…' or sorry for trying to go off and stick your head in a sewer where you'd almost certainly get murdered, leaving us to starve?" she listed off, scowling at me.

"Ah…well, no. Not really all of that," I admitted, shrugging. "I'm sorry for snapping at you, and at you, Mike," I said raising my voice so he could hear me. "I'm also sorry for laying down the law, but I honestly think it needed to be said; leaving it just 'out there' only leads to trouble later on. As to the sewers, you saw that thing. That was an 'Evolved' version of the Eidolon. I'm assuming that whatever escaped were kids or spawn or something…because when I first saw that thing, it was totally different to the version I ended up fighting in the end. Killing things like this when they're weak is the only way to go."

"So, sticking your dick in a meat grinder seemed like it'd pay off well in the end?" Mike asked, sticking his head out of the door and checking from side to side before gesturing for us to follow him.

"I wouldn't put it like that…" I growled, glaring at him, then abruptly stifling a grin myself when I saw the grin he was trying to hide. "Asshole."

"Hey, I just wondered…" he said, looking over and winking at me. I shook my head and looked over at Kelly, who'd totally missed the byplay and was looking down the street. I moved closer to her and inspected the street in the same direction, but I couldn't see anything.

"What's up?" I asked, and she shook her head.

"I thought I saw something, but I guess not." She dismissed it, shrugging blandly.

"Okay; let's get a move on. The store I'm thinking of first is about ten minutes away." I set off jogging, the other two catching up a few seconds later.

"So, how'd you make it up here so fast?" I asked Mike a few minutes later as we paused at a crossroads, all watching different sections of the road. The sound of our feet on the pavement had been the only thing I could hear all the way so far, beyond the occasional bird calling or dog barking in the distance.

"I ran," he admitted simply. "Me and a load of the others left the base; the Military Police had locked the armory down, so we had to do it unarmed, but a bunch of us with families left, cut the fence, and started running. I nicked a bike—pedal, I mean. Used that for about a day and a half, then it broke and I nicked a horse, just kept going really. It was a bit of a shitty trip, but I had my rucksack, I looted a few places as I went, a few good people fed me when they understood I was just passing through..." He shrugged and let out a sigh. "It really wasn't that bad until I got to about eighty miles out; last stretch, really. I met a couple guys who were hassling a young lad, I stepped in and they pulled knives. It...it ended badly. The kid who tried to stand up for himself got stabbed in the neck."

"Shit," I said, pausing and looking over at him.

"Yeah. Well, they won't be doing that shit again, that's for sure," he said grimly. "Until then, I'd been thinking I'd maybe made a mistake, and that the rumors we'd heard the first week at the base were just that, rumors. By the time I left, we were practically being kept on lockdown, full 'Rule of Six' on gatherings, you name it. The base Commandant thought that would calm things down; if we couldn't mingle, I mean. It made it worse. Two days, we lasted, then boom! We just all rushed the fence one night. Clippers out, cut our way through; half the lads on guard duty went with us. The last day, knowing how close I was to my girls, and running on blisters all the way, I kept seeing the signs of fights, houses burned down. People talking about murderers...One old dude pulled me aside in Gateshead, said there was a guy going around murdering anyone in a gang. He'd burned a house down and left a load of bodies behind. Horrific shit, mate."

"Uh...over by the 'Valley'?" I asked, and he nodded in confirmation.

"Yeah. Why? Third one I passed in two days."

"I...uh...heard about it." I muttered, swallowing hard. I wanted to tell them it wasn't like that, but our little alliance was tenuous at best right now, and telling them I'd gone all 'MurderHobo' twice already, if I included the gypsies in my flat, just wasn't going to go down well. Hell, I knew they seemed to accept what the Dungeon was for now, but the first time they saw people actually try it and die? That'd be a hell of a test for our group.

"Well, I knew it'd all gone to shit when I heard that. Looking back on the trip, I'd seen the signs all the way. I'd just not seen them for what they were. Smoke rising here and there, shouts, gangs that roamed and stared down everyone...I've seen similar in the sandpit, but here? I just didn't see it for what it was." He admitted, shrugging and looking away.

I thought at first that he didn't care, until he turned back and I saw the red-rimmed eyes. Then I realized he'd been blaming himself since everything had first happened for not being at home.

"Look…thanks for being there, alright?" he said gruffly, then he coughed and gestured forward. "Are we going, or what? I don't want Amy and Aly there too long alone, all right?"

"Yeah…no worries, mate." I reassured him. "Let's go." We jogged quickly across the main road, diving into an alleyway and up. We held our breath as we squeezed past piles of rotting rubbish and ignored the scuttling of creatures as they fled. "Might need to direct the squad this way soon…" I muttered, recognizing the signs of feral rats everywhere.

"What was that?" Kelly asked, and I smiled at her.

"Sorry," I chuckled. "Just thinking aloud."

"Oh…okay," she said, smiling back. "So, anything else you want to tell me?" I paused, reaching the corner and sticking my head out to look around, and turning back to face them.

"It's clear…the surplus store is three doors down on the right. Looks like it's been hit already, but to hell with it; let's go." I led the way, rifle in hand, sword on my back. It was less than two dozen meters to the door, and we paused, looking cautiously at the doorway.

"Well…" Mike said eventually.

"Yeah, this isn't looking promising…" I admitted, shaking my head.

The metal security grates that covered the door were wrenched up, but the part that had been padlocked to a loop in the floor was still attached. The rest had been torn open by something with massive strength, and judging from the marks in the slowly swaying grate, it'd been done by hand. There were clear indents for three huge fingers, as well as a little blood on the torn metal, thankfully dried.

"What the ever-loving fuck did that?" Mike asked and I paled, staring into the darkness intently before turning to the pair of them.

"I don't know, but this just got a whole lot more dangerous. You two are now officially 'overwatch', as I don't want you in there with me." I threw my rifle to Mike, who caught it and scowled at me as I held my hand out to Kelly. "I need the handgun, Kelly; Mike will give you his shotgun. You do close protection for him, and he'll handle ranged for us all."

"We already went through this…" she started to protest, and I shook my head.

"That was when we were possibly going into a sewer where nobody could see, and where a low roof meant we needed to use guns. Here, with that high roof?" I frowned, gesturing, "I'm going in, and you're my backup." I gestured again, and Kelly sighed and passed me the handgun, then tugging on the shotgun that Mike still held as he watched me.

"You know this is stupid," he said, glowering fiercely. "I'm trained for…"

"Monster hunting?" I demanded, cutting him off. "You got a sword, Mike? Ever used one in a fight?"

"*You* trained in it?" he fired back.

"Nope, but I've done it before, and I'm 'Billy-big-balls,' remember? Now, hush." I drew the sword and slowly entered the room, ignoring the pair and their indignant scoffs.

I blocked out the sound of their low argument as I stepped over the torn grate and through the shattered glass door, my foot crunching on the glass. The room ahead of me was a mess. What had once been a space filled with neat, regular racks on one wall, the middle filled with organized stands displaying clothes, MRE's, and various other items, had been smashed indiscriminately onto the floor. Claw marks down one wall ended in a dried blood spatter and a smear of blood, indicating that a wounded body had been dragged deeper into the building at one point.

"Well…that's not happy-making…" I hissed under my breath, leaning over and flicking a coat off the floor with the tip of my sword. The tip of a finger had been poking out from beneath. Disturbingly. the rest of a hand was exposed, ending in jagged flesh at the wrist, and the bones were clearly shattered by something with tremendous force.

"What do you see?" Kelly called out, and I flinched, hearing a growl lifting into the air from the back of the room where it was too dark to see anything. I heard Mike shushing Kelly quickly, but the damage was done. Deeper within the room, something stirred, accompanied by the sounds of hurrying feet and opening doors. I squinted, trying to make the shadows out, but the darkness back there, with the only light coming in through the shattered doorway behind me, and being shielded by the piles of debris, made it next to impossible to see.

After a few seconds, I could hear the sound of clawed feet approaching, lots of them, and more growls, as a lot of somethings started through into the main room from a back area. I slowly backed up, wanting to get through the door before they emerged, as it'd make a natural chokepoint. I wasn't so lucky. The growls picked up in fierceness as soon as I started to back away, with dogs suddenly appearing out of the gloom.

I paused, barely able to see their outlines, and wondering why they looked so wrong, until one moved ahead of the pack, stepping out into the light and snarling at me.

"Well, fuck," I blurted, taken aback. It was a huge Doberman, easily twice the size of any I'd seen before, but where a normal dog might have been a freak of nature or a cross with a Great Dane or something, this one was clearly not a natural evolution.

It stood as high as my chest at its head, with a spiked collar. Half of its skin and fur was missing on one side of its face, and worst of all…a small figure sat astride its back, balanced atop a saddle, glaring its hatred.

"Huuuuman!" It growled, its tiny pointed teeth flashing as it jutted a long makeshift spear at me. The weapon was blatantly a survival knife strapped to the end of a walking stick, but considering I was staring at a clearly wild goblin, one that was evolved beyond my own, and had not only tamed this huge fucking dog but had made its own weapons, I felt my balls shrivel up a bit. Especially as it could speak, and judging from the movements around it, as more dogs with riders stepped out, it was the leader of a pack.

From the back of the room, there came a bellow, along with a crunching noise as something shifted. A huge form slowly stumbled forward, shouldering the doorframe apart as it emerged, and I felt my blood run cold.

It was a fucking troll. It wore chains and a muzzle, with a saddle braced atop its shoulders. A small figure glared hatefully at me from where it hunched over, trying to avoid beheading itself on a light fitting. I was facing off against a troll that was being ridden by something that barely came up to its knee.

"Well massage my balls lovingly with a sandblaster…" I blurted, the words falling from lips that hung open in shock. Mike's voice sounded from behind me, his tone rough and clearly concerned.

"You've…uh, got this, right, boss man?" he said, swallowing past a suddenly dry throat.

"When it all kicks off, you take out any you can; then get you and Kelly the fuck out of here," I insisted, trying not to show the fact that I was seconds away from soiling my pants.

"Yeah, I don't think we're going to get far…" Mike said quietly, nodding to the dogs as they slowly moved out of the darkness, even as I backed up, shifting my sword from left to right warningly.

"I'll hold them in the door," I said. "Get back to the Dungeon and stay there. Do whatever you can to keep things together 'til I make it home."

"I don't…" Mike started to argue, and I cut him off.

"Just fucking do it, Mike!" I snarled. I heard him start to swear, and snap something to Kelly, who began arguing back at him.

"…his choice!" Mike snarled, my focus on the slowly advancing gang meaning I'd missed the first bit.

"But…" Kelly started, and Mike spoke over her.

"See you on the far side," he said, directed, I assumed, to me. "Firing!" And suddenly the crack of the rifle echoed repeatedly as he cycled through the clip at speed. Bullets flew through the air, and he lived up to his words, as the goblin rider was the first to fall, his head disintegrating under a direct hit just above the nose. Other goblins fell, then the dogs. The troll ignored the rounds that slammed into it, its rider squealing and hunching down lower as bullets peppered the thick skin beneath it.

"I'm out!" Mike called, and I yanked the clips I had, one full and one half, and threw them to him.

"Take them and go!" I snarled, firing my handgun at a dog that rushed forward. I heard Mike slamming the clip into the rifle, followed by an enormous boom that nearly deafened me, as Kelly fired the shotgun from her shoulder, stepping forward until the barrel was inches from my ear.

I flinched instinctively, gaping at her in shock as the dog practically exploded, a full round of buckshot taking it in the face. As it fell spasming to the floor, exceedingly dead, a second and third dashed forward, jostling each other in their rush to get through to us.

"We're off!" Mike screamed at me, and he yanked Kelly back.

"No, we have to help him!" Kelly shouted, and I stepped into the gap, spinning my sword to build momentum. I changed the pattern, flicking my sword around warningly as I holstered the handgun and slashed the next closest dog's throat.

"Kelly!" I shouted. "You know that dick measuring contest?"

"Y…yeah?" she said, pausing.

"I'd have won!" I snapped. "Now, go! Or I swear you'll never feel me prove it!" It was a stupid thing to say, especially in light of all the cool heroic things I could have said, 'I'll be back', 'Yippie-Ki-ay-Motherfucker' or even, 'I will have my vengeance, in this life, or the next' or a million of others, but nope, I had to think with my dick.

"You asshole!" she cried, but as I swung my blade hard, twisting low and cutting across from right to left to slice the second hound across the foreleg. The strike sent it flashing through the air, even as the dog screamed and hit the floor, thrashing around. I glanced back briefly and saw her, looking back at me, cursing at me from over Mike's shoulder as he ran.

"Jack, if you can hear me, get your metal arse to me!" I growled aloud, projecting the thoughts internally at the same time. I stabbed forwards, the sword glancing off the shoulder of the massive dog as it tried to get back to its feet, sending it skidding backwards as a second hound leapt over it, mouth opening wide as it tried to bite me.

I twisted my sword sideways, the blade out of the way already, unfortunately, and I slammed the pommel into its face, shoving it aside, though I was forced back a step by its bulk.

"Thank you, Markus!" I barked, thankful for his lessons on stance as much as anything else. Without them, I'd have gone under already, I had no doubt. Then it all went to shit as a dart flew out of the darkness, slamming into my right shoulder. I swore, recognizing it, as I moved to the left, ducking out of sight and leaning against the wall quickly. I yanked it free of my arm, throwing it aside, even as I felt burning pain erupt from the wound.

"Fuckers!" I ground out, switching the sword to my left hand and struggling to draw the handgun. I'd recognized the Flamedart spell that had hit me, and checking my notifications quickly, then dismissing them, I saw it was a far more powerful version than my own goblins had.

You have been hit by Diseased Goblin Mageling's Flamedart for 10 points of damage per second...
You have torn out Diseased Goblin Mageling's Flamedart, resulting in fifty points of damage!

"Holy shit!" I ground out, struggling to lift my gun and aim it. The barrel shook as I shoved it around the corner of the door and fired it three times into the room in quick succession. I heard screams and a snarl from something, before I felt the ground reverberate, and I swore, jumping back from the wall.

I barely moved in time, as the doorframe and a good part of the wall was smashed out by the troll shouldering its way through, screaming in rage at the holes I'd blown in its stomach. I backed up as it struggled out, shoving the disintegrating doorframe aside, stretching up to its full height, and raising its arms to the sky, screaming in fury.

I backed up, recalling that the saddle on its back was empty and a smear of blood was all that remained of its rider. Which meant no one was controlling it. Shit.

"Okay, then…time to even the field…" I muttered, backing away and getting ready to run down the road towards the south, as opposed to the west, were the others had gone. "Trolls didn't like fire in the games; is it true?" I asked aloud, unwilling to waste the mana to 'Examine' the creature when I could just cast a much more fun spell instead.

"Incinerate!" I whispered at it, deliberately focusing as hard as I could, ignoring the traditional game mechanics where it'd normally be used. The spell ignited on the creature's head and neck, and despite it being easily nine feet tall, with thick grey rhino-hide covering its body, it clearly had no defense against the spell, as it staggered suddenly, screaming in agony and clutching at its head before collapsing forward to hit the floor. Its skin and skull smoldered while steam leaked from its eyes, ears, and mouth.

"Oh yeah, motherfucker!" I snarled as it fell, and then, as more howls rose in the shop behind the fallen bulk, I started to run.

I sprinted down the street, zig zagging as best I could, clutching at my bleeding arm. I heard a horn being blown behind me, the sound rising into the air, mournful and long, and I could hear my breathing echoing raggedly as I turned the corner, skidding on a carrier bag blown by the wind. I just had to get away from them, and…

A second horn joined the first, echoing up from the distance to the east, as I headed west, and then a howl sounded from behind me, and I looked back. A huge dog had taken the corner and was bearing down on me, its rider, another small goblin, hauling back on a small bow, wild glee filling its face.

I didn't have time to dodge. I'd never hit it with the gun, and I didn't dare let it get any closer to use the sword, so I used the spell again, keenly aware this left me with only one final use.

As I aimed it, the little bastard fired his arrow at me, and I stepped aside, grunting in pain as it nicked a thin line across my cheek. I leveled my sword at it, screaming as I released the spell, pouring it out to hit the goblin, even as three more riders cleared the corner, shoving off each other in their haste.

The spell flashed to life, the ten centimeters it could cover being centered where I figured it'd do the most damage, right where the goblin and its mount met.

The little green-skinned bastard's screams rose in agony, filling the air as the others dove for cover behind parked cars. Thanks to the magic of, well, magic, I'd managed to hit my target…the goblin's crotch. I'd managed to cook its nuts and the middle of the dog's back, baking its spine. Both rider and mount tumbled to the ground, permanently crippled, as I ran for it, dodging around the far corner. A Flamedart barely missed me as it slammed into the stone, sending chips flying. I doubled down, pushing harder, heading north now, the screams of their companions not likely to hold them for long.

The street I was on, Grey Street, ran parallel to the street I'd been on before, and I knew I couldn't go far before they'd run me down. I needed to find somewhere to hole up, a shop, a pub, a doorway, for Christ's sake…and my eyes almost leapt from their sockets as I saw a sign on the building on my right. I'd totally forgotten about this place! I skidded to a halt as I gaped at the huge doors, the security grate still intact and holding them sealed. The windows were heavily reinforced, and as I froze in indecision, I heard horns rising again in the distance. My choice was made for me.

I channeled the last use of my spell into the grate, making the lock glow cherry red. I fired my gun, shattering the superheated lock, quickly hauling the grate up. I couldn't help swearing as I felt skin blistering, and I fired a second round, this time hitting the lock on the small internal door, damaging it.

I tried again, hearing the gun click on an empty chamber, and I swore yet again. With no other option left, I hauled back and booted the door, hard. Then again, and again. On the third kick, it splintered and gave way, letting me into a true goodie shop. Bagnall and Kirkwood.

THIRTY-ONE

I GLANCED DOWN THE street, seeing two goblins staring hatefully at me from around a parked car. I struggled to toss the empty handgun inside the shop, then gave them the finger before following it in, yanking the grate down behind me and slamming the door closed.

It was silent inside, but I gazed around, awestruck. The back walls behind the counters were covered with crossbows, single barrel and double barrel shotguns, and even a collection of hunting rifles. The place was a treasure trove of compound bows, recurves, an entire glass display case dedicated to knives…I just stood there for a few seconds, gaping, stunned by the amazing loot I was surrounded by and how much this could change my, and our, lives.

It was just pure dumb luck that the kind of people that shopped here usually weren't the kind of people that spent time in the city. They tended to have big estates out of town, while the rest of the plebes like me? We just looked in the windows, drooled, and shrugged, forgetting the shop existed by the time it was out of sight. I'd never have the kind of money to be able to buy toys like that, much less the land to play with them on.

That wasn't to say that nobody had tried to get in; when I'd been melting the lock, I'd noticed the signs of crowbars and other implements on the grates and door, including broken bits of picks sticking out of the lock. They'd just clearly not had access to magic that could melt steel, or, you know, cook a goblin's nuts at fifty feet.

I heard the horns in the distance again, and winced, shaking myself out of the distracted, frozen mess I was in. I grabbed a big old wooden display case full of lighters and firestarters by the entrance and tipped it over, shoving it hard against the back of the door and jamming it as best as I could. With that rudimentary barricade in place, I grabbed a lighter, sparking it to life and squinting around as I tried to decide where to make my stand.

I lifted the lighter higher, then grinned to myself at the sight of a sealed cabinet at the far end of the room. Proudly displayed was a shotgun marked as a 'CZ 550.' I had no idea if that was a good gun, but judging from the security around the cage, it had to be. I searched as quickly as I could, annoyed at finding a total lack of keys, but rather an additional obstacle in the form of a secure-looking wire that wound around the case, holding it closed.

Giving up on the case and hunting around, I found only one gun that wasn't locked away as securely, a 'GSG Schmeisser STG 44,' according to the display, but it'd clearly been put away in a hurry. The attached wire kept it chained to the desk securely, but I could move it around still, and in the glass display case below it…three full clips for it. It looked like an AK47, just a knock-off version, to my inexperienced eye, and I grinned as I smashed the glass and loaded it, cocking the gun and looking down admiringly at it.

The door had started shaking, the sound of harsh voices echoing in from outside as they argued. Growls of the dogs, or wolves, or whatever, joined the voices, punctuated by massive thumps as something tried to force its way inside. I grinned as I patted the gun, then twisted around, aiming carefully.

I fired a burst into the glass of the display case, just enough to shatter it. Ignoring the restraining bolts keeping the case closed, I smashed the rest of the glass out, and pulled the beautiful shotgun free, looking it over.

"Well, hello there…" I muttered to it, smiling. "You and I are about to become *really* good friends…" I said, using its butt to shatter the lock on a cabinet that held shotgun shells, boxes of them. I looked through them, seeing they were mostly Winchester boxes, I had no idea if that was good or bad, but when I saw the description of '.375 Caliber Controlled Expansion Cartridges' with a label specifying that they were part of the "Dangerous Game Series", I felt in my balls this was the troll ammo for me. There were ten boxes, and each box held twenty rounds. Hunting around, I also found a pair of twenty-five round clips for the shotgun on the rack, as well as plenty of ammo beneath the counter, and I grinned evilly to myself as I filled them with half buckshot and half hollow points, alternating between them, figuring I'd be able to remember what was in it after each shot.

I set the clips down on the cabinets and pulled out a box of .22 ammo. Pausing when I had five clips loaded, I pulled down a bullpup design rifle from another case. This time, the hollow point slug opened it for me, smashing the wire restraining lock into smithereens.

I pulled it free, pausing, then grinning as I noticed a lock on the trigger. I'd also seen the key, thankfully, hanging on a hook directly inside the case, and I had to grin at the laziness of whoever had set it like that. It was going to be a lifesaver for me.

I quickly unlocked it, then set it on the counter top with the relevant clips. Knowing I had mere minutes left, I began dragging the stands covered with expensive tweed jackets and posh hats away from the door, shoving them against one wall while ignoring the crashes as the wooden unit against the door started to break up.

As soon as I had a nice killing field cleared, I got a couple of the thickest jackets I could find and started piling them up around the gun case where I'd decided to make my stand, covering the front of the unit and creating a blind where I could duck down. With everything ready, I paused, looking at the door and waiting. In a movie, they'd have broken through at exactly that time, I reflected, just as the hero was ready, possibly after an intense training montage, as opposed to an idiot who really knew so little about the firearms he was about to use, standing there scratching an itchy ass.

I shrugged and pulled a thick protein bar out of the counter, idly munching on it, before spitting it out in disgust and trying to claw the remnants off my tongue. Whatever the hell it was made of, it was foul, and thick as oatmeal made with concrete.

Another few minutes passed, and while I waited for them to actually make it inside, I pulled free a crossbow, grunting as I cranked it, and loaded a bolt into it, setting it down with a sigh as I gently released the tension on the wire, half expecting it to go off.

I looked around one last time, then shrugged, amazed, and yet not so, that I'd forgotten this place was here, considering how useful the gear was. But then again, that was the way of it. It was such a high-end shop that nobody as crazy as me would have considered it, and looking at it from the outside, it was so plain and understated, it looked more like a secure office or expensive clothes shop than anything else.

A screech from outside broke through my musing, and something massive slammed into the window. Claws dug in deep, shredding the protective mesh and yanking it back and forth, until the entire piece tore free of the restraints and was catapulted away into the street.

I stared out in shock. The driving rain that had started was pelting down on a second troll, one that was easily half again the size of the first one I'd cooked earlier. I checked my mana, figuring I'd been resting for ages now, and swallowed hard as I found that I'd only regenerated thirty points…working it out, it'd only been about twelve minutes since I blew all my mana. That meant…

Shit.

I moved quickly, grabbing the bullpup rifle and sighting down it. It was only a .22 caliber rifle, but it was semi-automatic, and I guessed I'd need it. I waited until the troll ducked down, glaring into the remnants of the shop, and I opened fire, pulling the trigger as fast as I could. The small bullets chewed up its chest and the hand it raised to block my fire, but the tiny bullets merely had the effect of pissing it off, rather than hurting it. It grabbed something to the side, stood up, and swung it, throwing a howling dog and its strapped-in goblin rider in through the window.

They smashed to the ground sideways, the dog snarling as it scrabbled at the tiled floor, trying to get back upright, while the goblin hung on for dear life. I switched my aim, slamming three shots into the dog's head and taking it down before managing to totally miss the rider, my fucked-up shoulder slowing my switch in aim.

I ducked down as a barrage of small, wickedly barbed arrows clattered around me, and I growled fiercely, before jumping back up and opening fire, blasting two shots at the little bastard that was trying to hide behind the dog's corpse. One hit him in the face and ended his worries about his looks forever. Then I pumped the trigger twice more and froze as the gun clicked empty, before ducking down.

The second set of shots had missed everything, bar the troll, and the troll simply growled and threw another goblin at me. Thankfully, his aim was as shit as mine, as the goblin's head slammed into the top of the window frame, and the sickening crack that followed the body bouncing across the floor made me grin as he killed his own side for me.

I reached up and pulled down the shotgun, the rifle, the clips, and the crossbow, wincing at the pain in my shoulder, and I reloaded the bullpup, then slung it over my shoulder and rose with the crossbow, slamming a bolt into the face of the troll as it ducked down, glaring inside.

It screamed, rearing back, and bashed its left fist into a parked car, then grabbed another goblin and flung it inside, followed by a second and a third. I dropped the crossbow and opened fire with the shotgun. The first shot blew a hole large enough to see through the first goblin's chest, and I ducked back down as arrows rained down again, before drawing and throwing a knife from the counter at a goblin that stuck its head around the corner of the counter.

I missed, but its panicked squeak as it jumped back gave me just enough time to pull the shotgun around, and I fired three shots into the counter where it hid, each shot blasting straight through the wood and sending green-black blood flying.

I stood, firing at the gaggle of goblins that were climbing in through the shattered window while I was pinned down, their own bodies acting to halt the arrows as even their own kind seemingly didn't want to shoot them in the back at close range.

I snarled in fury at the temerity of the little bastards, striding forward and opening fire again and again, blasting the window clear, then switching to the rifle to aim at the troll as I hurdled the window frame. My first shot with the .375 slug took him in the knee, making it scream in anger, before the second slammed home inches from it, the kneecap giving way and the huge, grey-skinned, ugly-as-sin humanoid fell to its one good knee, howling in pain, as I switched my aim, hitting it once in the head and rocking it back, as a second shot took its rider in the arm, blowing the limb off to cartwheel away.

The barrage of hot leaden death I'd just unleashed had sent the goblins frantically scurrying for cover, over two-thirds of them dead, when I felt the rifle hammer come down on an empty chamber. I swore, ripping the magazine free and tossing it aside, before pulling out another and ramming it home, the angle being just wrong enough that it took an extra few seconds to seat properly, and in that time, the goblins returned fire.

Two arrows struck first, one slamming into my right thigh, the other into my stomach, and then a single Flamedart slammed into my left side, easily punching through the minimal armor I was wearing and sending me staggering.

I growled in frustration and pain, switching back to the shotgun and opening fire, slamming buckshot and then slugs into the car the trio were hiding behind, as I half limped, half collapsed to the side of it, shifting to a position where I could see them all cowering.

I half slid across the bonnet, sagging to the ground and facing them. The Mageling held its hands out as it gave its lifeforce to summon another glowing arrow. Before it could finish, though, I opened fire, the buckshot wounding all three, before the hollow point slug punched straight through the glowing arrow, into the Mageling's chest and out the far-side to take the final cowering archer in the face. A single long, floppy ear pirouetted into the air, blown free by the explosion of blood, brains, and viscera.

I sagged against the side of the car, my chest heaving and blood running from my wounds. I could hear little beyond the groans of the wounded. I braced myself on my shotgun, pushing up and forcing myself to my feet as I looked around. Pain radiated out of the arrows, especially the Flamedart embedded in my torso.

I was desperate to yank that damn thing free, as I knew it would just keep doing damage until I did, but the fear of the explosion it'd unleash while still embedded in my chest kept me from following through, at least straight away.

I forced out a breath as I grabbed the arrow in my leg, ripping it free and hissing in pain from between tightly clenched teeth. Tentatively touching the one in my gut, I quickly decided against it. I just didn't know what I'd damage ripping that free.

Limping along the car, I looked around, finding a goblin with one leg trying to drag itself away, and another one that was laid flat on the ground, its last breaths gasping out as it stared sightlessly, terrified and whimpering as blood seeped from a deep hole in its side.

I glared down at it and was about to say something suitably hardcore and badass, when I heard an earth-shaking growl from my right. The huge form of the troll, which had been slumped against the car, shifted, and its arm lashed out, smashing me from my feet to slam into the front of the shop. Blood sprayed from my wounds and my mouth as I heard and felt bones breaking.

"Fuuuck…" I whimpered, my right hand spasming weakly as the shotgun clattered down next to me. I tried to reach for it, but my arm wouldn't respond, and I blinked in fuzzy confusion, before registering the unnatural angle.

There is no way my arm is supposed to be that way around, right? I thought muzzily, seeing the way my elbow pointed forward, instead of backward, and realizing the blood that was slowly running down my arm to pool around my fingers on the floor was mine. My head sagged involuntarily, and I blinked, feeling like a bobble-head, as the pavement seemed to rise up to catch me. I blinked a couple more times, frowning, then realized I was laying on my right side, with pain radiating through me from a dozen or more places. Flashing symbols in my vision informed me that I had bleeding, concussed, and fractures debuffs, and I blinked as a large grey foot slammed down next to me, and something grabbed me by the head, lifting me into the air.

I howled as I was lifted, my entire body dangling and swaying. Bones in my neck popped as I was dangled in the air to look the troll in the eyes. It glared at me, and I glared right back, despite the fact that one of its claw-tipped paws was covering half my face, as well as my entire skull, more or less.

It huffed at me, opening its mouth and growling, as I frantically grabbed a stiletto dagger from a holster on my left hip. Blessing myself for grabbing it when I saw it, I drove it into the thing's eye, feeling the jelly pop and smush around the blade, and then my hand, as I drove it in deep.

It screamed in pain and threw me aside. My battered body flew through the air and slammed into a parked car, the windscreen shattering under me as I bounced over it and fell to the asphalt. Lying stunned and bleeding out, I stared up into the grey rainclouds that wept overhead.

I heard pained, furious howling, then a scream of rage, followed by the clatter of a knife hitting the pavement and the sound of a huge body staggering. It didn't make it far before half-collapsing against a car, glass shattering as it released a long, huffing growl.

A foot slammed down, somewhere out of sight, and I blinked, trying to peer up through the rain. I could feel the water running down my face, the hard solidity of the road underneath me, and the slight shake that accompanied the footsteps coming closer.

I remained staring blankly upwards, too numb and shocked to even turn my head at the sound of my death approaching, even though I heard the troll closing the distance…but then it stopped as something blurred overhead, slamming into the troll, just out of sight, making it scream in rage.

I blinked, trying to move, slowly tilting my head to the left. I could see the troll staggering, a crossbow bolt sprouting from its cheek as it snarled at something on the far side of me. I didn't have the strength to turn, I just laid there, staring at the Troll as it backed up, hissing.

Something black and bronze and silver, dripping stinking mud and blood, leapt over me, landing and jumping again, bracing off a car and bounding into the air, before slamming into the troll's chest, knocking it back. The damaged leg gave way again, and the enormous creature fell. The car behind it was completely crushed as its hands came up defensively, and I focused in, amazed to see Jack savaging the creature's throat.

It screamed, trying to tear my familiar free, before four goblins appeared around me. They were all injured and coated in stinking black mud, but they leapt atop the Troll, slamming their filthy clubs down and screaming their defiance as it lashed out with enormous claw-tipped fingers.

It managed to rip Jack free, throwing him across the road to slam into another parked car. His body dropped to the ground, a dent clear in the car door. The automata rose quickly, staggering, then attacked again, even as a goblin was shredded from head to toe by the troll's claws.

The troll howled in triumph, then kicked another goblin hard enough to send it flying into a parked truck. The impact rocked the vehicle on its suspension as the corpse slid down, leaving a trail of blood behind it.

I reached out with my left hand, scrabbling at the road, trying to get a grip, trying to pull myself along, and I screamed in pain as I jostled my injuries. I managed to turn myself onto my side, and I laid there, face pressed into the road, rainwater, dirt, and the blood of goblins and troll alike running down it. Digging in deep, I growled out in fury and forced my hand out, grabbing onto the edge of a pothole and dragging myself closer to the fight.

I didn't know what I could do, but I was determined that I was going to see that big bastard dead.

"There!" came a shout from somewhere behind me, and suddenly a pair of gunshots echoed out, bullets slamming home into the troll as it tried to fight everyone at once.

"There's more of the little ones; kill them first!" another voice rang out, and I growled, almost sobbing with fury as I heard my goblins being targeted.

I rolled myself over, waving weakly, and heard a barrage of fire, followed by a voice I recognized ringing out.

"Stop! Hold your fire!" Mike's voice bellowed, authority filing his every word, and the roar of gunfire staggered to a halt. "The big one, and that one ONLY!" he thundered. I heard a single shot ring out, followed by Mike shouting again. "What are you doing? Waiting for a fucking gold-plated invitation?! Fire!!!" he screamed furiously, matching action to words as he fired again and again, and I heard his footsteps coming closer. "Jesus, Matt, you look a fucking mess…" his whisper reached my ear.

"Still prettier than you…" I managed to wheeze out.

"Bullshit," he replied, grinning despite himself.

"So…can I…date…your sister…yet?" I wheezed out, coughing up a gobbet of blood as he ran out of ammo and slung his rifle, gunfire ringing out again from behind him.

"Hell no. Saving the world is a bare minimum first…" He grunted, grabbing me by the shoulders of my jacket and pulling me backwards, away from the fight.

"Hellfire!" I groaned at the pain tearing into me. "Who's…the… cavalry?" I asked.

"Local coppers. Turns out, there's a firearms team based in the main station. When I turned up with that rifle, they went a bit apeshit, though… it's a police one…you know that?" he asked me blandly, caution clear in his phrasing. He knew I'd gone through a lot and was asking if I'd killed a copper for it, without asking.

"I guessed," I said, coughing, then groaning in pain. "The assholes…in the park…they said they'd killed…a few. Seems…like they'd be…the best guns the coppers could have…"

"That's what I told them," he said, nodding to me with relief before aiming and firing his gun at the troll, making it stagger and scream.

I managed to get myself propped up against the side of a car, when a pair of paramedics, judging from their uniforms, arrived, and started looking me over.

"How the hell are you alive…" one of them muttered, wincing unconsciously, as the other glared at him, before smiling professionally at me. "So, looks like you've been in a few wars, mate. We're gonna get you patched up, though; don't worry!" he reassured me cheerfully as he tried to lie me back down.

"Leave…off…" I growled. "You know…how much it hurt…to get this upright?"

"We need to get these wounds tended, mate." He grabbed my shoulder and half-pulled, half-dragged me down onto my back. Whipping out a pair of scissors, he went to work on my top, cutting it away from the wound in my arm, then following the discolored skin across my upper arm, onto my chest and down to my waist.

"Uh…Dan…we've got internal bleeding and…multiple breaks…Jesus…" the paramedic trailed off, running practiced fingers across my chest and arm. "We need a tourniquet on that arm…and as to the chest…fuck…" He whispered to his companion, who knelt down quickly, pulling out equipment.

"Okay, mate, we're just going to give you something for the pain…" the second man said, pulling out a needle, and I shook my head, flexing my injured arm. I could already feel the increasing strength in it, as my insanely boosted healing took effect.

"Hell no," I growled. I took a moment to check on my goblins, finding that I was down to one, and that Jack was getting tossed all over the place. The various bullets that were slamming into the Troll were all small caliber, and they were doing little more than pissing it off. "Mike…" I called, coughing and spitting a congealed wad of blood onto the ground as I shoved back the paramedics. I twisted, groaning in pain as I forced myself back upright, and then Mike was there. Reaching out and gripping my uninjured hand, he pulled me to my feet and held me upright.

"I'm here, boss," Mike said, gripping my belt on the far side. "We doing a runner?" He asked me quietly. "Because the coppers agreed to come help because I swore I'd give them our guns at the end of the fight..."

"Well...that was a stupid...fucking thing to say..." I hissed, forcing myself to stand on my own two feet. "You see the rifle?" I asked him, nodding to where it laid against the wall, and he nodded. "It's...loaded with a magazine of....375 controlled...expansion cartridges. Hide...piercing. I'd nearly...killed the fucker with it when...I went after the last of the goblins..."

"Got it," Mike said, leaning me against the nearest car, where I'd be able to see the action. "You stay here; I'll go kill that fucker."

"And don't...give up...anything..." I ground out. "That...shop's full...of everything...we need. I'm keeping...it."

"Good luck with that," The first paramedic said, stepping in front of me as Mike shouted to warn the coppers that he was crossing the road. "Seriously, mate, you're badly fucked up here. If you don't let us work, you're a dead man." I felt my knees buckle, and I grabbed onto the car, clutching it for dear life as I forced my legs straight.

"Bandages..." I grunted out to him. "No drugs...and I need the top copper."

"Sarge!" The paramedic called out, and a few seconds later, a gruff older man responded, rifle held at the ready, his salt-and-pepper beard and weathered lines around his eyes clearly showing his years outdoors.

"You're the guy who stole our guns?" he asked me grimly.

"No," I ground out. "I'm the guy who...got shot at and hurt...by the guys who stole...your guns. I took their guns...when I killed them."

"Well, the guns are ours, and you'll be coming with us to answer some questions when all this is over," he said flatly, sighting down the rifle and firing off a few pot shots at the troll.

"Nope, wrong...again." I snapped at him. "The guns are mine, as...are the guns inside that shop, and...the one my man is getting...now. You need to keep...that big fucker distracted; then we'll...take him down." I took a deep breath, feeling new strength fill me as I straightened up and checked my HP. The time out of the fight had been just what I needed, allowing my accelerated healing to close the worst of the wounds, lifting me from the eighties back to one hundred and twenty.

I wasn't healed, or healthy, not by any stretch of the imagination, but I was alive. It was time to make sure that big fucker learned he'd made a fatal mistake in leaving me long enough to recover.

"Isn't going to happen," the sergeant said flatly, and I glared at him as I pushed the paramedic back and stood carefully on my own, facing them both.

"Tell me then, how do you think you're going to win this? Your guns are doing nothing more than pissing him off. I can kill it. I've been doing your job since the end of the fucking world, saving the people you fucking abandoned! Where were you? What the fuck were you doing, while I've been fighting and killing these creatures?!?" I stopped, swaying, the world suddenly filled with black spots and flashes, as I overexerted myself by shouting at the intransigent asshole. "Look…" I ground out, when I caught my breath. "I'll split the gear in there with you. That's because I know you need it, but the guns we've got in our possession now, the weapons and ammo? They're mine, and if you want them, it'll be over my cold, dead body."

"If that's the way it has to be," he growled in return, glaring at me. "I'm not leaving these weapons in the hands of civilians, and you're looting a shop. That's not happening."

"Tell me how you survive this, then?" I scoffed at him, gesturing to the troll, who'd just turned my last goblin into paste, having picked up a motorbike and used it as a club. "Look at that fucker. Not only is it healing, regenerating, even, but it's getting fucking stronger!" I snarled, then took a deep breath, wincing in pain as Mike made it to the rifle, sweeping it up and firing off a round into the Troll's back. Due to its hunched back and the poor angle, the slug wasn't as effective as it would have been with a clearer shot, but it certainly got the bugger's attention.

It spun around, swinging its mangled bike-club at him and he dove behind a car before turning and roaring in fury as the police continued to pepper bullets at it, getting its attention, but little more.

"Fuck's sake man, are you an idiot?" I snapped at the Sergeant, shouting out to his team. "Concentrate fire on the head!" There was a pause, then firing resumed, and the dozens of tiny wounds opening up across the body switched to the head, tearing furrows in the skin and making it scream in fury. It ran forward, hurling the bike-club across the road to smash into the car that three of the team were sheltering behind.

They ducked, and the Troll bellowed, the sound echoing off the surrounding buildings, then a second bellow, followed by a horn in the distance, responded, and I swore.

"There's more incoming," I growled at the Sargent and the pair of paramedics with him, who were gaping at my wounds in open mouthed shock. "What?" I asked, looking down. I grunted dismissively at the sight of the skin that was slowly re-growing at a visible rate. "Yeah, it's sweet, I know. Deal with it," I said shortly.

"Look, there's more incoming. The first lot I fought were goblins on giant dogs, with a troll, I killed them, but more came, and they brought their own troll. I'm gonna go out on a limb and guess that means that each group has their own troll. There's also goblin Magelings, and they can…fire…explosive darts. If they get into you, they'll make you bleed out, but yanking them free triggers the explosive, so it's a choice to see what's going to kill you the fastest, the bleed out, or the bomb," I explained quickly, choosing at the last second not to mention that magic was real now.

"You've got three choices, and you need to make it quick. Stay here and fight in the street, fall back and leave us to it, or join us. If it's the last, you do what I say, or we're all dead." Without waiting for a reply, I turned away, staggering across the street. My pain growing less and less as I went, but it was still bad enough that I knew what I was planning was suicide under any sensible universe's rules.

Mike had jumped up again, firing the shotgun into the Troll from behind, hollow points followed by buckshot making it stumble and fall to one knee, its massive form shaking the ground as it slammed its fists down hard.

It reared back, ignoring the minor wounds it was getting, and let out a scream of rage that vibrated the windows in the surrounding buildings, before lifting its clenched fists into the air and beginning to glow a sullen, ominous red. It slammed both fists down hard, and the ground shook violently. Ripples of force suddenly rolled outwards, the supposedly solid tarmac of the roads and slabs of the pavement acting like the surface of a pond when a rock is dropped in. Waves flowed out, flipping cars, making everyone stagger and fall. Some people were thrown into buildings, structures that started to crack and crumble. Awnings fell from shop fronts, glass in windows shattered, and streetlights collapsed, before the ability ran its course, and the street returned to its usual solid appearance.

The Troll sagged forward, huffing as it tried to recover, and for a minute, silence reigned, before the cries started up. Some of the police team had been trapped under cars that had rolled over. Others had been flung into windows, walls, barriers, or parked cars. Several were silent, crushed under rubble that had fallen from an ornate building, and I blinked and groaned as I half dragged myself, half crawled out from under a parked truck.

My last memory had been of trying to jump over a ripple I'd seen coming, and being caught by the following one, flying through the air and slamming into the ground, having just enough presence of mind to roll under the truck before smacking my face into the asphalt.

I forced myself upright, looking around and seeing the rest of the group doing the same. Mike appeared from nowhere, rushing forward to plant the barrel of the rifle against the back of the troll's skull, right where it met the neck.

He pulled the trigger. The troll twisted around, having sensed him too late as it recovered, and the blast blew most of its skull free of the neck, blood and viscera flying through the air as the recoil drove Mike back a few steps, before he sagged to his knees, panting.

The troll's body slowly toppled forwards, before slamming into the road with a wet, meaty thwack. Blood fountained out and gushed away, headed for the storm drains.

I sagged back against the truck, my notifications blinking frantically for my attention, and I pulled them up, seeing a wall of data as it recompiled.

Congratulations! You have killed the following:

- 1x Troll, Level 4, 200 XP
- 7x Goblin Rider, Level 2-4, 170 XP
- 2x Goblin Rogue, Level 2-3, 50 XP
- 2x Goblin Mageling, Level 4, 120 XP
- 7x Tamed, Evolved Dog, Level 2-3, 150 XP

Total XP earned: 690 XP

A party under your command killed the following:

- 1x Troll, Level 7, 350 XP
- 1x Goblin Rogue, Level 2, 20 XP
- 4x Goblin rider, Level 2-4, 110 XP
- 6x Tamed, Evolved Dog, Level 2-3, 130 XP

Total Party XP earned: 610 XP

As party leader, you receive 25% of all XP earned.

- Total XP awarded 690+(610x0.25=152.5) = 842.5

You have reached Level Nine!

You receive five Stat points to invest in your attributes, with one unassigned Skill point.

Current XP stands at 559/1000

I grunted, well aware that I had precious little time to fuck about with things, so I took a risk, putting my available skill point into Longsword, boosting it to level five, and put all five points into Agility. I was taking a massive risk, the more I thought about it, but that, combined with my 'Dodge' skill, boosted my chance to dodge incoming attacks by twenty-six percent. That gave me a one in four chance of dodging, and I was going to need that, badly.

"Uh…Matt?" Mike said slowly, as he walked over to me, the police around us gradually getting up and helping each other. "What the hell is this…" he asked, and I chuckled as I saw the way he was staring into the distance, eyes unfocused.

"That, my friend, is us having a chance," I said, and I mentally slammed 'accept.' I couldn't bite back the groan as my nerves seemed to erupt in fire for several seconds while altering themselves to make me faster. "Right…" I gasped, panting as I tried to get my breath back. "Any of you fuckers seeing words floating before you in the air?" I asked, holding my breath…and then letting out a relieved sigh when three of them held up their hands.

"Good!" I called out. "There's no time to go over why, or what this means. Long story short, you all gain an interface of sorts when you reach level one… if you haven't seen it before today, it shows how fucking little use you've been until now. That interface shows up once you leave active combat. Depending on how much 'XP' you earned in that fight, you'll have leveled up at least once. Think 'Stats' and give me a thumbs up if a new page appears…" I ordered, and a few seconds later, Mike and the other three had been joined by three more, who all held their thumbs up.

"Good, well it looks like you either earned experience from helping us to kill the troll, or it was from killing my goddamn goblins, in which case, you're all assholes," I snapped, before forcing myself to take a calming breath and shaking my head.

"You can see ten stats listed; the numbers correlate to how good you are at a specific thing, such as how strong you are. You start to get bonuses from level ten upwards. For example, your health is linked to Constitution. If you've got five stat points in that, you've got fifty points of health; if you've got ten, you've got two hundred health, as at ten points, each point invested becomes worth twenty, instead of ten. Don't ask me why!" I snapped, seeing a few brows furrowing and mouths opening.

"It just is, okay? Now, if you want to be able to run, add points into Endurance or Agility. You want to shoot better, try Dexterity or Perception… it'll sting once you make the change and confirm it, but it'll be worth it. I'll go over details with those who join me later. There's no time now. Judging from those sounds, we've got minutes, at best, so assigning the points to either Constitution, Perception, or Dexterity would be my advice to keep you alive through this fight. Bear in mind, if you have ten thousand points in health and get shot in the head, you're probably still gonna die. It's augmenting us, not changing physics and biology." With that, I turned to Mike and addressed him privately.

"How many levels did you go up?" I asked him, and he grinned.

"Three…I got five points per level…and I'm over ten in most areas; physical ones, at least…"

"Lucky bastard." I said, grinning at him and trying not to feel jealous. "Must be the military training; set you on the right path, right from the start, mate."

"What should I do with the points?" he asked, and I drew in a deep breath, well aware by the way they moved closer that the others were listening in.

"With you being as far ahead as you already are, honestly, I'd be tempted to do a 'min-max' build with the points…slam them all into one area, and make yourself into a god damn titan," I said honestly. "Fifteen points into Perception would let you spot anything coming far better than the rest of us, and…how many points have you got in there now?" I asked.

"Eleven," he responded, shrugging.

"Damn, I only have ten…" I replied, forcing a smile. "I'd be tempted to go all in there, because that'd increase your damage by a further fifteen points with each shot, meaning you'd probably kill most things, like goblins, even if you hit them three times in a finger…. That, or Dexterity, as those two govern your shooting skills."

"And my Skill Points?" he asked.

"Have you got any skills up yet?" I countered.

"No, just at level one for firearms…cool."

"Save it," I said bluntly. "You're a trained soldier. You'll leap up the levels faster than I ever could; then, when your progress starts to plateau, you can use them. They'll be more helpful that way."

"Okay, I'll trust you." he said, then groaned and started to shake. When he finally managed to catch his breath, I clapped him on the shoulder and grinned.

"Told you it stung!" I winked.

"Stung?" He groaned. "It felt like someone poured hot steel into my goddamn nerves!"

"What did you pick?" I asked.

"Dexterity, all fifteen points," he said. "Seeing great won't mean shit if I can't hit them."

"Fair enough, mate. Congrats on the 'Ding,' I guess." And before I could explain it, one of the police spoke up.

"Ding!" He said, grinning at me, although he looked pale and sweaty, hunching slightly.

"Congrats," I responded automatically. "What did you pick?"

"Strength, up to fourteen points now!" he said proudly, then shifted uncomfortably in his now too-tight tunic and harness.

"Well…there's a lesson to everyone. Strength makes your muscles bigger, but it also means you're slower now, and your gear doesn't fit. You have a melee weapon you wanted to use?" I asked him and he sagged, head drooping.

"No…" he admitted, and I snorted.

"Then you're a fucking idiot." I shook my head, noting a bit belatedly that I was now surrounded by the entire surviving force of police and paramedics. "Right, get your weapons and get your arses inside the shop if you're with us. If not, do whatever you want, and good luck," I said, moving to the far side of the road and leaning down to pick my sword up from where it'd fallen out of sight beneath a car. "Jack, hide here and get anyone you can." I ordered, the familiar hunching down and slipping out of sight between two parked cars.

"You're a real people person, you know that?" Mike said as he came up to me, grinning.

"Stupidity annoys me, mate." I sighed, shaking my head. "He literally chose the second worst stat to increase in this situation. Only thing he could have done worse was to choose Charisma…but yeah, I know, I need to be a bit more patient. Things have been like this for me since the first damn day, though, you know? He and his men could have been out here. He could have been helping, but instead they've all been hiding and pretending it'll all get better."

"Fair point. You'll have to explain all this shit properly later, though," he insisted, helping me as I clambered in through the open window of Bagnall and Kirkwood. "What's the plan?" he asked.

"We reload, and kill whatever comes this way." I said bluntly.

"What about the coppers?" He dropped his voice, noting the glare the Sergeant had shot my way, and the way he was ordering his men to stay clear of us, taking up position behind some parked cars.

"We'll save any we can," I said grimly. "Because I'm telling you now, they can't have much ammo left, and they're still staying out front, in plain sight. They didn't even strip the ammo from the dead."

"It's a hard thing to do, looting your mates…" Mike said, and I snorted.

"I'm sure it used to be, but the way the world is now? It needs to be done, and the dead don't care."

"Were you always an asshole?" Mike asked conversationally as he pulled a box of shells from the counter and started reloading my—clearly, now his—shotgun.

"Nope. Used to be a nice guy; then I worked in I.T, and that ruined me for most people. Only so many times you can ask an idiot why they thought writing a password on a post-it note and sticking it to a laptop was a good idea, before you lose hope. Then the world ended, and people tried to kill me. Like practically every fucking day, or so it seemed. Now I'm an asshole, but I'm alive." I focused my attention on reloading the bullpup rifle. "Doesn't help that people keep nicking my goddamn favorite guns, though…" I huffed, and Mike paused guiltily.

"Sorry, man; I didn't think…" he said, looking down at the gun.

"It's all right, Mike." I said, seeing the genuine guilt on his face. "You're probably going to be far better with any gun than I am. What happened to the rifle?" I asked, and he nodded out into the street.

"When all that kicked off, I dropped it for the shotgun. The sarge out there grabbed it when I was assigning my points, damn asshole."

"What, does he think harsh goddamn language is going to keep people safe?" I asked, shaking my head in irritation.

"Yeah and no…" He started, freezing as we both heard the guttural screams and howls from further down the street. The first shots rang out, and we hurried to the window as he continued. "As a copper, it's his job to make sure there's no guns on the street. He's just trying to stick to the old world, I think…hoping it gets better somehow."

"Doesn't look likely to me," I muttered as we watched a dozen or more goblins racing huge dogs up the street, with another two trolls in the back, pounding along steadily, trying to catch up. The coppers opened fire again, sporadic shots at first, with the Sarge clearly ordering them to hold their fire for as long as possible, trying to make the shots count, as goblin arrows rained through the air.

A copper went down, falling from cover into the road, clutching at an arrow that protruded from the side of his face, literally jutting from his mouth and cheek. He couldn't stop screaming. The paramedic that jumped out to help him screamed and went down with a glowing, sizzling dart in his back, followed by two more arrows as he was pulled back into cover by his partner.

"That one," I ordered, aiming as I spoke. "The Magelings are the most important first; then…"

A second scream rose from the coppers where they hunched behind the cars, as a thin goblin dressed all in blacks and greys seemed to appear from nowhere. Twin daggers reflecting the light as it 'Backstabbed' the Sergeant, tearing the knives out of his kidneys viciously, before pumping them back in, then out, and running for cover in the alleyway.

"Jack!" I snapped, having pretty much ignored the familiar until now, with everything that was going on. "Get the rogues," I ordered, and Jack bolted from cover between two cars, pouncing on the goblin as it tried to flee.

"I thought you were going to leave them to it?" Mike asked me, and I shrugged.

"I'm an asshole, not a complete bastard," I muttered, sighting with my small rifle. It wasn't much use, but even a single hit would help, I knew.

"What the hell?" Mike said, shocked, before starting to laugh.

"What's up?" I asked him, panicking as I hunted around, trying to spot whatever had made him comment.

"You just wait right there…" he said, and I heard the shotgun go off, once, twice, and then a third time, somewhere in the back of the room, while I continued to shoot single-fire at the oncoming goblins, who'd closed to less than a dozen meters from the coppers now.

The police were holding their own better now, the Sergeant having collapsed to the asphalt and the main group being seemingly led by someone with more common sense as they concentrated fire, taking down the dogs, then the goblins, which freed me up to fire pot shots at the Magelings. There were two that I could see, and they'd elected to stay at the back, ordering the trolls forward, both of which had riders.

The goblins sat astride their grey-skinned, fugly mounts on special saddles with what looked like spurs on their feet, grasping handles embedded into the trolls' flesh.

As I watched, one twisted the handles, guiding the Troll around an overturned car, and sank its spurs in, howling. The troll screamed in response, leaning forward and picking up speed. For the first time, I realized these two trolls were blind. A thin ring of serrated metal ran around their skulls, digging into the eyes and clearly preventing their regeneration. To my surprise, I felt the most disgust when looking at the goblins that screamed and hollered, jumping up and down on their mounts.

The trolls were the biggest threat, that was true, but they also looked to be slaves. The other two I'd fought weren't blind, but they'd had riders, and they'd killed the goblins as happily as they'd tried to kill me, once the riders were down.

"Change of plan," I snapped to Mike as I heard him approaching. "Take down the Magelings, and then the troll riders."

"Then drop the toy, and use this," Mike said, dumping a rifle on the counter next to me. It was a single shot, reloaded by a slot on the side, but it was much bigger and longer than the bullpup and other guns I'd used, and I saw the box of ammo Mike slammed down between us. He had a similar rifle to the one he'd given me; the only difference was that it had a clip attached.

"Oh, so it's like that, is it?" I asked, nodding to the rifle.

"Hell yes, it is! Sorry and all, but this is something I've wanted for years! Only way it'd be better is if it was a proper sniper rifle!" Mike said, grinning widely. "First one to ten kills gets the first quarters?" he asked, half joking, half hoping.

"Cool; I already killed more than twenty. Does that mean I get to date your sister?" I retorted.

"Nope, and it's ten from now..." he said, firing and rechambering, then firing again.

I hunched down around the sight, focusing in, and saw the second Mageling collapsing, blood spraying from its chest as a second 'boom' resounded from the rifle to my right, making me swear.

"This is so not a fair bet..." I muttered, opening my other eye and shifting, drawing a bead on the goblin riding the nearest troll. I pulled the trigger, hearing and feeling the click, instead of the shot, and then saw the goblin fly backwards, its head missing as Mike claimed the third kill.

"Seriously?" I cried, frantically grabbing a bullet from the box. "You even preloaded yours and not mine?"

"Don't forget the safety." Mike said, and I could feel the grin in his voice as I slammed the round home, closing the chamber and re-sighting.

"Utter bastard," I muttered darkly, just in time to see the second troll lose its rider. I shrugged and sighted in on the first troll, instead, leading it slightly. As it closed to five meters from the car that the coppers were hiding behind, I fired. My shot took it in the upper chest, staggering it and delaying its crushing rampage long enough for the coppers to move. Then it straightened and bellowed in rage, powering forward as it headed towards the screams and firing it could hear.

It slammed into the car, bouncing, and then screamed, lifting both fist and smashing them down on it, hard. The coppers had managed to kill most of the dogs and their riders, with one last goblin falling to a stealthed rogue, while Jack had killed three more of them.

The coppers fell back, dragging their wounded, and Mike fired again and again at the Trolls, as I reloaded and managed a single hit, taking the first one's knee out.

"Oh, fuck this," I growled, dumping the rifle and grabbing the shotgun. "Dibs!" I clambered over the chest-height barrier and out of the window.

"Crazy bastard!" Mike called, firing again and again, concentrating fire on the troll to the right, while I ran to the one on the left. I slowed as I stepped out between the cars into the middle of the road. The troll had paused a dozen meters away, sniffing for the coppers, its eyes eternally bleeding from the band across them.

"Over here, you big ugly bastard!" I cried out, firing at it. It was a buckshot round, and it merely peppered the creature, making it lift one hand reflexively to ward off the pain before bellowing and rushing in my direction on all fours. The loping run was reminiscent of a gorilla rushing through the trees, and I tried not to shit myself at the roaring, towering bundle of rage, muscle, and salivating teeth that rushed me.

"Come on, then…let's play a game…" I took aim, and as its right paw came down, just before its weight shifted, I fired, one of the last hollow-points hammering into the creature's right wrist, making it buckle and stagger as its weight came down fully.

The troll staggered to the right, slamming into a parked car and screaming at it, before lashing out with both fists, pummeling the vehicle over and over. I slowly clambered onto the car next to it, careful not to make any sound. The cars were parked nose to tail up the sides of the street, with barely a foot to two between them, and as the troll smashed the one it was working on into a battered hulk, I glowered at it.

"Come to daddy!" I whispered, running across the top of the car I stood on, crouching and kicking off to jump into the air and land on the car before the troll, just as it lifted both hands into the air for a smash.

As soon as my feet touched down, I was off, sprinting as fast as I could, running from the bonnet to the tail of the car and leaping clear. The only two thoughts in my mind were that I needed to avoid the damage, so I didn't trip and get smushed, and aiming, making sure my shot was right on target.

I passed its face at a range of less than a meter as it drew back to hit, its lips peeled back from long canines and molars. Strands of saliva and bloody drool flew as it screamed its impotent rage at the world…and I pointed the shotgun, pulling the trigger as fast as I could, and seeing the world seem to go into slow motion as the buckshot tore from the barrel, slamming into the creature's face.

I saw pellets sparking off the band across its eyes, ricocheting away, teeth cracking with the impact of dozens of small lead balls, the skin within its mouth being denuded by the impact and peeling backwards, shredding, exposing muscles and tendons, and a black glittering bone structure that seemed to absorb the light.

As my foot came down and I pushed off again, leaping forwards and landing on the next car, the troll that I'd targeted staggered back, hands faltering from their crushing trajectory, merely glancing off the car as it fell backwards and reaching for the shredded, shattered mess that was its mouth.

I ran a few more steps, skidding to a halt atop the roof of an old e-type jaguar and jumped off. Grunting in pain as I landed, I continued staggering as I walked forward. The anger that had driven me so far was now a steady hot burn in my stomach as I took aim. The next shot took the flailing right arm in the shoulder, a second buckshot round, followed by two more, then a hollow-point and the arm collapsed to the ground, severely bruised. Though my bullets weren't doing much to pierce its skin, the repeated blunt force impact had still taken its toll on the creature's joints.

I switched my point of aim, firing at the left hand as it blindly waved towards me, talon-tipped fingers reaching out hungrily. The hand had three fingers, with a single shorter thumb opposite them, and then I blasted it at short range, sending the offending appendage cartwheeling away from me.

The troll screamed, sagging and falling onto its back, the sound a mixture of rage, pain, and hatred. The cry was filled with bubbling agony as its amazing regeneration tried to heal it, even as its system went into catastrophic shock.

I stepped forward, covering the last meter to stand almost directly over it, ignoring the twitching arms, the bubbling, burbling cries and ruined mouth, as I aimed directly at the bridge of its nose…or what remained of it.

I pulled the trigger twice in quick succession, a double blast of buckshot ringing out, one practically atop the other to blowing the troll's eyes apart, fragments of blood and eyeball flying everywhere as the cumulative injuries overwhelmed its vital guard. Shielding my face from the worst of the mess, I grunted down at it.

"How do you like me now, motherfucker?" I shouted, before turning to the second troll, which was screaming and charging randomly as the police and Mike fired occasional shots at it.

"'That still only counts as one!'" Mike shouted the quote laughingly, and I bit down on a growl of frustration.

Where the police's small caliber firearms only caused the troll pain and annoyance, Mike's heavier hunting rifle did far more sustained damage, and it was staggering as he fired again and again at its legs, blowing whole chunks free.

I started walking for it, ejecting the clip and checking it, before shrugging, I had three rounds left. One was a Hollow-point, and the last two were something I'd not seen before, coated with a bright orange, rather than the dull red of the buckshot. I slammed the clip home and took aim, walking steadily closer.

"Oi, shitbag!" I shouted, and the troll turned towards me. As I closed the distance, I took careful aim, continuing to taunt him. "Yeah, that's right; I'm talking to you!" I cried out, and the Troll bared its teeth, snarling in my general direction, before Mike took a chunk out of its left knee, sending it staggering.

I fired, the hollow-point slamming into the top of its head and careening off into the distance, tearing a long furrow through the skin as it went. I aimed again, then nearly shit myself once I pulled the trigger.

The shotgun almost seemed to explode, a great fountain of fire erupting from the end. It took the Troll in the chest full-on, shredding, cooking, and butchering the creature in a single unbelievably aggressive display of power.

Whatever the shell had contained, it had sparked to life as it erupted from the barrel, growing to three meters wide and at least seventy long; a tendril of the fire slammed into the side of a building on the far side of the street, charring the sign for an abandoned restaurant into illegibility.

"Fuck me..." I whispered as the troll collapsed, screeching, while the fats popped and crisped, its entire body burning ferociously as it twitched in death. The street was suddenly silent beyond the sound of the flames, rain spattering down all around us and evaporating when it hit the fire. I turned to catch Mike standing open-mouthed in the window of Bagnall and Kirkwood's, and I shouted at him. "What the ever-living fuck was that?!?" I screamed, waving the shotgun at him, and he grinned, giving me a thumbs up.

"Dragon's Breath!" He called back. "Fucking illegal everywhere!"

"I'm not surprised!" I yelled, which, to be fair, was about the only volume I could hear for the moment.

"Found it in a drawer; probably hidden for a good reason, eh?"

"It's going into the Dungeon, I know that!" I cackled, grinning. If I ever had to fight another troll, I wanted some of that ammo.

"What the hell was that?!" a voice screamed at me from behind, and I turned seeing a copper stalking out of the rain. He, like the rest of the group, was dressed in black and dark blue tactical gear, helmet, and goggles, and he was practically apoplectic with rage. "You idiots are under arrest!" he screamed at Mike and I, and I cocked my head to the side.

"Are you for fucking real, pal?" I asked him, seeing the way the rest of the police were watching us, clearly unsure.

"You're damn right I am! You lunatics just shot the entire street up! You could have killed us all!"

"We could have left you to it, watched you get slaughtered, and picked off the trolls and survivors later. It would have been easier, and we'd have wasted less ammo," I shot back at him.

"You're criminals who robbed a sporting shop and shot the shit out of the area!" he snarled back at me. "Drop the guns and get on the ground!" He pointed his rifle at me.

"Not going to happen," I said coldly.

"Do it!!" He screamed, and of the four surviving coppers, one lifted his gun hesitantly to point it at us, while the other three simply looked from him to me. I glanced at them, recognizing, even beneath the gear they wore, that the three who weren't making a move, had all leveled up, and had been more appreciative of my advice earlier than the rest.

Clearly, it'd made a difference, as of the twelve who'd arrived, three of the five survivors were those who'd listened.

"Look, Danny..." one of them started to say, and the aggressive one screamed at him.

"Shut it!" he yelled, panting as he looked from the speaker and then back to me. "They've done this! More than half of us are dead, and they want to just walk off? Arrest them, college-boy, or fuck off while the real men deal with this!"

"What do you mean 'deal with this'?" the man who'd spoken up asked quietly.

"We've got no room in the cells...we can't let them go..." Danny shot back to him, his breath coming in gasps as he looked from the others to me and back again, obviously thinking he was being quiet, but with a helmet on, his voice was louder than he thought.

"You think that I'm going to just let you kill me?" I asked slowly.

"No, look, sir, that's not what he means..." the peacemaker said, holding his hand up to me, and making a point of releasing his gun to hang on its harness, showing he wasn't about to use it.

"It is!" Danny snapped. "We have to! You saw what he did! He probably killed Matrim and Burgess; you know it's one of our guns they had..."

"We don't know that, Danny..."

"Enough! You never had the balls to be a real copper, college-boy! Just walk away…let us…"

"There's no 'us,' Danny!" the young copper said desperately. "Don't you see? The world ended, it's all gone tit's up, and you're threatening to murder the only guy who seems to know what's going on!"

"It'll be all right…it'll go back to how it was…you'll see…" Danny muttered, licking his lips feverishly and sighting down his rifle at me. Sweat fogged his goggles and glistened on his cheeks, even as his rifle barrel trembled.

"Last chance," I said flatly, knowing that my mana had *FINALLY* hit one hundred. I released the butt of the shotgun and gently set it down on the ground. "Put your gun down and walk away. I don't want to have to kill you, but I will…"

"You see! He's threatening me…" Danny snapped, hunching in around his rifle a little closer and shifting his grip, his finger stroking the trigger.

"Don't do it!" Another one of the coppers called out. "Seriously, Danny, don't you fucking do it!" He lifted his gun and pointed at Danny instead, the others following suit.

"You're all with them…" Danny whispered, his voice hoarse as he glanced from one to another, eyes going wide as he licked his lips again. "You're all out to get me…"

"Drop it, Danny!" one of them bellowed, and Danny turned to glare at me again.

"This is all your fault!" he snarled, and I saw the tell-tale shift in his shoulders as he lifted the rifle, aiming at my chest.

"Fuck it," I snarled. "Incinerate!" I aimed at the base of his skull, even as I dove aside. The spell flared to life as he opened fire. His lips lifted in manic glee as he tracked me, just before his brain flash boiled in its own juices and he collapsed, a gout of steam erupting from his mouth as his skull blackened and charred.

"What the hell?" the peacemaker whispered, before shifting his gun to me. I slowly got up, dusting myself off. "What the hell did you do?" he asked coldly.

"I defended myself as that piece of shit tried to murder me." I snapped back at him.

"How?" he growled, and I felt my lips quirk into a sardonic smile as I lifted my hands and did a little 'jazz hands' wave. "*Magic*!" I said, before shaking my head in annoyance.

"Seriously, I've neither the time nor the crayons to explain this shit to you. The world has changed; ended, I guess. Now, if you learn how to do it, there's magic. Hell, there's a billion things I don't know about what's going on, and hardly anything I do know about, but this much I do know: holding onto the old world and its way of thinking will get you all killed."

"What…look, I need to know what you know, alright?" The copper said, stepping forward and lowering his rifle. "You seem to have a handle on this that the rest of us don't, so how about…whoa!" he said, snapping the rifle back up as he shifted to look at a Goblin corpse a dozen feet to my left. I couldn't see anything where he looked, but I could see above other corpses, a sparkling box phasing into existence.

It was about six inches high, in the shape of a black and copper pyramid, and it slowly rotated, faintly reflecting the occasional bit of sunlight that made it through the dreary cloud cover.

"What the hell is that?" he asked, aiming his rifle at the goblin's corpse. I still saw nothing. I glanced around, noticing that the others were fixated on other corpses, and of the ones I could see…they hovered above the two Trolls and a goblin that I was fairly sure I'd managed to kill over the course of the fight.

I turned, checking on corpses I knew I'd made, and sure enough, each one had its own slowly rotating, glowing Reliquary.

"Oh, shit…" I muttered, feeling my heart drop into my boots as I made the connection. "They were Dungeon Creatures…" I whispered, just as Mike stepped up beside me, having clambered out of the window.

"What does that mean?" he asked slowly.

"It means we're not alone, Mike…there's another Dungeon in Newcastle, and it's probably sent these hunting for us…"

"Well, shit."

THE STORY WILL CONTINUE IN

Age of Bronze

RISE OF MANKIND BOOK TWO

THANKS

At this point in the book its traditional to thank those who've helped you, supported and believed in you, as well as those who have inspired you, well that would be a huge list, seriously it would, so I'll keep this short.

To my wife, mother of my children, and the one who not only believed in me enough to help me to get this done, but when, after being told to 'shit or get off the pot' by two amazingly talented authors that I respected, actually said "They're right, what have you got to lose?"

...

Well, I know damn well that considering our financial situation at that point, it would have been much easier for my wife to have shot my dreams down, or put them off, told me to grow up, or have refused to invest any of our meagre savings into the project.

She did none of these things, instead she pushed me upwards and onwards, watched the two tiny sproglodites and kept the house, the family and the pets all together, while I sat in our home office and scratched my head about the best word to use.

Thank you, Chrissy. You are the best wife, partner and friend I can imagine, this...all of this...is because of *you.*

To my family, especially my Mother, who will probably be crying as she hears/reads this, depending on which version she chooses...thank you. You always gave 110%, working multiple jobs and insanely long hours to feed and clothe us all, yet still you made time to read to a small boy who was grumpy, upset and constantly in need of reassurance, when you must have been desperate for just a little time to relax...

Thank you, Mum. I love you.